INGERSOLL

a novel

INGERSOLL

a novel

Richard Samuel Sheres

Vendemmia
Press

Ingersoll

A Novel

ISBN: 978-0-9890602-0-2

Vendemmia
Press

Also by Richard Samuel Sheres

An Imperfect Certainty

Keeping Gideon

For my parents, who taught me that questioning is

a virtue, and uncertainty is not a vice.

A person will worship something, have no doubt about that. . . . That which dominates our imaginations and our thoughts will determine our lives and our character. Therefore, it behooves us to be careful what we worship, for what we are worshipping we are becoming.

Ralph Waldo Emerson

Foreword

Years of natural and manmade calamity have set the stage. Superstorms, quakes, terrorism, social disintegration—religious conservatives have had enough! They are determined to reclaim America's greatness as they see it and are within a hairsbreadth of amending the Constitution on marriage, abortion, and—most far-reaching of all—the formal declaration of the United States of America as a Judeo-Christian nation.

Thus was the stage set for *Ingersoll* when it was first published in 2013. And so it is today, with perhaps even greater relevance.

All during the writing of the first edition I felt under the gun to publish before the book's category had to be changed from fiction to nonfiction. Consider some of the major events of 2013. In Moore, Oklahoma a Tornado killed 26 people. The east coast was trying to recover from Superstorm Sandy. Race relations hit a latest low with the acquittal of Trayvon Martin's killer, who was "standing his ground." Meanwhile, efforts to deal with gun violence lost the sense of urgency that followed the murder of children and teachers at Sandy Hook Elementary. The Supreme Court stunned religious conservatives when it ruled that marriage was not limited to a man and a woman. The Boston Marathon was bombed. The federal government shut down. Sound familiar?

And yet, and yet . . . The country now is even more divided and at loose ends, unable or unwilling to confront its many challenges, whether natural or humanmade. As I write this, the nation—and the world, at a time when it increasingly appears to be deprived of American leadership—is in the throes of the greatest disease pandemic in a century. Storms of all types (including firestorms) have increased in frequency and intensity as the fight over human responsibility for climate change goes on. President Trump seems to unleash a fresh astonishment by the day. The war over women's right to decide what is best for their own bodies—and in particular to decide to terminate a pregnancy—has, if anything, gained ferocity and involved new forms of attack. Is it any wonder that Margaret Atwood's dystopian *The Handmaid's Tale* (and its sequel, *The Testament*) might seem more sensational—and more relevant—now than when it was published three decades ago?

In short, the time seems right to bring forth a new edition of *Ingersoll*. In the story, Ingersoll is the fictitious center of dogma-free research and learning created by billionaire Bryce Jones and named after Robert Ingersoll, the nineteenth century luminary sometimes called "The Great Agnostic." While Jones's desire is for the center to be apolitical, he soon finds that this goal is a victim of hyperpolitical times: It is impossible to be dogma-free in a determinedly dogmatic society. Ingersoll, then, must become a political counterweight to those who would subvert the nation's foundational ideals.

Jones has entrusted this mission to two leaders who are, at once, highly capable and humanly flawed. This contradiction is essential to the story and a reflection of the human condition writ large. If the United States of America is, as many assert, an exceptional nation, it is not because it has been divinely created or commanded to be so. There are no guarantees for our future. America will succeed or fail on the shoulders of its inhabitants

.

Richard Samuel Sheres
Alexandria, Virginia,
April 2020

Prologue

Candles That Do Not Flicker

THE CROWD ON THE National Mall is enormous. It is primed, ready to explode—a jarring reminder of how suddenly things can turn upside down.

The weather is still warm; it is a dying day of a summer that seems like it never was. There was a meteorological summer, yes, but that is not what stands out or is likely to be remembered.

The dissonance is caused by the timing of the attack, at the end of August, an event filled with horror and fresh warnings that great power does not equal great security. Until then, summer was almost normal, filled with enough of the usual diversions to give hope that things were settling down, the country finding its way again. In these circumstances it would seem logical that the whole summer could not have been lost.

But it will be remembered as lost nonetheless. How people remember pain depends on when the worst of the pain occurred. The summer ended in excruciating pain, so the whole summer is remembered as excruciatingly painful. Or as something best forgotten.

As if it could be.

The people on the Mall want to know how much they are supposed to take before they act on their convictions. How much calamity and general misfortune are they supposed to ignore or rationalize away? They want to know when the most obvious evidence of God's displeasure can be explained as anything *other* than His displeasure. That is the basic question, the subtext of all of the day's activity.

The attack itself was perhaps less spectacular than the one that occurred on Nine-Eleven. This time there was less innocence to shock. And the state of the country isn't what it was in 2001. This time it is exhausted, worn down from without and hollowed out from within. Especially from within.

To the people on the Mall the important signs were there long before the attack, which was merely the final vindication. First came the sudden, incessant wave of natural disasters that stripped the phrase Acts of God of its insurance-speak banality. The country has enough trouble dealing with disasters when they come one, or even two, at a time. But four or five?

The Gulf Coast devastated—yet again—by storms of unprecedented fury, one after another, and which this time didn't have the decency to remain in the usual Gulf playgrounds. Up the East Coast they went, soaking and flooding, spawning funnels, ripping off roofs built to withstand snow, not century-plus mile per hour winds driving horizontal rain.

In the West, to the usual cycle of forest fires leading to bare hillsides leading to mudslides leading to new growth and new fires was added the Bay Area quake and tsunami and devastation not seen in San Francisco since 1906.

In the center, tornados in the Alley that bears their name flattened towns, while the Rivers Mississippi and Ohio obliterated their banks, rolling over picturesque and not so picturesque towns alike, turning farmland to wasteland, and spreading disease.

Where was the people's government, their rescue of last resort? Nowhere. Spent, depleted on every level. Never fully recovered from the financial disasters of '08 and the endless political babble. Like the people it is supposed to care for, it is broke and broken down; it is inadequate, feckless and irrelevant—a coldhearted remedial lesson in the value of self-reliance. Is it any wonder that President Stuart's rote annual declaration to Congress that The State of The Union Is Sound brought him only embarrassing snickers from all parties and factions, no matter what side of the aisle they inhabited?

"What's next, locusts?" The hackneyed joke was a little too close for comfort. Certainly not very amusing to Believers with a capital B. Even semi-Believers, who claim to accept the Bible but not its literal truth, are less cavalier about dismissing it (the Book of Exodus in particular) as parable. And there is no longer self-consciousness in declarations that God had great plans for the nation—until it turned its back on Him: *We fell away, and He has his methods of communicating this to us. Obviously, it was taking more than one calamity at a time to get our full attention.*

To the people assembled here, the realization of God's displeasure has spun off a series of hard conclusions: Tolerance is not always possible. Compromise goes only so far. When you know the truth, you either stick to your guns or you don't. When you don't, God knows how to make His wishes known.

But perhaps, finally, the message was getting through, though not without a false start. At the very beginning of the summer it appeared things actually might be returning to what used to be called normal. Maybe the worst was over. And then . . . not the attack—not yet—but rather the clever run-up to the attack. The saturation of the ground ahead of the storm.

One might think that a nation that came into being using guerrilla tactics would understand how to fight a guerrilla war—how to avoid being stuck in rigid red-coated lines and shot at from behind trees. But while the country's security empire was preparing for The Big One, the enemies figured out that small was better. They figured out that it's not necessary to bring down a skyscraper.

All it takes is the occasional pop-up act of terror, the occasional assassination—and not necessarily of famous people, either. The odd cyclist shot on a bike path, a mother hit while loading her groceries into the car as the kids squabble inside, an elderly man strangled in his bed, a child snatched from school—any of these will do just fine if the objective is to create generalized fear—a national case of the jitters. Randomness is the key. The odds of a particular individual being hit are as small as the chances of hitting it big in the lottery. Creating a pervasive belief that no one is safe is huge.

And then, once credibility is established, a force multiplier: simple threats. *A bomb has been left at . . . so and so is to be killed or kidnapped . . . .* The beauty of it is that only occasionally does something actually have to happen to keep the pot boiling. The enemies understand that panic is a wondrous thing in the way it eats a society alive from the inside. Panic's ally, unfocused rage, is also useful. It leads to citizens devouring one another. It leads to even more bloated and ineffective security organizations. Big events only have to be carried out occasionally, and even then not necessarily directed against the kinds of symbolic targets hit at the beginning of the century.

All it took in August was a modest radiological event (as the emergency responders labeled it) in an obscure, indefensible place. The small—tiny, really, as such things go—dirty bomb went off in Evansville, Indiana. Who knows where it will be next time? It almost doesn't matter.

Technically, it's not even that Evansville couldn't have been defended; the problem is that, like most places, it was indefensible in the sense that not every place can be protected all the time. Casualties only need to be in the hundreds to overwhelm the hospitals. Meanwhile, no amount of security equipment—sensors, police vehicles, fire equipment and the like—is sufficient to deal with a real catastrophe.

And so here the people are, at the intersection of panicked searching for answers and absolute certainty about where the answers are to be found: America has gotten off track, they say. It has moved away from its God-given purpose. Isn't this clear enough?

They accept as given that Muslims must be opposed, and no longer will they submit to the soft liberal tropes of moral and cultural relativism, or to the naive belief that it is not necessary for Christians to assert their own identity.

The throng on the Mall is determined to retrieve all of it: the sense of national self and purpose, the confidence—the *We're-Number-One* swagger. The people are there to remind the world that the nation is great because God intends it to be so. He made this clear when He endowed the Founding Fathers with the wisdom to create a model for all humanity. It was the perfect example: a democratic republic that, like human beings, is flawed but has within it the power of redemption. The power to rise up and exalt itself.

No more! That is the message they have received all afternoon from speaker after speaker and singer after singer. America is supposed to be a nation where God is respected, where the holy union between man and woman is respected, where the spark of life is more than respected, it is sacred. If these things aren't clear, they will be made clear in writing, in the form of an amended Constitution, which at this moment is a hairsbreadth from becoming the law of the land. The amendments leave no room for interpretation or judicial parsing: no same-sex marriage, and no abortion for any reason.

But it is a third amendment that for this assembled mass will be the crowning achievement. The key words in the amendment are simple and straightforward: *No law or regulation will constrain beliefs and practices related to the preeminent place of Judeo-Christian principles in the nation's founding, or deny the role of the Creator in granting and protecting the nation's freedoms.* If this is not clear enough, the second section says that the people retain the right to pray and to advertise their religious beliefs everywhere, including schools.

Overnight, the movement has gained mass and thrust. This is obvious to anyone who looks out at the sea of candles beginning to illuminate the dusk.

What more proof can there be than thousands upon thousands—hundreds of thousands—of committed believers coming together to light up the sky—and this following a spectacular sunset, too.

They have been well choreographed. They have been told where to stand for greatest visual effect. They have formed their candlelit number into a great crucifix of humanity, which will be ever brighter as the sky darkens and more flames are added.

Only one thing is not happening as planned, and even this is for a salutary reason. The massive crucifix of people was intended to move. The cameras were to capture this symbol of the Lord as it surged toward the chancel of Lincoln's Memorial, thousands of the faithful parting at the long reflecting pool, flanking it on either side to create a dark center in the watery nave of the cross, a symbol of the hurt in the Lord's heart that the people are meant to fill. And the mirror of candles shows the way. The cross is there, but it cannot move as planned. There are simply too many people. They cannot move, nor do they need to.

The Reverend Morgan Fitzgerald stands before them on the Memorial's steps. This event is his doing, more than anyone's. It is his church in California that took the bit, took God's message and used every opportunity and every trick of modern technology to spread it.

As a leader, Fitzgerald embodies the perfect combination of zeal, intelligence, and affability. Anyone can approach him and get a fair hearing.

Even from a distance he is easy to see. He is tall. His weight bounces between two hundred fifty and three hundred pounds. At the moment, it appears nearer the high side.

He is surrounded by other leaders of the movement. It is obvious that they defer to him.

He looks out upon the great human-candle crucifix and prepares to speak. There is no extraneous sound to signal this intention—no tapping on the mike, intake of air, or clearing of the throat. His audience silences itself all the same, and looks to him. When he begins, it is without hesitation.

"'I have put before you life and death, blessing and curse,'" his voice rings out, full of confidence and honey. "'Choose life, that you and your offspring shall live.' This is what the Bible tells us. In these few eloquent words God tells us most of what we need to know. He has given us choice, but there is really only one choice that makes sense." The Amens reverberate in the open space, joyous shouts and low murmurs combining into a rumble of purpose.

"Follow, then, to our Lord and Savior Christ Jesus, who gives us the rest of the great instruction: Choose life in this world and for all eternity. Choose life, that you and your offspring shall live for ever and ever." More Amens follow. Already many in the crowd have begun to weep.

"Today, our nation faces this very question. Shall we choose life here and now and for all eternity? Or shall we make the wrong choice, with all the anguish this entails?"

Fitzgerald stands back and surveys the crowd. His fervor turns into a smile. "Now," he tells his listeners, "some people might reasonably ask, well, what took you so long?"

A man who recognizes the need for a bottle of wine to breathe, Fitzgerald pauses to let the laughs and cheers ripen in the crowd. "It's a good question. We certainly took a lot of whacks on the head. How could we not have followed the signposts that God so clearly set out for us?

"Brothers and sisters, at last the scales have fallen from our eyes! Shall we ensure that every living thing that contains the spark of God is preserved and protected?"

The masses before him have no doubt.

"Shall the United States of America, given to us by God, now make the right choice?"

Yes!

"Ladies and gentlemen, on this wondrous evening I submit to you that it must!"

Amen! God bless you, Reverend!

"It must—*we* must—because there is no other reasonable choice. We have come to that point where we as a nation can go only one of two ways. We can let things go on as they are and lurch from tragedy to tragedy as the very fabric of our society is shredded. Or we can choose life, that we and our offspring shall live."

* * *

Not far from here, two men and a woman are watching the proceedings in fascination and, despite their deep antipathy, something approaching awe for Fitzgerald and the movement he inspires. Whatever considerable differences may define these observers, they share a certainty that Fitzgerald and his followers are wrong, and dangerous. The threats he speaks of are as much as anything the product of the things he advocates.

In a sense, they have learned the same lesson as the believers: It is long past time people stood up—really stood up—for their convictions. They understand that in the end their biggest challenge may not be Fitzgerald, but rather their own side: If the believers are characterized by spark, steam, and unity of purpose, those who might oppose them are freighted with the ballast of smugness, indifference, denial, and petty fractiousness.

The three would not have chosen this battle, and they have come to it late, but for many reasons they are in the best position to wage it. Before long, they will offer a unique rallying point to confront the challenges, both outside and in.

Richard Samuel Sheres

The Amendments

Amendment XXVIII

Section 1. Marriage is defined as a legal union between one man and one woman.

Section 2. Congress and the several States shall have power to enforce this article by appropriate legislation.

Amendment XXIX

Section 1. The right to life is a paramount and most fundamental right of a person.

Section 2. With respect to the right to life guaranteed to persons by the Fifth and Fourteenth Articles of Amendment to the Constitution, the word "person" applies to all human beings irrespective of age, health, function, or condition of dependency, including their unborn offspring at every stage of their biologic development including fertilization.

Section 3. No unborn person shall be deprived of life by any person, provided, however, that nothing in this article shall prohibit a law allowing justification to be shown for only those medical procedures required to prevent the death of either the pregnant woman or her unborn offspring as long as such law requires every reasonable effort to be made to preserve the life of each.

Section 4. Congress and the several States shall have power to enforce this article by appropriate legislation.

<u>Amendment XXX</u>
Section 1. Congress shall make no law and the Executive shall make no regulation abridging the free exercise of religious belief or practice; nor shall they by law or regulation undermine or constrain beliefs and practices related to the preeminent place of Judeo-Christian principles in the nation's founding; nor shall they make laws or regulations that have the effect of constraining or denying the role of the Creator in granting and protecting the nation's freedoms.

Section 2. The people retain the right to pray and to recognize their religious beliefs, heritage and traditions on public property, including schools.

Section 3. These Articles supersede only the first clause, respecting the establishment and exercise of religion, in Amendment I. All other clauses in Amendment I remain in force.

Chapter 1

Ingersoll, September

FROM HIS POSITION AT center stage, the man in the dark gray suit with precisely aligned pinstripes looks out over the auditorium. His is the calm confidence of the highly accomplished or the very rich. It is a ceremonial kind of day, but he is not one to stand on ceremony, so there will be no flowery introductions. He has not made a grand entrance. At the appointed time he will begin to speak.

Still, to understate the significance of the event would be a mistake. The man has been working toward it for years, largely in secret. His planning has been meticulous, and this again is misleading, for while the man is well known for the kinds of splashy surprises he will attempt today, he is not usually known to be invested in the details, which he places in the hands of others; his powers of concentration are normally focused on choosing the right others. But for this project he has had to control even small things. It is the only way it could work.

The man is C. Bryce Jones, known simply as Bryce both by those who have met him and those who have not but who for any number of reasons need to feed the illusion of easy familiarity with money and celebrity. He is standing at the podium on the stage of the auditorium of the town he has built on the banks of the Potomac and called, formally, until today, the Potomac Institute for Research and Development, but widely known simply as The Institute. The stated ambition of The Institute is progressive, unfettered research in the service of human advancement.

Begun a mere four years ago, The Institute is already a sprawling complex of buildings just south of Washington, D.C., on the Maryland side of the river. In the pursuit of speed, Bryce never failed to remind people that the Empire State Building was raised in a year, and that the colossal commercial project next door called National Harbor seemed not to take much longer than that.

The Institute is completely Bryce-funded; it wants for nothing. The best for the best and the brightest, he said. This was shortly after he declined to follow Buffett's example to put his billions in the service of the Gates Foundation. He said he would prefer to provide the world with a Plan B alternative made up of Plan A players. Science, philosophy, medicine, the arts—nothing is off limits if it can reasonably result in progress, broadly defined. What the world needs is intellectual seed corn, he said. The combination of high salaries, independence, low-to-zero teaching loads and the best facilities created an instant draw.

The seats are beginning to fill. There are members and guests of The Institute, a surprisingly large representation from local churches, and a decidedly junior delegation from local media outlets; most of the reporters cover the everyday business beat and are there to witness the latest Bryce acquisition or bright thought for the cable news digest, blog, social network, or inside newspaper pages. It is to be an easy day for them, the very essence of quotidian—an announcement, a schmooze, a quick file, and an early dinner.

The notes in front of Bryce are not extensive. At 73, his eyes, once the color of avocado but now the gray-green of a depleted ore, still focus well. He may wear the mock tortoise reading half glasses with the high-arch bridge out of habit, but he will not need them. He has always been comfortable speaking extemporaneously, and he has been so immersed in the project for so long, he can speak clearly to it and address any question that arises. The bullet points in front of him are only for unknowable emergencies; chance favors the prepared, as Pasteur said.

Looking out at the faces of this junior press corps, Bryce wonders if he hasn't made a mistake by not hyping the event. Seated at a table behind him are two people who are keys to the day and to the entire enterprise. One is a long-trusted associate who is well known in the business community for managing Bryce's most challenging projects. His name is Ansel Frye, and no one who has followed Bryce's activities will be surprised to see him.

To see him in this context, once the context becomes clear, may be another matter. The Institute may have begun as a pet project, but to Bryce it has become a passion, the nearest a nonreligious man will come to a calling. Profit is not the motive. By all means run it well; it must be run well, as any Bryce project must be, and there is no question that Ansel will play to this strength. But this is a time of crisis, and the general must be not only a planner. He must be a believer in the cause, and for the first time in their long association, Ansel has had to be persuaded to take on a project—a fact that is deeply perplexing to Bryce.

No such persuasion was needed for the woman to Ansel's left, and if there is any tipoff that this is not to be a routine occasion it is her presence.

She is India Ruiz, who is to liberal causes what oxygen is to fire. However much Bryce wants Ansel's steady hand, he knows that the times require a crusader who can devote all of her steam to a project. Ansel can rein her in if necessary, but give him a need to rein someone in.

Without a doubt, if India had her way this day would be a spectacle. It was Ansel's idea to tone it down. Let the media heavies catch up to the news, he reasoned. They always overcompensate. Besides, if the big church presence is any indication, the fuse has already been lit.

India's presence aside, there is only one hint of the explosion to come. It is in the image projected on the stage and the walls of the auditorium, floating slowly as if reflected off a mirrored ball. It says, "Welcome to Ingersoll, Cradle of Freedom and Progress."

* * *

The front rows are reserved for press. Ansel recognizes a reporter from a local TV station who is having trouble keeping his eyes open.

Another, who Ansel does not recognize, has apparently given up the fight.

"I wouldn't mind seeing a little more anticipation from the media," Bryce says to Ansel in a low voice, his brow furrowing slightly in a way Ansel has come to understand expresses more displeasure than Bryce will let on. He knows that India will take satisfaction in the remark, if she has heard it.

"They'll regret it," Ansel responds. "Just wait until the map goes up." He says this with a calm confidence that betrays no doubt.

In some ways, even more than Bryce, Ansel projects an image of command. At fifty-one, he is in his prime. His shape has thickened, but not softened. His hair, half grayed and still full, is a secret source of pride. He believes that rigor must compensate for losses in youthful exuberance and endurance.

The auditorium has filled quickly. There is a growing energy in the room that the reporters can't account for, but at any rate have begun to notice.

Ansel looks over to India. The two are close in age, Ansel a few years older. She is a small woman, but not fragile. Her skin is inclined toward olive and in addition suggests a permanently faded tan, like that of someone who was too much in love with the sun for the first twenty or so omnipotent years of her life. She has a large freckle below her right eye, near her nose. Her hair is cut practical-short, something not to be bothered with, but it is stylish. At one time it would have been shockingly black; now it is transitioning to silver. When she smiles, she reminds people of a certain age of a young Joan Baez.

Bryce looks at Ansel, then at India, and asks if they are ready. They nod, but he does not really need a response. Tom Whist, Bryce's personal assistant since he graduated from the University of Richmond the year before, anticipates him and mouths that the electronics are right, and the house lights dim.

Bryce leans in slightly, half glasses sliding toward the tip of his nose. A thinning shock of white hair falls onto his forehead, and he reflexively pushes it back. "I'd like to welcome you to The Community of Ingersoll," he says, and the remaining audience chatter falls off.

"For those of you who don't know, more than a century ago, Robert Green Ingersoll was America's foremost advocate of agnosticism and what was widely known as freethought. Both of these things are in short supply today, to the point where our nation is threatened as it has not been since the Civil War. Our most fundamental freedoms are at stake, as are the precious commodity of unfettered thought and the nurturing of new ideas."

In the audience, the reporters are exchanging glances. This is not what they were expecting. But this is not the case for many others scattered in islands throughout the auditorium. Many of these people lean forward in their seats, as if awaiting a signal.

"This nation was founded on the principle—born out of necessity—of church-state separation. There have been many attempts to rewrite this history. Indeed, the American Revolution has been recast as a story of American exceptionalism, and an exceptionalism of a dangerous kind— not of a nation's preeminence based on merit, but of one that reflects a supreme creator's desire to kindle a national point of light in the world. Some of the most distorting of these efforts have portrayed the Founding Fathers as devout Christians—which the most important of them were not—intent upon founding a Christian nation, which they were not."

Throughout the room there are pockets of restlessness as people shift in their seats. But some of the disquiet is not easily defined; it is a free-floating energy that seems to be awaiting release. In the seats behind the podium, India eases closer to Ansel, who leans in so he can hear what she is about to whisper.

"There are too many people out there who have been prepped for what we're doing," she mouths.

"There's nothing that doesn't leak in this town," Ansel mouths back as Bryce goes on.

"In reality, of course, the guiding principle of our nation was wariness of state-sponsored religion and fear—a fear fully subscribed to by Christian denominations themselves—that the state would do precisely what our Constitution forbids—create an established, favored faith."

India shifts impatiently closer to Ansel. He can see she is not satisfied with his rote response.

"This is a very selective leak," she says, almost too loudly. "The press members seem clueless, and most of our own people don't know what's going on either. It's only the churchers scattered around the room who are in the loop."

"How do you know that?"

"I recognize some of them. They're prepared for something."

Ansel puts out his hand palm down to suggest India should lower her voice. He nods in acknowledgment of the point she is making, and returns his attention to Bryce.

"Unfortunately," Bryce is saying, "it is also telling that one of our great patriots, Thomas Paine, went from being the foremost champion of the revolutionary cause to a man reviled and determinedly forgotten for the crime of choosing to advocate reason over unthinking subservience to God. But that is the legacy of a large segment of Christianity in this country, and it is a legacy whose effects we are feeling acutely today."

"You are a liar and a perverter of the truth!" The woman's words pierce the auditorium.

Bryce has anticipated such outbursts, and intends to ignore them. There will be plenty of opportunity to wage the fight. Still, his reflex is to look up to see the source before he continues. What he sees are assents and mouthed Amens by the people around the protester—ripples around the stone's point of entry.

"In recent years, the efforts to undermine our constitutional freedoms have become ever more craven . . ."

"You are the one who is craven! You are a blot in the sight of God!" This time there is no difficulty identifying the speaker. The woman has stood to make her declaration, and now sits down.

Only someone close enough to see Bryce's face clearly will catch the ghost of anger that passes. Some may notice the briefest flicker in his delivery. However, Bryce is a disciplined man, and there is no chance of his being deterred. "Like Thomas Paine, freethinkers throughout history have had to contend mightily with the forces of dogma and"—he adds this in pointed tones—"bullying, sometimes violent repression."

In another part of the audience, a man stands. He is dressed neatly in olive Dockers and a checked long-sleeved shirt. "This *was* a Christian nation, and will be again!" His voice is strong, well rehearsed and not shrill, and he says this as if to point out a matter of fact. He is bearing witness, making a correction.

Bryce starts to go on, but stops as the still-standing man gets the better of him. The man seems to have said all he intends to say, but his erect posture suggests he will remain standing, and others in the audience join him.

Bryce looks down at his notes, taking a moment to collect his thoughts. But before he can continue, Ansel steps up to the podium and leans into the microphone. "Sir, there will be an opportunity for questions after Mr. Jones has finished his remarks. We ask you to be patient and courteous."

This time it is a woman who stands. "Not when our precious souls are in the balance!" This woman is shrill, but it is more difficult to tell whether she is rehearsed (the remark is, after all, not quite on point) or spontaneous.

Reporters in the front of the room crane their necks to see what is going on behind them, but by now they may be the only ones in the room who are surprised by the sharp rise in temperature. Some of them have a quizzical look, as if they had been sent to cover a flower show but encountered a race riot.

In the audience, others stand but remain silent, heads bowed, one hand over heart, the other raised to God.

"If people insist on interrupting the program," Ansel begins, still leaning into Bryce's podium mike. But Bryce holds up a hand, preventing him from delivering the consequences part of the sentence.

Bryce covers the mike with his hand and leans toward Ansel. "If their plan is just to stand, let them."

Ansel nods, but he is skeptical as he returns to his seat. As he does, he sees that the security people have made themselves more obvious in the auditorium.

One of the reporters turns to another. "What the hell . . ." he mouths.

Bryce looks around and goes on. "Although it may surprise some people, the current efforts to formally declare the United States a Christian nation are not unprecedented. In fact, there have been many proposed constitutional amendments over the years. All of them have failed."

"Not this time!" a woman shouts. A security guard, an immense black man in a tent-size royal blue Ingersoll blazer, gray pants, crisp shirt and rep tie, his head shaved and shined, moves toward the woman and tells her what Ansel had started to announce—that if she can't sit quietly, she will be removed. He is polite but firm, managing to command a baritone voice in a way that is at once clearly audible and not in itself disruptive.

"You can throw every last one of us out," the woman says, as the guard comes closer, "but the soldiers of God will not be defeated this time!" She moves toward the aisle, and the guard seems to relax as she apparently will leave voluntarily. Nevertheless, he places the guiding hand of authority near her elbow, until she spins and tells him, loudly, "You don't have to touch me! I'm leaving!" But she hasn't gone far before she turns again to announce, "You will not have a community dedicated to wickedness here! We will not allow it!"

Bryce waits for the auditorium door to close behind the woman. "As you will see in a moment," he continues, "today's announcement is more than a statement of intent. Ingersoll has been in the making for some time. Under the banner of our original name, the Potomac Institute for Research and Development, we have established a place for rigorous thought, reflection and research, free from the preconceptions and certainties of religion or dogma of any kind. Today, we officially begin the next phase of The Institute's life. As its name has changed to The Community of Ingersoll, so will its activities and its place in the national debate expand."

As Bryce has been speaking, more people have been standing in choreographed pose, with heads bowed, left hand placed over heart and right hand raised to heaven; not raised in stiff-armed salute but with a sharp break at the wrist that opens the palm in a way that might be interpreted as a contradictory desire simultaneously to receive God and to hold His wrath at bay should they somehow have provoked it. They are quiet, but their presence is clearly unsettling to Bryce as he pauses, lips pursed, and surveys the audience.

"Ladies and gentlemen, in the coming days much will be revealed about Ingersoll. For today, however, we want everyone to understand one simple message: We will not permit zealots to take our country without a fight.

"When I say 'our country' I am talking about the America that at its best has been, in fact, the city on the hill that the early religionists spoke of. We speak of it not in religious terms, but in the model America has presented to the world as a light of freedom and human progress." Bryce pauses to scan the audience, anticipating an outburst. People are still standing, but they remain quiet.

"Today, there are many who would try to extinguish that light. Some are enemies from abroad. Some are people at home who, out of fear or misguided notions of security, would respond to our enemies by giving them what they want—the weakening of our own freedoms from within. And then there are those in the religious community who would use the country's weakness and pain—especially since the disastrous August terror attack—to further their own narrow aims.

"A century and a half ago, a brave man named Robert Green Ingersoll argued tenaciously and eloquently that human progress can come only with free thought. He advocated humanism, and these words from his Humanist Credo are words our own community pledges to live by:

'We are not endeavoring to chain the future, but to free the present. We are not forging fetters for our children, but we are breaking those our fathers made for us. . . . We are the advocates of inquiry—of investigation and thought. . . . We know that doing away with gods and supernatural persons and powers is not an end. It is a means to an end, and that real end is the happiness of mankind.'"

Under her breath, India says, "Shit, he took out the best line."

Ansel knows the one she means. It was his idea to take it out—there will be more than enough opportunity to slap the face of the religious community.

India quietly says the line now, her jaw taut, her eyes wide and focused on Bryce's back. *"We are satisfied that there can be but little liberty on earth while men worship a tyrant in heaven."*

But Bryce has gone on. "Many of you are familiar with the research institutions that have been established here over the past four years. Today, I am proud to unveil the rest of our community."

Bryce motions to his assistant. The lights dim further as a map appears on screens around the auditorium.

The room is mostly quiet as the people in the audience seem not to understand what they are seeing. The map shows an aerial view of several square miles adjacent to the existing site of The Institute. The original area appears in dark green; the larger adjacent area is shaded in a slightly lighter green. Superimposed is the word "Ingersoll," and beneath that, in smaller typeface, the legend "The Community for Human Progress."

"What you are looking at," Bryce continues, "is our expanded community. Building upon our existing center along the river, the larger community will provide space for a range of living situations and activities, including residential housing, recreational facilities, commercial and some light industrial activity, and so forth."

"Excuse me, Bryce . . . Mr. Jones," a reporter calls out. "Forgive me, but I don't quite understand what we're looking at. Precisely what part of this area is Ingersoll?"

A buzz of concurrence follows as Bryce holds up a hand. "Allow me to finish, and I think it will become clear. The short answer to your question is, all of it."

At this, the room becomes a hive. The previously listless reporters are on the edge of their seats, hands in the air. Even the religious standers apparently have not been tipped off to the extent of what they are seeing. Their outstretched arms have fallen to a slightly lower angle, as they squint toward the screens. On the stage, Ansel and India smile at one another, then return their attention to Bryce.

"As you can see," Bryce says, "most of the area south of Fort Washington and west of Route 210, the Indian Head Highway—about ninety-five percent of it—that is privately held, will be incorporated into Ingersoll. The area surrounds, but for obvious reasons can't include, some federal park lands, to which of course we will ensure public access. We already had considerable river frontage, but we've also purchased key transportation and infrastructure facilities, such as the small airport at Bennsville, which was already privately owned and which we intend to upgrade."

"Wait!" one of the formerly sleeping reporters calls out. "Who do you mean when you say *we*?"

"The land is owned by me directly or by several companies that I control. We have begun working with local authorities to incorporate the properties under one private community—that is to say, Ingersoll—and have made considerable progress toward this end."

The sound in the room is now coming in disconnected bursts, as some in the audience speak animatedly to their neighbors and then pause to study the map. One of the reporters turns to another in the row behind him. Caught by a sudden ebb in the sound, he says, more loudly than he intended, "The son-of-a-bitch has gone and bought himself a county."

Bryce skips a beat, with a wisp of a smile, as pockets of laughter emerge and several people lean in to their neighbors to ask what they had missed.

"Above all, as a community, we intend to fight any and all efforts to bridge the separation of church and state, which has been at the root of our national existence and success. This of course includes the current proposed constitutional amendments that are making their way through the states for ratification.

"As befits the name, Ingersoll is a community that actively encourages what has often been called freethinking, unencumbered by pressures for conformity. Above all, we actively discourage the forces of religion—all religion, I might add, not just Christianity as some of our detractors have claimed—which we believe to be on the whole a negative aspect of human existence.

"This does not mean that the people who work here cannot hold or express religious beliefs. We do not, after all, want to impinge upon human progress by adopting the very strictures that throughout history have been imposed by religious institutions. It does mean that our community has a clearly stated philosophy of non-belief, and that none of our facilities will be in any way sectarian. The only object of worship here will be unfettered human progress. Ingersoll will devote political energies to ensuring that our nation preserves the freedoms envisioned by the founders and enshrined in the Constitution. The current effort to declare the United States a Judeo-Christian nation is particularly egregious.

"I am sorry to say that we have come very late to this mission. As you know, only a few more states must ratify the proposed amendments for them to become law. But let me be clear: We will do everything in our power to defeat them. Among other things, this means we will proceed much sooner than planned to make Ingersoll more than a concentrated research and learning center; we will work urgently to realize the comprehensive community for freethought that you see on the map today, as well as to make it a political action center.

"Now, when I speak of leadership, I hope you'll understand that I don't mean leadership that is limited to a nonbelieving community. That would be a recipe for failure. Crises like the present one tend to focus on the extremes. We need to remember that most people are neither atheists nor radical fundamentalists. Our community rejects unquestioning belief of all kinds. We must convince a majority of our compatriots that what we stand for is freedom—freedom of choice and freedom of belief.

"On a personal note, I'd like to say that of all the ambitious projects I have undertaken in my life, this one is the most vitally important. Accordingly, I will devote my time, reputation and whatever resources I have at my disposal to making Ingersoll—and, more to the point, the mission of Ingersoll—a success. I will provide the resources to get Ingersoll off to a good start. However, in the long run Ingersoll must become self-sustaining, which is one reason I want it to include a larger economic base.

"Finally, I intend to begin the retreat into the background immediately. In truth, had we not been faced with the present national crisis, I would have handled the entire project anonymously."

In the audience, hands are already shooting up. "And to show I mean what I say, I'm joining you in the audience and turning over the stage to Ansel Frye and India Ruiz. They will answer your questions. Thank you."

Chapter 2

Forfend Heaven

ANSEL LEANS TOO FAR forward into his microphone, causing a brief feedback screech before he can adjust his distance. "Before we go any further, I'd like to thank Bryce for the confidence he has shown me and India in leading Ingersoll at this critical time. And with that, we'll take your questions." Ansel points to a reporter.

"I'm Brad Johnston, CNN," the man says, standing. "Mr. Frye, could you or Ms. Ruiz elaborate on the timing question. From Mr. Jones's remarks, I understand that the Ingersoll project, by which I mean the original research core and until-now secret commercial and residential area, was rushed into operation. Why now? Why not, say, six months ago? And what is the significance of the larger area? Could you not have operated from the existing core?"

"Frankly, we underestimated the speed with which the Christian Coalition would be able to push the amendments through the state ratification process. Bryce mentioned the importance of engaging the great majority of people who don't identify directly with any side. It will be our challenge to convince them that they cannot afford to be a silent majority.

"To some extent we have to blame the climate of fear and extremism and the rapid deterioration in every area of national life that coincided with the introduction of the amendments in Congress. There was the long-sour economy, of course, and its many manifestations such as increased poverty, suffering and crime, and also the pronounced loss of national purpose. The August terror attack was the final shot of adrenalin needed by the amendments' supporters.

"Anyone who has followed India's career knows her reputation as a leader in the great social causes of our time, including of course the freethought movement. We're now down to a few battleground states, and there is no time for delay. We also realized that we needed someone like India to lead the political effort."

The reporters jockey for the next question. India holds up a hand to indicate she wants to say something, but before she speaks a question is shouted. "Are you an atheist, India?"

"Yes." She answers without hesitation, and pauses to let the word speak for itself before she adds, "I don't think I've ever been unclear about that. To answer the earlier question, we could have conducted our program from the original center, but we wanted to make a statement, now and for the future."

A reporter's question penetrates. It comes from one of the business beat drones familiar to Bryce and Ansel, who is in the process of tunneling in to bury the lead. "What kinds of facilities do you plan to build?" he asks.

"Not houses of worship, you can count on that," India responds quickly, eliciting low laughter from the audience.

"Susan Price, NBC Media Group. If you lose Virginia, do you lose the fight? And how do you fit with other civil liberties groups that are pursuing similar goals?"

"There's no doubt that losing Virginia would make things much more difficult," India says. "But we're confident that we won't lose Virginia. Virginia symbolizes the very essence of American revolutionary ideals. It led the way to our country's founding, and we believe strongly Virginians won't fail to meet the challenge today. As for the other organizations, we hope to work closely with them to achieve our common goals. We will offer them resources as appropriate, but they are, and will remain, independent."

Another anonymous shout: "You're pro-abortion, aren't you Ms. Ruiz?"

Before India can answer, Ansel leans in to his mike. "I'd hoped we'd made this clear, but we won't answer shouted questions from unidentified sources."

A reporter stands quickly. He is tall, wiry, with an austere aspect to him. "Steve Carlsbad, Christian Broadcasting," he says in a clarion voice that Ansel associates with evangelical preachers.

The reporter is handed a microphone. He glances at an index card. "Ms. Ruiz, can you explain why Americans, traditionally a religious people, should accept your interpretation of history? Only a small—and, I might say, fractious—percentage of Americans don't believe in God. Why should they concern themselves, let alone fear, what could be called the latest in a long line of failed atheist experiments?"

Ansel jumps in, but lightly: "Mr. Carlsbad, I think you're getting ahead of yourself, aren't you? We are extremely confident in our future, and in the good sense of the American people."

"Whatever Americans believe or don't believe about God," India adds, "they believe in freedom."

"But you would impose atheism as the country's religion," says an unidentified female voice from the back.

Ansel looks up to find the violator of the rules, and lightly puts a hand on India's to keep her from responding.

"Sorry," the voice says. A middle-aged woman rises. "Judy Bascomb, Christ the King Church, right here in the middle of your atheist badlands." The remark gets a laugh out of the audience. "One of the few property islands to resist the billionaire Jones's tempting pieces of silver," she adds. In a more serious tone she asks, "You don't really think you can require people to be atheists, do you? I assume some lawyer has told you that you can't have an atheist residence requirement here, or much less impose one on the rest of the country."

"We have no intention of imposing anything on anyone," India says forcefully. "I think it's fair to say that imposition of belief, often upon pain of excruciating death, is the province of religious people, Christians and Islamists chief among them, not freethinkers."

At this, Ansel shoots Bryce a quick look. In a couple of brief sentences India has encapsulated what he hopes for and what he fears. She will raise the temperature of the argument . . . and yes, she will raise the temperature of the argument. He is concerned about her deliberate—he knows from talking to her that it is deliberate—conflation of Christians with, not Muslims, which in the present hostile climate would be bad enough, but Islamists, the accepted shorthand for radical Muslims, which is to say, terrorists. "What is to be gained by equating Christians with terrorism?" he had asked her.

Ansel knows that Bryce is counting on his steady hand to balance India's aggressive advocacy. India is to have considerable leeway in the Nonbeliever versus Believer contest, but Bryce is concerned that she have some brake on her, and that brake is to be Ansel. Whatever her strengths, India carries heavy baggage in the form of divorce from her husband and remarriage to Karen Walker. Combined with her record of radical activism, these things make it easy for the conservative religious establishment to paint her as an emblem of the evils of nonbelief. On almost every count Ansel is thought to be a good counterbalance to India: exemplary professional reputation, loving husband, winning personality.

Ansel is concerned that India's rejection of religion—organized religion, above all—is so strong that it makes her suspicious of all forms of organization—or perhaps structure would be a better word. To her, organizations almost inevitably become autocratic and repressive. She has a serious libertarian streak; her attitude is, you don't bother me and I won't bother you.

Ansel worries that she doesn't fully grasp that her certainty, confidence and independence from religious moorings are not common in the general population, and that, lacking these attributes, most people feel a fundamental, often unspoken need for some sort of spiritual connection and some sort of ritual. He believes that when people pray—particularly when they are in dire straits—they are doing more than beseeching a higher power. Whether the occasion is a Catholic Mass or a Muslim call to prayer, as much as anything it is a chance for people to find an area of peace and certainty in their lives. It is a chance for them to find a place of order, where they feel they have some control; whether or not their prayers are answered, at least they can control what they ask for.

India would say (and Ansel would largely agree) that this solace is achieved in the service of a lie (God, His prophets, and so on), and that when individuals combine in the service of their personal spiritual needs, they become assertive, insufferably righteous, and often violent.

Ansel is acutely concerned (and he thinks India should be more concerned) that their project suffers under the weight of a great paradox: It champions individualism and then asks the individuals to combine to defend their right to be individuals. And, to India's point, if they succeed in organizing, nonbelievers risk the same sorts of excesses they associate with believers—intolerance, compulsion, violence, and all the rest. Ansel is mindful of these dangers, but he and India do agree that their cause is at grave risk of being overwhelmed. As Franklin said, they must all hang together, or assuredly they will all hang separately. Yet, Ansel fears that India's "with us or against us" attitude compresses the area for compromise and drives people to the extremes.

Ansel thinks that, as a practical matter, believers benefit from their faith on an organizational level. After all, religion is more than belief in a divine being. It is a reason to have community and comforting rituals. It is a way for people who are not comfortable with ambiguity to order their lives. It may go against the purism of many nonbelievers, but if the world is to be made safe for nonbelief—if Ingersoll is to have a chance of success—ways must be found to meet the needs of believers.

India's response—which makes Ansel nervous even though he does not necessarily disagree—is that it is too late for tepid debate.

"Let me make something clear," Ansel interjects now. "There will be no religious tests for buying a home in Ingersoll."

Yet Ansel knows that the truth is more complicated. He knows, for example, that over the years, as Bryce has bought up property and homes, he has given many of these things away, either as outright gifts or in attractive but murky lease arrangements. They have gone to friends and friends of friends who have been quietly vetted for their religious views.

Bryce has, to use his phrase, seeded the area with progressive nonbelievers. This, combined with Bryce's refusal to approve the creation of any religious institution within what amounts to the country's largest gated community, will create an environment that will be inhospitable to believers. "You don't have to break the equal opportunity laws," Bryce said. "You only have to make Ingersoll a place where religious people wouldn't want to live, any more than you or I would want to live in a community where ninety percent of the people are Evangelical Christians."

India is about to add a comment, but before she can do so, Kay Littleton, the Reuters business correspondent, identifies herself and hits on a subject that Bryce, Ansel and India all agree is a crucial unknown. "What makes you think nonbelievers will rally 'round you?" she asks. "However fragmented Christians are, they can agree upon God as a kind of basic organizing principle. What have nonbelievers got? I'd venture that they aren't very good at joining things—they are nonbelievers, after all."

Ansel and India join the audience in soft laughter. "Let me take this one as the designated atheist," India says with a smile. "When we speak of ourselves as nonbelievers or sometimes as freethinkers, we in fact refer to people who hold a wide spectrum of belief, from militant atheists to doubting, prove-it-to-me Catholics or Jews.

"We call ourselves by the historical term freethinkers because we believe in the freedom to be curious and to find our own philosophical and ethical way in the world. Of course, when I say we believe, I'm using the word in a certain way. In this respect, I'd like to quote from someone who is reviled by true believers but who has captured the essence of what we are and what we are not: Christopher Hitchens." At the mention of his name several people in the room groan, while others laugh in apparently happy anticipation of combat and a good story. India makes a stop sign with her hand and goes on. "I repeat, if you want to know in brief what we stand for, it is this. I have it written down, but I know it by heart:

"'Our belief is not a belief. Our principles are not a faith. We do not rely solely upon science and reason,'—as," India interrupts herself, "our opponents charge—'because these are necessary rather than sufficient factors, but we distrust anything that contradicts science or outrages reason. We may differ in many things, but what we respect is free inquiry, openmindedness, and the pursuit of ideas for their own sake.'

"You can be sure that I'll have this quote inscribed on some marble wall around here. You ask why we will unite when we have not united before. The answer is that if freethinkers can't get together now, they never will, and if they don't recognize the threat to their country and to their own freedom of belief or nonbelief, we are all—believers included—in a very sad situation.

"In short, to nonbelievers out there who are also non-joiners, I quote a recent comment by Mr. Jones when he said that you might as well get used to beginning your day with a public recitation of the Lord's Prayer."

Chapter 3

Godless

THE WEATHER SUGGESTS A return to summer. The overnight temperature has not gone below a humid sixty-eight degrees, and the forecast is for an afternoon high in the eighties. When he sees this on the early morning Channel Four report, Ansel Frye reaches into his closet for a lighter weight suit.

His wife stirs and cranes her neck to see him. She is Erika Frye, and they have been married for just over twenty-one years. "I'm getting up," she says, as if he'd asked.

"You don't have to."

"Of course I do. Things to go, places to do."

He hears the TV news announcer's bubbly caffeinated tease about the items upcoming after commercials. Local officials are planning for a confrontation in the new town of Ingersoll, he says. The crawl asks, "Atheist Challenge?"

Ansel looks up expectantly. He is pleased. The announcement might not have gone off as hoped yesterday—he knows well that Bryce is upset with the interruptions by the demonstrators—but there has been nonstop coverage of the story.

The news programs are divided on the lead. CNN, the NewsFirst Network, and other national outlets report that billionaire C. Bryce Jones is mounting a late challenge to the Christian right, hoping to stop their amendments from final passage. The local stations and network affiliates go with the local story, the revelation that Bryce has been secretly buying up huge swaths of land in Prince George's County.

One of the local reports says the purchases are reminiscent of the surprise announcement by Disney decades before that the company had been secretly buying land near the Civil War battlefields in Manassas, Virginia to build a theme park. The reporter reminds that the Disney project ultimately was defeated by preservationists, who mounted a huge campaign whose slogan was a model of simplicity and clarity: "No Mouse." He points out that it is not unusual for wealthy individuals or corporations to buy real estate secretly, out of fear that if word were to get out, prices would skyrocket.

What is unusual, the reporter says, is the scope of the project. In this, the owners were aided immensely by the collapse of real estate prices during the foreclosure crisis that began in 2008. For all practical purposes, Ingersoll stands to be a county within a county. Moreover, there is no historic preservation stake this time. "What there is," he concludes with his best TV flourish, "is a looming battle between believers and nonbelievers."

Erika rolls to the edge of the bed and without fully sitting up plants her feet on the floor. She exhales deliberately, and stands with a grimace, holding on to the night table for support. At just shy of six feet, she is almost as tall as Ansel, but she finds it increasingly difficult to straighten to that height.

"How are you feeling this morning?" Ansel asks. It's not that he isn't really concerned, but asking the question every morning has given the tone an absent quality, which is mirrored in her reply.

"Been better. Been worse." An old aluminum cane with a shepherd's crook cork handle is propped against the night table. Erika calls this her raising cane to distinguish it from the more elegant ones she will use during the day. She places the cane in her left hand, grasps the night table with the right, and pushes off. She wobbles slightly. Ansel moves to help, but she steadies herself before he can reach her and takes the first careful steps toward the bathroom, exhibiting the typical MS shuffle.

Erika considers herself lucky, though. She was diagnosed over ten years ago, and except for a yearlong period during which her symptoms worsened, she has stabilized at a point where she can function reasonably well. She can predict with confidence that the shuffle will become less pronounced as the day goes on until, late in the day—sooner if she has overtaxed herself—she will tire and it will gradually return. She calls the shuffle her energy-fatigue barometer, and sometimes Ansel is more observant of it than she is, though possibly she is more aware than she lets on. Ansel is more vigorous than even he knows, and she is self-conscious about relying too much on him, slowing him down.

She has no complaints, however. Ansel is sensitive to her condition. Despite it, they are good together. Her inability to have children is the only void that remains unfilled. Ansel is sympathetic on this point, too, but it is not in his power to fill it.

"I'll be gone when you get out," Ansel calls to the closed bathroom door. There is no reply, only the sound of spattering water. Ansel knocks once and cracks open the door. He repeats what he just said, and this time gets a burbled "okay." He turns and begins to leave, but then knocks, opens and calls in again the heads-up that, depending on how things go, he may have to stay at Ingersoll for a night or two.

* * *

He is getting a late start. Even ten minutes can make a big difference in the always-miserable commute from his estate off Foxhall Road. Ingersoll is not far as the crow flies, but there is no good route, and Ansel has tried them all. He has recently set up an apartment at Ingersoll, and he envisions spending much more time there.

This morning he's looped around from the Virginia side, crossing the Wilson Bridge into Maryland. The drive has actually been smoother than he expected, until he approaches the entrance to what the sign on the gate still refers to as The Potomac Institute. Despite the early hour, protesters have gathered in force. It is not lost on Ansel that they have organized so quickly. The local churches were ready for them yesterday, and they're ready today. The protest signs are up to date as well: they all refer to

Ingersoll. Several of the graphics show the word with a big red slash through it, overwritten with the word Godless.

As he had ordered, there are more guards at the gate, and there are county police cars as well. One of the protesters recognizes Ansel. A few press in toward the car, blocking Ansel's vision with their signs. But that is as far as they go, and they back away when the Ingersoll guards wave Ansel through.

The executive offices occupy the top of a ten-story building overlooking the river. Like the rest of the complex, the building has been erected within the last four years. The urgency of the construction came not long after Bryce had a cancer scare. Bryce denies the connection—he says a pure research community like Ingersoll was always in the back of his mind. He points out that he began the large land purchases before the personal crisis (a suspicious abdominal mass that turned out to be benign).

Still, Bryce never made a secret of wanting to make a mark in the world, and Ansel believes the scare was the impetus for a change in direction. Legendary success in business was not enough. At the same time, Bryce is too controlling to apply his billions to a typical philanthropic foundation. What he wants—insists he always wanted—is a living monument to his core beliefs: The power of fine minds to alter the world if these minds can be given the resources they need and placed in an environment free of dogma—organized religion in particular— except faith in the possibility of human progress.

So Bryce began to build his legacy. The part he did not anticipate was the surge of the religious right, and the emergence of Ingersoll (the name itself only a recent inspiration) as a focus of opposition.

Ansel walks in just after seven. From his office he has a good view as the early morning sun illuminates the growing protest crowd. It will be another clear day. The leaves have begun to change color. Three of the maples on the property have already turned a shocking red; the snap of warmer weather makes them seem particularly out of sync.

Ansel spies Bryce's modest car passing through the gate. The protesters were slow to converge on it, until they noticed Bryce in the back seat. His new driver belongs to a personal security detail that Ansel has insisted on and Bryce initially resisted. Ansel believes Bryce has a blind spot as far as his personal security is concerned, and he knows Bryce will continue to fight him over it.

India is waiting in the project room, an enlarged conference room outfitted with extra desks and electronic equipment. Predictably, as the Ingersoll rollout approached, the space became widely referred to as the war room.

India has already moved into an apartment in the complex, and has only to walk across the street. Which, to Ansel's mind, is irrelevant—India is the kind of person one expects to live on the job site. He has done his share of such living himself, though in less noble causes. India's strength is that she will do what Ingersoll needs to be done to succeed at this precarious time. His concern is that she will overdo what Ingersoll needs to be done.

They exchange good mornings. She is sipping black tea from a large Ingersoll mug bearing a stylized portrait of the Great Agnostic himself over the legend "Reason and Progress." Whatever their differences in personality and philosophy, she is hard not to like. She exudes a sense of will, an optimism somehow never drowned by adversity, and a faith that persistence will be rewarded. Ansel thinks of it as the kind of enthusiasm one sees in college student leaders, but which almost always fades. On less kind days he is reminded of the adage that he who is not a radical at eighteen has no heart, but he who is still one at fifty has no head.

For his part, he likes to think that he has found a happy medium, a sort of sensible radicalism. But he fears he may have shifted toward thoughtful pragmatism at precisely the time when a rebellious heart is needed most.

Chapter 4

India

I WAS ASTONISHED TO receive Bryce's call, and even more astonished when, a few days after we met, he asked me to become Ingersoll's "director for secular life," as he called it. We're still not quite right with the title. It needs to convey a nonreligious philosophical outlook, but not one that is hostile to spirituality. Bryce also mumbled something like "director for epistemology," which might be accurate but is not exactly a tip-of-the-tongue sort of thing.

It's not that I don't have the right credentials: Degree in philosophy from a respected university, JD for practical applications (one to feed my soul, such as it is, the other my stomach and to get things done), author of three books on secularism, including a biography of Ingersoll himself (maybe that's where Bryce got the idea of calling me), and director of the U.S. Forum on Secular Humanism. And then there are the grassroots movements that I'm really better known for.

In most ways this is a dream job. I've fantasized about leading a community like Ingersoll, but I couldn't imagine scraping up the funding—or at least not on the scale that Bryce can do it.

Bryce did his research about me—did his due diligence, as they say. I would expect nothing less. He knows I'm stubborn and a lightning rod, and I was determined not to mislead him by suggesting I would magically become pliable. It may be my dream job, but I am unwilling to make the kinds of compromises that one usually has to make to take on such a job, and which then usually lead to disappointment all around. I can do great things for Ingersoll, but I wanted Bryce to know what he's getting.

First of all, I am not a wishy-washy agnostic. I am a full-bore atheist. I have trouble dealing with believers, because however much I would like to be polite, I'm impatient with minds blinkered by tribal custom, general superstitiousness, the need to believe in salvation or a better future, and so on.

When I was younger, I thought in terms of carefully, deliberately explaining to these people why their beliefs are so illogical. Surely they would see reason! But the older I've become—and the more religious the country has become, especially after the latest round of terror attacks (talk about an amygdala-based response to danger!)—the more restive I've become. So much for mellowing with age! If my initial position was arrogant, my more mature one might be described as arrogance augmented by impatience.

Sometimes this gets the better of me, such as when I asked a TV interviewer why the "esteemed" Reverend Falwell should be esteemed, or for that matter, why he was qualified to participate in any deliberations on public policy when his expertise was in a spiritual load of crap.

The remark set off a firestorm, even within my own organization. But I wouldn't back down. I regret the choice of words, perhaps, but the idea is correct. I don't see what credentials a surgeon would bring to a debate on public school financing, and I don't see what credentials a doctor of divinity would bring to a committee on science textbooks.

I would have thought that this dustup and innumerable others like it would have disqualified me for the Ingersoll job. But Bryce made it clear that he was looking for precisely the qualities I have of substantive knowledge, self-assurance, and willingness to fight for freethought. He did add not in so many words that he hoped I could do the female equivalent of keeping it in my pants! He said this is essential, because

Ingersoll needs to walk a fine line between unapologetic secularism and gratuitous provocation.

So, speaking of gratuitous provocation, I asked him if it was wise to appoint a married lesbian like me to the post.

Bryce had the right answer, as far as I'm concerned: Ingersoll will stand for humans and human progress in all of its forms, and nothing is more fundamental than the right of human beings to choose their mates. This may be provocative, but there is nothing gratuitous about it.

There is one thing I'm not so thrilled about: I report to an overall director, Ansel Frye. Bryce tried to play down my concern, describing Frye not as my boss as such, but as a kind of *primus inter pares*—which as far as I'm concerned is Latin for I have a boss! What he has in mind is for me to focus on advocacy, secular outreach and the secular life of the community, while Ansel has the big picture as a sort of mayor or county (Ingersoll really is a small county) commissioner. Advocacy in its many forms is the first order of the day.

I also have come to the frank conclusion that part of Ansel's function will be to keep me from going overboard (well, good luck with that)! I'd never admit it to Bryce, but this may not be a bad thing. My impulsiveness has gotten me into trouble before (viz., "spiritual load of crap"), and I don't want to mess this up.

I think I can live with this arrangement. Much will depend on the chemistry Ansel and I establish. I know him only by reputation, and (big surprise) I don't take direction well. I view my job as synonymous with Ingersoll's purpose. Ingersoll is an amazing opportunity that may never come again, especially if the Christian right has its way. If Ingersoll succeeds merely as a traditional "new town," like Reston in Virginia or Columbia in Maryland, then it will have failed. The point is to be an outpost of secularism in a burgeoning theocracy.

As far as the future of the country is concerned, everything is riding on its success.

Chapter 5

Erika

WHEN I FIRST MET Ansel—or maybe I should say when I realized I loved him and that something serious would happen between us—I felt quite sure about what I was getting.

But not about what I was getting into.

What I was getting: A man who is handsome (let's be honest, that's the first thing that registers, even if it doesn't end up being the most important), terrifically self-assured (the two go together, I suppose), and very bright in a Type-A, hyper-focused sort of way (I figured I'd have to work on cultivating the romantic, sensitive side of him—women always convince themselves that such transformations are possible).

I see Ansel's drive as a legacy of a very fraught upbringing. On the surface, it would appear he grew up with every advantage. His family had money. (I tease him that this goes without saying—who but moneyed people give their children names like Ansel?) He went to the right prep schools, which led to the right colleges, and so on, but this in itself is revealing. The right colleges as far as his parents were concerned were not, as you might expect, Princeton or Stanford. They were Jesuit. Notre Dame would be fine. Boston College or Georgetown would be fine. Daddy had studied for the priesthood and to this day berates himself for not having the necessary faith—the calling, as they say—to succeed.

There was no insistence that Ansel compensate for dad's shortcomings by becoming a priest himself, though of course this would have pleased his lower-case father no end. But to say that religious expectations were a part of Ansel's life would be a gross understatement. As far back as he can remember, it chafed, and by the time college came around he did everything he could think of to sabotage the required applications to the Jesuit places. This tactic didn't work with Notre Dame, where his family had connections strong enough to overcome the poorly written essay he substituted for the one his father approved.

But Ansel refused to attend, and chose instead to accept a scholarship to the Wharton School at Penn.

Those years were the beginning of the rift with his parents that still has not completely healed. As Ansel fell away from religion, his parents fought him every step of the way. It's amazing to me that such otherwise bright people wouldn't grasp the long-proven parental truism that their opposition would drive their son away, not inspire compliance.

As Ansel moved down what he calls the underground railroad to nonbelief—taking baby steps away from Catholicism, on to flirtation with Episcopalianism, and on down the stations to Unitarianism, Ethical Culture, and finally, his present wilderness state of what he likes to call charismatic agnosticism—he became ever more estranged from his family, who finally all but disowned him, even against the advice of their priest, Monsignor Benton.

And here we are, deep into the cause of Ingersoll, which might represent the final station in Ansel's rebellion. As I understand it, India Ruiz has a similar background in terms of rebelling against wealthy parents. The difference is that they managed to remain a family.

Ansel goes a little squirrely when I say it, but Bryce perfectly fills the parental void. The match was a natural. For Ansel's part it's no surprise that he is the kind of person Bryce would want to take under his wing, though of course I'm biased.

Before I leave the subject of what I was getting, I should also say that Ansel was not—and is not—as clinically robotic as I've perhaps made him seem. True, he was never going to win a prize as Mr. Emote, but he definitely has a sensitive, thoughtful side. In any case, I am not, nor was I looking for, someone whose eyes well up every time he watches *Casablanca.* The two of us are romantic in a workmanlike way, feeling deeply without fanfare, though we could be quite sensual, at least near the beginning, and predictably less so now after twenty-some years and the not so predictable turns of my MS.

But what was I getting into, and was it really so different from what I was getting?

To answer this question it has to be made clear that I fit the stereotype of my name and Nordic heritage. I was loved by my parents, and despite a lack of effusiveness, I never had reason to doubt this. However, I was also the third of four daughters, all of whom came after a five-year break that followed the two one-year-apart brothers. Some epiphany must have occurred to my parents during the break, but I don't know what it was. Perhaps they realized they could use more manly labor for the family business and simply assumed the male line would continue.

So, I ended up being the fifth of six, the two boys clearly in the royal line of succession, followed by the four ladies-in-waiting, who were loved and wished the best of things in life in a general way, without the clear expectations dealt to my brothers.

The modern, formulaic response to this is to condemn my parents' gender bias. I didn't resent it; I took it for granted. I suppose some children might even consider this a fortunate position to be in, with the pressure off. Anyway, it's not that simple. First of all, to say there were no *clear* expectations for the girls is not to say there were none. To the contrary, a little more clarity might have been helpful; and while the goals might not have been clear, the general standards of conduct and accomplishment were high. The boys were expected to enter the professions (medicine or engineering being preferred). We could become whatever we wanted (or so we were told, though I always had the feeling from my mother that her occupation, raising a family, was really the preferred one), but whatever we did, we were expected to do it well.

This is not the optimal environment for a late bloomer, which I was. Not until my sophomore year of high school did I come close to meeting acceptable academic standards. Not until college did I completely shed the gawky-gangly appearance that doomed my early romantic life, as well as anything that required grace or what they now call physicality.

Though I might not have realized it at the time, what I was getting into when I met Ansel (the gawkiness had passed by then, and was even replaced by a modicum of gracefulness) was a situation in which as long as I was with him I would almost certainly have to sublimate my un-self-assured psyche and haphazardly underdeveloped life plan to his very self-assured, driven presence.

All of this is subtext, of course, reflecting for both of us the light-bending power of early experience. For Ansel, this meant probably greater self-estimation than would have been supported by the facts; for me, the opposite. For both of us, these things resulted in self-fulfilling prophecy: Ansel became Bryce's right hand, with all that entailed, and never even considered that this should not be his fate. I became somewhat successful as a research psychologist, and the more Ansel excelled, the more I came to accept that somewhat successful would be my just fate.

Perhaps oddly enough given our differences, Ansel and I have done well as a couple. I don't think either of us doubts our love for the other, and though I've never really understood it and it sounds strange, Ansel usually puts a positive spin on my insecurities, interpreting them as humility.

Our relationship underwent a significant change about seven years into the marriage. First, after having made the mental adjustment of accepting the inevitable compromises between career and family, we tried to become pregnant, and couldn't.

The reasons were not easy to figure out. Biomechanically speaking, we were both pronounced sound. My ovularity, as it were, was well complemented by Ansel's motility.

Still, it wasn't working. And the sex wasn't working very well either, from a pleasure standpoint. For both of us it was hard to enjoy what had become a moon-and-tide-driven obligation, and a futile one at that.

It wasn't until certain other physical symptoms—which I won't go into here—began to appear that we deepened our immersion in the world of medical diagnostics. There, after almost two years of testing, I was told I had MS, a disease that is, in fact, not easy to diagnose or, for that matter, to predict its course.

Since then there have been good and bad times—periods of remission when I thought I might not really have the disease (perhaps the diagnosis was wrong after all), and disheartening periods of deterioration. MS can be cruel in that way. It gives you hope and then steals it, almost always keeping you on the downside of the slope where the only thing that varies is the angle of descent.

Through it all Ansel has been wonderful. I sometimes think it's ironic that it took my condition to fulfill my desire to make him more openly sensitive and loving. At least where I'm concerned he is sensitive and amazingly solicitous—sometimes to a fault.

Paradoxically, our connection to one another has become smaller, and I don't pretend to completely understand this. Too often I feel we are going through the motions of real togetherness—the right motions, perhaps, but motions nonetheless.

Chapter 6

March on Richmond

THE REVEREND ROLAND PETERSON is surprised by his good fortune. He had expected to stay with several of the others at the Quality Inn or Hilton Garden Inn across town and be shuttled with them back and forth to the conference. Instead, he is checking in at the conference site—the venue, as people liked to say, as if it lent more authority to the proceedings—at the Jefferson. On all counts such luxury is an unusual experience for him.

Looking around at the chandeliers and time-burnished wood, Peterson's pleasure is not guilt-free. His congregation certainly would not pay for such a place, nor would he have the effrontery to ask them to do so. Moreover, he is not comfortable with the symbolism of a Christian organization holding a well-publicized meeting in a place like this. There might be a certain logic to the organization choosing to project an image of power and success at this time, but to his mind it is hard to get around responding to the pop question "What would Jesus do?" with the answer, "He wouldn't."

At the reception desk he places his hands lightly on the cool, creamy marble and leans forward. This is a habit, developed he doesn't know when, this leaning inward on a barrier when he approaches an official. It could be a clerk or a vice president; rank is not the issue. It is as if he wants to suggest that nothing artificial need separate two people of good will. Sometimes he is aware of it, aware that this posture conveys a sense of eagerness, urgency, or presumed intimacy, whether he intends it or not. It is almost never perceived as threatening, because almost always he is smiling when he makes whatever request.

It is a smile that is hard to miss, full white teeth parting a face a few shades shy of ebony that on close inspection reveals old acne scars and a kind of wind-chapped complexion. He tells the clerk in a resonant voice that he is Roland Peterson and that there should be a reservation, made for him by Reverend Fitzgerald's office. "Peterson of Christ the King Church, in Maryland," he adds, in case the extra information might be helpful.

"Yes, I have it right here," the clerk says with an unforced smile. "The request was for a superior room, but we don't have any available at the moment, so I took the liberty of upgrading you to a deluxe. I assume you don't mind?" he adds in a friendly rhetorical tone.

"Am I to understand, then, that there is nothing lower than superior in the hotel's pecking order?" Roland says pleasantly as he signs the registration form.

"That's right," the clerk responds in a more defensive voice than Roland's facile question requires. "Superior is the lowest we go here," he adds more lightly, as if he has just caught on. He hands Roland the room key and an envelope. "Reverend Fitzgerald's secretary left this note for you," he says.

Roland slings his suit bag over his shoulder and opens the envelope as he walks toward the elevators. He declines a porter's help. It is just one more service to which he is unaccustomed. He stops by the elevator and unfolds the note. It is handwritten on NCCR letterhead, an invitation to join Fitzgerald and a few colleagues for a brief pre-dinner repast in his suite.

The initials stand for National Coalition for Constitutional Reform, and it is only one of Fitzgerald's action coalitions. At the moment this one commands most of his attention. Roland is fairly certain of the reason he has been included among the board membership at the Jefferson, and he is not entirely comfortable with it. He represents a large congregation, and is well known and popular among congregants and fellow clergy alike. But he is not a national figure, nor does he have national aspirations, and the only logical explanation for being invited into the inner circle, however brief his inclusion may be, is that his church is the largest of three that have been enveloped by the new Ingersoll project.

Roland steps onto the elevator, the dark wood paneled interior of which continues the lobby's theme of genteel opulence. Before the door can close he is joined by a man and a woman, both wearing black suits and clerical collars like his own. They smile at him, and he asks if they are in the hotel for the conference. They nod and say yes in cheerful unison, and Roland is made more comfortable by the momentary snug of comradeship. He says "my floor, see you later" as the elevator hits four and he steps out into a brightly lit vestibule. He catches himself in an antique-looking English mirror mounted on a crimson wall, but doesn't linger as he turns to the right and looks for his room.

The corridor is more typically hotel-corporate than luxurious, but Roland's room meets any definition of deluxe he has ever considered. Again he feels guilty pleasure as he surveys the period furniture and heavy celadon drapes, and sinks into the carpet plush under foot. He drops his bag near the closet and walks around the room, lightly touching things at random. He eyes the king-sized bed and flops on his back on top of the white bedspread, kicking off his shoes as he lands.

Anticipating the meeting with the NCCR leaders, Roland feels awkward and unprepared. He can only assume that Ingersoll will be discussed, but he doesn't know what specifically Fitzgerald has in mind. Others might view the get-together as an opportunity to bring news from the top to their congregations, or even as a chance to see if something might present itself on a larger, perhaps even national stage.

Roland is not above wanting to stand before his flock and tell them of his high-level reception. If nothing else, it will justify his extravagant lodgings. Mostly, however, he doesn't want to feel embarrassed by not having thought of the wider implications of the Ingersoll announcement, or not having a clear plan of action in mind. He is angry about Ingersoll; he thinks he has been deceived by Bryce Jones. Like many people in the area, he was familiar with—and occasionally interacted with—the research campus of what was then called The Institute. He had suspicions about the existence of a more ambitious plan. At several meetings, Bryce had given assurances that the wider community would be considered and kept informed about the project's future.

In the event, Roland had only brief notice of the vast Ingersoll plan that made his church part of an archipelago of three, and this information came not from Bryce but from his people who had obtained jobs at The Institute. Calls to Bryce and to his apparent alter ego, Ansel Frye, went unanswered.

Before the announcement Roland did not consider The Institute to be particularly threatening. Roland is naturally optimistic, and he half jokingly considered a community of scientists and thinkers as a challenge for conversion, or at least as open to persuasion. He would have been happy to engage the people there in discussion forums or other events.

Ingersoll was another matter, a slap in the face made all the more invidious by the surprise. The NCCR will no doubt want something to be done, but it is not yet clear what can be done. The church's lawyers are looking into several avenues of challenge, but it is unknown whether any of these might be successful or how long the legal process might take.

As Roland sees it, there are two issues, both involving timing. He is not particularly concerned about the long-term prospects for a community of nonbelievers. Christianity is resilient. In the natural course of time it will overcome such a community as it had conquered so many challenges over the millennia.

The more urgent question is how to confront Ingersoll's political agenda, which no doubt will be well financed. The Ingersoll people had issued the challenge. They would do everything in their power to block the amendments. Perhaps in the end that wouldn't amount to much, but no one wanted bumps in the road when the amendments were so close to reaching their destination.

Surely the leaders will expect Roland to do something. He has no real obligations toward them, and he sometimes has misgivings about their decisions—holding this conference in as showy a place as the Jefferson being a prime example. Still, when it comes to the basics, he is very much on board and would like to help. The only hope for the country is to return to its Christian roots. The nation is in crisis, and a strong statement about the future is the way it can be saved.

* * *

Roland wakes with a start, checks the time, and sees that he has half an hour before he has to meet with the leadership. He falls back and rubs his eyes. He has been making a mental list of the kinds of things his church might do in response to Ingersoll. Most of them involve some form of organized protest. He weighs his approach to the church leaders, who he knows only by reputation. He suspects they will want him to arrive with a plan of action, but he decides to hear them out first. He reasons that, after all, he doesn't know absolutely that Ingersoll is the reason for the invitation.

Roland takes a few minutes to freshen up and heads for the elevator. He pauses at the door of Fitzgerald's top-floor suite and listens to several voices rushing over one another. The voices meld into a form of urgency, but it is not clear whether they are angry or simply eager. He is surprised when the door opens before he can ring the bell.

The equally surprised man on the other side of the door seems familiar to Roland, who then recognizes him from the earlier encounter on the elevator. The other man has reached the same conclusion, and says, "I saw you before."

"On the elevator. You were with a woman, also a preacher," Roland says.

"Marcia Gladstone," the man responds. "You'll see her inside, the only bit of estrogen in this group. Thank God for her."

"You're not staying?" Roland asks.

"No, I've finished my business. Or maybe I should say they've done my business," he adds over his shoulder, with a butterfly laugh.

Roland enters the suite, following the voices. There are several men sitting around a coffee table. Two in clerical attire sit on a sofa; the others, looking more like business executives, have pulled up chairs. Two of the executives are immediately recognizable.

One is Morgan Fitzgerald, who appears even larger in person than he does on television. His tie is loosened and his sleeves are turned up to reveal thick dark hair on his forearms.

The other is Richard Carter, director of the NCF, the National Christian Foundation, and a leader in the pro-life movement, who is absorbed in papers on his lap.

The woman he had just heard called Marcia is also there, standing off to the side in quiet conversation with another cleric. They are both sipping what appears to be club soda. Roland is the only black man in the room.

"You must be Reverend Peterson," Fitzgerald says, standing and then approaching with his hand extended.

"Roland. Please call me Roland," he answers. Roland is not a small man, but his hand is enveloped by Fitzgerald's.

"I'm glad you could come," Fitzgerald says, as he places a hand on Roland's shoulder and leads him a few steps toward the group. There are introductions all around, including a terse greeting from Carter, who quickly returns to his reading.

So far, the two top leaders are playing to type. With Fitzgerald, this means an almost instant sense that you are in his comforting embrace. He is easily the most popular leader in the American Christian movement, and even his most cynical critics credit his apparent sincerity and good works. Together with his wife, he leads efforts to aid battered children, and they have adopted four special needs kids themselves. India Ruiz has been among the first to credit him with being, in her words, not hypocritical.

Fitzgerald's immutable opposition to abortion for any reason surprises no one, least of all his antagonists (except to the extent that he mystifies them by seeming otherwise so reasonable). The real dissonance occurs over subjects like evolution and creationism, with his liberal opponents apparently truly baffled at the notion of a seemingly intelligent person making a fortune selling books whose central idea is the temporal coexistence of humans and dinosaurs.

Carter's curt introduction suggests that what Roland has heard about him also is true. Carter is viewed almost universally as a no-nonsense-take-no-prisoners leader who doesn't know why anyone would ever suffer fools gladly. Three years ago he left the board of his mega-church to assume the NCF directorship. Beneath a wiry frame and an acerbic demeanor is what Roland has heard is an even more wintry personality.

Carter has progressed more by getting results than making friends. He is variously described as brilliant, flinty, obsessive, effective, and occasionally, unprincipled.

Fitzgerald waves Roland to an empty chair. "Please," he says. "Make yourself comfortable."

Roland thanks him and sits, tugging lightly on the creases of his pants as he does. He notices that this part of the suite is being used as a command center for the conference. There are additional computer hookups and phone lines, and several stacks of paper, the top sheets of which are labeled in large black letters that he cannot make out from where he is sitting.

"There are a few things we'd like to discuss, if you're willing," Fitzgerald says.

Roland responds "of course," but notices that Carter seems to be annoyed, or perhaps distracted, by something.

"This business of Ingersoll, as they call it," Fitzgerald begins after the requisite small talk.

"I assumed that's what you wanted to discuss," Roland interjects, leaving it to Fitzgerald to go on. Which he is about to do when Carter interrupts.

"How is it possible that so many people failed to anticipate this business even when they live cheek by jowl with Bryce Jones and his merry band of heathens?"

Roland is taken aback but ignores the implied personal criticism and says simply that Jones apparently went to great lengths to hide what he was up to.

"I have a sense of sleight of hand," Fitzgerald says. "Jones's proclivities have long been known, but—tell me if I'm wrong, Reverend—attention was focused on his research center. The Potomac Institute, that's what it was called?"

Carter continues reading whatever has his attention. Without looking up he says with what could only be a sneer, "Leave it to the super-rich to claim ownership of the very idea of community."

"Listen, Reverend Peterson," Fitzgerald resumes.

"Roland, please."

"Roland, the leadership council is not overly worried by what Bryce Jones is up to."

"Pimple on our arse," Carter volunteers. Except for Marcia, Fitzgerald and Roland, the others in the room laugh.

"If you'll excuse our indelicate friend here," Fitzgerald continues with a pleasant smile, "he has a point, if not much decorum."

Carter looks up with a fast-evaporating smile and gives Fitzgerald a shrug.

"I think it's fair to say that we're close to passing our amendments," Fitzgerald continues. "That's really the thrust of this conference. We have to make sure the pieces are in place. When the Virginia legislature meets in January, we want our victory to be in the bag. If Virginia ratifies, we will almost certainly go over the top, Ingersoll or no Ingersoll. But we want media attention on Richmond, not on a sideshow in Maryland. Ingersoll is a distraction."

"Richard and I are not completely on the same page about Ingersoll," Fitzgerald says, nodding toward Carter. "In my opinion it is more than a . . . blemish. It's one thing to proclaim a philosophical outlook—nonbelief, as they put it in this case—and another to be an effective voice for that outlook. I am concerned about India Ruiz's appointment. People tend to dismiss her because she's so bluntly in your face, but she has a record of success in pushing her various causes, and I think it would be a mistake to overlook her or what she and the others plan to do regarding Ingersoll and the amendments."

"I agree about India," Roland responds. "Actually, I've worked with her in the past."

"Really? Why would *that* happen?" Carter asks.

A flash of annoyance appears on Roland's face. He's all for solidarity with his Christian brethren, but he has no intention of becoming supine to get along. What's more, he is ever mindful that the black Christian community has needs to which the white community is often blind. Still, he is a courteous man—however much people may mistake this for weakness—and he answers in an even tone.

"My congregation reflects a mixture of solidly middle class and economically struggling members. And before I came to Christ the King, I ministered to mostly poor people. I may differ completely with India

Ruiz where religion is concerned, and also concerning matters such as abortion, but she is a sincere person, who among other things cares deeply about social justice, equality, and human rights. We have considerable common ground on these issues." Looking over at Carter, who seems to have lost interest once he made his point about India, he can't resist adding, "As I'm sure you do, too, as a good Christian."

Carter looks hard at Roland. "No one really cares about human rights if they don't care about the rights of the unborn."

The sidebar chatter of the others in the room has ceased, as their attention has been drawn to the growing intensity of this conversation. Before Roland can respond to Carter, Fitzgerald waves the air and says with determined brightness, "Let's not get distracted. We need to remember that we're here in Richmond to accomplish something historic. Our concern is that the events in Maryland remain tangential to what we're doing here. Reverend Peterson, I'd like to know if you have any ideas about that."

"A few," Roland says, his manner noticeably more frosty. "First of all, India Ruiz aside, I think you are right, Reverend Fitzgerald, to be concerned about Ingersoll—excuse me if I use their given name as shorthand, but one of the problems is that it is an easy name for people to remember; it will stick."

Fitzgerald nods agreement, but Carter has returned once again to his paperwork.

Continuing, Roland says, "I think it would be a mistake to underestimate Bryce Jones."

"Why not? You did," Carter says without looking up.

This time Roland won't ignore the slap. "Mr. Carter," he says, and pauses until Carter looks at him, "I've been asked to come here to express my views on the events around my church. Is it too much to request the common courtesy of your attention?"

The only evidence that these words have had any impact on Carter is a blink and his continued gaze at Roland.

"Please go on," Fitzgerald says in a reassuring voice.

"Let me be clear. I am angry and embarrassed. I feel I have been misled by Bryce Jones. However, in the great scheme of things I am not particularly concerned about Ingersoll. These are frightening times, and people are turning to religion for comfort as they always do in such times; they're not turning to frothy intellectualism. In the long run Ingersoll will join the ranks of countless failed experiments. After all, the man for whom the community is named, no matter how eloquent he might have been, didn't change much in the end.

"Nevertheless, I am concerned about the short-term problems that Jones and Ingersoll pose. Most state legislatures, Virginia's included, don't return for their new sessions until January. That gives the Ingersoll people a few months to rally opposition to the amendments."

"That's not really much time," the woman Roland thinks of as Reverend Marcia says from the periphery of the group.

"I think it could be enough," Roland responds, looking toward her.

"To act as a focal point?" Fitzgerald interjects. "Is that what you mean? We know there is significant opposition to the amendments, but that it is fragmented."

"Yes," Roland answers. "The usual liberal groups—the ACLU, People for the American Way, Americans for the Separation of Church and State, and so on—are working hard, and I wouldn't be surprised if they are garnering support. But they've never been able to command the sort of broad backing that would make them a cohesive national force. Ingersoll could change that."

Fitzgerald nods encouragement for Roland to continue.

"Bryce Jones certainly has the resources—and a willingness to use them—to have an immediate impact. You in the national spotlight probably know more about this than I do, but as I understand it, he has already reserved huge amounts of media space to run commercials and print ads. I don't know exactly what he has in mind regarding the ACLU and the others, but they wouldn't have to waste time raising funds. Assuming he wants to, he can make billions of dollars available instantly, and draw them into a crusade led by him. Or India Ruiz, or whoever. It may not be a lasting coalition. But it may last long enough to be an effective wrench in our works."

For once, Roland seems to have captured Carter's attention.

Chapter 7

Roland

MY GRANDFATHER WAS A preacher of the old school, all fire and brimstone. When he spoke of the crown of thorns, you could feel them piercing the flesh, see the rivulets of blood. He was a fierce opponent of what we call moral relativism and he called milquetoast Christianity. (I also like the more recent phrase "Worshipping at the Church of Benign Whatever-ism," penned by Kenda Creasy Dean, who has a way of hitting the nail on the head.)

My father was a preacher, too. He relied less than his father on frightening his flock into virtue. As a result, he was more successful than my grandfather in building his church, but this caused lasting divisions between them. As far as his father was concerned, this was an unacceptable surrender to modern vices.

Yet whatever their differences, my father also opposed relativism. Our covenant with God requires that we be strong in our faith and our behavior. "Thou shalt love the Lord thy God with all thy heart and with all thy soul and with all thy mind." This is how Jesus summarized the Ten Commandments. He was as clear as could be about the requirements of our faith. The basic message is timeless. It was for my grandfather as for my father and for me.

Where we differ is in the method of conveying the message—of spreading the Word and the Gospel. Times change, and if setting the Lord's Prayer to music helps bring people to God, I say so much the better—it is still the Lord's Prayer. If convention centers and satellite feeds are replacing the revival tent, that is fine with me, so long as the effort is sincere and truly in the service of spreading the Word. (I'd like to think I've seen the last of the for-profit preachers and their yachts and air conditioned doghouses paid for by the faithful.)

Thus we three are different in our form but identical in our devotion to God. God Himself takes many forms in our lives, but He is still God.

The three of us differ in another way. My father and grandfather had the calling from day one. I took a more circuitous route. I'm nearly fifty years old, but if you knew me at thirty you would say I had turned my face from God entirely. We may all be sinners, but some are farther from God than others, and I was certainly far from Him.

My grandfather died while I was in this state of disunion with God. My father was dispirited, fearing I would not turn my life around, and that my eternal reward would be as the wages of sin.

But indeed, God's ways are sometimes mysterious, and nothing could be more mysterious than my transformation from sinner to Saved. The time, really not so long ago, has passed since I ridiculed my father's ministry and particularly his desire that I follow in his footsteps. My grandfather would have exulted in my change (and no doubt does so, as he looks down upon me), even if he would not exult in my methods. He would have said I threw Satan out. As did our Lord before me, I declared "Get thee behind me, Satan," and resolved to work for God and the Kingdom of Heaven.

I have been doing so ever since. In the last ten years, my Church of Christ the King has become one of the largest in the area. It is gaining ever wider attention as we have used modern tools of mass communication in the service of the Lord. I believe our ministry could have global reach, entering millions and millions of homes and lives. I would be less than honest if I failed to mention that such rapid success is an elixir. I have not yet succumbed—and I hope I never will—to the siren of fame. Not that I'm so famous, mind, but we've been successful enough to taste the possibilities delivered by the Internet, and to understand why so many preachers—honest ones—have had their heads turned.

Recent events have placed our church at the forefront of the battle to reclaim America as the Christian nation the founding fathers envisioned. We will not have done our duty if we fail to convince unbelievers that the United States of America enjoys the blessings of freedom and prosperity precisely because this is the will of the Creator. There can be no better proof of this than experience. As the nation turned its back on this truth, it fell on hard times. It was visited by catastrophe after catastrophe. We fell upon one other and suffered the terror attacks, while the bounty we had known withered. Having awakened to these warnings from God, it is our mission to redeem our nation in His eyes, and at the same time to redeem each and every one of our eternal souls. We are modern Crusaders, saving souls and taking back the country not by the sword, but through the power of law and democratic persuasion.

We are within a hairsbreadth of amending the Constitution to reflect our values and thus reclaim our place as the light of the world, as our Creator intended from the start. Our country's guiding charter must state clearly that we are a nation based on Christian values, tolerant of others but unyielding in the primacy of our faith. We define marriage as a holy union between a man and a woman. And we cherish all life from the inception of the Creator's spark. This is the essence of the three amendments we will shortly enshrine into law. It is a practical triune for our times. If we succeed, the true Godhead will be realized.

But a threat to these goals has emerged in the form of the Community of Ingersoll, as it calls itself after a famous nonbeliever. The leaders of this misguided effort claim they are seeking some sort of enlightened progressivism and (taking an old name for their movement) freethought.

Progressivism and freethought—it is a tantalizing message to those of weak conviction. It demands little of us; it is endless research without the need to draw a firm conclusion. It is the balm of low expectation. C.S. Lewis said it best: "The safest road to Hell is the gradual one—the gentle slope, soft underfoot, without sudden turnings, without milestones, without signposts."

The nonbelievers say all things can be explained by science and reason. They say our existence is explained in the language of subatomic particles. Yet, they are woefully unable to explain the very essence of humanity—consciousness. They are totally unable to account for our unique awareness of our selves. They refuse willfully to understand the spark of God and His gift.

We know that what they will do—whether it is their intention or not—is drag the country back into a state of darkness and ignorance. Joining with others, I have pledged every bit of effort to ensure that they do not succeed. We must do whatever it takes. Nothing less than the Kingdom of Heaven is at stake.

We have armies on our side. And we have Truth. Unlike our opponents, we do not confuse reason and faith. Faith *is* our reason. It *is* our science. It *is* our future. The person who lives a righteous life has no need to fear for the future. To him, the future—the real future—is a known quantity. I was reminded of this today when I saw a news report on a man who had demonstrated notable bravery in confronting an armed criminal. After it was all over, the man said he had no fear because he knows where he is going—he knows heaven awaits him. What great power this is! A person who lives a truly righteous life in Christ has the comfort of that life, but also the wherewithal to rise to the extraordinary occasion, armed with the certainty of grace.

I confess I was slow to comprehend the threat posed by Ingersoll. I admitted as much to Fitzgerald and Carter in Richmond. And I tried to make clear to them that, in their own way, they may fail to appreciate the threat. Ingersoll will never win people over en masse. Rich men are as entitled to their follies as anyone. They just do it on a grander scale, as I believe Bryce Jones will discover. But as I said in Richmond, the true danger is that Bryce will use his enormous resources and perhaps—as with the false face he showed me—deception and even treachery to stop our amendments from passing.

I have no wish to be treacherous in response, but nor do I want to be played for a fool. I may not have the ability, or necessarily even the desire, to join Fitzgerald and Carter on the national stage (indeed, Carter exemplifies some of the worst traits of our national leadership), but C. Bryce Jones and his acolytes will find that neither I nor my church is a pushover.

My congregation and I are already making life difficult for Ingersoll. We have mounted ever larger demonstrations—peaceful demonstrations, I should add—to make our presence felt and disrupt their operations. This evening I will meet with area church leaders, including the pastors of the other two churches here in what our own Judy Bascomb cleverly called the atheist badlands.

Chapter 8

Another Universe

IT IS A SHORT walk from Ansel's office to the temporary apartment that has been set up for him. It is all he can do to tear himself away after a scheduled 6:30 p.m. conference call. He has told Erika he will not make it home; she understands the pressures he is under, and says she'll see him the following evening, assuming he can get away.

Eventually he will arrange for a nicer place to stay within Ingersoll. In the meantime, the apartment, in a residential building named for suffragist Alice Paul, is more than enough for his needs. In some ways he prefers it to one that is larger or more elaborate. There is something comforting about the certainty of these modest boundaries. His choices are limited to three rooms—bedroom, combined living room-dining room, and small kitchen—all pleasantly appointed and with an expansive view of the river.

It is already almost eight, and as he changes into casual clothes, Ansel wonders if it pays to continue with his evening plans. With a stop at the supermarket, he won't arrive at his destination until after ten. A glance in the mirror quickly reveals the fatigue that is settling in on him. But he has promised, and so he forces himself to quicken the pace of his changing. Fifteen minutes later he is out the door and in his car.

Ansel hopes that leaving through the main gate will be smoother than it was when he arrived, but if anything the number of protesters has grown, and the security people have to push them back after his car is recognized. He thinks it might not be a bad idea to change cars until the furor dies down.

Finally, he pulls away from the knot of people, gaining speed as he heads toward the Wilson Bridge into Virginia. In recent days he has taken to checking his rearview mirror more frequently. So far there has been no indication that anyone is following him, but who could know with this religious crowd? For a moment he is aware of headlights that have stayed with him, but the car passes him and speeds off.

* * *

He makes better time than expected, and soon is within about fifteen minutes of the house in what is still called horse country, even though suburban blight, complete with a high proportion of foreclosed-upon houses, long ago besieged the area. He spots the last real supermarket before the road narrows, and decides to make a quick stop for some flowers and a bottle of wine.

He is in the wine section, where faux sale tags in front of every bottle make finding anything difficult. He is about to settle on a familiar label when he glimpses two people pushing a cart at the end of the aisle. They have crossed his line of sight only briefly, but he is nevertheless fairly sure that one of them is Bryce's personal assistant, Tom Whist, and another young assistant, Jeanette Castle.

Ansel knows that Tom lives somewhere in this area—one of the legions who regularly trades commuting time for sleep—but he is still surprised to see him, and Ansel himself would prefer not to be seen. He also wonders if Tom—assuming it is Tom—also would prefer not to be seen. Perhaps there is a budding office romance?

Now Ansel wonders if they have not in fact seen him. He decides to avoid them if he can—he wants to get back on the road anyway—and only to speak to them if their paths cross unavoidably. But they are nowhere in sight as he takes his wine and flowers through the express checkout and gets back into the car.

Soon the road narrows to two lanes. Neat wooden fences appear near the roadside, and the silhouettes of venerable homes can be seen far enough away to suggest the considerable size of the properties.

Close to the road he passes an old stone mill and a row of antiques shops, some with rusting agricultural or equine-related objects—an old plow, a wagon wheel, and an entire buggy missing only its horse, the horses having long ago been put to more glamorous use in jumping and dressage.

Just before entering tony Middleburg (tony seemingly the only adjective ever used, as if it were part of the official name), Ansel turns into a tiny lane, dark for its lack of street lighting and made even darker by old trees that have held on to most of their leaves in the unseasonably warm weather.

He pulls up in front of a large stone house. There are dim lights in a few windows and a too-bright porch light that momentarily blinds him. He retrieves a small suitcase from the trunk, juggles the wine and flowers, and slams the lid with more force than he intended. He doesn't look back, but hears the car's relatively benign security beep and sees the brief reflected flash of its lights confirming he has locked it.

At the front door he sets down the suitcase and lifts the heavy brass doorknocker, but the door opens before he can let it drop. The woman who answers holds a finger to her lips. "The kids just fell asleep," she whispers. She kisses him on the lips as he eases past her into the entry hall.

She is Melinda Staunton, a petite woman, about ten years younger than Ansel. She has auburn hair, cut extra short in the manner of women who are athletes or simply have too much to worry about to fuss. Both conditions are true for Melinda, though her athletics are of the amateur variety, limited to running the occasional 10K. She is an artist, a watercolorist mostly, who has a gallery in Middleburg, where she spends whatever time she can when she's not caring for the children.

"You look like hell," she says, shaking her head and taking the wine and flowers.

"Unavoidable," he answers with a shrug.

"These are pretty," she says with a nod toward the flowers. She means it, but would say something like it even if she didn't. She is imbued with politeness; she considers it one of the essential things in greasing the rails of civilization, and insists it does not diminish another defining quality—her toughness.

She has the wholesome looks of a Midwesterner, which she is, with evenly set features and a slightly upturned nose, which she insists is definitely not cute, and protests (again, honestly) that it lacks character. Her polite directness has always been one of the biggest charms for Ansel. His WYSIWYG girl, he calls her—what you see is what you get—though she usually finds a way to take a positive angle.

"Quite a mess you guys have unleashed, though you can't say you didn't know it was coming. Let me open this wine and you can tell me what's really going on."

Ansel pulls up a chair in the kitchen, which is large and in need of updating, though Melinda doesn't seem very interested in doing this. The house, or the main part of it anyway, was built in the early 1830s. Melinda says it has already gone through too many renovations—like the shrink-wrapped face of a star who is losing her character. The kitchen cabinets, defying natural wood tradition, have been painted in a pale green enamel (no chips evident), and are old, as are the appliances. Melinda says she likes the nostalgic feel of the place.

She reaches into a drawer and pulls out an old-fashioned corkscrew, the kind where the wings rise in dutiful anticipation as the worm is screwed into the cork, and turns her back to him as she begins her work on the bottle. She peeks at him over her shoulder, then returns to her task.

Ansel looks up to see a small child peer into the room, half hidden at the door. She has Ansel's clearly defined features, beautiful in an impermanent, childlike way, meaningless as an indicator of how she will look when she is older. Her sleep-tangled, shoulder-length hair is transitioning from blond to brown. One hazel eye is visible as her rosebud fingertips grasp the door frame.

Ansel's broad smile entices his daughter into full view. She is in pajamas and bare feet, and gains confidence that she won't be chastised for being out of bed as she heads for his cartoonishly outstretched arms. "Come to me, Cara mia mine," he says in a lilting almost-song, hoisting her onto his lap.

Melinda turns and wags a mock-serious finger. "You were supposed to be asleep."

"I couldn't," Cara responds with simple plaintiveness.

"Five minutes, then," Melinda cautions.

"That's enough time for some fatherly hugging," Ansel says, taking Cara in a bear hug and eliciting a squeal. "I missed you very, very much," he says.

Melinda shushes them. "You'll wake Sam."

"Too late," Ansel responds, nodding toward the boy who has entered the room suddenly and without the reticence exhibited by his sister.

Sam is almost ten, and tall for his age. He is beginning to take on Ansel's sharply defined facial characteristics, where until now he has more closely resembled Melinda.

"Join the party, pal," Ansel says, drawing Sam toward him.

"It's a school night, Ansel," Melinda reminds.

"So it is," Ansel confirms. "Just a little family time, then. Speaking of school," he adds, turning to Sam, "how is it going?" He gets the expected, dismissive "fine" in response, and starts to demand a fuller explanation, but changes his mind. This is one of the problems of part-time fatherhood. Needed discipline is often trumped by the desire not to be viewed as the visiting ogre. This, in turn, frequently annoys Melinda, who complains that she must be the mean one.

"You're coming to my game on Saturday, right?" Sam asks, backing away from the reception hug.

"If I can," Ansel responds. "I'm very busy at work right now."

"You promised him, Ansel," Melinda reproaches, impatiently. "It's the semifinals and you told Sam you'd come."

"I'll try. I really will."

"A woman came into the gallery today," Melinda says, clearly not mollified but determined to change the subject. "One of the locals, which you can tell reliably because they either dress to the nines before they open the door to pick up the morning paper or are so wealthy they don't give a damn how they look. She was the second kind. If I hadn't seen her around, I could have taken her for a shelter resident. Anyway, after looking around with apparent distaste, Mrs. Stock Option in her ten-year-old, made-in-Bangladesh velour tracksuit looks at me and, instead of saying something about the art, says, 'Can you believe the nonsense going on across the river?'

"I said no, I can't—a politely ambiguous lie is best in these circumstances; there isn't a safe answer to such a statement."

This brings a smile to Ansel's face.

"I thought that would be the end of it—a how about this weather kind of thing—but she went on for at least ten minutes about how all of the atheists at *Intersoll*, as she kept calling it, will poach or sizzle when they appear before Saint Peter."

"She's only saying what a lot of people are thinking," Ansel says.

"Into bed," Melinda commands to Sam and Cara as she hands Ansel a wineglass. "We'll tuck you in soon."

"Kisses first," Ansel says, ignoring the beginnings of a small protest. Cara responds without reservation, planting a wet kiss on his cheek. Ansel tells her the kiss won't do—it's not wet enough—which prompts a laughing slobber in the same place. "Good, that will do the trick." Sam follows with a brush of I'm-too-old-for-this compliance, and Ansel settles for tousling his hair.

"He's reaching that age," Ansel says after the children have gone.

"Actually, he reached it awhile ago. You just weren't around to notice."

"Not fair, Melinda."

"No, I suppose it isn't," she says, turning away.

"What is it, then? What's wrong?" His voice is sharper than he intended. Fatigue has once again taken over his face.

Melinda looks at him. She is still standing. "Ever since you agreed to handle the Ingersoll rollout—had it thrust upon you, or whatever—we knew we wouldn't be seeing much of you. To be honest, I wasn't prepared for how little time we'd have together, and the children are feeling it too, Sam especially. He's too old to be put off by the weak explanations we've been giving him."

"What has he said?"

"It's not so much what he's said as it is the dismissive, *whatever-ish* attitude he takes when the subject comes up."

"Comes up how?"

"You know, why can't you or I do this or that—the other fathers *always* are there even if they are busy at work." Melinda puts hands on hips to emphasize the *always* to suggest she understands this to be stereotypically youthful hyperbole.

"Always," Ansel echoes with a smile.

"Still and all, Ansel, we can't ignore this for much longer. We're going to have The Conversation with him, so we ought to get on the same page about what we'll say."

Ansel nods. "We will. Things will ease up after we get past the amendments business. After that I'll either have to leave the country or I'll be able to delegate more of the basic running of the project. By the way, with all the furor of the churchers, you wouldn't believe how many people on our side of the argument—or so I assume—are applying to move into the place."

"Which will only anger the believers more, I suppose, but don't change the subject. The fact is, not for the first time you've made promises you can't keep."

"That certainly wasn't my intention," Ansel says, before taking a sip of wine.

She is about to argue, but stops herself and takes a breath, then exhales audibly. "I know. You never intend it." She says this matter of factly, resigned. "You always believe you can do what you promise, even though the rest of us know it's impossible. Some sort of superman thing."

Melinda crosses the room to him, runs a hand softly through his hair, then tips his face up so she can kiss him. "I agreed to take of you what I can get, so I guess I overpromise too. Anyway, if that means I only have you between tonight and tomorrow morning, then for now that's what I can get. Or what I'll have to settle for. So I hope you've come ready to make long, lingering love to me," she adds with a smile.

Ansel returns the smile and laughs. "Honey, all I'm good for tonight is some passionate sleeping."

"Forget that, Buster." She takes the glass from his hand and pulls him up from the chair.

With Melinda trailing behind, Ansel cracks open Sam's door and sees that he has already fallen asleep. His room is a jumble of sports equipment, clothing and various unidentifiable objects that can only have come from organic surroundings. "Nice mess," Ansel whispers. "Reminds me of my room."

"Not now, I hope."

Cara's room bears the marks of a mother's organization. "She still lets me come in and straighten up, the little darling," Melinda says with a low laugh. "That won't last much longer." Cara stirs. Ansel kisses her and smooths out the covers.

"Come to bed," he says, after easing the door shut.

"Two minutes. You go first. I just have to jot down a few to-dos for tomorrow before I forget."

When Melinda returns Ansel is sitting up in bed with his back against the headboard, drowsing. Melinda tilts her head, regarding him. "Hmm. I'm looking for that final burst of energy I know you keep in reserve somewhere." As she says this she is removing her top and stepping out of her jeans.

He reaches for her, pulls her to him. "Just the right height," he says as she frees her breasts from the bra. He kisses first one nipple, then the other, tugging gently on each.

Still standing, Melinda reaches over, slowly unzips his pants and begins to stroke him. "It appears we've located that secret energy source," she whispers. He smiles as she undresses him, straddles him.

"Where to begin?" he asks, slyly, and answers his own question. "I know," he says, as he reaches for her hips and guides her forward along his torso, lifting gently, kissing the inside of her thighs along the way. When she is within range, she leans forward, grasping the headboard for support while he continues to flick his tongue and tug gently. His tongue parts her, swirls, as she breaths heavily, pressing herself into his mouth while with his free hands he reaches to touch her breasts. She moves her hips, slowly then fast, until she is almost there and as if by unspoken signal slides her body down and inserts him deep inside.

When they are done and Ansel has fallen asleep, for some time she is awake in the dark, propped on an elbow, studying him. When she awakens scant hours later, he is gone, having taken pains not to be observed.

Chapter 9

Melinda

MY FEMALE FRIENDS—THE few who know—think I'm a complete fool. How could I have a family that's a family only ten percent of the time?

I understand why they don't get it, but in my opinion what they leave unsaid is the strange situation many of them are in, where because of divorce, abandonment, or what have you, they are even more alone than I am. At the end of the day, quality ten percent beats nothing . . . or less than nothing if you're simply stuck in a bad marriage.

Some of them would say ten percent doesn't beat nothing, especially when nothing allows them the freedom to get out and find a hundred percent something. Yet I know that for most of these women this is a pipedream. They are trapped by a lack of money, exhaustion, and fading looks.

In any case, I am as free as they are to find something/someone else/better. Ansel could hardly place restrictions on me. But if it happened, the circumstances would be completely serendipitous, as was my meeting Ansel.

The fact is, I'm not looking. I love Ansel, and I'm certain that he loves me within the limits of his situation. I understand his situation, or at least

I always thought I did. He was—and is, though few people would understand it—in a good marriage. At no time, even before Erika became sick, did he make any of the usual fatuous declarations about leaving his wife.

We both deny the constraints of traditional relationships. Not that either of us is promiscuous. We simply believe in the capacity of humans to love more than one person at a time, each in her own way. In only one respect does the arrangement pinch: Erika and I compete for time, and if there is a conflict, the possession arrow (as they say at Sam's basketball games) is in her direction. I'm grateful to have two fine children with him, and I do regret that he can't spend more time with them.

The thing is, I like my freedom, and I always have. Just as I'm not looking for a husband now, I was not looking for one when I met Ansel. I was in fact exploring the possibility of single parenting, in-vitro style.

When I became pregnant, Ansel said he would support whatever decision I made about aborting or raising the child. Money was not part of the equation. I was doing well enough before I met Ansel, and he could easily support us, and of course Erika, too.

And for the record, Ansel is both able and willing to support us in a very fine lifestyle. I have been adamant about resisting. I have no problem accepting financial help with the children—they are his responsibility, too, after all. Because of Ansel, they will always be able to go to the best schools and have the best opportunities.

But I will not put us in a position of dependency, where I or the kids get used to a lifestyle that could change suddenly. I will not live looking down the gun barrel of hugely changed financial circumstances. As I said, I was doing fine before we met, and I'll do fine if we have to part ways. This gives me great comfort. And, not that I care overly much what other people think, I don't want to be seen as a kept woman. I'm not his mistress. In everything but law I am as much his wife as Erika is.

When I found out I was pregnant, I never had any doubt that I would keep the baby. How could I not, if I was looking into single parenthood anyway? Ansel may not be able to spend much time with me or the kids, but he loves us and the kids love him. Sam was an accident, but we planned Cara.

There was a time early on when I might have wanted Ansel to leave Erika. This didn't last long. As I said, Ansel never promised to leave her, or for that matter said that he did not love her—unlike many men who will promise anything just to get a woman to go to bed with them. I value this honesty.

Yes, honesty is a strange word to use when speaking about a situation of basic dishonesty. But once you accept the premise that most people are more susceptible than they think—or are willing to admit—to any number of things, including falling in love the way we did, you start thinking about honesty in a more complicated, nuanced way.

Some would say that this is naive rationalization—that I'm selling myself a bill of goods—and maybe I am. They would say if Ansel can be dishonest with Erika on such a fundamental level, his character is seriously flawed, and he could be just as dishonest with me. After all, the only real certainty I can have that he doesn't have still another family out there somewhere is that there are only twenty-four hours in a day! But it's still worth something that he loves Erika and says so to me. In any case, after Erika's MS was confirmed, there was less than zero chance he would leave her. Having realistic expectations—that is to say, what one should reasonably, honestly expect in a given situation—means a lot.

It helps that I've never been possessive. As I said, I've always believed that it is possible to love more than one person at the same time. I always believed this in theory, anyway. Until I met Ansel I never had to put the theory to the test. Some of my friends used to proclaim often and loudly their belief in open (not free) love, especially during our libertine youth, when multiple, sometimes simultaneous lovers were the order of the day. Most of these friends have recanted in the face of marriages to (and children with) wayward husbands.

I'm the unusual one, I suppose. So far, my belief has withstood the test of time. This is not to say I don't occasionally get jealous, or that I don't think I'm doing anything wrong. It may be right for me, but whether it hurts the children remains to be seen. They seem pretty normal despite our strange living arrangements. But I can see that soon things will be more trying. Sam's a bright kid, and even now I sense he may only be holding back on the tough questions because he's afraid he won't like the answers.

Erika is a more complicated question. I have no reason to believe she knows about me and Ansel, and basically, I think it's his business. He is with me with eyes wide open—and has been even before Erika got sick. I would hate for her to be hurt, though.

So, this has gone on—happily, in my view—for over ten years. But Ingersoll changes everything. Ansel is very visible, which raises the threat to the secret (which, I must say, has been kept pretty damned well) and the near certainty that the discovery would be used very publicly against him. This is something we didn't think through well enough. Ansel did try to turn down the job, and I don't think Bryce Jones has ever figured out why it was necessary to persuade Ansel to take it. I still think it was a mistake to give in, though I know how persuasive Bryce can be and how much Ansel believes he owes him.

I have no reason to think we have, in fact, been discovered. But Ansel's life has never been under the scrutiny it is today. There can be no doubt that his enemies would love to discredit him in this way.

I believe Ansel is in denial about this. His commitment to Ingersoll and Bryce and his determination to meet his current responsibilities have blinded him. He has convinced himself that the secret can be kept. I'm more inclined to think that discovery is inevitable; we just don't know when.

The children are another matter. I am very worried about fallout as far as they're concerned.

And, really, Ansel is in a no-win situation. If the secret comes out, he will be reviled by the hypocritical Christians for immorality (never mind the likes of money-grubbing, sex-crazed preachers). If he breaks things off with us—which I don't believe he's capable of doing, if for no other reason than the children—they will also revile him for abandoning his responsibilities.

And Erika—I would hate for her to find out. I mostly have the life I wanted. Because of her condition and inability to have children, she doesn't. That is very sad. I truly wish her well, and I have always been prepared to share Ansel as we have for a long time, maybe forever.

∞

Chapter 10

Rule of Four

IN RICHMOND, INDIA STEPS off the elevator and into the smiling embrace of one of her oldest friends and colleagues. "Welcome to the foxhole, comrade," Rachel Kennedy says, infusing the Marxist salutation with the self-mocking irony they had shared when it was routinely hurled at them, without irony, an unvarnished epithet. On the pale fabric wall behind her, a sign in formal, dull brass letters that suggests more history and permanence than is possible, says "Ingersoll Foundation."

"It's been too long, comrade," India replies, returning the smile. Rachel is a good seven inches taller than India, who tilts her head back more obviously than necessary to look into her face. "Aren't you old enough to start shrinking?" she asks.

"Close. It won't help. We'll shrink in lockstep. Besides, elegant beauty is timeless."

"Ah, I see, said the sprite. We might as well head to the barricades, then," India says. "Nice digs," she adds as Rachel leads her down a carpeted hallway.

"One of the few positives of hard times—nice office space, available quickly and cheap. This place is a real find."

They pass an open area in which several people, most of them young and most (or so India assumes) volunteers, are engaged in the fundamental generic rituals of political activism, however much updated to accommodate technology—working the phones (traditional and smart), laptops and pads, bombarding the social network sites, collating multiple copies of this or that.

A huge, old fashioned black and white paper calendar with six-inch squares for each day dominates the far wall. Critical dates have been crudely circled with a broad-tipped, emphatic-red marker and cluttered with scrawled reminders, asterisks, and goals that spill over their datelines.

The calendar is a source of internecine humor between what Rachel calls the e-pups, the under-twenty-somethings who staff the Richmond office, and what the e-pups refer to as the e-pops, loosely defined as people (Ansel, India and Rachel, in particular, of course) who don't fit into their demographic and who are derided for an attachment to Paper-&-Pencil 1.0. To the former, grown up on digital calendars, PowerPoint and the like, the wall calendar represents clutter, inelegance, and minds in disarray; to the latter, wistful comfort found in the anachronistic minimalism of large-button hard-wired telephones.

A few of the volunteers smile as they recognize India, who smiles back and gives a small wave. "Our successors on the barricades," India adds lightly to Rachel.

Rachel half turns as she walks a step ahead. "They're light years ahead of us at that age," she says. "We had heart. They have heart and brains."

"Or tech savvy at any rate, which often passes for brains," India says. "And no shortage of self-esteem, which is a mixed blessing. If you want to make a profit, buy them for what they're worth in the morning, and sell them for what they think they're worth in the afternoon," she adds with a laugh.

"It's all those trophies they've won just for participating," Rachel says. "It goes to their heads."

She shows India into a large office. It is well-appointed but not elegant, what the office furniture rental catalog calls Level B-Plus.

"I like it," India says. "It suits you—middle age comforts without ostentation."

Rachel notes that there is much more office space than they need. India says Ansel suggested the extra room so that resources could be in place for the push on the legislature. "He also wanted it in case any of our partner organizations want to co-locate for the duration—a practice he is encouraging. Similar space has been reserved in three other states that could be pivotal, but the focus is on Richmond. We all think Virginia holds the key to victory or defeat of the amendments."

"You look quite the professional," India says, nodding toward Rachel's simple dark green dress and pumps. "Different," she adds with a sly smile.

"And you," Rachel says with an exaggerated sidewise look at India's pantsuit.

"It's Calvin Klein, darling. T.J. Maxx, forty-nine dollars. Do you like it? It *is* strange. When I took the job, Karen—no-nonsense love of my life that she is—told me I had to stop dressing as if I were organizing lettuce pickers in California. The pantsuit and a few identical outfits in different colors are as much of a concession as I'm willing to make."

"That's a relief," Rachel laughs, showing evenly spaced teeth and the beginnings of crow's-feet at the corners of her eyes. She has let her dark hair grow out almost to shoulder length and made no effort to hide what she calls her experiential gray.

"What can I say? I'm in my glory when I'm organizing lettuce pickers in California. Two pairs of jeans, a bunch of tee-shirts, a pair of hiking boots, and an office consisting of castoff desks, battered filing cabinets, chairs that recline every which way except back, dot-matrix printers where you have to tear the perforated edges off the paper—that's what I'm comfortable with. Karen wasn't buying it, though."

"How is she?" Rachel asks. "I haven't seen her in ages."

"She's great," India responds, recalling the conversation over her wardrobe. "She hasn't changed much in appearance, by which I mean still girlish, damn her, still my opposite in looks—still natural dirty blond, fair-skinned and apparently demure until you get to know her stevedore ways. 'Don't give me this mythological worker's paradise crap,'" India mimics, hands on hips. "'You always secretly wanted to be a well-heeled union boss, admit it! Well, at any rate, you'd better think about a nicer wardrobe before Mr. Big Bucks Capitalist C.B. Jones sends you to the basement with the rest of the char force.'

"I told her maybe she was right, and I could begin to improve my image by divorcing my dikey wife. So, she looked at me deadpan and said, 'Listen, first of all, I'm not dikey, I'm just fit, which you might try being more of. Second, I'm not the one who wants to look like Cesar Chavez.'"

"Sorry, no lettuce shards on the floors here," Rachel exclaims with a laugh. "I could have some delivered if it would make you feel better."

"It might, but then I'd realize it was delivered by some poor sub-minimum wage non-union guy, and that would get me depressed all over again." A bemused expression remains on India's face as she looks around at the corporate Potemkin village and thanks Rachel for doing such a good job of putting it together. In more serious moments India has in fact wondered whether she might be seduced by such surroundings, and whether Bryce's money was a mixed blessing. She has never had the luxury of full funding, and she is seriously concerned about losing her edge.

"Is Ansel coming?" Rachel asks.

"Maybe later. He got held up at Ingersoll." India is reminded that this is not the first time lately that Ansel has been delayed for reasons he chose not to explain.

"How are you getting along with him?"

"Not bad. I think he needs to be more aggressive, but I also strongly suspect that that's the point. It's unspoken, but Bryce wants him to keep me from going off the reservation, as it were. So there's some natural tension. No major blowups so far, though."

India takes a proffered seat on the sofa, a sleek piece with maple accents and taupe upholstery, while Rachel takes a matching armchair opposite. They are separated by a faux marble-top coffee table. "Give me a rundown," India says.

"We're moving along much more briskly than we imagined," Rachel replies. "It helps not to have to spend most of your time trying to cadge funding. We're running ads on TV, radio, in the *Richmond Times*, and some of the more popular online sites. Facebook is churning. The whiz kids out there in the bullpen are playing pied piper on Twitter. Lots of reaction, but of course much of it is unfavorable."

"Well, I guess just so long as we're not being ignored. Unless things have changed in the last forty-eight hours, we're still working under the assumption that the House of Delegates is a lost cause, so all of our efforts will be focused on the Senate. We've discussed it a lot at Ingersoll. Based on what you've told us and on our own nose count analyses, there are three senators in play—Reich, Armstrong and Harper. We can discuss them further at the meeting this afternoon."

Rachel nods. "We're on all of their calendars before they show up for the next session. We're cautiously optimistic. There's a possible fourth target, David Bernsen. We're on his calendar too. I think we have a shot at him."

"Good," India says.

"We feel like we've got time to work on these guys. Nothing definitive will happen before the hearings in January. We've already made sure Ingersoll will be represented. The committee chairman said he wants Bryce to testify."

"Yes, we know, but Bryce would prefer me and Ansel to do it, and it looks like that will be acceptable."

"In the past couple of days, a few of the Republicans have been talking about petitioning the governor to call a special session to consider the amendments. They're probably right that the advantage would be theirs if the vote were held today. We're fighting it. I think we can hold them off, but we might have to fall back on Bryce to pull some strings."

"He's willing to do what he can," India responds. "But he's made it clear that he wants to be in the background as much as possible. The amendments are the immediate concern, and Bryce understands that, but he's always had a longer view of the Ingersoll project. He keeps reminding us that he's not going to live forever, and he doesn't want the project's success to depend completely on him."

"I understand," Rachel says. "It's a sound philosophy. I wish some of the causes we've been associated with over the years had been less dependent on their leaders. Present company excepted," she adds with a smile.

"Definitely," India says. "I was concerned when Bryce first contacted me about the job. It's hard to ask someone who says he's prepared to commit billions of dollars to a cause whether he's really serious about it, but I did ask him. I was polite—I really was!" she adds, responding to Rachel's bemused expression. "I was hoping he would make a convincing case, because I was more excited about the job than I wanted to let on."

"All kidding aside," Rachel nods, "I do understand what you mean. You have to change your perspective when you're dealing with certain types of people. To us, the thought of frittering away a few billion is ridiculous, but to a Gates, a Bryce, a Buffett, I'm sure they look at it differently."

"Exactly. I wasn't so much afraid that he would fritter it away as that he would shift his enthusiasm elsewhere. If you can afford to put a few billion into a project and still have lots left over, you can afford to walk away from the investment, too. Well, not walk away so much. Bryce is not flighty. But I did want reassurance that he was in it for the long haul. There are no guarantees, of course, but I really did put it to him straight—polite but straight—and I felt he was sincerely committed. He said he'd rather die broke . . ."

"Whatever broke means to someone like him," Rachel interjects. "Down to his last couple of hundred million, probably, the poor guy."

"True. But I was reassured by what he said. I think he has an honest sense of history, and I think he meant it when he said he'd rather die broke than go down on a footnoted list of plutocrats in a failed national experiment. Maybe I was too eager to be convinced, but that hit home. Despite what some of my critics say, I'm not looking for glory. But I am looking to make a difference. That hasn't changed, except for the part of me that's getting older and feeling the time pressures more acutely. We all want to be remembered in a certain way, and if Bryce doesn't want to be relegated to a failed plutocrat footnote, I don't want to be the footnote that says inconsequential social activist. Anyway, enough of this," India says with a sweep of the hand. "How do things stand with the other organizations?"

"It's a mixed bag. You know how it goes. You'd think like-minded groups would be more eager to join forces when they're under attack."

"We could solve most of the world's problems if we could abolish ego," India says with a rueful shake of the head. "What's the quote? Something like, there's no limit to what can be accomplished by a person who doesn't care who gets the credit. Anyway, this is one area where Bryce has been more forward-thinking than any of us knew. He's made huge contributions over the years, and developed close relationships with many key players in the liberties and good governance movement, but has kept his profile low. He's not on any of the boards, though presumably he could be if he wanted to.

"Bryce is uncomfortable with all the hoopla over Ingersoll. Not that he doesn't want influence, but he almost always prefers to fly under the radar. I'm sure he would have been content to let Ingersoll grow organically, slowly entering people's consciousness. The recent events, the amendments in particular, forced his hand."

"As they did for many of us," Rachel says. "A few of the groups have been great," she continues. "People for the American Way, Southern Poverty Law Center and Americans for the Separation of Church and State have been very cooperative, though some of the proprietary ego thing does creep in. They're smart enough to realize that if we don't row together, we'll all sink. And they know that a rapid infusion of Bryce's resources can mean the difference between failure and success. Still, even when they agree, there is an undertone of resentment at the low frequency end of human perception."

"I understand," India says. "Last week, I met with some of the Americans for Separation people. We invited them to Ingersoll. There was a lot of bonding, bonhomie, unity of purpose, and all that. But there is that edge. I was trying to be careful not to project my own feelings onto them. But one of the board directors, an old acquaintance, did say privately that he resented the power of Bryce's money and the presumption that Ingersoll should lead. He said it irritates him that Bryce should be in on the landing when he wasn't in on the takeoff. Of course, Bryce would argue that his money has been on the plane all along."

Rachel leans forward in her chair, fingers interlaced. "That may be true, but the larger point is also true. Look, India, you and I know as well as anyone that financial backing is crucial, but it will never be viewed by the foot soldiers as equal to being on the frontlines. The key to dealing with the other organizations is to make sure that we don't fail to recognize their standing and long history of contributions in many areas of rights and liberties, not just those related to gender equality or religion.

"For instance, PFAW and Americans for Separation realize that at this moment Richmond is the primary battleground, and have taken us up on the offer to work with us here. They've both seconded high-level people within their organizations. But I'm careful not to suggest in any way that they must defer to us.

"There's a somewhat different problem with representation from the Secular Coalition for America. Despite the Coalition's umbrella role, some of its member organizations want to work with us independently and be given their own space. American Atheists has been most vocal about this. We're working it out.

"As I told you over the phone, the ACLU is giving me the most heartburn. The people I've spoken to there have a pronounced top dog attitude."

"As opposed to our top dog attitude," India interjects with a smile.

"Well, right, I do try to play that down. The thing is, they might like to have our resources, but they don't really need them for this fight. They're not enticed by our offer of free office space, either. They have affiliates in every state, and their own offices here in Richmond, down on East Main."

"We have other concerns about the ACLU," India rejoins. "Actually, I'm speaking more for Ansel when I say this, but we're worried about some of their high-profile cases going forward and becoming lightning rods to further unite the right."

"Such as?"

"The suits they've brought on gay rights, including gay marriage, for one. And a big issue with the defense of Ibrahim Odah and other Muslims arrested in connection with the August attack."

"What's the rub between you and Ansel?"

"Ansel thinks the right will use these cases to bludgeon us, especially tying them to freethought, as if there were some link between human rights, rational thought, and terrorism. I agree this could be an issue, but I don't think it's as important as Ansel does. He wants to go to the mat with the ACLU and get them to put the suits on ice, at least until the amendments issue is resolved. I don't want to hold up movement on other issues. We shouldn't be the only ones worried about having to fight a multi-front war. Let the right split off some of its resources."

"But, you know," Rachel says, pursing her lips in reflection, "if they won't freeze the suits, it might be just as well that we're publicly on the outs with them. The right already demonizes the ACLU at every opportunity. That's not likely to change no matter what. In comparison, we'd look like the responsible party, the voice of reason—not a bad place to be in this mess. By the way, American Atheists may put us in a similar bind. Self-censorship is anathema to their leadership. I think it's a legacy of Madalyn Murray O'Hair."

"My idol," India laughs, recalling how often she has been compared to O'Hair, and not as a compliment.

* * *

The afternoon is devoted to a strategy session with some of Ingersoll's allies. Ansel has arrived for the meeting, explaining he was able to extricate himself from Maryland at the last minute.

They go around the conference room making introductions and providing brief bios. India already knows most of the people, at least by reputation, and is impatient with such pro-forma corporate rituals—even a corporate body like Ansel would agree that nothing is really learned about the participants, and anyway, the time to learn about them is before the meeting. But she defers to what she believes are Ansel's sensibilities, and sits back while the ritual proceeds.

The ACLU has sent a representative after all. She is Janine Portner, a thirtyish lawyer who India at once concludes may be bright but is also powerless and most likely is there only to ensure that her organization is not ambushed.

Rituals aside, India is determined to engage these people in as informal a manner as possible. She is concerned that Ansel's presence will change the tone. Real progress is made when people push up their sleeves and become a little frazzled—that is her experience, anyway. She is too young to remember the ultra-egalitarian planning sessions for the antiwar marches of the late sixties and early seventies, but that is her heritage on both sides of the family; it is in her blood as surely as post-Second World War children identify with Pearl Harbor or D-Day.

She perches on the corner of the rectangular conference room table, and the minute introductions are over launches into her plan of action. "We've just started our media campaign, as I hope some of you have noticed."

Ansel nods. "There's no question that we're going full bore on media buys. That's one area where we're ahead of the curve."

"A rare thing," India adds with a rueful smile.

"As you'd expect," Ansel continues, "we're concentrating on the battleground states. But taking a fatalistic angle, Bryce thinks we have to fight for public opinion across the board even if we lose on the amendments."

"Especially if we lose on the amendments," interjects the representative from American Atheists, Steve Fein. "We won't have much else."

"Let me add something here," India says, looking at Fein. "There's no doubt that we—all of us at Ingersoll—are committed to freethought, above all regarding religion. But however much we may like a good fight, we're not looking to make enemies just for the hell of it—some of you may be surprised to hear me utter those words—and as a practical matter, we have our partners to consider. For several of them . . ."

"Definitely for us," interrupts the ACLU's Portner. "Our priority is freedom, not a nation free of religion."

"That's my point," India continues, softening her tone to hide annoyance over the interruption. "Each of our groups has a particular focus, but freedom binds us all together."

"You don't have to be an atheist to believe these amendments are reprehensible," Ansel says.

India hits a command key on her system, and three photos appear on a screen. "Let's talk about a few other things we agree on," she says. "First, focusing on Virginia, there's no point wasting time on the House of Delegates. It's not close enough, and time is too short. We're writing it off.

"That leaves the Senate. It's close. We think we have a shot, and the photos you see on the screen and in the bios in your individual folders are of the three people we believe we have the best chance of winning over. That's Ingersoll's assessment, and I hope you will agree, though of course if any of you know of anyone else we can get, by all means let's talk about it. Of the three, we need to have at least two of them take our side. Naturally, this doesn't mean that we're giving up on persuading others. We'll fight for every vote we can get. But these three are the most promising swing votes."

At this Ansel appears perplexed. "Rachel said we had a fourth? Bernsen?"

"We don't have enough information yet to present on him," Rachel responds. "Sorry, I thought you knew."

"No." It is only one word, but there is an edge to Ansel's voice, which he quickly tries to minimize by elongating the word to end in a rising note of inquiry—a ski jumper in mid-air correction.

India tells the group blandly that she's sorry for any confusion. In any event, they could still include Bernsen in the discussion.

"Let's begin with Barbara Reich," India says, pointing to the lone woman in the group. "Reich is 46-years old, married with two teenage children. She served two terms in the House and is in her second in the Senate. She's a Democrat, representing a district that's traditionally held by Republicans. It will surprise no one if I say that she isn't successful because she has managed to convince her constituents of the fundamental truth of liberal ideals."

This draws a snicker from around the room, and India uses the pause to invite comment at any time, "especially from those of you who are steeped in Virginia politics."

"So," she continues, "we have a quite conservative Democrat whom we think we can win over on the main issue, the Christian nation amendment. We may lose her on the others. The key is that Reich is a conservative of the old school. She is a student of American history, and probably will not support a constitutional amendment that goes against the grain of American tradition."

"We see her as someone who would be a strict constructionist if she were on the Supreme Court," the ACLU's Portner adds. "She preaches family values and probably believes in them, whatever that means, but she may not think it right that family be defined in the Constitution. Also, you haven't mentioned it, but she's Catholic."

"Saving the best for last," India says with a smile. "Her Catholicism may be an advantage on the Christian amendment, as I'll explain, and this is true as well for Carl Armstrong, who I want to discuss next.

"Armstrong carries less ambiguity baggage than Reich. He's a conservative Republican in a Republican district. But from what we can tell so far, the Christian amendment makes him uncomfortable, and in this both he and Reich are reflecting something we've picked up in polling elsewhere in the country: Catholics are not so far removed from their roots in America that they've forgotten what it's like to be discriminated against by fellow Christians. In this sense, we're seeing considerable support from alliances, mostly informal, of Catholics and Jews."

"Keep in mind, however," Rachel says, "that the people who crafted the amendment were clear to focus on the Judeo-Christian heritage. In other words, they went broad with the language, even if they didn't mean it."

"That's true," Ansel volunteers, "but there are lots of people, including Catholics and Jews, who are perfectly capable of reading between the lines. They understand that when it comes down to it, Judeo-Christian won't necessarily apply to them."

"And that's what we're hoping for from Reich and Armstrong," India adds.

"Moving on, Jack Harper is a 40-year-old Democrat with a moderate-to-liberal voting record. So, one might ask, why is he included in this group? Why is he even in play and not a definite vote with our side? The answer is that he has put himself in this camp with his public statements. He's never gone so far as to support any of the amendments, but he talks about keeping an open mind in a way that, frankly, suggests—unlike Reich and Armstrong, who will probably make decisions based on principle—that he may take a more cynical, what's-in-it-for-me stance. Disturbing, but true. We should be able to count on him, and we can't. But if it comes to it, we may be able to buy him off."

"If we can figure out what he wants," Rachel adds.

"Yes," Ansel agrees. "The good thing is that the clock is ticking. If Harper is angling for something or other, he'll have to make it clear before the ratification votes."

"The bad thing," India says, "is that we could be outbid." Turning fully to Ansel, she asks whether he'd like to discuss David Bernsen.

"At least let's air some of the basic issues," Ansel responds. "It's all too obvious that we can't count on any of the swing votes. We can use all of the maybes we can get."

India turns to Rachel. "Why don't you take this one?"

"I don't have a photo handy, but if you're not already familiar with him, take it from me, he's young!" Rachel says, turning to the group. "He'll be thirty-one next week, to be precise. He's in his first term. The reason I didn't include him today is that we keep hearing conflicting things about him, which I suppose is what you'd expect of someone who has no record to speak of. Originally, we wanted to go after him because the first few people we interviewed labeled him a moderate Republican. One used the word progressive.

"But in the last few days others who supposedly know him well have said that he is conservative to the core. He comes from old money, and that money was pretty clearly the deciding factor in his primary win— probably not in the general, though, since the district is solidly Republican. Bachelor's and law degrees from Georgetown. He's Episcopalian; we're not sure how observant. He's getting a lot of pressure from his constituents to support all three amendments. He hasn't come out one way or another, but he's ambitious, and there's no reason to think he'll buck a trend."

Ansel appears downcast as he shakes his head. "So, we may have gotten bum information on him early on. This is very distressing. Having to persuade two out of four, if our head-counting is right, is tough enough. Two out of three . . ."

"Let's not give up on him yet," offers PFAW's Brian Bayliss. "I have a couple of friends who live in his district—outcasts all," he adds with a smile. "We may be able to get a better fix on him."

"Right," India responds. "We weren't giving up. Our earlier interviews could be the right ones. But we need to find out before we waste too much time on him."

Chapter 11

Keeping Time in a Second Dimension

IT IS A SUNDAY afternoon, a time for family and typical post-meridian pursuits. If an observer were to think about it at all, it would likely be as a fleeting, almost subliminal note of approval, and perhaps envy: the handsome, self-assured couple, mother and father; the precious young girl, wondrous at the festive tumult around her, her hand enveloped and protected in the father's; the pre-teen sports-addled boy leaping ahead two steps at a time.

The place is Redskins Stadium (never mind whatever latest corporate legend is actually on the facade or the latest failed attempt to change the team name to something less offensive). It's a big game. The Giants are in town. Whatever else is going on in the world, in Washington this is the place to be.

The family members excuse themselves one by one, and people stand either graciously or absently to let them pass and take their seats. They change order: Ansel, Redskins cap securely on his head (even though he won't be disappointed if the Giants win), makes room beside him for Sam, who is not quite swimming in a Redskins jersey (he's between sizes), and Melinda, who has Cara, her face already food-smudged, on her other side.

They are laughing, in high spirits, teasing each other and watching pregame theatrics. All morning Ansel has observed Sam go through one mood shift after another, alternating between the present carefree playfulness and histrionically sullen withdrawal. Within any fifteen minute period, it's difficult to know which Sam will be the operative one. He couldn't contain his laughter when Cara knocked over a glass of juice at breakfast. An antic slide into all-things-are-funny followed. Less than five minutes later, nothing was funny, particularly if credit for the humor would go to Ansel or Melinda (but especially Ansel).

Ansel might have dismissed Sam's behavior as routine preadolescent hormonal mania, except that ever since receiving Melinda's heads-up that they had better be prepared for sharper, more skeptical questioning from Sam, he has been alert to signs that this reckoning might be imminent.

Ansel is a strong believer in preparing for problems, but this is a problem he tends not to dwell on, as every scenario is unpalatable. The most common one goes something like this:

Ansel: Something bothering you, pal?

Sam: Several false starts, ending in, If I ask you something about you and mom, will you tell me the truth?

Ansel: Don't we usually tell you the truth?

Sam: Silence.

Ansel, frowning: Well, why don't you just ask me?

Sam: Are you and mom fighting?

Ansel, seeking clarification as a delaying tactic: What makes you ask?

Sam, with a shrug, sensing Ansel's motive: I don't know. You're hardly ever here.

Ansel: You know how busy I am. I can't get home every night.

Sam, quiet.

Ansel, recognizing Sam's dissatisfaction, but wanting to avoid giving him fodder for further discussion: We've talked about this.

Sam: My friends' dads are busy too.

Ansel: I can only speak for myself. I get here as often as I can. You know that.

Sam, giving up, attention wandering: Uh huh.

The Redskins emerge onto the field from a huge inflated team helmet, to the accompaniment of fireworks. Cordite-scented smoke drifts into the stands.

Ansel promised his family he would be here today come hell or high water. He has season tickets to these seats, but his place is often vacant, or occupied by a stand-in. As good as the seats are, they are not the only ones in the stadium for which he has season tickets. He has a bloc on the opposite side of the field as well, which he sometimes uses, mostly in the company of business associates, and even more often gives away.

For all the precautions he takes to keep his lives separate, there is always the worry that something will go awry. He believes it's the small things that trip you up—being recognized in the random panning of the TV cameras over the crowd, the casual reference at some social event with Erika (*didn't I see you at . . . could have sworn it was you*); over a decade of experience trying to keep their relationship secret, this is possibly the biggest truism Ansel and Melinda have affirmed. They have tried to control the big things they can anticipate. That is why, for example, Ansel decided that even his closest friends would not be let in on his parallel life. They can't slip up if they don't know. But the other things . . .

Neither of them is certain of the precise moment that their furtive romance turned into something more, and then into what it is now.

For Melinda, the moment probably occurred when she revealed to Ansel that she was pregnant, and he, instead of taking the news as a problem to be solved, as she thought he might, saw it as an unanticipated wonder to be somehow embraced. She never thought he would be angry, show her less affection, or blame her. But she was prepared to fend off soft-spoken discussions about terminating the pregnancy; what she got instead was an enthusiasm that may have exceeded her own. She would never say so, but it did occur to her that his attitude toward the pregnancy, which was truly unplanned, may have been affected by the simultaneous realization that he would never be able to have a child with Erika.

For Ansel, despite his pleasure at the news, the realization that they would be more than a secret couple with a child, but rather something closer to a real family (or as close as he could make it), didn't really hit until later, when Melinda, well into the pregnancy, was preoccupied with setting up a nursery.

In retrospect he thinks that not until that moment did he fully appreciate just how well his mind was suited to the compartmentation of his lives. He always knew he was good at focusing on whatever was at hand; now he found that he could easily pay full attention to the very different areas of his life, without one channel bleeding into another. Time was the biggest constraint, especially the huge amount of time devoted to his professional life, and however much the tight rationing may have bothered him, it was the one thing both Melinda and Erika understood and accepted at face value, at least until recently.

Melinda and Ansel also accepted that despite their best efforts, discovery of their parallel life could happen. However, this understanding was always of the "we'll cross that bridge when we come to it" variety, and always in the context of damage to private lives. The imagined scene was both vague and almost pathetically banal; it would be dealt with in the tedious ways of all lovers placed in this position, with tears, apologies, and perhaps promises to change.

And then came Ingersoll, or more to the point, the national struggle that put Ingersoll in the crosshairs and had caused Melinda to lobby hard in what she knew would be the losing cause of persuading him to turn down the job. Neither Ansel nor Melinda doubts that the stakes are far bigger than either could have imagined. If before, the only people who would have cared about their secret lives were those directly affected or who had some relationship to either of them, now, discovery would hurt their cause, and at the very least would magnify the personal embarrassments and make the pain public.

And yet, both were determined that the higher risks would not prevent them from being the family they had committed to. So, here they are, standing to cheer the good plays and boo the bad ones, to yell at the refs, to eat and drink sports cuisine. For minutes at a time Ansel forgets (or at any rate doesn't think about, which is almost as good) the binds and mires that at present comprise the core of his existence.

The Redskins running back takes the ball, gains four and is about to be tackled, when he slips the grasp and charges like a wounded wildebeest into the end zone. Ansel high fives his son. They are all smiles. Ansel's smile is still on his face when they have retaken their seats. Only for the briefest instant is he conscious of wanting to be that running back.

Chapter 12

The Atolls

THE MOOD IS ONE of frisson and snap, the latter at least in part due to the tardy arrival of late September weather. More important, Roland thinks, is the anger that permeates the congregation. There is a sense of betrayal and reprisal in the air. Roland feels it even before the beginning of Sunday's late morning service, the last of the day.

The pews are full, but Roland would put as much of himself into his sermon if there were only a handful of worshippers. It is a legacy of his father and grandfather, who never made a distinction between saving one soul or a hundred—all must get your best.

His single-mindedness isn't reciprocated. Despite what Roland believes to be a well-delivered sermon, it is clear that the congregants' minds are on other things. There are more than the usual number of asides and conversations (some of them quite animated, though occasionally punctuated by neighborly reminders of where they are), and fewer than the usual number of chins on chests. And there are more people than usual—many more.

Seated behind Roland are the Reverends Schweig and Liston. Karl Schweig is the pastor of the Blessed Name Lutheran Church, Liston of the Holy Gospel Baptist Church. Along with Roland's Christ the King, these constitute the three churches in the newly formed Ingersoll Sea that have come to be called, collectively, the Atolls.

Surprisingly large numbers in all three churches have been making it clear to their ministers: Lead or get out of the way! Speak up for the faith or stand aside! The proposed constitutional amendments merely provide the lyrics to an old melody. This *is* a Christian nation, they say in unison (and not *Judeo*-Christian, either)!

Founded by a small group of German immigrants at the turn of the last century, Blessed Name has steadily lost members as the demographics have changed; it now comprises mostly old people and a few of their obedient adult children. It is *their* children, on the cusp of less obedient adulthood, who are demanding young blood in the pulpit. Never mind how many generations have been baptized by Rev. Schweig. The time for change has come—is long past, if you ask any of them.

Schweig, in his late seventies, has only recently gotten around to choosing a potential successor. The Young Turks in his flock forced the issue during the last fundraiser, when they threatened to lobby against contributions if he didn't look toward a more energetic, activist future.

Rev. Jeremy Liston has a similar situation. His congregation, consisting primarily of lower middle class blacks, is becoming younger—and more outspoken—by the day. But unlike Schweig, Liston is a firebrand, born anew even by evangelical standards. If he were a Muslim cleric he would preside over the kind of madrassa that routinely draws scrutiny from the authorities. Still, at 45, he fears he may be losing ground to even more radical youth. It will be a challenge to stay in front of his congregation without being run over.

Roland himself is not insensitive to such danger. At the moment, Christ the King is by far the largest of the three churches. Roland is well aware of what he refers to, blandly, as the racial generational shift in his congregation. Its new members are an amalgam of old time revivalism and new age entitlement, impatience and activism.

To some extent Roland dismisses the problem as one of size. A massive new tabernacle built four years ago is able to accommodate throngs of the faithful and a sea of their cars so large that shuttle service has to be provided from the outer reaches for the less fit. On approach, the church itself appears as an island. With over five thousand members, any faction becomes significant and yet, paradoxically, this factional significance is buffered by the very size of the overall body.

Nevertheless, Roland sometimes feels as though he is riding the tiger. The large mainstream congregation—and its money—is the lifeblood of the church. But especially these days, evangelical activism is its beating heart. In particular since the August attack and among its youth, that heart has beat faster and faster.

Any healing or return to normalcy that took place in the years after 9/11 has now gone entirely. There is no small degree of anti-Muslim sentiment here. There has been quite enough cheek-turning, thank you.

After the joint service there will be a potluck lunch followed by a meeting to discuss the response to Ingersoll. Roland and the other ministers are worried about the meeting getting out of hand.

Already there are signs. As the service comes to an end with the week's announcements, Roland closes by mentioning almost in passing (as if it were necessary) that they will reassemble at two o'clock. He doesn't think much of it as he concludes his remarks and begins to descend from the pulpit.

But it quickly becomes clear that even this seemingly banal announcement will be challenged. The congregants have begun to file out when Makembo Smith, one of the more prominent firebrands, booms out, "The Atolls are not in a sea, Reverend! We're being told to live in a cesspool!"

Roland looks up, and simply nods when it becomes apparent that this is meant as a rhetorical correction, a contextual placeholder for later. Smith is already walking out, accompanied by several others, one of whom has given him an encouraging slap on the back.

Even more worrisome to Roland are murmurings from Rev. Liston's church that some of the members are talking up a violent response. Threats have been rumored against Bryce, Ansel and India—the unholy trinity, as they're called—and against newcomers to Ingersoll. *You think you can buy up our neighborhood and fill it with atheists? We'll just see about that! You think your kids will play in their nice suburban backyards? Think about how it will feel when none of you—not a one—is safe!*

Chapter 13

India To Ansel

CONFIDENTIAL / INGERSOLL INTERNAL USE ONLY

To: Ansel Frye
CC: C.B. Jones, R. Kennedy
From: India Ruiz
Subject: Update on Virginia Senate Contacts

Ansel, I want to update you on the state of play regarding our lobbying efforts in the Virginia Senate.

As we discussed in Richmond, we've gone ahead with meetings with Reich, Armstrong, and Harper. We've also tried to get a better read on David Bernsen. Because Ingersoll is in the news, we have an advantage in getting face time. But the edge is likely to be temporary as our novelty fades. Following is a blow-by-blow on each of the senators, along with some notes on the state of play within our own camp.

1.<u>Reich</u>: Reich was visited at her home by Rachel, Matt Doyle from Americans for Separation of Church and State, and Bayliss from People for the American Way. We had a minor dustup putting together the delegation. I wanted to limit the size to three, which seemed an appropriate number for a visit to the senator's home. This meant politely turning down a request to participate from Rob Mescek, of the Secular Coalition. He wasn't happy, but he went along with it.

As I think I've mentioned, a few of the organizations under the Secular Coalition umbrella have been pushing for individual involvement. Some are acting completely independently, which of course they have a right to do, however much it may complicate things for us.

American Atheists (the *other* AA!) is being pushy, giving us heartburn, but probably also not helping the digestion of the Secular Coalition. I was contacted by a woman from AA named Cary Morehouse. She must be all of 30, but she fashions herself the successor to the O'Hair legacy (there was no shortage of audacity, I can tell you that)!

When I explained to Morehouse why we were trying to keep the meeting with Reich small, and that I had coordinated this with Mescek (a bit of a stretch, since I hadn't actually met with him yet), she said she is happy to work with Mescek (note the Royal She, presuming an authority I doubt she really possesses), but was obliged to make clear that her organization has its own agenda. She then went on to say, flat out, that she (again, that *she*) believes AA is being deliberately excluded from the meeting because we're afraid they will offend Reich.

I denied this, of course, but there is some truth in it—even more so after meeting Morehouse. I'm afraid she'd go off half-cocked and make some ridiculous remark about Reich's Papist leanings or such, which is the last thing we need considering that a main point of our strategy with her and Armstrong, the other Catholic, is to appeal to the vulnerability of Catholics if the Christian America amendment passes.

In the event, the meeting with Reich was limited to Rachel, Doyle and Bayliss, and the results were mildly encouraging. On Christian America, we believe that Reich is, as we've hoped, receptive to the arguments that the amendment runs counter to American constitutional tradition and that it is this very tradition that ultimately made it possible for Catholics to thrive.

Reich made the point that these are different times and that, especially given the "nature of the threat to the country" (read Muslim) and the "sophistication" of modern religionists, it is important to make a clear statement about our Judeo-Christian heritage.

Rachel took this as an opening to argue that the most valuable aspect of that heritage is not religion, per se, but freedom of belief—or nonbelief—and that "difficult times" are both inevitable and, by definition, temporary, but constitutional amendments are much harder to alter.

They kicked this around for some time. Rachel didn't leave with the impression that Reich was persuaded, but she does confirm our original judgment that she is thoughtful and serious, and will weigh the arguments carefully.

The other two amendments are a split decision with Reich. She is leaning toward us on the marriage amendment. She says she does in fact believe that marriage should be between a man and a woman, but she doesn't think this has a place in the Constitution. It didn't come up in discussion, but one of her brothers is openly gay, and this may have affected her views.

On abortion, however, she's clearly against us. She's joined at the hip with the Church on this one. Rachel's sense is that trying to convince her otherwise will be a waste of time.

2.<u>Armstrong</u>: The same three-person delegation visited Carl Armstrong, on the same day. As you know, Armstrong is a conservative Republican in a conservative Republican district. His position on the Christian amendment tracks closely with Reich's. He has a strong sense of American history and is clearly uncomfortable with the direction of the amendment.

Armstrong hasn't committed himself one way or the other, but we have the impression that more than any of the others he sees himself as a direct descendant of the Virginia founding fathers. He cares about his legacy, and we think he might be open to arguments that suggest (i.e., not beating him over the head with them) that he would not want to go down in history as the "anti-Jefferson" or "anti-Madison."

The biggest threat is that his stalwart nature will work against us in the form of party loyalty. He has never broken ranks with his party on a significant issue, and when it comes time to vote, he may not be able to do so on this one either.

As for the other two amendments, forget about it. He's on board to vote the party line.

3.<u>Harper</u>: This was a quick meet and greet (we agreed to call it preliminary) in order to catch him during an out-of-session visit to his office in Richmond. I went to see him myself, along with Mescek from Secular Coalition.

Unfortunately, Harper is shaping up as the most problematic of all our targets. You'll recall that at our meeting in Richmond we said that his votes may be for sale. Nothing at the meeting with me and Mescek changed that judgment. If anything, we may have underestimated his corruptibility. Moreover, he hasn't made clear what his price would be. Depending upon how one reads him (and he's cagey as hell) he could be angling for large contributions to his political war chest (or his personal war chest?), endorsements in future campaigns (he's unquestionably ambitious), or some kind of direct connection to Bryce. Or all of the above. Stay tuned.

In a sense Harper has the luxury, politically, of voting either way. He's a Democrat, but in the genteel southern Virginia sense. The combined urban-rural makeup of his district means that his constituents are fairly evenly split on basic issues, (though I suspect they're more in the pro-amendments camp) so he'll have a sales job no matter how he votes. He's winsome and personally popular, however, so he can probably pull this off.

My bottom line is that we can't trust him. He's got an oily sheen to him, and unlike Reich and Armstrong, principle and a sense of the moment aren't part of his makeup. My guess is that he'll try to play us until the very end—and even then we won't be sure we haven't lost the auction until the hammer falls.

4.<u>Bernsen</u>: I thought I'd end with a possible bright spot. Per our earlier discussion, we tried to get a better read on Bernsen through our sources. This hasn't provided much enlightenment, so Rachel and I decided to pay him a visit. (FYI, we didn't mention this to the others in order to avoid squabbling over the composition of the "delegation.")

We visited Bernsen at his home—which would more properly be called an estate and which adjoins the "real" estate, occupied by his parents. There is no mistaking his wealth.

Rachel and I came away with identical impressions. First of all, you can't escape being struck by how amazingly young he is. He just turned thirty-one, and looks twenty-five. But he's not callow, and is in fact rather complex.

Bernsen is handsome and personable—his life of privilege gives him a golden child aspect. He's bright, articulate and well-informed. He (or someone) even did his homework on me and Rachel, which was especially impressive given the short notice of our visit. He was knowledgeable about my activist past (and present, I hope), and actually engaged me on it, asking, for instance, about some of my human rights and labor campaigns. The cynical side of me immediately smelled noblesse oblige, but I have to admit, if he wasn't sincere, he made a good show of it.

Our main issue with Bernsen is the unexamined life of a thirty-one-year-old child of privilege. As we discussed the amendments, he made it clear that he intends to vote yes on all three—hence, the initial judgment that he's not worth our time.

Yet it's also clear that Bernsen has a bright, inquisitive mind. He seems to be more thoughtful than his down-the-party-line positions would imply. One has the sense that he is on the verge of becoming his own man—of thinking for himself, rather than falling back on cant. Whether there is sufficient time for the metamorphosis to occur is another thing.

I repeat, it's just a feeling (though Rachel seems to have reached the same conclusion independently), but we shouldn't be too quick to discount him. He may be more malleable than we thought. It's hard to tell, but it's worth a shot—all the more so given the uncertainties regarding the others.

Chapter 14

Eye for Eye

H E PREFERS TO DRIVE himself, but for Ansel, as for the other Ingersoll principals, this has become difficult. In the short time since the announcement of the wider community, the number of protesters at the gates has risen steadily, and they have become increasingly rowdy. Between the protesters and the swelled number of guards and police to deal with them, the simple act of driving in and out has become a time-consuming ordeal.

To believers, the very idea of Ingersoll—and particularly at this time—is an affront. Two weeks ago, this insult was the theme of a megachurch sermon by Morgan Fitzgerald. "There is never a good time to offend God," he had said, "but at this time, when He is locked in epic battle with the forces of evil, it is particularly egregious. It is as if the founders of this Ingersoll deliberately chose this time to demean the Lord. Perhaps they thought that our Lord was down and vulnerable, but we know He is never down for the count. His armies will always win out in the end."

Following the sermon, Ingersoll became even more of a national focal point in the fight. At the White House, when asked to comment, President Stuart said only that he hoped all sides would treat one another with civility. Nevertheless, he had found several ways to make his sentiments known, not least by his foursquare support of the amendments.

To the many demonstrators living near Ingersoll were added believers from across the country. The hotels filled up, sometimes five to a room, and the locals opened their homes to welcome the visitors.

Bryce, Ansel and India now rarely go anywhere by car without being sandwiched between Land Rovers filled with Ingersoll security. The fact that the security details are armed is a source of friction with county officials and police, who offer frequent assurances that they are fully capable of maintaining safety and order.

Ansel is thinking of these assurances as his black sedan, accompanied front and rear by the security vehicles, crawls through the crowd at the gate. He spies three county police cruisers, but they are on the perimeter, the officers sitting inside with no evident desire to assist. From the beginning Ansel has doubted the county's ability to provide real security. Fair or not, he thinks of the officers as being conservative and Christian, and assumes they will be unenthusiastic in protecting them. Thus far they have given no reason to change his mind. He is certainly not inclined to reevaluate this notion as objects strike the car. It seems the demonstrators are no longer satisfied to march and chant; in recent days they have upped the ante with various missiles, mostly of the edible kind, though one object last week hit with enough force to leave spider cracks in a car's window.

There is a positive development in all of this. Ingersoll has become a rallying point for nonbelievers as well. On one level, Ansel is not sure why this should surprise him. After all, his own faith in their cause is strong, and they have done a good job of calling others to the fight. Beginning with the announcement and press conference, the issues at stake and their crucial importance have been well articulated.

Still, if there is one thing about which Ansel has not been confident it is the willingness of agnostics and atheists to commit themselves—more to the point, to unite—in a cause. He and India have been sweating this from the beginning. The churchers have their great, erroneous organizing principle; the rituals may be as complex as the underlying theologies, but the fundamental message of their faith is clear.

How, then, is his side to organize around a negative? India describes the problem as one of trying to herd apostate cats. To some extent Bryce confronted this question at the press conference: It has become a war of necessity, he said. Join with us or submit to the tyranny of the believers.

But Ansel is surprised that this message has had as much resonance as it appears to have had. Like the churchers, the religious freedom people have joined the fight. (Here, too, the phrase "nonbelievers" puts them at a disadvantage as far as image is concerned—the churchers always seem to have the upper hand in bumper sticker wars, witness pro-life versus pro-choice.) Many have called, written and contributed. Many have simply shown up; in fact, there have been more of these volunteers than Ansel and India have known what to do with, at least until they can get ahead of the curve. Many have inquired about living in Ingersoll.

Nevertheless, Ansel worries constantly about the staying power of these people. He often reflects on the experience of the Unitarians in this connection. He believes that, logically, the Unitarians should be more successful than they are. They have a long tradition of liberal thought, embracing believers, nonbelievers, fallen away Christians and Jews, intellectuals, and activists. In Ansel's opinion, religion should never have to be the motive force behind ethics or right action, but if it must be so, the Unitarian Church should be a natural home for thinking people, deist or not, who are curious about their place in the cosmos, who want or need to belong to something bigger than themselves, or who want a place to work for worthwhile causes. And indeed, it has succeeded in these things. As India puts it in her none too subtle way, if humans are too weak to give up superstition, this is what the crutch should look like—a dogma-free (or dogma-minimal, at any rate) zone.

So how is it that such an attractive institution should not be the preeminent church in the land? He asks how Baptists, Pentecostals, Catholics and the like can be so thoroughly dominant. And then he answers his own question in the most disheartening way. The Unitarians encourage thinking, while the others tell people what to believe. People are essentially told to check their powers of reason at the door, and many—perhaps most—are obviously willing to do so. In so many ways it is easier, after all.

This dilemma has weighed heavily on the Ingersoll leadership. Ansel and India have been working hard to find that elusive organizing principle—one that can outlive the imminent danger after the danger has gone. What is the argument that will get freethinkers to work together, and stay together? What is the positive argument, the one that replaces God with something concrete to work for—the one that doesn't end with the trite proclamation, "You're free! Free to think and be all you can be! Go and conquer the universe by the power of your mind!" The one that says, "Here is something you can believe in that has nothing to do with The Word handed down by nomadic shepherds, the universe explained by flat-earthers, or justice defined by witch-burners." The one that says more than that something is *not* the way forward, but that *this is*.

In the meantime, his problem is far more mundane. As they inch through the sea of demonstrators he wonders in frustration how to get past them before the car looks like a dead fruit sampler. "Can't we have these people pushed back?" he asks his driver, a former army bomb tech named Carlos. "We shouldn't have to run a damned gauntlet just to get in or out of our own community."

"We've tried, sir," Carlos responds, his dark eyes addressing Ansel in the rearview mirror. "Mr. Roark spoke to the P.G. cops," he says, referring to Ingersoll's increasingly consequential security chief. "You can see how much good it's done over there," he adds, pointing to the parked patrol cars. "Mr. Roark said we shouldn't be too pushy—that we don't want to give the picketers a reason to go nuts. Personally, I wouldn't mind flattening a few of them for effect."

Ansel emits a small laugh. "I'm afraid Mr. Roark is right," he says, as the car finally starts to break free. "But I know how you feel."

Ansel picks up his phone on the second chorus of "Bette Davis Eyes" (having briefly toyed with his preference for "Sympathy for the Devil"). "Yeah, Tom," he says, impatiently, then "shit." Carlos's eyes appear again in the mirror.

"Hold on," Ansel tells Tom, leaning forward to tap Carlos on the shoulder. "Pull over as soon as you can. We have a change of plan." He sits back, and says into the phone, "I'll be right there."

"Where to?" Carlos asks as Ansel signs off.

"Do you know where the southeast construction site is?"

"I think so. Do you have an actual address?"

"Tom wasn't sure. He said it's going to be pretty obvious when we get there."

"Sir?"

"Apparently, some of our friends of the religious crusader persuasion decided to make a point by using some of our new homes to light up the sky."

* * *

Finding the site turns out to be a simple matter of following a fire engine. The homes under construction are part of a mid-price development. When Ansel arrives, the fire is under control. It's clear, however, that two homes are a total loss.

Ansel steps from the car and heads toward the incident commander, who is directing some of his men to a spot on one of the houses. As he approaches, Ansel is surprised to see Roland Peterson standing next to the commander.

Ansel extends his hand and introduces himself to the commander, who takes it and then quickly excuses himself, giving a half turn to address a subordinate. An ambulance is slowly leaving the scene, lights flashing but no siren whooping.

"Mr. Frye, Roland Peterson," the pastor says, offering his hand. "We met shortly after you arrived."

"Yes, of course," Ansel says.

"My church isn't far from here. I heard about the fire and thought I'd see if I could help."

"Has someone been hurt?" Ansel asks with a nod toward the departing ambulance.

"I understand a fireman suffered minor injuries of some kind. I don't know the details."

"His face was singed in a flare-up," the commander says, turning back to Ansel and Roland. "It doesn't appear to be serious."

"That's a relief," Ansel says. "Do you know how the fire started? My company owns these properties," he adds.

"You work for Mr. Jones, then," the commander says. Ansel judges him to be in his forties. An intense, but not particularly threatening, gaze emanates from a well weathered face. His hands are rough and meaty, with nails cut to the quick.

"Mr. Jones is the foundation's chairman. I'm the CEO."

"The investigators should arrive shortly," the commander says. "I'd prefer not to prejudge the situation."

"You must have some clue, based on experience," Ansel presses. "Frankly, it's hard to see how this could be anything but an intentional act."

"All I can say, sir, is that fires are not always what they seem to be. There's all kinds of things that can get a fire going."

"Right," Ansel says in a tone resigned to the bureaucratic nonanswer.

"I think what Mr. Frye has observed," Roland says, "is that none of the usual suspects, so to speak, are possible in this case. Only the frames are in place. There's no electrical or gas hookup yet. Of course, the investigators must have the final say, but wouldn't your professional experience suggest something intentional?"

"I suppose so, Reverend," the commander says. "I suppose I'd have to say that, yes. That's my unofficial opinion, of course."

"Of course."

Ansel is struck by Roland's diplomatic manner, but also by the commander's change of tone. He seems more deferential, but Ansel isn't certain whether this is out of respect for the pastor's position or a mirrored response to the way he put the question.

"Not exactly the circumstances I had in mind," Roland says, turning to Ansel, "but I'm pleased to run into you. I had been thinking it would be a good idea to get together."

"Yes, I'm sorry we haven't done it sooner. Events have gotten a little out of hand."

"As we see," Roland says with a glance toward the houses. The fires are out, but there is an acrid smell of damp ash in the air. "To be honest, Mr. Frye . . ."

"Ansel, please."

"To be honest, Ansel, from the viewpoint of the churches in the area, such meetings are long overdue. I feel I must tell you that there is considerable resentment toward Mr. Jones and his project."

"Let's set it up," Ansel responds briskly. "How many churches are involved, in addition to yours?"

Roland cocks his head, suggesting surprise that this is not readily known by Ansel. "Two. Blessed Name Lutheran and Holy Gospel Baptist."

"Not a Catholic church? I thought there was a Catholic church near here."

"Yes, near here, but not technically within the borders of the proposed community. If we are the Atolls," Roland says with a drawn smile, "I suppose the Catholics are located on the continental shelf. Anyway, Father Gresk has his own bureaucracy to deal with."

"I met Reverend Schweig when I arrived," Ansel says. "I gather there's another—a Reverend Liston, I believe—who wasn't available at the time."

"Yes, that's right," Roland replies. He seems to reflect for a moment, then says, "I wonder if you would consider joining me now for a cup of coffee."

"Why don't we do that?" Ansel responds. "Let me just check with my assistant to make sure I'm not supposed to be elsewhere. I can also have him set up a meeting with the other pastors, if you suggest."

"That would be good." Roland pauses, appearing to choose his words carefully. "A meeting with all of us would be helpful. But if you can spare the time, you and I still might take advantage of this chance meeting."

"Yes, certainly," Ansel replies, curious about what Roland has in mind.

* * *

Roland's office is open and orderly. The walls are covered with neatly spaced plaques and certificates, which Ansel scans as he is led to a small sitting area. From here Ansel can see the church parking lot below, illuminated faintly by blue lights, and a treed area behind.

They have entered through a back staircase. Ansel can hear the echo of purposeful voices from somewhere in the building.

"Demonstration shift change," Roland says matter of factly.

"Ah, the armies of God," Ansel says with a wry smile.

95

"They *are* mighty," Roland responds with less irony as he motions Ansel to a seat and offers coffee or tea, apologizing that it will take a minute. "Geneva is gone for the day, so I'll have to fetch it myself."

"Don't trouble yourself," Ansel says, finding pleasure in the deep timbre of Roland's voice. "I probably shouldn't stay long anyway."

"Oh, don't think that you're not welcome," Roland nods. "It's just a little awkward because the other pastors and I have agreed to coordinate our activities, and frankly, I don't want to be seen going behind their backs."

"I understand." Ansel wonders about Roland's choice of words—*seen*, as in witnessed, or seen, as in perceived or seeming to be. It occurs to him briefly that perhaps their meeting wasn't entirely by chance.

"That's why I suggested taking advantage of our encounter," Roland adds, removing his jacket and taking a seat opposite Ansel. "There are a couple of things we might best keep between us, and running into you at the fire provides a convenient excuse."

Roland leans forward in his chair and clasps his hands. With someone else, the posture might seem false or gratuitous, but Ansel thinks it makes Roland appear genuine and earnest.

"Let me say a few obligatory things on which I'm sure I can speak for the other pastors. First, it will come as no surprise that we are upset by what we see as a seriously divisive plan by Bryce Jones, and at a time when things are already too divided."

When it becomes evident that Ansel is not going to respond, Roland continues. "We intend to keep up the protests until the amendments are approved—which we believe will happen soon enough—and you back off this, if you'll forgive me, misguided Ingersoll business."

Ansel leans in, mirroring Roland's posture. "Since you're speaking forthrightly, Roland, which I respect, let me return the favor. First of all, we believe we have a decent shot at defeating the amendments, and intend to oppose them with our last breath. You may think a constitutionally defined Christian America is a good thing, but we think it is a disaster. We think it will end in the death of American democracy—and since you don't know me well, I feel obliged to add that I am not given to overstatement.

"Second, all of us—Bryce above all—are determined to make the progressive ideal of Ingersoll a success. We have bold plans for this place, it's true. Ingersoll is the foundation stone of progress. We see it as a beginning, not an end in itself."

Shaking his head, Roland says that he is truly mystified that anyone can believe that a life of denying God and Jesus Christ can represent progress.

"And yet," Ansel says with a tight smile, "there it is."

"Yes, there it is. But I would like to think that we can address our differences peacefully."

"That is certainly our hope as well."

"Unfortunately, I don't think it's everyone's hope."

"As we probably witnessed this evening."

"While we're at it, I'd like to get something personal off my chest."

"By all means," Ansel says with a sweep of the hand.

"I feel thoroughly deceived by Bryce Jones. It is, frankly, somewhat embarrassing when dealing with colleagues to appear as if we have been cuckolded, so to speak.

"When the entity called the Potomac Institute was established, Bryce gave me his personal assurances that progressive didn't mean anti-Christian. Of course, Bryce was long known for his agnosticism, and I had no illusions that The Institute would be particularly hospitable to religion. But to have Bryce, you and India—whom I've not yet held a meeting with, by the way, which is irksome in the circumstances—essentially declare war on religion and drop this bombshell about Ingersoll's dramatically expanding presence is deeply offensive to all of us here."

"I'm sure there was no intention to offend, and whatever our problems with religion, it's unfair to characterize what we're doing as declaring war on it," Ansel interjects. "And I am sorry about India. I can only assume that she's been overwhelmed. I'll make sure she corrects the oversight. As far as the new community is concerned, I'm sure you can understand why Bryce couldn't afford to be too revealing. If nothing else, it would have made the land purchases prohibitively expensive.

"But the real issue—the heart of the matter—is that the only way Ingersoll could avoid being stillborn was to make sure its gestation period, if you'll forgive the metaphor, was not cut short."

Roland's blurted laugh takes Ansel by surprise. "Ansel, please, I love the metaphor, especially its pro-life implications! I hope you're not trying to get me to say something in support of abortion!"

Ansel returns the laugh, struck anew that things are always easier when people—antagonists above all—can bring humor into the arena. "Listen, Roland, we believe we are strong enough to survive opposition, including the protests; that might not have been the case if we had announced prematurely. As it was, we announced earlier than we wanted to because of recent events . . ."

"The amendments . . ."

"Among other things. The atmosphere has become poisonous for nonbelievers. I hope you can see that."

Ansel pauses to let Roland respond, but he seems intent upon listening. "I hope you understand that I—and I'm certain I can speak for Bryce here—deeply regret any embarrassment you were caused within your community. I truly hope we can work together amicably going forward."

"I hope so," Roland says, his lips pursed. "I'm sure you must understand that many things are beyond my control."

"You do have the largest church in the area," Ansel points out.

"True, but inadequate. Christians are anything but monolithic. In fact, that's why I wanted to speak with you alone."

As Ansel cocks his head, quizzically, Roland continues. "Our friend the fire commander notwithstanding, it seems clear that the destruction of the new homes is no accident." Holding up a hand to stop Ansel from interrupting, Roland goes on. "Let me answer the question before it's asked. I have no knowledge of who the culprit is."

"But I'm guessing you have suspicions."

"We all have suspicions, Ansel. I can't be too specific, but I do want to help prevent violence or further destruction of property."

"Then I think you need to tell me—or the authorities—what you suspect."

"I'll only go so far as to say that there are hotheads in our congregations who are not being restrained."

"Hotheads? Just a general category?" Ansel adds with a note of skepticism. "Surely you can do better than that, Reverend, before someone gets seriously hurt."

"Actually, I can't. I will only say that it's well past time you called on the one pastor among our island churches whom you have not yet met."

Chapter 15

First Alarm

IT IS THE FIRST meeting of a chockablock morning, shoehorned in at seven o'clock at the urgent request of Roark, the security director, who has asked to meet alone with Bryce, Ansel and India.

They gather around the table in Bryce's office. Bryce's assistant, Jeanette, who has taken over for Tom while he works fulltime for Ansel, sits poised with a notepad, separated from the others by a few empty chairs. India looks bleary-eyed, having driven in from Richmond late last night.

Bryce, as usual, is at his best first thing in the morning. Ansel tells him that this is how he became successful, gaining advantage over the later-performing and coffee-deprived. "Let's get this show on the road," Bryce says to Roark.

A self-possessed, sinewy man who long ago resigned himself to a pinstripe suit culture in which he would never feel authentic, Roark nods and quickly surveys the room. With a world-weary expression he runs his fingers through thinning, legacy-red hair, letting them slide off momentarily to knead the back of his neck. He has thick eyebrows that seem to be trying to compensate for the shortfall on top and which might be comical if not offset by a no-nonsense, often combative visage.

"Is something wrong?" Bryce asks to Roark's uncomfortable hesitation.

"I'm sorry, Mr. Jones, but I asked for a closed meeting with only the three of you."

"Oh, well, you know," Bryce shrugs, "Jeanette is the fly on my wall, my shadow."

"Still," he replies, letting the word hang. "There's no offense intended—it's a need to know thing."

"No problem, Mr. Jones," Jeanette offers, standing. "I'll just wait outside."

"Thank you, Jeanette," Bryce says. "This won't take long," he adds with an unmistakable edge that suggests Roark had better not have embarrassed her for nothing.

"I'm sorry," Roark repeats when the door closes. "This really won't take long. You'll understand the reason for limiting attendance in a moment."

Ansel hopes Roark isn't being overly theatrical, as he sometimes is. He is the one who brought Roark on board in the first place, pressing, over Bryce's occasionally cavalier objections, that security would have to be taken more seriously following the Ingersoll rollout. Bryce has a reflexive resistance to sky-is-falling drama, and Ansel wants to ensure that Roark provides no fodder for his dismissive tendencies.

"I assume this isn't about clearing the crowds from the gates," Bryce interrupts. "Ansel has already approved your plans for dealing with that."

"No sir." Roark's tone now hints at impatience. "There are two things all of you need to be aware of. First, we have good intelligence that violent attacks on Ingersoll are in an advanced planning stage. The arson incident was just a taste. Some seriously well trained people have moved into the area to do this, and they have local support."

"This *is* based on good intelligence, right?" Ansel interjects. "It's not speculation?"

"How do we know?" India presses.

"The information is solid. One thing is that they're getting support from one of the local churches, including a pastor named Liston."

"From Liston, personally?" Ansel asks. "I've just scheduled a meeting with him. Are you sure he's personally involved?"

"Yes, but I'm not sure of the exact role he's playing. I'd say that, at the very least, he's looking the other way."

"You're meeting with him soon, I hope," Bryce says to Ansel.

"Day after tomorrow."

"Make sure you feel him up good."

"As well as I can. Listen," Ansel says, turning back to Roark, "Roland Peterson at Christ the King hinted that something might be going on. He wouldn't be specific, though. Before I meet Liston, you should get me up to speed on anything you've got to help me ask the right questions."

"Will do, Mr. Frye."

"You said there was a second issue," Bryce interjects.

"Yes. All three of you should consider yourselves targets."

"Really? That serious?" India puts in.

"Yes, that serious. I'm going to spend some more of your money, Mr. Jones. Beginning tomorrow, all of your security details will be 24/7."

"That seems excessive," Bryce says with undisguised annoyance. "I won't be my own prisoner. I'll let Ansel and India speak for themselves."

"I'm sorry, Mr. Jones, but as far as I'm concerned, they can't. You can't." To Bryce's surprised expression, Roark adds: "I know you're not crazy about these things. I try to be accommodating on all kinds of things. This isn't one of them. Nobody dies on my watch—that was my law when I was Secret Service, and it's my law now. It's your show, Mr. Jones. I understand that. But this is serious. I'm not exaggerating the threat. If you can't go along with me on this, you'll have to find someone else to be security director."

"Well," India says with a tight smile. "I guess we've been told."

Looking hard at Roark, Ansel says, "What do we know about these people and who is supporting them—aside from Liston, I mean?"

"Some of the names I've been given are people I know or have heard of. Serious paramilitary types, mostly from out west. I don't know who's backing them. I assume they're not freelancing, but you never know. I think we all understand that there's no shortage of religious nuts willing to ante up the resources, or do bad things themselves."

Ansel glances at Bryce, who gives a reluctant nod, and turns back to Roark. "Okay, we're running late. Here's where we are. We'll go with stepped up security for now, including the personal details."

"With one qualification," Bryce interjects. "I expect them to be unobtrusive. I don't want us looking like panicked potentates on the run."

Roark holds up a hand, with a nod of comprehension. "I can keep a lot of it in the background, Mr. Jones. But some will be more obvious, simply because I want these clowns to know we're not a soft target. They need to know we're on to them, and to suspect that what they see is the tip of the iceberg."

"Okay," Ansel says, picking up. "We'll reevaluate after the amendment votes. You'll brief me and others as appropriate before I meet with Liston, and you'll keep us informed. Agreed?" he adds, looking around the table.

"Agreed," Bryce says.

"Sorry, I need to be somewhere," India says, rising.

"Thanks for your time," Roark adds, as the rest of them stand.

"No," Bryce says. "Thank *you*. I apologize if I gave you short shrift. Sometimes I probably need a good swift kick in the rear on these things."

India takes a step toward the door, but stops suddenly and turns back to Roark. "One more question. I've been on the receiving end of these kinds of threats before. To be honest, I've had my fill of waiting for some crackpot to act or not act. So let me just ask you hypothetically, if we didn't want to be passive about this . . . if we didn't want to hold our collective breath . . . What I mean . . ."

Roark holds up a hand. "I think I understand what you mean. I'll just say that there are things that can be done proactively, let's put it, but that's a whole different conversation, not something you want to discuss when you're running out the door. I suggest we drop it for now."

"By the way," Ansel says, "with regard to the secrecy question, this is not something we can hold too closely if others are in danger."

Roark looks up as he gathers his papers. "Understood. I'll get a handle on things ASAP."

"Was it really necessary to exclude Jeanette?" India asks, her hand still on the doorknob.

"Unfortunately, yes. I'm not as confident in my judgment about this as I am about the other thing, but I believe we may be penetrated."

"Penetrated as in spies?" Bryce asks with a start. "Don't you think this was worth discussing?"

"I do. I was hoping to. None of you seems to have the time today. And as I said, I'm less sure about it."

"We'll make time," Bryce responds. "For now, in thirty seconds or less, who do you suspect?"

"I don't know for sure. I've been made aware of certain things that have leaked to the churchers."

"What kind of . . ."

"Things that are known by relatively few people at the top."

"Jeanette?" Ansel asks.

"I don't know. It's possible, but she's not the only possibility."

"I sure as hell hope she's not involved," Bryce declares. "I'd be royally ticked off."

Chapter 16

Common Ground Eludes

WHAT STRIKES ANSEL AS his car pulls up in front of Holy Gospel Baptist Church is that it looks nothing like what he thinks of when he thinks of radical evangelism. There is nothing of the big brick tent that defines Christ the King. Rather, the main part of the church is a substantial gray stone structure with a sharply pitched slate roof, rooted in place for over a hundred years. Graceful pointed-arch milk-glass windows are outlined by crimson frames. The building has been expanded front to back more than once, as evinced by slight changes in the color of the stone.

Ansel has convinced Roark to let his security detail pull up out of sight, though he feels slightly abashed over having issued what he thinks of as an India-worthy blast. (*For Christ sake, Roark, Liston's not stupid enough to off me in his own church! Besides, this is supposed to be a neighborly call. I'm not showing up with an entourage and a fucking Plexiglas Pope-mobile!*) Also, he's pretty sure he's offended Roark, who claims to be a lapsed Catholic but Ansel suspects is not so lapsed as to take slights to His Holiness without flinching.

The front entrance is locked, but the outlines of people are visible through the windows. Ansel knocks, and a moment later, the door half opens, held in place by a kind-looking middle aged black woman with pewter hair, who says that Reverend Liston can be found in his office, which is entered through the side door.

Ansel is accompanied by Tom. He has decided that whatever Roark's suspicions about Christian spies in their midst, there is no point to behaving oddly. And in a lighter, unguarded moment of stoicism, the small part of his brain given over to paranoia, which he acknowledges but rationalizes as being within the bounds of normal human prudence, also told him that if Tom really is connected to the ring, he might be useful as a shield when the bullets start to fly—though he takes no comfort in the image of a dead Tom, lionized for his bravery by his church sponsors, frozen in some stained glass window and suffused in Godly light.

Liston is dressed in his black coat and clerical collar, a brilliant white against the waxed mahogany of his skin. He has an uncontrived dignity, and exudes a friendly warmth that belies the image of bomb-throwing anarchy that has preceded him.

"This is a lovely old church," Ansel says as he takes a seat beside Tom.

"I fell in love with it at first sight. I was told India Ruiz would be with you," he adds.

"She intended to be here. Unfortunately, she was held up at the last minute. She sends apologies and says she'll reschedule as soon as possible." All of this is true; the part Ansel doesn't mention is that the holdup involves India's organizing of counter-demonstrations of Ingersoll Freethinkers, as the volunteers have called themselves. He hopes they will choose another name, one that, as he put it to India, doesn't sound like a high school debating society.

"I worked with her once," Liston says. "Did you know that?" He laughs and adds, "I know it must not seem the most likely of pairings."

"I didn't know," Ansel says with genuine surprise. "Did you ever hear her mention it, Tom?" he adds, feeling wrong-footed.

Tom shakes his head. "I haven't."

Liston waves it away. "I wouldn't be surprised if she doesn't remember. There were so many of us. It was at a huge anti-poverty rally. This must have been, oh, twenty years ago or more. She was very young—so was I, for that matter—but anyone would have told you she was special. People just followed where she went."

"And now you find yourselves on opposite sides of the barricades," Ansel observes lightly.

"Indeed we are. It just goes to show, alliances are not permanent, and adversaries don't have to be either. I think I've just paraphrased our first president," Liston adds with a laugh.

After talking with Roark, Ansel wants to feel out Liston as far as he can regarding any possible violence. He is hoping that Liston might give him an opening, and decides that this may be a small one. "I suppose there's no doubting we're adversaries for the moment," he says.

"And possibly much longer," Liston responds, a smile still on his face, fainter now. "Eternity is a long time, after all, and even longer if it's not spent in heaven."

"Did you hear that, Tom?" Ansel asks, returning the smile. "Reverend Liston is afraid he might not be going to heaven."

Liston shares the joke with a big burbling laugh. "Touché!" When the laughter dies down he says, "I understand you met with Roland Peterson recently."

Ansel wonders what Liston knows about the meeting or what was discussed, or if he suspected that Peterson had pointed a finger at him. "We ran into each other at the fire."

"He's a good man. Possibly not in the good graces of the church hierarchy, such as it is."

"Is that so? I take it for granted that they all oppose what we're doing. I don't know why they would be displeased with Peterson."

"I don't know either, but I know why I'd be displeased if I were in their shoes." Liston takes a sidewise look at Ansel—sizing him up, Ansel assumes. "It's strictly speculation, of course, but my guess is that first, Reverend Peterson, pastor of the largest church in the area, is caught with his pants down concerning your community, to choose an expressive, if possibly inappropriate, metaphor. And then he's slow to use the power of numbers, and presumably other resources, to get on it."

"The opposition doesn't seem wanting from our perspective," Ansel says.

"Perhaps so. But it came late, and my guess is that they think it's inadequate—not to mention a distraction from the real work of getting the amendments passed."

"What does inadequate mean?"

"It means that, at the end of the day, even with the amendments passed, your community will still be there as a visible obstacle to our work for the American people."

"I must say, Reverend, that sounds like more of a political ambition than a spiritual one. Anyway, from your mouth to God's ears, as you would say. I hope you don't think this is an ill-considered, fly-by-night project on our part."

"To the contrary . . ."

"We believe Ingersoll's success to be vitally important."

"Oh, I don't doubt your commitment, Mr. Frye. Again, I was only speculating on why some people might be dissatisfied with Reverend Peterson's efforts."

"But you don't feel that way yourself, heaven forfend!" Ansel says with not much of a smile.

"You keep using the words of believers," Liston says with a mock stern wag of a finger.

"It's a problem we all face," Ansel replies. "It's a cultural-linguistic problem caused by many years of religious influence. But don't worry. We'll find our own metaphors. For the record, I'm not one of those people who believes the Bible should be banned or placed on the upper shelves, like a bootleg copy of *Lolita* or *Lady Chatterley's Lover*. I have no problem stipulating that the Bible contains some of the most beautiful language ever written."

"Just not truth, eh?"

"It's not devoid of wisdom, like the best of literature. It's just not divinely inspired. And the wisdom tends to be lost in the weeds planted by your vengeful God."

"Well, anyway, Mr. Frye, I have my hands full dealing with my own flock; I can't worry about Reverend Peterson's."

"So," Ansel ventures, "continuing our hypothetical discussion, since you apparently share concerns about Ingersoll's long-term presence, what would you do if you were in his shoes—and less hypothetically, in your own?"

"It's hard to imagine being in Reverend Peterson's shoes. For one thing, there is no clear hierarchy of authority in this. The men in Richmond may be influential, but that's different from giving orders. As for me, I've never been associated with a church as large as his. My guess is the size makes the congregation drift toward the center . . . away from the edges; the extremes cancel each other out."

"On this issue?"

"On every issue. So Reverend Peterson will probably just keep on keepin' on, at least until he's derailed by some petty internal bureaucratic issue, such as how powerful the music committee is relative to the membership committee, which seems to be the fate of all of us at some point or other. In the meantime, Reverend Peterson can be our statesman—the voice of reason," Liston adds with a chuckle.

"And you, Reverend? Keep in mind that our community seeks nothing more than peaceful coexistence, which is one reason why the Christian nation amendment is such a big deal to us."

"Ah, now, Mr. Frye, that's a bit of an exaggeration, isn't it? The average Ingersoller—is that what you call them?—is probably willing to live and let live. But a sizeable minority is in an evangelical mode of its own, wouldn't you say? Even more so as the call to arms has gone out. I'm not unaware of Ingersoll's force augmentations, let's call them."

Ansel observes that Liston says this with markedly less mirth. "Every movement has its fringe. If I may say so, I've heard it said that your congregation is less open to discussion and compromise than, say, Reverend Peterson's is."

"We don't peg ourselves on a sliding scale, Mr. Frye."

"Nor do we. But we both know such scales exist, figuratively that is, and as astute observers of our communities we have a pretty good idea of where people fall on them."

Liston sits back, eyeing Ansel, as if wondering how forthright he should be—a posture Ansel unconsciously mimics. He has a sense they're getting down to brass tacks, when Tom's phone rings.

Ansel turns to Tom, visibly annoyed at the interruption.

"I'm sorry, Mr. Frye, it's my 911 number."

"Well take it outside, please."

"The nemesis of the reflective life," Liston says with a nod as Tom exits the room.

"Sometimes I don't know if the pros outweigh the cons," Ansel says, seething at the timing of the interruption. For the moment he wants to leave the discussion open, with some ambiguity and room for maneuver—to leave more space for nuance and compromise—but his annoyance gets the better of him, as he says, "Look, Reverend . . . Jeremy, let's not play a dangerous game if we don't have to. Frankly, you can talk all you like about equal lunatic fringes; the fact is that the religious fringe has a far longer and far more sordid history of reprehensible acts than the nonreligious."

Liston leans forward, appearing eager to respond, when Tom comes back into the room and signals to Ansel.

"What, Tom? Can't this wait?"

"No sir, I'm sorry. Your wife has been taken to the hospital."

"What?" Ansel shakes his head as if to rid himself of some disorienting cobweb. "What happened? Is she all right?"

"I don't know. She seems to have had some kind of seizure. She's at Sibley. That's all the information the office had."

"I don't understand. Why wasn't I called?" Ansel asks, standing.

"Your secretary said your phone is turned off."

"Forgive me, Reverend, we'll have to continue another time."

Liston stands, concern on his face. "Of course, not at all. Go. We'll reschedule soon."

"We really do need to pick this up again," Ansel says, gravely.

"I know. We will. I'll pray for her," he adds without irony as Ansel closes the door behind him.

It doesn't occur to him to mind.

Chapter 17

Limb from Limb

ERIKA IS DOZING WHEN Ansel arrives. What had begun as a sunny day has gradually turned cloudy-blustery, and now there is only the gloaming through the window and the soft artificial lighting directed toward the ceiling above her bed. She is alone in the private room, a television news channel giving off white noise.

He stands over her, stroking her arm. An I.V. drip is surgically taped to her hand. There is a large red welt on her left cheek.

She looks at him through slit eyes, says drowsily "Sorry to be such a bother."

"Don't be absurd, Erika," he says, bending to kiss her forehead. "The E.R. doctor told me you had a seizure," he adds, not certain she's listening.

But she's making an effort to wake up, and asks for a sip of water from the flimsy plastic cup on the nightstand. "I'm okay," she says. She pats the bedding around her, searching. "The bed up-down thing?" she mumbles.

"It's here," Ansel answers, picking up the remote control from where it is just out of her reach. "Up or down?"

"Up." She holds out a hand as her head is raised. "Too fast," she says. "A little dizzy." After a minute: "A little higher. Okay. Better."

"Do you remember what happened?" he asks, still stroking her arm. She looks more alert.

"Some. I was in the bedroom. I'd gone to get something or other. Things started to go wonky—a little spinning, but also in a herky-jerky kind of way. I vaguely remember the ambulance guys taking me out.

"They said they responded to my Life Alert. But I don't remember pressing the button. The only thing I can figure is that I hit it somehow as I fell."

"I guess that's not all you hit," he says, grazing the welt on her face. "Does it hurt a lot?"

"Not too bad. It throbs a little. I didn't know it was there until a nurse in the E.R. showed it to me in a mirror."

"You were alert when you arrived, then?"

"Alert enough to feel embarrassed by all the fuss."

"For crying out loud, Erika . . ."

A brisk voice from the doorway pronounces, "You look like you're feeling better." The voice belongs to a woman, Dr. Kovac, as she introduces herself, the staff neurologist. She is young, probably finishing her neurology residency, Ansel thinks. She has a Central European look, with chiseled, angular features more interesting than pretty. "We've contacted your doctor . . . Markowitz . . ." she says after a brief hesitation. "Right, Markowitz," she confirms to herself ahead of Erika and Ansel. "He'll be here to check on you soon. It looks like you're okay, though."

"What can you tell us?" Ansel asks.

"We assume you had a seizure of some kind, but our tests so far don't show anything out of the ordinary. I understand you've been diagnosed with MS."

"Some time ago," Erika responds. "Do you think the seizure is related to that, or something else?"

"I can't say for sure. Seizures are not that commonly associated with MS, though they do occur. It could also be related to the medication you're on."

"I've been on it for a while. It's not new."

"Well, I've scheduled some tests, including an MRI. There's nothing unusual on the EEG, EKG or CAT. Until we know more we're assuming you had a grand mal seizure."

"Why are you assuming that?" Ansel asks. "She could have just blacked out and hit her head on the way down, right?"

"It doesn't seem that way." The doctor is clinical-friendly, conveying the tone of someone who is happiest playing games of diagnosis. "First of all, let me reassure you that we see no signs that you had a stroke. It might have been a TIA, but I doubt it. We should know more later."

Kovac takes Erika's arm and turns it to reveal a small strawberry on the elbow. Then she raises the sheets and points to abrasions on Erika's thigh, just above the knee. "The reason I suspect a major seizure has to do with the carpet abrasions on your arms and legs."

Erika issues a surprised laugh and says she didn't even know about them.

Kovac removes a digital assistant from her pocket, and focuses on it for a moment. "According to the admitting record, you told them you don't have a history of seizures, is that right?"

"Not like this. I've had . . . um . . . parox . . . paroxysmal—I can never get that word out—symptoms. Unusual posturing, that kind of thing."

"How about drop attacks, when you feel like your legs are wobbly? Sometimes MS patients have incidents that can appear to be grand mal, epileptic-type seizures, but the cause is different."

"I've never had anything like this," Erika says, looking at Ansel for confirmation.

"I've never noticed anything," he responds. "She does get wobbly sometimes, but I've never seen her fall and thrash about."

"Anyway," Erika says, "when can I go home?"

"Well, your doctor will come by this evening, so at a minimum I would suggest you stay overnight. Possibly one or two days while we run some tests. We can keep an eye on you that way."

Erika frowns, but Ansel says decisively that it's a good idea. "If we're lucky, this was a one-off, but we should stay on top of it."

When the doctor has gone, Ansel strokes Erika's hair. "I love you," he says. "It scared the hell out of me when I heard. I'm sorry I couldn't get here faster."

Erika gives him a drowsy smile. "I didn't notice. One of the good things about whatever happened is that it's easy to lose track of time."

"I still feel bad. My phone was turned off for a meeting. I usually turn it to vibrate just in case of something like this. The office called Tom, who was with me. I rode him pretty hard at first because of the interruption. I'll have to make it up to him."

"Important meeting, then?" she asks.

"The good Reverend Jeremy Liston, from one of the island churches. I'm worried about his flock getting out of hand."

"Not dangerously so, I hope," she says, appearing more alert.

"I hope not. If there is anything going on, I want to nip it in the bud."

* * *

When Ansel arrives at the Foxhall Road house, where he plans to spend the night, he is concerned to find the garage door gaping, then remembers that this is how the EMTs got in without breaking down the front door. Erika said she thought she might have left it open when she returned from the supermarket.

They have been in the house for about two years now. It's the kind of stately place that would be used as a residence for an ambassador whose country needs to make a good impression (we want your aid but don't really need it). Built in the 1920s of brick and stone, with sharply peaked slate roofs, despite its size and large property, it has an intimacy that was lacking in their last, even larger home, in Connecticut. Erika professes to be happier here.

The following morning, an Ingersoll driver is waiting for him. The commute is mercifully light. Even at the gate, the demonstrators seem to have less urgency. Perhaps it's the cold, Ansel thinks, now that they're into November. It's hard to see how they could keep up the level of fervency they had displayed from the start. He likens it to a let's-go-team chant at a stadium, where the crowd claps at an ever faster pace until there is nowhere left for it to go, and the chant comes to a fractious, entropic halt.

In any case, on the assumption that the lull is temporary, India has been organizing counterdemonstrations. It didn't take her long to tire of the press coverage showing an endless loop of Ingersoll's opponents without viewers also seeing its supporters.

India has asked Ansel to put in an afternoon appearance in the auditorium with some of the volunteers and squad leaders, as she calls them. The purpose is to keep them motivated while they subordinate their passion to Ingersoll's—that is, India's—command.

She has also convinced Bryce to attend briefly, despite his reluctance to be involved in the day-to-day activities of Ingersoll. He understands that he can't detach himself completely at this point, but he tells India he has to draw the line somewhere if Ingersoll is to be freestanding and self-sustaining. "I really won't be alive forever," he reminds her.

"But you're here now, and this is the critical moment for Ingersoll. We need these people motivated."

And so he agreed.

* * *

Ansel is weary as he joins the others in the auditorium named for women's rights pioneer, abolitionist and atheist firebrand Ernestine Rose, and the site of the announcement launching Ingersoll. He plans to leave for the hospital as soon as he can get away.

His energy begins to return as the buzz of the mostly college-age crowd crosses the blood-brain barrier. Ansel is impressed by how effectively India has spun them up.

It strikes him that the increasingly vocal contest with the believers' world has created a strange duality. The first four years of Ingersoll's existence as The Institute had been defined largely by a sedate, scholarly atmosphere. The daily work had a serious, substantive tone. Now there is an energy more in keeping with a fully active college campus. The scholarly work is continuing, but the mood is one of high dudgeon.

Ansel and Bryce are sitting together on the stage, waiting for India to introduce them. She has been going on about the tradition of freethinking and the need for twenty-first century humans not merely to know, but to act on the knowledge, that the earth is not flat and that what keeps us from floating off into space is gravity, not the ballast of superstition.

With a start, Ansel feels the vibration of his phone at his chest—he has jammed it into his shirt pocket so as not to miss a call from Erika.

As he glances at the screen, he catches the word hospital. He excuses himself to Bryce, turns obliquely to the back of the stage and raises the phone to his ear. What he hears, however, is not Erika's voice, but

Melinda's, which immediately disorients him. Melinda knows not to call him without prearrangement. He wonders how the wires (or the signals or whatever one says nowadays) must have been crossed. How is it Melinda's voice when the readout on the screen says hospital? He pulls the phone from his ear to look again at the screen, but returns to listening before he has a chance to read it as Melinda again calls his name.

"You're at the hospital?" he whispers, still confused.

"Yes, Loudoun. They took Sam here."

"What?" He is still trying to make sense of this, and his voice must betray the confusion and anxiety.

"He was in a car accident."

"Sam?"

"Yes, Sam. Who do you think I'm talking about, Ansel? Where are you?"

"In a . . ."

"You have to come now. It's serious." Her voice is more than anxious; she seems barely in control. "He was being driven home from school . . . they took him right into surgery. I haven't seen him yet."

Ansel looks around, at a loss. "I'll . . . come. Of course. . . . I'll figure something out."

He turns to Bryce, says he must go. Bryce understands immediately—he has just sent flowers to Erika.

But as he stands, India is looking at him, questioning. Unaware anything has happened, she has just introduced him to the audience. In confusion, he walks toward the podium, intending to make excuses and leave.

But the audience has been expertly worked up, and he doesn't want to be the cause of their crashing, and so he will seize the moment . . . give them a minute or two—the time that might be taken by missing a traffic light.

His first words are halting, but there is a symbiosis with the crowd, and he quickly finds his voice. He tells them that the future of the nation is in their hands. He tells them that they are privileged to be here at this particular moment in history, when they can make a decisive difference. He tells them that just as the nation's first patriots lived at a similar critical moment and responded by pledging their lives, fortunes, and sacred honor, it is now in the hands of a fortunate few to preserve their sacrifice. It is a speech full of such clichés; he has given it many times. But the confluence of the crowd's enthusiasm and his distraught state of mind fuels a new, passionate urgency. And then he can't locate a good point to cut it off. The seized moment turns into five, then ten, and almost fifteen before he can tear away.

And now it is rush hour as he drives himself out the gate, having told his security detail—ordered them, actually (he will deal with Roark tomorrow)—to stand down.

Chapter 18

A Reckoning

HE FINDS HER IN the hospital chapel. It is a small, nondenominational space with comforting-familiar pews and diffused light, but without the trappings of an altar or anything else that might suggest more than the echoed ambience of formal religion. She is in the front pew, trying to console a woman even more bereft than she is. It is when she notices him that he sees the expression of hostility.

It is a look he has never before seen on her face. At that moment, words fail him; later, he will think of her expression as baleful, full of anguish that is understandable and animus that is incomprehensible.

"Where have you been? I called you almost two hours ago!" Her voice is harsh and raw. She has pulled away from the other woman, who also turns toward Ansel. There is no reproach in the other woman's look. It is all grief and, Ansel will learn, guilt.

He ignores the question, overriding the impulse to say she is exaggerating, it has not been two hours. "What happened?" he asks. "Where is Sam?" He is startled, suddenly aware and ashamed that only now does he fully comprehend the gravity of the situation. On the phone Melinda had said Sam had been taken into surgery. What was it that convinced him that it was less than life-threatening? Even now he can't really believe Sam's life might be in danger. "I got here as fast as I could," he adds, his stomach turning over at the guilty thought that the time he spent talking to the volunteers might have made some kind of difference.

Melinda stands, momentarily losing her balance. She lurches toward him, holds him desperately, rigid fingers stabbing his back. The other woman watches, her face bloated, her makeup streaked, caked and blotched.

Melinda pulls away. Before she turns to the other woman, Ansel is shocked to see in that split second something more than pain, but a confirmation—is it really possible to see these things in such a brief time?—of fire and resentment.

"This is Carol," Melinda says.

"Sam," Ansel says with barely a nod. "What about Sam?"

"Maybe we can see him soon," Melinda replies, and now her voice seems vacant. "I'll take you to him. Carol, could you leave us for a few minutes?"

The request starts a new round of sobbing. As Carol moves to leave, she must pass close to Melinda and Ansel. Melinda grazes her arm. "Carol," she says, "this is" . . . and here she hesitates before she says "this is Sam's father. I'll talk to you soon," she adds, not giving her enough time to do more than nod at Ansel and turn quickly toward the door.

"Carol was driving the car," Melinda says when they are alone. "She pulled over to the side of the road to let another kid out. The car was hit from behind. Sam was in the rear passenger seat behind her. That part took the biggest hit."

"For Christ sake, Melinda, how *is* he?"

"Not good," she says, her face again dissolving into tears, and this time they seem to be only tears of grief, unadulterated with blame or anger—or so Ansel reads them. "His head hit the rear pillar. There's been some internal bleeding. Some broken bones, too, but it's the head trauma they're worried about."

Ansel stares at her and blinks. In his shock, all he can think to say is, "Was he wearing a seatbelt?"

Melinda looks at him, momentarily perplexed, but she doesn't ask what difference it makes. She gathers herself—tries to get the words out. She takes a deep breath and forces it out in one blow. "The doctors may have to induce a coma, depending on the outcome of the surgery. Sam" . . . and now that she's said his name again she begins to lose control.

Ansel feels unsteady on his feet. He holds on to the end of the pew for support. "What else do the doctors say?" he asks at last with desperate certainty in his voice that she has not told him everything. "There must be something that can be done. We can get him to the best specialists. We can fly him anywhere . . ."

Melinda hunches her shoulders as if she could withdraw her head into her chest. "They probably should have airlifted him to the trauma unit at Fairfax from the accident scene. But they brought him here first, and then there was no time. They said they had to relieve the bleeding in his brain. I don't know if it would have made any difference," she adds with a tone of defensiveness, as if she might have somehow altered the chain of events.

"But what can be done now?" Ansel's voice has become constricted, reedy, unfamiliar to one so used to the idea that there is always something that can be done.

"I don't know." And there is that look again. Her face is hardened and accusatory. "It's touch and go." At this, she begins to sob, until she can get out the words, "In case of the worst, they want permission to take his organs."

Ansel takes a step back. He sits—more of a collapse—into a pew.

"Where were you?" Melinda asks again, and now Ansel is no longer startled by her tone. He resents that she is displacing everything onto him. He is at rapid turns numb, disbelieving, sick to his stomach. He is fixed on the word *you*. *You* needed to be with him. "I got here as soon as I could," he says again, weakly.

"We should find out if we can see him yet," Melinda says, vacantly.

"One minute," Ansel responds. "Just . . . one . . . *minute*. I need one minute."

As they leave the chapel, they pass a lounge where Carol is sitting. She has her back to them, and is being held by a man, her husband, Ansel guesses.

Melinda speeds up, pushing Ansel along. "I couldn't deal with her again," she says after they've passed. "Not now."

"Was anyone else hurt?" Ansel asks.

Melinda shakes her head no. "Carol blames herself. She says she didn't pull far enough out of the roadway . . . left her rear sticking out. When she was struck, Sam's seat took the brunt. She says maybe he would have been okay if the car had side airbags, but it was an older model. Who knows? Maybe it wouldn't have made any difference."

"Mrs. Staunton . . ." A nurse approaches on soft shoes. She is middle-aged, with an amorphous shape and a face practiced at rapid alternations between empathy and brisk competence.

"This is Sam's father," Melinda says.

The nurse gives a sympathetic nod. "Dr. Brinkman is the surgeon," she says. "He'll be with you soon."

"But how is he?" Melinda asks urgently.

"The surgery went well. He's in post-op. With head injuries, it takes time for things to be known. Come, I'll take you to him," the nurse says gently. She leads with a purposeful walk that stops short as they approach Sam's bed. The bed is curtained off, but in any case there is no patient nearby. The only sound comes from the regular rhythm of a ventilator.

They stand together in stone cold silence until Ansel nods toward the ventilator. "Is he dependent on it?" he whispers. "What happens if it's turned off?"

The nurse seems taken aback by the stark question. "I wouldn't dwell on that now. We'll cross that bridge if we have to, Mr. . . . . Staunton?"

"Frye. But what will happen?"

"It's hard to say. Head trauma is just like that. Sometimes the patient will breathe on his own and things improve rapidly. And to be honest, sometimes the patient breathes on his own and that's not the best outcome . . . for anyone."

The expression on the nurse's face suggests to Ansel that she regrets imparting this last bit of information, which is confirmed when she adds, "But really, Mr. Frye, let's not get ahead of ourselves. The doctor said the surgery went well. Let's go with that for now. I'm sure he'll give you more information when he sees you."

"I understand." Ansel's voice is empty. Next to him, Melinda is using the palm of her hand in a losing fight to push tears away.

The nurse passes her a tissue. "I'll leave you alone for a few minutes."

Sam's head is heavily bandaged, but Melinda gently places her hand and then her own head up against his forehead. "I love you," she says. "If you can hear me, know that I'll stick with you for as long as it takes. I'll fight with you. For as long as it takes," she repeats.

Ansel steps around to the other side of the bed, puts his hand softly on Sam's arm, and murmurs to him in a trance-like, stream-of-consciousness way. More than the words, the tones convey both sorrow and encouragement. After a few minutes of silence during which the only things he is aware of are Melinda's low sobs and the pounding of his heart, he looks up absently. "Where's Cara?"

"With Susan, next door. You took so long," she mumbles after a pause, as if talking to herself. She stares at a vague point in the near distance, looks at Sam, and then looks away again.

"Please, Mel, don't make this even worse by putting a barrier between us. I didn't realize how serious it was, and I don't know how much faster I could have gotten here anyway."

"I needed you, Ansel!" She has raised her voice, now lowers it. "I'm . . ."

Ansel thinks she is about to say she's sorry, but she stops, and only sobs. She grabs a tissue from the box next to the bed and blows.

They are both startled by the purring vibration of Ansel's phone. "Erika," he mumbles, looking at the screen. He pushes the call to voicemail.

"You'll have to take me home," Melinda says vacantly. "I don't trust myself to drive." And then, "What am I saying! I have to stay here with him!"

"I need to clear my head . . . figure out what to do . . . how to deal with this," Ansel says, staring blankly at his phone.

"You have no choice. You have to leave," she responds. But there has been a clear change in her voice. Usually, when she says something like this it is with an acceptance that this is the deal she made. Not now. Now what Ansel hears is frustration and futility, regret over having made a deal she can't escape. "There's nothing you can do now anyway," she adds.

They arrange for her to spend the night in the bed next to Sam's, and for a friend to bring some things from home. Ansel says he'll wait to meet the surgeon and then stay for as long as he can, and promises to be back early in the morning; sooner if necessary. He'll do what he has to.

Later, when he leaves, the air outside is cold, but it's exactly the kind of brace Ansel needs. As he walks to the car he listens to Erika's message. She is being discharged. If she can't reach him in time, she'll find another way home.

He will have to drive to Foxhall to be with her. He calls to tell her this, but he is afraid of what his voice will convey and is hugely relieved when he is able to tell her voicemail instead.

But he doesn't get off that easily, not today, as the phone vibrates. It's India, and against his better judgment he answers the call.

"How's Erika?" she asks. He thinks she must have assumed that was where he was going this afternoon.

"Better. She's being discharged," he responds after a beat.

"I'm glad. Please give her my best. Listen, Ansel, we have to get together tomorrow, early. It's important."

"I . . . I can't tomorrow. I have to do something."

"I've already set it up; there was a blank in your calendar."

"You'll have to unset it." His voice is harsher than he intended. "I can't do it tomorrow, India," he adds more softly.

"Are you all right? You don't sound good."

"I'm fine. I just can't tomorrow."

"All right, I'll cancel. We need to do this ASAP, though. The Richmond people, too."

Ansel is about to ask what the urgency is, but quickly backs off. He doesn't want to know. Not now. It's irrelevant. Whatever the answer, he has to find a way to be with Sam and Melinda.

When he returns to Foxhall Road it is all he can do to hold himself together and convince Erika the problem is only work-related and exhaustion.

The real test comes at three in the morning, as they are both jerked awake by the ring of his phone. "I'm sorry," he mumbles to a suddenly alert Erika. "I'll have to take this. Try and go back to sleep."

In the next room he hears Melinda's voice, as if from inside a bell jar. She tells him that Sam has awakened briefly. He's shown some positive signs. He's breathing on his own. "I hope you can explain the call to Erika," she adds after a pause. "I thought you'd want to know as soon as possible."

"Yes, of course."

He hears profound sobbing. Followed by fathomless silence.

Chapter 19

Course Correction

O N A COLD, SULLEN morning, Ansel is sitting at his desk with the chair swiveled 180 degrees so that he faces a wall of glass. His eyes are focused on the far distance.

In reality, his eyes are focused only in the strict sense of the word, as a camera lens might be set to infinity. Ask him a question and it will quickly become evident that he sees nothing.

In his history of executive jobs Ansel has been known for thoroughness and the quality of his preparation. He is rarely blindsided.

Now he thinks he has been caught unawares from every direction. There is Sam, of course, above all. He can barely bring himself to think about Sam, and on those occasions when the image comes, unbidden, he is squeezed short of breath all over again. The impending arrival of Christmas makes it all the worse. Not that he was ever able to spend much time with Melinda and the children during the holidays, but usually he was able to steal some.

There is also the loneliness—the keeping of the pain to himself and the sense of shouting into a vast, empty chamber. He is afraid he might explode; afraid that if there is no relief, something will blow.

His only possible space for relief, Melinda and their few friends who know, has been denied to him. Blindsiding number two: Melinda doesn't want to see him. He believes she knows—must know on some level—that he bears no responsibility for what happened. Yet the accident and the fact that he was not available when she needed him has changed the entire calculus for her.

He is angry too. Some of the anger is scattershot, inchoate; he doesn't know how to cope with it. Some of it is aimed at Melinda. He thinks there is an unexpected betrayal here—a one-sided voiding of the compact. From the moment they fell in love there was a mutual understanding of the constraints they would face. They both understood the rules, even when they chafed. They had even discussed at length the changes that would occur if Ansel took the Ingersoll job. Before, discovery of their secret lives would have meant scandal and pain to several people. Now, with so much on the line for Ingersoll and, to his mind, the very future of the country, discovery would be used as a cause célèbre—a high-profile distraction. *This is the kind of morality and family values you get from the Community of Godless!* The assertion would be fatuous and easily rebutted by publicizing endless examples of religious hypocrisy. (*Let's hear it for whoring pedophiles!*) The problem is that the circus would besmirch Ingersoll and draw attention from the real issues at stake.

How cavalier—how bloody arrogant—he had been in thinking that the whole business would be managed and finessed!

There is encouraging news. Against the odds, Sam is doing well, though the prognosis for a complete recovery is unclear. At the very least there will be a lengthy and arduous period of rehabilitation—time Ansel should be there to help but until the amendments crisis is resolved will not be.

He tells himself he will take full responsibility for his actions, but he expects Melinda to do the same. He reads many things into her reluctance to see him, but the one that hurts and angers him is the implication of blame, or so he construes it.

And another complication: The possibility of discovery is no longer an abstraction. He has been knocked sharply off kilter by a handwritten note he received in the mail at home. It said, simply, "Our prayers are with you in this hour of darkness. May your son recover in the fullness of the Lord's grace." There was no signature, and no indication of who it came from. Thank goodness it wasn't opened by Erika. But who knew about the accident and would send such a note to his home?

Ansel's thoughts are interrupted by Roberta, his secretary of the last fifteen years, who sticks her head into the office to remind him that the board meeting is beginning in five minutes.

* * *

Ansel is the last to arrive. Without apology, he takes his customary seat at the table. India looks at him, her head cocked slightly.

Bryce calls the meeting to order. Rachel has joined them from Richmond. He thanks her and the board members for making it on short notice, promises to keep the proceedings as brief as possible, and turns the floor over to India.

India thanks him, and seconds his appreciation of the members' responsiveness, especially in light of the approaching holidays. She explains that, unfortunately, there are matters that cannot wait until the next regularly scheduled meeting.

"Let me put the issues to you bluntly," she says. "After getting off to a dynamic start in September, recent polling shows we are losing steam. This is happening just as the legislative sessions are fast upon us. It is particularly significant in Virginia, where the governor has been asked to hold early hearings on the amendments. We have indications that the declining polling data is affecting the positions of senators we badly need to hold or capture. To respond to these problems, I believe we need to alter our fundamental strategy.

"First I want to look at the data." Turning to Bryce and Ansel, India notes that this is the material she sent them yesterday. "I hope you had a chance to digest it."

Bryce nods and says he has. Ansel nods as well, though he has not read it.

"The good news first," India continues. "The polling indicates that there is still significant enthusiasm for Ingersoll. These results are supported in the real world by the overwhelming number of requests we've had for information, including information about living here.

127

"As has been true since the start of The Institute, there is broad support for the idea of Ingersoll as a center of dogma-free research. This support extended to the religious community, broadly defined.

"However, after the announcement of Ingersoll in September, we began to see a sharper dividing line. There is still strong support for the original mission, but as you would expect, there is a big falloff in support for the broader, explicitly antireligious mission, especially among believers. This held true for Christians, Jews and Muslims who self-identified as active believers, and also, sad to say, even for a small minority of nonbelievers who for one reason or another don't think there is a need for a community like Ingersoll.

"People who believed, pre-Ingersoll, that religion should not dominate public life still believe it; opponents are as unmoved as ever. The only area in which we might be making some headway is in convincing people opposed to religion that it's safe to come out of the closet."

"Except that it probably isn't," says the military man on the board, General Medved, to concurring laughter.

India glances at Ansel, who is less amused, and possibly not even engaged. "As you know," she continues, "the opposition has been vigorous in countering our media offensive, especially in their television, radio and online advertising. Unfortunately, they have hit upon a theme that seems to resonate with people. Their ads—some of them quite clever—keep hammering home the idea that a moral society is not possible without religion."

"Ah, yes," Bryce says, "the age-old you need religion to be good canard."

"Sorry to say," India continues, "it's a winning argument out there. Not only in general, but with the particular targets we have in the state legislatures. Rachel might want to say a few words about that."

Rachel is known to most of the board members; she takes a moment to introduce herself to those she hasn't met. Her expression is anxious as she begins, looking around the table. "We are at a pivotal moment in Richmond," she says. "The recent poll numbers are worrisome. Simply put, we have no margin for error; we can't afford to lose momentum now. If our head counts have been correct, the Senate will probably come down to a vote or two either way. I'm very much afraid that a mood swing away from our cause will make it easier for senators who are currently in our column or leaning toward us to switch sides."

"So much for profiles in courage," General Medved adds.

"Well," India says, taking back the floor, "with a few exceptions, such as the ever-venal Harper, we hope senators will vote their conscience. The problem is that many of them are truly conflicted, as ridiculous as this may seem to those of us who think the issue is clear-cut. If there is a momentum shift, they may be caught up in it." India scans the room to make sure she is being understood. Ansel is looking down at the papers in front of him and absently twirling a pen.

"Is there no possibility of stepping up our campaign—more or more targeted advertising and so forth?" asks Meredith Sienese, a public health expert.

"Good timing, Meredith," India responds with a smile. "We have a saturation problem. Keep in mind that once the public has sat for all of our stuff, it has plenty more to sit for. Our ally organizations are pumping resources into parallel campaigns. And then, of course, there's the other side, spending considerable fortunes to get out their message that the country will fall apart without a formal declaration that Christ is on its side.

"I think we've reached the point where it's necessary to conclude that there is a problem that goes beyond the medium. There is also a problem with our basic message."

"Now, *that is* troubling," Ansel says. He realizes that he's picking things up on the fly. Since the disaster with Sam, he has not been available to India when she requested him to be, and he's barely skimmed material he received from her. He chooses his words haltingly. "A few times now, India, you've used the words basic and fundamental to describe the message or approach that needs to be changed. I don't want to prejudge what you're about to propose, but I'm very much worried about making strategic changes when there's barely enough time to change tactics."

India pauses before responding. She looks questioningly at Ansel, perhaps wondering why if he is going to oppose her he has not done so before now. After all, she has sent him memos describing what she is about to say.

"We're coming up on Christmas," Ansel continues, "which is hardly the time when people want to listen to serious debates, let alone one that gives pride of place to an anti-Christ message."

"I'm very much aware of all this, Ansel," India responds, her tone noticeably more crisp. "What I want all of you to understand is that right now we're on a losing glidepath, and if we don't change it, we're done for."

"All right, India," Bryce says, holding up a hand. "Let's not get hung up on generalities of strategies, tactics, or glidepaths to loss. Tell the board what you have in mind, specifically."

India bears down on the conference room table, her hands pressed flat and arms locked at the elbows. "The issue as I see it is the absence of a positive message. Religious people push their religions while we counter with nothing, literally. Yesterday, I saw a protester's sign, which captured this neatly. It said, 'Ingersoll—The Crusade for Nothing.'

"All we do is ignore people's religions or tell them that their religions are nothing more than ridiculous superstitions and they should stop being suckers. All right, call religion what you will—call it a crutch for weak people, call it bullshit. But the bottom line is the same: We are trying to take something positive—and by positive I don't mean something good, I mean something tangible—and tell people they should give it up. In the meantime we offer nothing to fill the void.

"We tell people they should not let superstition rule their lives. We want them to look reality in the face. We'll tell someone who has nothing in his life but religion that his only comfort is a crock, so give it up and be strong."

She looks around the table. "It just won't do, folks. It doesn't matter how much sense we think we make and how little is made by the churchers. We need to stand for something more than the absence of a thing. We need to fill the void," she says again.

"And we do this how, exactly?" General Medved asks, irritably. "The essence of what you're saying is that there is no answer to be found in religion, but people need something in its place. Well, tell us something new. Oh, and by the way, while we're dismissing the value of religion, let's not forget that whatever their motives, religious people are considerably more generous than nonbelievers when it comes to supporting charitable causes."

"That's exactly my point, General. We need to stop acting as if *we* have nothing positive to offer. *We* need to be aggressive in pushing an idea that has been implicit since the founding of our community, namely that reason and systematic study—call it scientific method, if you want—is capable of helping people live their lives in a productive, moral, and fulfilling way. And we need to make this the basis of our community for the long term, even if we lose the current battles.

"I don't claim this is a new argument. It's made far more eloquently by people like Sam Harris. But we must convince people that science is not only for conquering disease or making faster microprocessors. It is capable of informing our fundamental values. It is capable of explaining the practical benefits of human cooperation. It is capable of explaining why the golden rule works. You don't have to follow the Ten Commandments or some Biblical exhortation. You can get to many of the same places—better places, in fact—by actually demonstrating the effectiveness of something real, instead of by slavishly spewing myths propagated by old men who knew nothing of a physical world that, along with the rest of the universe, was created for them alone.

"We all know that you don't need religion to be good. It's time to explain to people why this is so. Otherwise, all we're doing is what the churchers are doing—expounding beliefs based on nothing more than the intuitive sense that they must be true . . . basically, our own dogma.

"Let me be clear: I'm not suggesting that we stop being assertive. To the contrary, we have to put the believers on the defensive. When they say the only way to heaven is through Jesus Christ, we must say, 'tell me why you believe this.' And when they say, because it is written in the Bible, we must say, 'why do you believe the Bible to be true?' And when they say it's true for . . . whatever reason, it almost doesn't matter, we must repeat, 'but why do you believe this?' We must stick with it until they have no place to go except to resort to the final line of defense: we believe it because we believe it; we believe it because we have faith. And we must hammer them over and over, until the emptiness of this response is evident to anyone who is even slightly inclined to question.

"At the same time, we need to do more than respond to religious people by saying their beliefs don't make any sense. Our ads should—in a clever and appealing way, I might add—tell people that we stand for more than the absence of something."

"India, I don't disagree with you," Ansel interjects. "There's no problem with what you're suggesting, but I think you're losing focus. In the long run we may want to convince people of our wisdom. For now, we're not trying to get people to vote *for* us. We're trying to get them to vote *with* us. By all means let's give believers a positive alternative. But the immediate issue is not belief or nonbelief per se. It's freedom. The Constitution needs to allow people to believe or not believe as a matter of personal choice and freedom of conscience."

"Wait a minute, Ansel," Sienese says over a pointed index finger. "The pro-amendment people will say flat out that they have no intention of taking away this choice."

"That's exactly right," India seconds.

"Of course that's what they'll say," Ansel responds, palpably impatient. "But we know that's not the reality. The point is that we have to drive home the falseness and disingenuousness of their arguments, not get sidetracked into explaining what we hope to offer as a substitute for God."

Ansel looks at India, whose face is pinched and angry at his opposition. "Look, India, I repeat, I'm not disagreeing with you on the need to offer a positive message, or even that we should begin doing so immediately. I'm only saying that this won't help with the five hundred pound senatorial gorillas in the room. The way to do that is to keep our opponents focused on the issues of freedom and the need to remain true to the country's greatest traditions."

Whether or not she agrees, India doesn't appear to be mollified.

Chapter 20

Melinda

I DON'T OFTEN THINK about the things that can turn our lives upside down in a moment. Or, rather, I try not to dwell on them. Sometimes it's because doing so is too painful, sometimes because I'd have to do something if I thought about them—take some kind of action—and sometimes because there isn't any action to take, so why worry twice?

As much pain as I have over Sam, I don't blame myself for the accident. I took all the responsible precautions. He was being cared for by someone I knew to be trustworthy. Carol isn't one to have too many glasses of wine over lunch and then go pick up the kids. Sam was in the "safe seat" in the car. And yes, Ansel, it turns out he was wearing a seatbelt.

My mistake goes much deeper. It goes to the heart of my most basic assumptions. Ten years ago, I was ready to have a child on my own. Aside from the seed, no man need apply.

Enter Ansel. I altered the plan to accommodate him. Basically, I wanted him and I took him the only way I could have him. All very blithe and I-am-woman-hear-me-roar-ish. It's easy to be confident when you're young and everything is going your way.

And so, there was nothing but pure bravado when I told my friends (the few I was sure of) about Ansel and about how I planned to raise our son pretty much by myself. I brushed aside their questions and objections. Of course I could do this! Single women raise families all the time, and I had at least some of Ansel (and yes, a guaranteed financial cushion if it came to that—not that I was eager to think of this as anything but insurance for the most dire emergency).

How much more wrong could I have been about . . . everything! The most obvious mistake is that I failed to think about others who might be affected by my "avant garde" philosophy. Since my first pregnancy was an honest accident (I hadn't yet had enough time to act deliberately on my misguided philosophy!), I suppose I can say in my defense that single parenthood (with whatever plus-up from Ansel) was the only possibility. There was no way I was going to have an abortion. It's a weak defense, I suppose, but it gives me something to hold onto.

But Cara? We planned her. The arrogance is mind-boggling!

At one point during the crisis with Sam, Ansel asked that I not create a barrier between us. I can't even remember what the barrier might have been. All I know is that right now I can't look at Ansel—can't be in his presence. I know this isn't fair. He didn't cause the accident, after all. I can't look at him because he's a flesh-and-blood reminder of my foolishness. I liken it to a spoiled bite of a favorite food that puts me off it from then on.

It's not only unfair to him—it's cruel, I understand this. I at least can cry openly and lean on my friends. Ansel has no one.

So, it's unfair and it's cruel. I don't want to be either of these things. Right now, I simply can't help it.

Where do we go from here? *Is* there anywhere to go from here? I can't shut Ansel out forever. I don't want to, really, and it wouldn't be fair to the children. I need some time, that's all. I need time to allow my emotions to catch up to my rational side.

Chapter 21

Young Senator Bernsen

WAITING IN THE SENATOR'S reception area in the legislative office building across the street from the commonwealth's Capitol, Rachel is mindful that she owns an indelibly cartoonlike image of a southern politician—two images, actually. One is the blustering Huey Long (in her head really Broderick Crawford) or sometimes LBJ, either one of whom might be bloviating about bringing electricity to his *consitooents*; the other is the genteel late-model (i.e., post-KKK) Robert C. Byrd, with weathered features and silver Wildroot-cast pompadour.

Thus, when she is told the senator will be right with her she makes a point of reminding herself that the senator in question could be her son, and that he probably spends more of his time on social media than at prayer breakfasts, and she marvels at the ability of an out-of-kilter world to undermine preconceptions. Just as there is death out of order, there is success, power and influence out of order. She can resent this, and often does, even as she knows there is nothing to be done about it.

When she is told she can go into his office, she walks in briskly, extends her hand midstride, smiles broadly and proclaims it is good to see him again. He, presumably likewise on autopilot, leads her to a small sitting area in front of his desk and tells her yes, it's been too long and he's been looking forward to seeing her again. She won't remind him, then, that it has been only weeks, and hopes she will not have to reconstruct their last meeting for him from scratch.

This proves to be unnecessary when Bernsen asks after India, volunteering that he is disappointed that she is not here too.

"You'll probably be seeing more of her than you'd like," Rachel responds lightly. "She's busy preparing for the hearings after the holidays."

Bernsen smiles and says he's happy to note that what he calls "you Ingersoll people" still acknowledge the holidays.

Rachel is pleased that his mood is light and that, as in their first meeting, he doesn't take himself too seriously. This is followed quickly by the thought that he should not be underestimated or his youth taken gratuitously. "Oh, we acknowledge that they exist," she says, returning the smile. "We just don't think they mean anything. . . . Well, except for New Year's—we'll observe New Year's in the sybaritic spirit people expect from us pagans."

He laughs. "Sounds about right."

Rachel says she realizes it is late in the day and promises to keep the meeting brief. As if on cue, Bernsen's secretary sticks her head in to remind him he has one more appointment, a late addition to the schedule.

"We won't run too long," he says. After the secretary has withdrawn he adds, "Don't worry, long enough," in apparent response to concern on Rachel's face that she might be given short shrift. He follows this with a happy laugh, leans in as if he's about to break a solemn confidence, and tells her that the big appointment in question is with his girlfriend, who has threatened to steal him away for dinner.

"I know we just sat down," he says suddenly, "but would you mind walking and talking? I've been stuck in this stuffy place, elegantly appointed though it may be, all day."

Rachel says that would be fine, and suggests putting coats on if they're going outside, adding that it was getting colder when she arrived.

He suggests walking across the street to the Capitol and asks if she's been inside recently. He says she should see how a hundred-plus million dollars of citizens' tax money was spent renovating the place.

"Anyway, the hearings," he resumes as they step onto the elevator. "You do know that they don't fall under any of my committees?"

"Yes, of course, but we're hoping you'll attend anyway. We need thoughtful people there."

"You don't find Senator Yost to be thoughtful, then?" He says this with a hint of mischief. Yost is widely regarded as a conservative ideologue, not particularly well liked even within his own party, and routinely excoriated by the opposition.

A gust of cold air hits them as they leave the building. "This would feel really good if it didn't feel really bad," he says, shielding his face with his hand.

"It's an impressive structure," Rachel says, nodding toward the Capitol as they cross the street. "Shining city on a hill and all that."

"It inspires me, actually, though I don't mean to sound hokey. The middle building—the original before the wings were added—was designed by Thomas Jefferson, based on a Roman temple in Nimes. He intended it to represent the majesty of Roman law. The two wings are for the Senate and the House of Delegates, as you probably know. They were added on in the early nineteen hundreds. We can go in over here," he says, leading her to the main entrance on Broad Street. "Very special for elected officials and other muckety-mucks—including freshman senators," he adds with a self-deprecating smile that Rachel finds endearing.

They take a short walk toward the rotunda and its focal point, a marble statue of George Washington. The floor in the rotunda is a glowing black and white marble checkerboard. Washington stands on a pedestal in the center, encircled by a glossy black wrought iron fence to protect him.

"You may have seen it a hundred times, but I make a point of bringing visitors to the Washington statue first," Bernsen says with a sweep of the hand, adding, "though in truth less to pay tribute to the great man than to the sculptor, Jean-Antoine Houdon. Like Michelangelo's David, Washington was carved from a single block of Carrara marble, but more expertly carved. Really!" he adds with an innocent exuberance. "Just look at the detail work—the buttons along his thigh, the soft leather and the seam in his gloves that are so perfectly captured."

Rachel says "Yes, I see what you mean," and walks slowly around the statue. "It really is wonderful. Did Washington ever get to see it?"

"It was finished before he died, so he could have seen it, but he probably didn't. He sat for Houdon to do facial masks—the only time he ever did such a thing, so it's believed to be a true likeness—but as I understand it, he never saw the finished product. The story goes that some years later the Marquis de Lafayette cried when he saw it and remarked on its perfect resemblance. Come, I'll show you to the Senate chamber. Do you know," he continues as he leads Rachel along, "that India Ruiz is something of a legend in my parents' house?"

Rachel is momentarily taken aback by the apparent non sequitur. "You're not going to make me feel ancient, are you?"

"Not at all. I don't mean legendary in a good way, in any case. It's just that when I was growing up . . ."

"There's that phrase . . ."

"Whenever India was in the news leading this or that strike or boycott—it usually seemed to be something like that, and it didn't really matter, since it got to the point where all you had to hear was the name India Ruiz—my father would become apoplectic. He'd say she was a perfect example of the ills of socialism—Big Brother, the death of the individual, and all that."

"And how did you feel about it?"

"Honestly, I didn't give it much thought. Mostly, I thought it was funny that it was so easy to get my father all worked up. So it was fun getting to meet the devil in the flesh. To tell the truth, she didn't seem all that satanic—a little disappointing on that score."

"She'll be sad to hear it," Rachel says with a laugh. "How about your mother? Was she on the same page with your dad?"

"I don't think so. Not that crazed, anyway. One of my family's dirty secrets is that my mom was a bra-burner back when. It's hard to imagine if you see her today. Although, come to think of it, maybe not so hard. She may not look like a radical, but in her way she's still big on women's issues. She's totally against abortion, but she gets her back up when she thinks men are trying to tell women what they can or can't do.

"This way," he says, touching Rachel's elbow lightly. They walk slowly toward the Senate chamber, taking in the portraits lining the walls.

"And you?" Rachel asks. "Your mother may be opposed to abortion, but if she's concerned about women's rights, she'd probably oppose the sweeping amendment under consideration. Yet I gather you support it."

He stops and seems to stiffen at this, a nerve hit.

"Rachel, let me make something clear. People have a tendency to think that because I'm young I'm not my own person. You need to understand that I'm not my father and I'm not my mother. I believe abortion is immoral, and whatever they think, I have no problem having the U.S. Constitution say so."

Rachel is momentarily put off stride by the force of his conviction and the probable accuracy of his candid assessment of how other people view him. "I do understand that," she says softly, recovering. "But I hope you realize that there are profound moral consequences—immoral consequences, actually—to banning abortion the way this amendment does."

Bernsen holds up his hand to interrupt her. "Yes, it discriminates against the poor, causes back-alley problems, and so on. I understand. I get it. I don't want you to think that I'm totally hard over. I don't believe life starts at fertilization—not meaningful life, at any rate. I'm not big on abstinence, and I'm okay with the emergency contraception stuff, not that these are the kinds of things it's smart for me to go around advertising in my district. But once it's too late for contraception, emergency or otherwise, abortion shouldn't be an option."

He resumes walking slowly down the corridor. They pause to open the glass doors to the Senate chamber. Rachel turns her head quizzically. "Then I guess I don't really understand your position. If you don't believe life starts with fertilization . . ."

"Meaningful life," he corrects.

"All right, meaningful life. At what point does life become meaningful, then? If you'd use emergency contraception—let's call a spade a spade here, you're talking about very early-stage abortion—why not allow a woman the right to choose, say, two weeks later, or a month?"

Rachel notices that Bernsen shifts uncomfortably before he says, "I can't give you that precise an answer. All I can say is that I find abortion morally objectionable, and as for the time . . ."

"The old Catholic time of quickening?" Rachel interjects.

"Maybe. Or maybe it's just one of those things where you know it when you see it."

They glance around the room, which could be a pristine monument to the eighteenth century if not for the electronic touches. A bright digital sign board at the front of the room notes that the Senate is not in session and that it will resume on January 9th. There are forty desks, one for each senator, and an electronic voting panel on each one. Bernsen points to the panel on his desk. Buttons for yea, nay, speak, page and something labeled R69, which he explains is for instances when the senator recuses himself because of a conflict of interest.

Rachel nods, says with a smile that it seems to be the least worn of the buttons. She points to the nay button. "That's the one you hit on the amendments," she tells him.

He laughs, says "you wish," and adds that he wants to take her into the Capitol's original legislative chamber. "We'll have to make it quick. I need to get back to the office."

"Ah, right, your next appointment. Can't keep her waiting."

Despite Bernsen's obvious continuing discomfort with the abortion topic and the shift away from her priority concern over the Christian amendment, Rachel decides to press him on abortion. She wonders in passing if his openness to emergency contraception might stem from a pregnancy scare of his own, and whether some discrete digging around might be useful. "Aren't you concerned that the I-know-it-when-I-see-it standard may not be good constitutional law? I would urge you to consider that the amendment under consideration has not the slightest bit of flexibility. If it passes, emergency contraception won't stand a chance, either."

Bernsen nods, then begins to respond but stops short. "Let's just say I'll give it some thought."

Rachel concludes unhappily from his abrupt finality that this is all she will get from him at this point, and segues into the next issue on her list, hoping for some flexibility there. "And gay marriage?" she asks. "What's your current position on that?"

They walk into what Bernsen explains is the original legislative chamber. A larger than life statue of Robert E. Lee confronts them as they enter. "We don't have much time. I just wanted to give you a glimpse of this room, in case you haven't seen it. I think of it as a sort of heroes of Virginia room—paintings of all of our presidents . . ."

"Jefferson Davis, too, I see."

"Yes." He looks up with an expression Rachel takes for truculence. "And a bust of Stonewall Jackson, and also busts of other Virginians like Meriwether Lewis and Cyrus McCormack. My current position on gays is pretty much what it's always been. I can go with civil unions that are marriage in everything but name. But marriage is not only a religious issue, it's a historical one. There's a marriage context."

Rachel purses her lips and shakes her head, pensively. "But again, as a constitutional matter?" She is having trouble coming to terms with what she is hearing and seeing from Bernsen, and is concerned that she is too much a product of her sensibilities, which are pure Yankee. To her, the last of the lions of Virginia history died with Jefferson, Mason, Madison and the others of the founding generation, not Robert E. Lee (if pressed, she might make an exception for Woodrow Wilson, and even he is falling into ever greater disfavor the more she learns about him).

What she has seen in the Capitol does little more than reinforce her opinion of Virginia's inexorable slide into reaction. To her mind, the land that led to a world-altering democratic republic under Virginia's early leaders had wallowed in the primacy of states' rights—and slavery—and had shown no leadership worthy of the word since.

She wonders if Bernsen's desire to show her this room reflects a reverence for the founders she cares about, or if he takes his history whole as a single venerable relic—something to be proud of, to identify with, to accept in its entirety after being graded on a forgiving curve, like modern Greeks genuflecting before the Acropolis as they begin a day of feckless self-government. *We're number one!* goes the chant in America, *Even if we're not!* Is Ingersoll's evaluation of Bernsen as thoughtful and persuadable accurate, or in the end is it an incorrect presumption based on his youth and affability? The question would not be so vexing if it were not so crucial.

"Even if you believe in a historical marriage context," she says as they turn to walk back to his office, "is the Constitution of the United States the proper place to express it?"

Bernsen pauses before he answers. "A few years ago, I might not have thought so. But as the consensus has vanished over what America is, or should be, I've become more willing to assert my own vision."

"Did such a consensus ever really exist, or was it a myth?"

"It existed more than now, I think. We need to get it back. What's the point of having a country if the country doesn't stand for something?"

"We couldn't agree more, David," Rachel says, slipping without thinking from the unnatural senator appellation she has been using. He doesn't seem to notice. "The question," she continues, "is what does it stand for? You know, it's not that long ago that the consensus said that separate but equal was acceptable. I hope you agree that we needed a different consensus then."

"I do."

"And now?"

The wind is still cold and blustery as they leave the Capitol. Rachel and Bernsen reflexively grab their collars shut at the same time.

"The issues before us now are different," he answers into the wind. "After all, some people would argue that stopping abortion is an extension of civil rights."

"The so-called rights of the unborn, you mean." Rachel is drifting toward annoyance with Bernsen's formulaic responses. And she hasn't yet broached the critical amendment.

"Not so-called. I don't believe all rights are conferred at once. The right to vote doesn't exist in childhood. The right to existence itself is something else, and that's what's at stake here. It trumps a woman's right to choose. Taken together, the three amendments reaffirm the founding fathers' notion of what the country should be."

Now Rachel is getting really nervous. Bernsen may insist that he is independent, but his views seem anything but. "Forgive me, David, but you really need to review your history and pay less attention to the Christian right's cant about this." She is suddenly afraid that in her irritation, her tone has become patronizing, or perhaps even maternal, and that she may be pushing past what is acceptable in dealing with this young senator. But he does not seem to object, and she decides not to pull her punches.

"I must say, David, I'm tired of hearing us, and the courts in particular, criticized for straying from a supposedly original interpretation of the Constitution only to hear these very same critics go on without missing a beat to grossly reinterpret constitutional history. After all, a woman no longer counts as three fifths of a man, and we don't have slavery anymore." Even as she says this, she is concerned that she has chosen perhaps her weakest argument. And Bernsen doesn't fail to pick up on it.

"We don't, but that's not because the Constitution was reinterpreted. It was amended. Amendments have always played an important part in keeping the Constitution vital."

"Nevertheless," Rachel pushes on, trying to get past the mistake of serving up such an easy pitch, "it's not right to attribute to the founding fathers views that they never held. Virginians probably should appreciate this as much as anyone. You just showed me the people you say you venerate, but I'm sure you know that the authors of the Constitution and Bill of Rights were not religious men as the term is being defined today, just as the separation of church and state wasn't the marginal issue it is being portrayed as, or an abstraction. The irony is that as much as anything it was intended to protect religious people. I'll remind you that Jefferson's famous letter to the Danbury Baptist Association, the one with the phrase 'wall of separation between church and state,' was a response to their concerns over threats to religious liberty. Here in Virginia, too, it was religious groups that supported the religious freedom act. It was a matter of self-interest, David," she says forcefully, turning to him as they come to the crosswalk. "The last thing they wanted was a state religion not of their own imposed on them."

As they reach the elevator in the office building lobby Rachel fears Bernsen is losing patience having to defend what from his point of view is probably an obvious and straightforward position. "But Rachel," he objects as the elevator door opens and they step back to allow passengers to exit. "The current amendment threatens no one. It does nothing more than acknowledge the historical reality of the role of Judeo-Christian precepts in the nation's founding. The various sects might have feared for their independence, but at bottom they were Christian."

They are alone in the elevator, among the few people arriving as the short out-of-session workday is ending. "David, I disagree, and I hope you will consider strongly that words have practical meaning, and these words in the amendment do not merely express a historical reality. They distort that reality."

"I don't see how."

"By omission, that's how."

They have stepped off the elevator and are approaching his office, and Rachel is afraid she will not get a chance to make her point. She rushes her words even as she slows her steps. "To say that the majority of people identified themselves as Christians may be true, but it leaves out the essential history of religious freedom. Our forebears *came* here fleeing religious persecution in the first place. No one wanted more than they to ensure they would not be discriminated against by a state-sponsored religion. So to lump all the sects together now and gloss over their concerns by stating simply that they were all Christians and therefore this is a Christian nation is a gross distortion."

His smile brings Rachel up short as they reach the outer office. "I didn't think I said something funny, did I?"

"No, no." He gives a dismissive wave. "I was just thinking that if I didn't know better, I'd say you've been hanging out with my girlfriend. Except for the gay marriage issue, she's in your camp all the way—a real pain in the butt, to tell the truth," he adds, refreshing the smile.

"Obviously I *should* be hanging out with your girlfriend. I hope she's having more success with you than I seem to be having."

"Not yet." Now as he pushes the door open he smiles broadly and adds, "She has more things to withhold, though, so we'll see. And speaking of the devil, she's here in the flesh. I hope I haven't kept you waiting too long," he says to the pretty young woman who has just put down her magazine. "This is Laura," he adds, turning to Rachel.

"A pleasure," Rachel says, taking Laura's extended hand. She has a vague feeling that she has seen her before, but she can't pin down a memory. "Ordinarily I'd fight for more time, Senator," she says turning to Bernsen. "But in this case Laura might be the more effective advocate. Anyway, I hope we can get together again soon."

"Sure," he responds, offering his hand. "Just get on my calendar. And say hello to India for me," he adds, lightly.

As Rachel turns to go, she stops and turns back toward him. "I do have one more point I'd like to leave you with," she says, looking at him evenly. "When we talked about amending the Constitution for the better—to grant missing rights—you said that this is how change is accomplished. I failed to remind you that Virginia doesn't have such a great record in this regard. Among other things, I should have reminded you that Virginia voted against women's suffrage. I urge you to keep that in mind and put Virginia back on the right side of history where individual liberty is concerned."

"I will keep that in mind," he responds, apparently mirroring her gravity. Rachel is not sure how seriously to take him but is glad to have made the point.

"Work on him," she calls over her shoulder to a perplexed Laura, and lets the door close behind her.

Chapter 22

Forming Lines

INDIA HAS ASKED HER driver to take her through the Ingersoll residential community rather than go directly to the main compound (she hates this word, evocative as it is of standoffs with rightwing paramilitary crazies, but in the absence of other widely accepted shorthand, it has insinuated itself like a weed in the garden).

She has not been driven this way for a week, the last time being to visit the scene of yet another attempted arson at yet another construction site, this one a neighborhood shopping center that is nearing completion. The plan went awry when a timed propellant failed to ignite. Nevertheless, this fourth attack since the one that drew Ansel and Roland Peterson together is having the intended purpose of keeping people on edge.

The Ingersoll leadership is gratified that so far such attacks are not having another effect presumably desired by the culprits, that of discouraging prospective residents. Applications to live in Ingersoll (especially Ingersoll Town, where this shopping center is located) have, if anything, increased as the fight has heated up. There are considerably more applicants than can be accommodated.

More worrisome is that the radical churchers have upped the ante. They have supplemented the arson attempts with gunfire. Twice in the past week someone took potshots at construction workers. Roark assumes that so far these attempts either have been made by irate believer entrepreneurs or, of greater concern, some of the imports from out west whose misses were deliberate and who might at any time choose to be more accurate. The FBI has launched an investigation, but law enforcement of all types has been stretched to the limit since the August terror attack, and the prospects for persistence in the matter are not good.

Chain link fencing, motion detectors and cameras have gone up over large sections of the perimeter and at key points within Ingersoll. Bryce had made a point of not erecting such barriers, ugly chain link in particular, which was probably never realistic given the even uglier climate, and this was the quickest response available to meet the security threat. Any skepticism India had during that first warning meeting with Roark has been undone. She hates the obvious security that surrounds her now—in particular the caravan in which she often travels—but she is relieved to have it.

Now India is struck by the juxtaposition of the fences and the many hospitable signs they had put up shortly after the rollout. "Welcome to Ingersoll, a Community of Reason and Progress," they said. Of course, many of the signs have been defaced, including some that have been ripped apart and left lying next to new wooden crosses of the type often planted at the scene of fatal car crashes.

There are signs by the volunteer Ingersoll Community Action Committee, the ICAC (called by everyone Ick-Ack). Created within weeks of the rollout, the ICAC has presumed the lead in the defense of Ingersoll (sometimes only half jokingly referred to as "homeland defense").

The essence of the ICAC is stridency. Early banners calling on citizens to Stand Up For Your Right Not To Believe and declaring All Thought Is Freethought quickly gave way to more ominous messages in response to the arsons and threats of violence against Ingersoll.

The ICAC has become an object lesson in the limits of orchestration. The creation of Ingersoll included no less than nine committees or similar bodies sanctioned under—or, as was often said, "given the imprimatur of"—the founding charter (sometimes referred to snidely as "Genesis" and accompanied by no shortage of Sistine Chapel-like illustrations of Bryce blowing the winds of life into his creation). The committees had various purposes, ranging from the practical, quotidian aspects of community life (sanitation, beautification, and so forth) to the epistemological or doctrinal aspects, often under the rubric of community outreach.

The committees dealing with practical matters got off to a good start. There has been no shortage of eager volunteers from among existing or new residents.

Not so regarding groups on the philosophical issues. These committees have languished, in part reflecting the inherently less well defined objectives under their purview. What, after all, is appropriate outreach for a community of nonbelievers? In short order factions appeared, some of them taking on the self-righteous air of revolutionary committees. The factions themselves splintered into new, ad hoc organizations, the ICAC being the largest of them, leaving the original Ingersoll-sanctioned bodies to wither.

India passes new banners and posters done up in primary colors and recycled American Revolution symbols (the Don't Tread on Me snake is a big one) and even more pointed images of fist-held weapons thrust in the air and bearing the legend, Freethought Thus!

Yet another concern is the growing radicalism of some outside atheist groups that have at least nominally allied with Ingersoll. Joining groups named for famous atheists, freethinkers or skeptics, including Madalyn Murray O'Hair and Charles Darwin, and the established groups, such as American Atheists, are newer groups and offshoots that have tended to take more misleadingly generic, anodyne titles, such as The Coalition for Religious Freedom and the Antiestablishment Forum. Having spent most of their existence on the fringes of American consciousness, these groups now seem determined to seize the moment. If their claims are to be believed, their membership is growing faster than any of Ingersoll's mainstream constituencies.

However, it is not only the proliferation of the groups or the stridency of their rhetoric that is worrisome. Of even greater concern is their apparent willingness to use violence. This is a source of alarm to Bryce and Ansel, who are worried not only that this is precisely the kind of thing that gets out of hand, but that some of the groups are trying to co-opt the fledgling Ingersoll brand.

Bryce and Ansel have made it clear that they draw a line between forceful advocacy and violence. Neither of them was ready for the declaration of two of the splinter groups that violence or threats of violence against Ingersoll, including the arsons and near-miss gunfire, would be met by "equal and greater" responses "near and far." The leader of the benign-sounding First Amendment Protection League has said in a recent interview that "the believers aren't the only ones who know how to use high-powered rifles."

Despite her reputation as an advocate of nonviolent protest and civil disobedience, India surprised Bryce and Ansel with a pensive, sotto voce declaration that maybe this development isn't such a bad thing. "As long as we're not seen as sponsoring or condoning these groups, maybe it's not so bad to put the opposition on notice that they can't attack us with impunity. Let them know that the famous vengeance of their righteous God cuts both ways."

Ansel didn't buy it. "That is really dangerous territory, India. I agree that there might be some positives to sending them such a message. But we're not looking for civil war."

"And if our adversaries are?"

Bryce held up a hand. "Hold on." His demeanor was calm but commanding. "Even if that's true, India, we can't afford to be sucked in. Ingersoll stands for reason and progress, not militant atheism."

"But Bryce, what if the other side is determined to use militancy or violence to shut down reason and progress?"

"That would be a calamity, certainly. Thankfully, we're not there yet. I think Ansel's point is that we can't win a civil war, so let's not be drawn into one."

"Yes," Ansel said. "We may have our crazies, but you know as well as I do that we'll never out-crazy the churchers, particularly if it starts to look like we're the aggressors."

"That's not likely," India said.

"Not impossible, either. Once the pitched battles start, there's no telling how things will develop. The only thing certain is that we are vastly outnumbered and outgunned."

* * *

India enters the main compound through the new Northeast Gate (still awaiting the name of a martyr to freethought), which they use because it is most convenient to their present location, not because there are fewer demonstrators trying to block it. Here, too, the activists are out in force. As at the main gate, the demonstrations are constant. The local churches, especially the Atolls, have done a good job of motivating and organizing them. Even during this Christmas holiday period there is never a shortage of people and enthusiasm. Finally, India muses, they have found an antidote to the perennial complaints about the commercialization of Christmas and over-shopping.

One thing that has changed at the gate is the presence of large numbers of pro-Ingersoll demonstrators. They have responded to the calls of the Ingersoll leadership—in fact, responded with greater alacrity than any of the leaders might have hoped for, yet another manifestation of growing militancy.

For the most part the pros and antis are respectful of one another, but fights and confrontations are becoming more frequent as the amendment votes draw closer. In one instance, pro-Ingersoll demonstrators responded to rotten produce attacks on Ingersoll cars by throwing their own "growage" (as one of them called it) at the churchers. As a responsible leader India should object to both sides' transgressions, but she is happy that the churchers can finally share the Ingersoll experience of high laundry bills.

Chapter 23

Legislative Testament

THE DAY WILL BE devoted to preparing for the Virginia legislative hearings. India, Ansel and Rachel will represent Ingersoll. They will be coached by two consultants who have long experience supporting national political campaigns. One is Peter Link, founding partner of Link-Brady Associates, who has provided debate coaching to three presidential candidates, two of whom won the election.

The other consultant is Margaret Sayre, whom India wanted for her specialization in pushing liberal social issues, especially environmentalism and family planning. Sayre has shown herself to be particularly adept at anticipating the opposition's arguments, a track record Ansel found compelling enough to have him stop pressing for a red team coach with conservative credentials, at least for the moment.

They are meeting in one of Ingersoll's media studios. The consultants have arranged the space to approximate the setting anticipated for the hearings. Chairs for the legislative panel (about five of them, with the understanding that they represent a real expected total of about twenty) are arrayed facing the witnesses and about a hundred audience seats.

Three chairs are arranged for the witnesses behind a polished, heavy wood table. Microphones and pitchers of ice water are set at each place.

Link and Sayre are studies in contrast. Link, in his late fifties, is short, hawk-eyed, overweight and three-quarters bald, traits that possibly nowhere but in a place like Washington would be characterized positively as reflecting sagacity and cunning. Sayre, in her mid-thirties, is lithe and animated (depending on the context, some would say flirtatious). She is a political wunderkind, who like all wunderkinds who survive long enough is facing the challenge of meeting mature expectations.

Ansel says he wants to get started; they have a lot of ground to cover.

India observes that whatever had been distracting Ansel must somehow have been addressed, as he has been more obviously present over the last week or so. Still, there are unpredictable times when he seems to tune out, and she is at a loss to explain this.

Of course, India has no way of knowing just how much force of will it has taken Ansel to continue his work in spite of the private, unsharable anguish for which he is unable to find an outlet even with Melinda, and which he must be extra careful to disguise when he returns home to Erika. Sam has begun what will be a long rehabilitation with uncertain prospects. Ansel is doing his best to find time to be with him, but it has not been easy.

He has had only perfunctory meetings with Melinda. About a week ago she consented to see him at home, but the only good to come out of it was the time he got to spend with Cara. Toward the end of this short visit his profound sadness metamorphosed into anger when Melinda decided to unburden herself to him—something that perhaps would be better tolerated at a later time, when some of his rough edges might be worn off. As it was, he was forced to sit through what she called an honest admission (viewed by him as another of those times when honesty is overrated) that she was tearing herself apart over the "life choices" she had made. Not that she blamed him, she was quick to add. It was as much her fault as his, absolutely.

Except that reason is an unreliable ally. Whatever she said, only one thing came across: None of the woes that had lately subsumed her life could have occurred if it were not for him. That was her subtext, wasn't it? In the circumstances, it seemed the only interpretation.

Melinda dumped all of this on him even as she had other outlets—that's what angered him, or another thing that did. It was unfeeling and selfish. She could unburden herself to the small number of friends, mostly women, who were in the know. In other times he considered some of them his friends too. But now their loyalties were aligned with her.

Even those who didn't know the truth could still offer her sympathy and support. Sam's school held a rally for him, which was streamed to the rehab center. Melinda attended, of course, and said she was frequently moved to tears. It was for all to see that Melinda, the poor struggling single mother, had now had another rock inserted into her pocket.

Ansel might have had the support of either of his two best, oldest friends. He might still have it, except that he had long ago decided to keep his two lives utterly separate, and revelation now would require so much time and explanation, and risk to the friendships, too, if either was hurt by the earlier lack of confidence.

So there was no one. No friend, no colleague, and the added fears of hurting Erika and giving Ingersoll a giant fucking over at a most critical moment.

Unfortunately, the possibility that the secret would be revealed was no longer remote. Clearly someone already knew. Someone had sent the letter, after all. That was jarring enough. When there was nothing further over the following week, Ansel could almost convince himself that the threat had faded—a powerful thing, wishful thinking. Then he received two new messages. One was an email and the other a get-well card with an Idaho postmark that was mailed to his office (not opened first by his secretary, thank goodness—a bit of luck not likely to be repeated).

Like the first letter, the new messages were not explicit. The email said there were many people in his corner who were hoping for the best during his personal time of trial. The card was accompanied by a newspaper clipping, a feature article on reckless men. It offered a good sampling, from a recently exposed televangelist to the cruel public infidelities of several politicians. The article was quite balanced in that way; its theme was that self-destructive tendencies know no party, cause or premise, except perhaps their universality.

* * *

Ansel misses a beat when India nods to him to indicate she is ready to get started. She cocks her head curiously and this time he says okay, let's begin. There are brief pleasantries, and Ansel turns the meeting over to Link and Sayre.

"As we understand it," Link begins, "you will have an opportunity to make a brief statement at the outset of the hearing."

"That's right," India says.

"Good. We don't always get a chance to lay out our position before the committee tears into us."

"That's true," Sayre adds. "The opening statement is important not only to get our position on the record. The real value is in shaping the rest of the session. The legislators will have arrived with their prepared questions, some of which will be deliberately tendentious, to put you on the defensive and embarrass you—not always because they disagree, mind you, sometimes just to grab the limelight. The statement gives you a chance to turn the tables on them and frame the subsequent proceedings your way."

"The focus—our strategy"—India notes, "lies in shaming them, for lack of a better term. Rachel can address this in greater detail, but a good part of our lobbying has been devoted to convincing the relatively small number of senators who we see as swing votes that Virginia has strayed from its revolutionary heritage."

"To put it mildly," Rachel adds.

"The point," India continues, "is to convince them of the need for an act of courage. This is true regarding all of the amendments, but particularly the religion one."

"Right," Ansel says. "Of course, as with most hearings of this kind, our target audience goes beyond the legislators themselves. We will want to bring public opinion to our side and give the legislators political cover for supporting us."

Link clears his throat and says, "Two key points here, Ansel. First, just because the hearings will be broadcast, don't assume anyone will see them. You need to reach beyond the policy wonks who read blogs in the bathroom and keep C-Span on as white noise. You need to do or say something interesting enough to go viral. Second, while you're appealing to this wider audience, you need to be careful not to embarrass the legislators, which I suppose is part and parcel of giving them political cover."

"With the possible exception," Sayre adds, "of those who are obnoxiously against you. With them, embarrassment may be your only weapon. But even then you have to be careful not to embarrass them in a way that makes their colleagues feel obliged to defend them, or that makes you appear mean-spirited or petty."

"True," Link affirms, nodding at Sayre. "But let's not get ahead of ourselves. The first thing is to set the tone and get it right. A general point worth making here: Don't ever be self-conscious about what you're doing, in particular about the need to make the same point repeatedly. Don't ever assume that people can see through you."

"Forgive us if this is old hat to you guys," Sayre adds, "but we encounter it often. Clients tell us it bothers them to use the same catchy phrase over and over. They worry that people who see them say the same exact thing in three different interviews will conclude that they're robotic. Forget that. Just look at any successful politician. People need as much repetition as they can get. Their memories are as short-lived as ice cream in July."

* * *

Link explains that, with the hearings coming up quickly, he and Sayre wanted to create a practice setting that was as realistic as possible. "With this in mind, we have asked a random group of Ingersoll employees and volunteers to participate as audience members."

Link signals to the rear of the studio, and an assistant opens the doors to let the group in. "As you see," he continues, "we have arranged to have you sit at a table like the one you will probably occupy in Richmond. Before you move over there, however, we're going to let the opposition, as it were, take a turn.

"So, if you would take seats in the audience for a few minutes, allow me to introduce our two speakers, the Reverends Morgan Fitzgerald and Roland Peterson."

Laughter goes up in the room as two men who bear a striking resemblance to Fitzgerald and Peterson nod and take their assigned seats at the table. "Peterson" is wearing his usual ecclesiastical suit; Fitzgerald's stand-in, as large as the man himself, is dressed in gray flannel slacks and a cashmere sports coat.

"We must have cornered the cashmere market," Ansel says with a nod toward Fitzgerald.

Sayre says, "We know we can expect testimony from the other side, of course. We want them to go first, on the theory that last impressions are more important than first ones. You'll want to do what you can to arrange it that way. For today, just to get into the mood, we will have them give a truncated opening, and then you three can take it. Peter and I will play the parts of legislators. However, we'll feel free to step out of our roles to interject comments and critiques.

"We'll also hope you can pack the audience for the real thing," Sayre adds, without mentioning that the audience participants pressed into service for the practice session have been asked to favor the pro-amendment side in their reactions.

Sayre and Link take their seats on the rostrum. "Okay, let's start," Link says. "Reverend Fitzgerald, we understand you would like to make an opening statement. For the sake of brevity today, I'll ask you to focus attention on the religion amendment."

"Thank you, Senator," the Fitzgerald stand-in says in a voice convincing enough to draw a murmur from the other participants.

The pastor is only a few words into his statement before applause goes up in the audience.

Link, putting on his most officious face, holds up a hand and intones, "We recognize that this is an emotional issue. However, observers are requested to refrain from responding to the witnesses. Thank you. Continue, Rev. Fitzgerald."

"Senator, what we hope you will take away from this hearing is the understanding that since the introduction of the amendments, their opponents have not missed an opportunity to misrepresent them and the majority of Americans who support them.

"Opponents of the amendments would have you believe several things: First, that Christians are trying to take over the country and turn it into a theocracy—a Christian version of Iran. These are nothing but scare tactics. Second, that Christians in America are intolerant. Some go further, suggesting flat out that we are bigots. Third, that religion has somehow become irrelevant in today's world—and this assertion's corollary: People don't need religion.

"Senators, we could not disagree more with each and every one of these assertions, as well as many other distortions that are repeated over and over in big lie fashion. I am confident that by the time Rev. Peterson and I finish today, you will understand the hollowness of our opponents' arguments and the urgent need to ratify the amendments that are before you."

Fitzgerald and Peterson continue, and several times are interrupted by cheers from the studio audience. At first the audience is admonished. However, as the proceedings go on, the admonishments become fewer, until they are offered up in only the most egregious instances. By the time the Ingersoll troika is called to present their case, the room appears to have been won over by the clerics.

"Okay," Sayre says, "let's assume that Ansel has just read his opening statement. I think you may have a sense here of its importance in changing the tone in the room, as we discussed earlier."

"Ms. Ruiz," Link begins, resuming his senatorial stand-in role, "for the sake of convenience today, I assume you won't dispute your oft-stated position that you are an atheist? It's fair to refer to you in this way?"

India pulls the microphone closer, but before she can respond, Senator Link continues. "Do you acknowledge that Christianity has played a profound role in the creation of our country? I mean to say . . ."

"With respect, Senator, before you continue I'd like to answer your first two questions."

"Good," Sayre says. "Nicely done. You firmly but politely kept him from getting on a roll and making a speech."

India nods and goes on. "To your first question, Senator, you are welcome to refer to me as an atheist. I'm confident, however, that you will be courteous enough not to do so in a pejorative way."

"Smaller words, India," Sayre interjects. "It's a good response, but try to stay away from words like pejorative."

"Negative, then, Senator. I'm confident you won't attach a negative meaning to the word."

"I wouldn't dream of showing you anything less than Christian charity."

The audience laughs enthusiastically, and India smiles as well.

"Good on the smile, India," Sayre comments. "It shows you can appreciate humor without getting your back up."

"Actually, I *can* do that," India responds lightly.

"I have a senatorial question," Sayre continues, in her role.

Once again, India interrupts. "I'll be glad to take your question, Senator. In deference to your colleague, let me just finish answering his. I do acknowledge the fundamental role Christianity played in the founding of the country. But it was one of many factors that made us what we were and are. I would maintain that this isn't the real issue. Contrary to Rev. Fitzgerald's insinuation that we are trying to demean religion and Christianity in particular, what made this country great is its unique ability to make room for believers of all stripes, but also for minority peoples and views, including nonbelief. Certainly, the course of minorities and nonbelievers has not always been smooth."

Sayre leans in. "Some would argue that the proposed amendment in no way restricts these rights, but only acknowledges the overwhelming faith of the country. Some might also argue that the community you represent is not benign in its championing of atheism. So let me ask you, given your personal belief or lack thereof, and given the profound role of religion in America, as well as the avowed antireligious purpose of the community you represent, can you tell us why Americans should listen to you?"

Rachel taps India on the arm, indicating that she wants to respond. "Speaking for myself, I'd like to say that, like many in our community, I'm not an atheist. I'm an agnostic—and yes, there is a difference—and I am open to the idea that there are many things in this world that are beyond my understanding. However, conventional religion simply does not answer my questions or address my sense of wonder. There may be wisdom in the Bible, but I do not believe it to be divinely inspired, but rather the inspiration of men who, however wise they might have been in some ways, were woefully ignorant about the world they inhabited."

"And I would emphasize the word *men*," India interjects.

Link raises a finger. "Careful, India. That's the kind of self-indulgent thing that will change the message."

"Well, sorry, but it's true."

"I'm not disputing it. And if you want to make the point that men have controlled the world, you can make it. But treat it as a serious issue that deserves attention, not a throwaway line—don't just make it appear like you're indulging in a petulant screw-you moment."

"I agree," Ansel says. "We have to be firm but nonthreatening. Our purpose here and Ingersoll's purpose generally is not to convince believers not to believe, however much I would personally like to spend our time doing that. The point we have to get across is that our purpose is to protect the freedom of believer and nonbeliever alike."

"Mr. Frye," Link says, resuming his official voice, "there is nothing in the proposed amendment that in any way infringes on your right not to believe."

"We must respectfully but vehemently disagree. There is no way a country can establish a state-favored religion without implicitly making all who do not belong to that religion second-class citizens. Whether stated or not, for many people that is in fact the objective of this amendment."

"The point is worth making, Ansel," Sayre says. "But I would make it slightly differently. Rather than say the *objective* is to make nonbelievers second-class citizens, I would say something like, whether stated or not, that will be the *result* of the amendment. In other words, it's better if we don't malign the opposition's intentions."

"Point taken."

"In any case," Link goes on, "my response might be that we have no desire whatsoever to treat non-Christians as anything less than equal."

"What, after all, is the point of the amendment?" India rejoins. "It is an official endorsement of Christians, who are the majority and need no such endorsement. To the contrary, it is the message sent to others—a message that says you are not a full member of this nation if you don't believe."

"Yet some might say we are tired of having to fight for *our* rights as Christians," Link responds. "No matter what our denomination, we agree on the betterment of humankind through faith in our Lord and observance of God's commandments."

"If ever there was cherry-picking, Senator, it is in how Christians define the word of God. Thou shalt not kill, but thou may commit genocide in my name, enslave people in my name."

"Hold on India," Link says. "I'm sure you can see that this is precisely the kind of confrontation they will want to draw you into. You can't win an argument with them, much less their religious backers, that defames their religion. You can argue why religion is not necessary to be a good person, but even that risks playing their game, whereas your game, India . . . your game . . ."

"Please stop calling it a game."

"All right. Your purpose, how's that? Your strength is the freedom argument. Don't let the opposition distract you."

Chapter 24

Fractious Atolls

ROLAND PETERSON IS SLOWLY pacing his office, moving from window to sofa to window, trying to settle on a way to broach a sensitive topic. Over the years he has become a thoughtful, methodical man who mistrusts impulse—it is a legacy of his impulsive youth, a tale he likes to tell as a parable. The things in his life he is most proud of—and nothing more so than the growth of his ministry, which has sunk deep roots in the community—are the product of persistence. Progress is achieved by building up, not tearing down.

Now his conscience—his sense of responsibility—says that he must lead as a voice of reason. Fervency has its place, but it must be tempered if it is not to lead to anarchy and destruction. This is the essence of the problem he faces.

The pastors of the other Atolls, Reverends Schweig and Liston, will arrive momentarily. It has been difficult to arrange this meeting, and Roland strongly suspects that there is more to the difficulty than conflicting schedules.

In truth, it is only Liston with whom Roland wants to meet. The invitation to Schweig is a courtesy—the three were forced into the same boat by the creation of Ingersoll, and there is no reason to throw any of them overboard—and it can't hurt to have Schweig as an ally, though it might not be of much benefit either, given the small size of his congregation.

No, the real problem is Liston. It is his congregation, under his leadership, that has emerged as the source of violence and possibly even terrorism. No doubt this is why it has been so difficult to set up the meeting. Liston must suspect what Roland wants to discuss, and he is not likely to be receptive.

They arrive at the same time. Liston, solicitous of the older man, steps aside to allow Schweig to enter first. Roland notices that Schweig seems more than usually unsteady on his feet. He greets him with as hearty a welcome as the situation will allow and guides him to the chair usually reserved for himself. His greeting of Liston is more perfunctory, and is returned in a similarly guarded manner.

Roland urges Liston to take a seat and orders coffee and tea. He thanks both of them for making the time for him, and assures them he wouldn't have asked just now if the matter were not urgent.

"As I'm sure you both know, we have just experienced our third case of arson in a week," Roland begins.

"We?" Liston asks with a paperboard smile.

"Yes, we, Jeremy. I believe we all live around here?" Roland is actually relieved that Liston has joined the argument so quickly, sparing them all the rote meandering pleasantries and getting to the heart of the matter. "And, of course, the arsons are just a part of recent activity. There's hardly a wall, bridge, pillar or post that hasn't been defaced in some way."

"Roland, if I may anticipate you, you may be a bit hasty in implying that our congregants are responsible for this?" Schweig suggests, cocking his head, the rising tone of the question softening what otherwise might have been a confrontational assertion.

"I don't think so, Reverend. And however one feels about this Ingersoll business, our churches are located here. I think we owe our neighbors, some of whom may not have been consulted any more than we were about their submersion within Ingersoll, common courtesy, not to mention a good example." Roland looks from Schweig to Liston, who he can see, unlike Schweig, has no interest in challenging the implication of complicity in the violence.

The three men look up in response to a knock on the door, followed by the secretary's unsteady entrance as she tries to balance the coffee tray. Roland rises to hold the door, and thanks her as she sets the tray down.

"Let's not be coy here," Roland continues when they are alone again.

"I quite agree," Liston interjects as he leans over to stir sugar into his coffee. "As far as graffiti and protest signs are concerned, I don't believe any of us has tried to rein in our congregants, including you, Roland. If you want to argue that it's gone too far, you can—though I must say I disagree—but please don't suggest that my church or Reverend Schweig's is particularly culpable."

"As a matter of fact, Jeremy, I didn't especially want to discuss the graffiti. My main concern is the violence. To begin with, I do have good reason to believe the arsons are being carried out by members of your church."

"It's not true," Liston says, staring hard at Roland. "But even if it were, I don't condone it, and I resent the suggestion that I do."

Roland sits back in his chair and eyes Liston with undisguised skepticism. What he can't say is that he has recently been visited by Ansel, accompanied by Ingersoll's security chief, Roark, who presented unassailable proof of the culprits' actions. They were prepared to confront Liston but wanted Roland's thoughts first, and wondered if, as the head of the community's largest church, he might intercede. Roland committed only to giving the matter some thought, and to his mind this meeting is at his own initiative. It is certainly not in his interest to be seen as doing Ingersoll's bidding, even if they do share an objective.

"I don't know what you mean by 'reason to believe,' Roland," Liston continues. "If you know something, tell me what it is and I'll deal with it."

Again, Roland is concerned to make his point without revealing too much about the source of his information. It will do little good to provide details, given Roland's strong suspicion that, notwithstanding his assertion, Liston would not seriously deal with anything. For several reasons—including Roark's evidence but also his own experience with

Liston—he is certain that Liston, if not directly complicit in the violence, at least condones it.

Now Roland is annoyed when Schweig plays into Liston's hands, saying, "These are serious matters, Roland. I don't think Reverend Liston is asking too much for you to provide details if you have them."

Roland goes for the soft, misdirecting lie. "The details in my possession are indisputable, Reverend. However, I have promised to protect the identity of the person in my congregation who brought them to my attention."

"It's not true," Liston responds. "In any case, there has been no serious violence."

But Roland is not willing to let Liston off the hook. "Perhaps not violence, per se. No one has been seriously hurt in the arsons. But how long until someone is? Already there has been an escalation, from arson against homes and businesses under construction to the most recent case, a store that was ready for its grand opening. And then there is the rash of potshots, which I suspect have not hit anyone—yet, at any rate—by design, not incompetence or luck."

"My church has nothing to do with those shots!" Liston intones over a pointed index finger in his best baritone hell-and-damnation voice, leaving Roland to consider the absence of such strong denial with regard to the arsons. Moreover, Roland knows almost certainly that what Liston says about the shootings is only true to a point: The shooters are not members of his church, but they have benefited from his church's hospitality.

"Don't let your fifteen minutes of fame go to your head," Liston continues angrily.

Roland shrugs off the comment as irrelevant, and quite possibly sparked by envy. "Please, Jeremy, don't. You know full well that I never sought the limelight with Fitzgerald or Carter, which is what I assume you mean."

"Whether or not you did, I also know full well that they're displeased with you and not happy with events here."

"Who is?" Schweig interjects lightly, perhaps hoping to lower the temperature.

Again, Liston's remark is true, but goes only so far. Fitzgerald is concerned, and has told Roland so (and Roland has learned this from other sources as well), and apparently Fitzgerald has had conversations with Carter that parallel the one he is having with Liston, to wit: Fitzgerald doesn't want the situation in Ingersoll to get out of hand, but Carter doesn't mind giving Ingersoll the suggestion that things could get nastier, and not necessarily in a nonviolent way. At any rate they all agree that Ingersoll should not be the focus of media attention while they make their final push for ratification in Richmond, and this is what Roland now tells Liston and Schweig.

Insisting once again that he did not ask for his role in Richmond, Roland says Ingersoll has already hogged too much of the media spotlight, and this won't be helped by the unwelcome appearance before the Virginia legislators of India and Ansel—an appearance everyone assumes Bryce Jones is responsible for engineering.

Still, Roland is nettled, feeling that Liston has successfully put him on the defensive. Trying to regain the initiative, he holds up a hand and says to the others, "Look, my purpose today is not to make presumptuous allegations. But we all know that our community is becoming, quite literally, a tinderbox. The larger political picture aside, this simply can't be good for us. Moreover," Roland continues before Liston can interrupt him, "there is an element out there—and I'm referring especially to the shooters—that is capable of causing real tragedy and chaos."

"Well," Liston says with a grim expression, "I have to agree that there is a heightened risk. As for the crazies, it would be particularly bad if one of them were to assassinate one of the Ingersoll leaders."

"Indeed it would," Schweig says with an automatic grave tone and solemn nod of the head that suggests to Roland that he doesn't really understand the menacing implications of Liston's comment.

When the meeting has ended with the predictable mutual assurances of responsible church leadership, Roland is even more unsettled than when it began. Above all, he wants to know how much of Liston's remark on assassination reflects more than speculation. Does he know something? The only certainty is that the meeting accomplished little beyond getting his own views on the record—and there is no reason to believe that his views were ever unknown to Liston.

Chapter 25

Richmond, January

THE EARLY DAYS OF the new year are marked by a freak heat wave. People arriving with clothing suitable for the thirties are shedding layers to accommodate the mid-seventies. It is a gift, this weather, if only as a reminder in these fractious times that there are such unexpected gifts. To the air of high tension is added one of carnival.

Beneath it all is a sense of the moment. All sides believe this is where the country's future direction will be decided. More than a century and a half after the Civil War, Virginia once again will be the crucial battleground. A loss of the battle here will not necessarily spell the end for either side, but the amendment opponents are closer to the brink than the supporters. The consensus is that Virginia presents the opponents with their best chance to turn the tide. If they fail here, they will be unlikely to win the remaining states. And the contest here couldn't be tighter.

The hotels are filled within a twenty-five mile radius of Richmond. Top of the line, middling, fleabag and everything in between, it doesn't matter, the No Vacancy signs are out. Most of the rooms were reserved months ago by parties that were clear-sighted or just lucky, reserved by churches, organizations of all stripe, committed individuals, and those who simply like a good show.

The churches have the advantage in housing their supporters. Many who can't find hotel rooms or are on a shoestring budget are finding space in church basements, offices, and even pews. Congregants are opening their homes and purses to the modern crusaders.

The antis can't compete on this front. The various anti organizations want to import supporters. Only a few have tried to do this methodically, as the churches have. Ingersoll has come closest. India and Rachel have long experience boarding the sleeping bag and crash pad set, and began early to work the problem. Still, the churches have the advantage, not only in size, but in access to their communities. Nonbelievers rarely have reason or opportunity to register as nonbelievers. Their mailing lists are a hodgepodge culled from all over.

One thing everyone has is enough money for outreach. Bryce has lived up to his pledge to personally cover any excess advertising costs, and not only for Ingersoll. Commercial time on all media is spoken for. Many people are complaining that the drumbeat is even worse than in the closest elections they can recall. For all practical purposes, there is no other radio or TV advertising on offer. This is most visible in the drastically reduced number of automobile commercials. Newspapers are enjoying a brief renaissance in bulky editions. All parties are taking full advantage of social media. India routinely reports increases in the number of her followers on Twitter, Facebook, and the newest rage, Reap, though she is the first to admit that she hasn't a clue what the numbers really mean.

Denizens of Richmond say they can't remember ever being courted so aggressively, ignoring the fact that it is a courtship once removed. It is not their votes that are the prize, but the votes of their representatives, and more specifically their senators, since the fate of the amendments in the Republican-controlled House of Delegates is not in question. However, this is not to say that the voters are powerless. There is an election coming next November, and even voters with short memories may remember to settle scores then. Hence the keen competition to woo them.

The city is enjoying an unexpected boom in visitors' dollars. Some Richmondites say they're sick of it and wish everyone would just go home. But Richmond has been economically depressed for years, so most residents are happy to be civic boosters. Some say this is a chance to show off the city. It's the kind of advertising that can't be bought—an Olympics moment without having to build the stadiums or the village. Others are wary, fearing that the spotlight will reveal, not Los Angeles 1984, but the humiliating Scopes trial of Dayton, Tennessee 1925.

Billboards—legal or not—are sprouting up everywhere. The churchers have an advantage in this arena as well, since they have never stopped using them to spread the word of God. Our Lady of Siena Church has one urging people to call an 800 number "to hear your personal message from the Blessed Virgin." The Bethlehem Baptist Church has expropriated Norman Rockwell's iconic Thanksgiving dinner, superimposing the legend "This Is What Our Lord and Savior Wants For Us."

The local flying club couldn't resist "God Is My Copilot" placed over a fuzzy spectral image of Jesus hovering in the cockpit. Predictably, United Atheists couldn't resist the dyslexic rejoinder that "Dog Is My Copilot," with the image of Jesus replaced by one of a beneficent golden retriever.

Such responses have caused Bryce to complain irritably to Ansel that "these idiots don't understand that sarcastic or offensive messages, even ones that any normal person would consider humorous, play into the churchers' hands."

Ansel reminded him that they had no way of controlling United Atheists. And anyway, how is this any more ridiculous than the Church of How Jesus Would Do It predicting on billboards that the Rapture would coincide with the ratification vote? "And do you know that there is an honest to goodness organization called Jugglers for Jesus—I'm not kidding, Bryce. The website talks about a guy who is a 'full-time Christian juggler' who can spread the Word of God at parties and what not."

Bryce was not assuaged. "The churchers are the majority. It's easier for them to argue that their lunatic fringe doesn't speak for them."

When Ansel recounts the conversation to India, who is sleep-deprived and as irritable as Bryce, she wants to know why he's so opposed to their side punching back. "And besides, he's supposed to be hands-off . . . though I suppose The Money can't ever really be hands-off."

"I understand Bryce's point," Ansel responds. "It's not that we shouldn't push our case forcefully. We're doing that. But we get nothing by trying to humiliate the other side."

"Sometimes ridicule is the only suitable response to ridiculous people."

"The problem is that the religious people obviously don't see it that way, and it does nothing for us when the churchers paint us as elitist."

"Well, tell Bryce we're not in control," says an unmollified India. "He's not the fucking pope, and Ingersoll is not the fucking Vatican, unless what you mean is that neither of them is obeyed on subjects like birth control."

"He has a point, though, India, especially considering that our main goal is to convince a few politicians."

"Yeah, yeah, I know. Once again we're in the stupid position of trying not to offend people who see nothing offensive in calling us immoral and telling us we're damned for all eternity. We've been over this a hundred times. Don't tell me that putting up a billboard showing a happy family with the legend "This Scene NOT Brought To You By Religion" is too offensive."

"That's not what we're talking about. The example you give is fine. But I don't see what we gain by portraying the believers as low-forehead knuckle-draggers. Don't forget that the swing votes we're trying to capture in the Senate belong to people who are believers, and it doesn't help us to make them feel foolish and defensive. That's where Bryce and I agree."

"But we're *not* doing that, Ansel. None of our advertising has been disrespectful. Bryce doesn't seem to understand that Ingersoll doesn't own the trademark on nonbelief. We can try to make our case with the guerrilla-atheist types, but we can't tell them what to do. Plus, Bryce is supposed to be staying out of the day-to-day stuff, and I'm more than a little pissed off by these phone calls."

"Oh, please, India, you said it yourself. The money can't really be silent. Bryce may want to be hands-off, but he's got his reputation and a hell of a lot of money at stake. We're probably lucky he hasn't interfered more than he has."

Chapter 26

Fire in the Hole

ANSEL AND INDIA ARE together in Richmond. It is past nine on a Friday night and they are headed for their rooms on the fourth floor of the Jefferson. Exhaustion is plain in their drawn faces and slow gait as they cross the lobby. The Jefferson has become the de facto ground zero for the campaigns. Both sides long ago took up rooms for their senior leaders, and more recently scrambled to reserve any available meeting and conference room space.

Even at this hour the hotel, and particularly the enormous lower level, is a roiled sea of competing colors, red for the pro-amendment factions, white or blue-and-white for the antis, with splotches of uncoordinated primary colors denoting various independent interests.

Tired as they are, Ansel and India decide to take a walk through the organized (planful is another word heard frequently) chaos around them. The national movement leaders from both sides have tried to arrange contiguous space for their constituent organizations—an effort that has fallen victim to limitations on the hotel's planners, as well as the autonomy (real or imagined), initiative, zealousness and general moxie of the various organizations themselves. The result is a jumble of competing colors and groups. Only a few are packed, or packing up, for the night.

The raucous Gay-Lesbian-Bisexual-Transgender-Queer-or-Questioning Alliance table, fitted out in rainbow colors and seemingly determined to keep the proselytizing going even in the absence of people to proselytize, somehow ended up cheek by jowl with the table manned by the Christian Coalition for Traditional Marriage. Mutual disbelief at the space assignments (*you've got to be kidding . . . there must be some mistake*) at first led to clumsy, formal (less formal on the Gay-etcetera's part) exchanges. But as often happens when the theoretical collides with the practical, the chilly awkwardness gave way to social accommodation and even occasional unguarded bonhomie (*we're ordering coffee . . . can we get you some?*). Richard Carter was reportedly irate to find one of his pro-life shock troops engaged in what appeared to be a civil exchange with pro-choice reps.

India has been practically living here since the beginning of the year. The original plan was for her to coordinate the national effort from Ingersoll and leave the Richmond campaign to Rachel. But as the importance of the Virginia vote grew, with each side pumping ever more resources into it, she decided it would be better to be based in Richmond. She was confident that she worked well enough with Rachel to avoid friction.

Ansel is still shuttling between Ingersoll and Richmond. In the past few months he has been reassured by India's professionalism, the occasional (and not wholly undesirable) dramatic flare-ups notwithstanding. His presence in Richmond at this time is mostly required for the hearings, which have if anything grown in importance along with the national spotlight on the Virginia ratification votes.

No election campaign in memory has exceeded the competition on display all over the city. Pros and antis are going door to door, trying to convince people to pressure the legislators. Sometimes one doorbell ringer leaving a house crosses paths with someone arriving to make the opposite pitch. (*Don't bother with this house. They're hard over against you. Thanks but I need to give it a shot anyway. Can't just take your word for it, now, can I?*)

Armies of young people deliver or hand out flyers for freedom of religion. Many of the flyers are stolen and torn up or dumped by trailing followers of the opposing camp, only to have the roles reversed the following day. One result is a blight of paper—colored, broadsheet, black and white, slick, home-printed with and without typos—that must cause all of the authors to question the effectiveness of their output even as they fear that letting up on production will give an advantage to the other side.

Phone banks, robo-call, and robo-contact equipment are getting a good workout; however things turn out now, this is a useful rehearsal for the November elections. The scripts vary only in a few diametrically opposed places: *Just a reminder that the House of Delegates and Senate will soon be voting on ratification of three constitutional amendments that could not be more important for the nation's future. Please take a moment to contact your representative and tell him/her to vote yes/no on marriage (sanctity or freedom thereof), pro-life-choice, and a Christian nation/freedom of belief (or non).*

* * *

Ansel and India head for the elevators, agreeing they will each take a light meal in their own room, crash for the night, and meet for an early breakfast to start the whole business over again.

As they step onto the elevator, they hear a commanding "Hold it, please." India stretches for the door open button and presses it just in time.

Both look up in mild to surprise to see that the voice belongs to Richard Carter.

"Sure you want to be seen with us?" Ansel offers with a thin smile.

"Trapped," India adds.

"Former Marine," Carter says. "I'm good at close-order combat."

It occurs to Ansel that this might be a light moment but for Carter's perpetual intensity and natural mean-spiritedness, which would undoubtedly run up against India's reflexive determination to take no guff, as his mother used to say.

"Press three please," Carter says.

India nods and hits the button. "Four for us," she says with the barest hint of hotel strata superiority.

"Nice of Bryce Jones to put you up in these lovely digs," Carter says, facing the closing door.

"Nice of your needy parishioners to do the same for you," Ansel replies, bringing a smile to India's face.

"It's been a pleasure," Carter says without turning around when the elevator stops on three.

"See you," India says.

"Oh, Ansel," Carter exclaims, turning back just before the doors begin to close. "Forgive me, I almost forgot. I hope everyone is feeling better at home." His "Regards to the Missus" gets in just under the wire as the elevator begins to move.

"Has something new happened with Erika?" India asks in surprise as they reach their floor.

Ansel is flustered, but hopes it's not visible as he recovers. "I don't know what he was referring to. Maybe Erika's hospitalization a few months ago—it seems like ages ago, actually."

"Strange."

"Yes, but then, he's a strange guy."

"Not the first person I'd want to be trapped in an elevator with," India smiles.

They say goodnight, reconfirm their meeting time in the morning, then both conclude that a half hour earlier would be better.

But Ansel is shaken as he swipes his key card and watches for the green flash that tells him he can enter the room. Wishful thinking had gotten the better of him when the cards and emails about Sam stopped arriving, making it possible to move the threat to the back of his mind.

Now he knows without doubt how things stand. In the brief span of the elevator encounter with Carter, he understands clearly that the bomb has been armed and awaits only a go order.

Chapter 27

Pressure Point

WITH ONLY DAYS TO go until the hearings begin and with a full schedule of preparation and lobbying under way, India is irate that Ansel has to make a sudden trip home, and worse, has offered only vague explanations—less than that, really—for the disruption. She feels faintly embarrassed at being unable to explain it to Rachel, who must hurriedly rearrange schedules. It suggests India is not in control of something she should be in control of.

Both of them would have understood if there had been some emergency involving Erika. Clearly, only the most serious matter would cause her to interrupt Ansel at such a crucial time. But, coincidentally, Erika has just contacted India, looking for Ansel, who was not responding to her messages. Erika was surprised to hear that Ansel was on his way north, leaving India to wonder whether she had revealed something she shouldn't have. Her curiosity deepened when she took a call on a separate matter from Bryce, who also apparently knew nothing of Ansel's whereabouts. The one thing about which India is certain is the angst that suffused Ansel as he was leaving. Nothing was spoken, but his face was haggard and his manner unusually distracted.

* * *

The call had come from Melinda that morning.

"It's a note, Ansel, and it's not good." Her voice was stern, accusatory (or so he interpreted it).

"What kind of note?" He had a good idea what the answer would be—had been wondering since the encounter with Carter what form the threat would take—but asked anyway.

"Handwritten, in block letters, placed in the mailbox early this morning. Very early; I found it at 5:30. I was on my way to Sam's rehab before work. I suppose it could have been dropped off last night."

However much he had tried to steel himself for this moment, or something much like it, the reality was knocking him for a loop. "Read it to me."

"Whoever wrote it mentions Sam . . ."

"Don't summarize it, Melinda, read it! Please," he added after a pause.

"Yeah, it's short, anyway:

"'Dear Mr. and Mrs. Frye'—cute, huh?—'We were so glad to hear about the progress Sam is making. We understand he'll be coming home soon. That's great. You'll be able to spend a lot of quality time with him over the next couple of weeks. Mr. Frye in particular has a lot of catching up to do! This will be a good opportunity for everyone, and will make it possible to continue along the present road—smoothly, unruffled, without complications. All the Best. Your Concerned Friends.'

"So, if we had any doubt that someone knows—including the recent news that Sam is coming home—we don't anymore."

Ansel was silent long enough to make Melinda think the call might have been dropped. "Ansel?"

"I'm here."

"I take it to mean whoever it is will keep our secret if you . . . what? Stay out of the way in Richmond for a couple of weeks?"

The disgust in his voice was plain. "Just long enough to get through the ratification votes."

"Or until the next time they want something from you. You knew this day might come." She added this matter of factly.

Ansel was relieved that at least she had dropped the bitter tone, but he resented her placing the onus entirely on him. It's not as if she had been an unwilling participant in the arrangement. "It doesn't make it any easier," he answered.

"What difference can it make to them if you sit it out?" she asked. "Can it really affect anything at this stage?"

"I don't know. The votes will be very close. Everyone is trying for any edge they can get. Considering the timing of the note, I suppose it's the hearings they have in mind, though I don't know how much difference my not participating in them would make. Then, again, they don't have much to lose by trying this bit of extortion. If I stay away, maybe that helps them, maybe it doesn't; in either case they're no worse off. If I don't stay away, they can expose us whenever it suits them. At a minimum they get to throw mud over all of us. *Just look at how tawdry and immoral these nonbelievers are!* But in truth, it probably wouldn't matter to our side if I didn't participate in the hearings. India and Rachel will do fine."

"Unless they have something on India too."

"Yes, though who knows what it could be, considering that she's already self-tarred as an ultraliberal atheist activist divorced lesbian."

Ansel didn't particularly intend this to be humorous, but it got a good laugh—sardonic, but still a laugh—out of Melinda, and one out of him in turn.

"Fuck, whatever we do, they might expose us," Melinda said. There was silence for a moment before the resentment crept back in. "You may be focused on Ingersoll, but what about the kids? How do I shield them? You need to do what you can to keep this from happening, Ansel. Even if it means giving the cretins what they want."

* * *

Ansel is on his way to see Melinda now. He's not really sure why he's going. There's probably not much more to be learned or to say to her. India is none too pleased. He's already caught flak from Roark over leaving his security detail behind. But he concludes it's important to make the trip anyway. If nothing else, during the drive he has a chance to think things through.

Not that it matters much at this point, but he's still troubled by not knowing how things were exposed. He goes over and over the same ground, looking for a slip-up. He assumes that over ten years there

178

simply must have been something. Yet nothing obvious comes to mind. They have been discrete. They have been careful. There is always the possibility that one of Melinda's friends said something to the wrong person. He can explore this with Melinda. But then he thinks again, what's the difference now? The secret's out. The only real issue is damage control.

Still, it gnaws at him. The most likely explanation is that he has been watched . . . followed during one of his visits to Melinda, for instance. But something must have tipped off his enemies . . . must have caused them to look.

Unless all of the key people at Ingersoll have been under surveillance—that's another possibility. Considering the groups they're up against, it wouldn't be surprising. Then, don't overcomplicate it, he tells himself. The simplest explanation is often the right one. The trouble is, in the circumstances, there could be many simple, plausible explanations.

And then he's whipsawed back to the reality that the only question to be answered now is what, if anything, to do. Maybe he carries on as usual and hopes his enemies won't follow through on their threats. Maybe they would rather keep their powder dry. But would this accomplish anything more than postpone the inevitable? They would still have the power, and they could use it at any time, for any reason.

There are only two things he must consider. What will be the impact of the revelation on the movement? And what will be the impact on the people he loves? He resents Melinda's suggestion that he's only thinking about Ingersoll. As if she and Erika and the kids hadn't crossed his mind!

And then he has a moment when he allows, maybe they hadn't—not really, not in a way that could have caused him to alter his course. He might have rationalized his actions as being a necessary sacrifice that must be shared by all. It is never only the soldiers at the front who suffer, after all. The larger issues now at stake are hardly less important than any war or battle. This is what he tells himself. And he believes it, even as a part of him recognizes it may be nothing more than base self-justification; believers in causes just and unjust alike always find a way to excuse what they do.

His entire being clenches when he envisions the children and Erika finding out. It is one thing for the kids to have had to get used to his irregular presence, and another for them to absorb the idea that his absences are the result of other claims on his affections. And the thought of hurting Erika is almost unbearable.

Of course, no one will understand how he could do such a thing. They will talk about it as if the whole matter—ten years' worth of a loving relationship with Melinda and a family to show for it—could be bound up as one big singular act. But this is wrong. The criminal sneaks up on the crime, and the crime sneaks up on the criminal. Each strand builds to the large edifice. The politician may not intend to do wrong; he convinces himself that the small favors traded are for the greater good (or nothing would get done, after all), as are the subsequent favors traded, and so on, until the web is woven.

Clearly there was a point at which Erika was betrayed, but there was never an explicit decision to betray her. Like many betrayals, this one started small, almost innocently (*why don't we have coffee-lunch-dinner-run into each other at . . . kiss? yes kiss . . . you'll be there too? great . . .*).

But just as his finding a culprit in the crime's exposure will make no real difference to him in the end, the cause of the act makes no difference either. There is no real justification. He knows it. So does Melinda. He will remind her of this. He's willing to pay the price, though only now does the price seem so high. He didn't want the Ingersoll job, fearing precisely this kind of danger. But he did take it, didn't he? Yes, Bryce knows how to turn up the pressure. But he's not a child. He did succumb, didn't he? He did convince himself that the risk was manageable.

Still, almost all of the consequences he envisions can be dealt with one way or another. Except Erika . . . whom he does love . . . has always loved . . . and now . . . what?

The drive north has not been for naught, however. By the time he arrives at Melinda's he's decided what he must do.

∞

Chapter 28

India: Update

CONFIDENTIAL / INGERSOLL INTERNAL USE ONLY

Memo For: Ingersoll Board of Directors
From: India Ruiz
Subject: Update on Hearings and Virginia Senate Contacts

The format of the hearings has finally taken shape after a good deal of negotiation between the House of Delegates and Senate. What began as a fairly straightforward exercise in creating an ad hoc commission on the amendments (now called with upper case formality the Special Commission), became increasingly complicated and contentious as the public spotlight on the decisive role Virginia may play has become more intense.

It was never considered a routine matter, but Virginia's growing prominence as a make-or-break state was matched by legislators' growing interest—for reasons both seriously substantive and opportunistically political—in being on the commission. No doubt there will be lots of speechifying for the cameras. We might be able to use this to our advantage if we can steer the participants toward appearing statesmanlike and wise for posterity.

The commission consists of eighteen legislators, ten from the House of Delegates and eight from the Senate. The Republican majority in the House is reflected in their numbers on the commission; six of the ten are Republicans. The Senate representation is evenly split, four and four.

There are a few wild cards in this arrangement. For example, we were anticipating having to make our case at separate House and Senate hearings. The dynamic may be changed somewhat—for better or worse—at a mixed social.

As far as the votes among the commission members go, at this stage, prior to the hearings, of the ten House panel members, six—possibly even seven—are for the amendments in various combinations—i.e., not all reps will necessarily vote yes on all of the amendments. We believe the religion amendment would pass six to four in this group.

The Senate, where we've pinned our hopes, presents a problem as far as commission membership is concerned. Although we still think we can prevail in the full Senate vote, of the eight commission members four to four would be optimistic; five to three against us is more likely.

Of the four senators we have targeted for particular attention, two are on the commission: Reich and Armstrong. (Seniority counted for a lot in determining membership.)

Nothing has really changed with Reich. We've kept up the pressure on her to the point where I'm afraid if we don't back off, she'll vote against us out of pique. Fortunately, the churchers are making an equal nuisance of themselves. In the end, we think she'll vote with us on religion and same-sex marriage, and against us on abortion.

Armstrong is driving us crazy, as we predicted he would. As a Republican, he's under a lot of pressure to vote with the party—which he almost always does. But we also have been keeping up the pressure. (FYI, Rachel and I, and probably some of our allies, are meeting with him again tomorrow.) We're pulling out all the stops to convince him he's a latter day George Mason—strong, manly, independent, and committed to individual liberty.

Armstrong may not want to disclose his vote beforehand, but he might have an "alphabet problem:" He could be the first to vote in a roll call (if they go by name, not district), in which case he'll have to show his hand early.

Harper is driving us crazy too, but for different (alas, also predictable) reasons. I met him alone and made sure to move our discussion out of the office where we would not be overheard/observed. We continue to throw promises his way, staying right on the line of legality. What I'll say for the moment is that he's crafty and venal, and he knows how much his vote is worth. No matter how much we offer, he will refuse to commit himself. We can only hope that he's playing our opponents in the same manner—which he probably is.

Either way, Harper has a lot of wiggle room with his evenly split constituents—one vote is as good as another from a political POV. We need to keep pressing him, though. I hate to say it, but we may have to sweeten our already sweet offer.

And finally, young Sen. Bernsen. As with the others, we keep dropping in on him. Unlike the others, he is not so obviously sick of our attentions. Rachel did yeowoman work engaging him when they took their "Capitol Stroll" last month. He is sincerely interested in the substance of the issues. Sometimes he gives the impression that he's in an Oxford debating society event and simply enjoys the give-and-take. However, he does also seem to have a sense of the moment.

Bernsen almost certainly will not go with us on abortion, and he won't commit on the other amendments. He came tantalizingly close to doing so the other day, when he told Rachel that she "won't be disappointed" by his vote. We can only hope so.

Two interesting observations from Rachel: At their first meeting, Bernsen mentioned that his mother went through a "liberal phase" (who didn't?) in her college years. We don't know how far she's moved ideologically (I would guess pretty far, at least on the surface, and father Bernsen is definitely not in our camp), but maybe she's a closet liberal. Apparently, Bernsen is closer to his mother than his father, so there may be some kind of influence opportunity for us there.

The second observation is that Bernsen is crazy for a girl he's been going out with. Again, we can't be sure, but from what we've been able to find out so far she's shockingly liberal. Maybe another angle to play here (*Lysistrata* solution, anyone?!), but of course, we're running out of time.

Chapter 29

Ansel to Bryce

FALSE SUMMER HAS ENDED when Ansel's car pulls up to the gate at Ingersoll. He has been driven through a cold rain from Richmond; once again, the security detail accompanies him. No reason to argue with Roark now. Besides, if anything the mood has become uglier. This is true across the country, where it seems there is not a kind word to be found by or for anyone.

Within the short few months of its formal announcement, Ingersoll has become a national flashpoint. For both sides it has become a convenient shorthand for any aspect of the debate. Depending on the speaker, Ingersoll is the perfect crystallization of hope or despair for the country's future.

As soon as he returned to Richmond after seeing Melinda, Ansel warned India he might have to leave again suddenly, and that she should be prepared to handle the hearings without him. Once again he gave no excuse, but this time at least he made it clear that the potential emergency has nothing to do with Erika. He added vaguely that he might have to meet with Bryce on short notice. India can't really dispute this, but she's none too happy at the prospect of yet one more plate to keep spinning in the air, or that anything important involving Ingersoll is going on without her, especially now.

The rain has done nothing to depress the demonstrations at the gate. According to Roark, the organization and logistical support for the churchers no longer depends on the Atolls. Professional organizers have taken on the task, drawing volunteers from the entire metropolitan area and beyond.

Ansel is impressed with Ingersoll's response: India deserves praise; she's no slouch when it comes to organizing counterdemonstrations. Ingersoll may not have the demographic base to draw from that the churchers have, but India's troops turn out in constant, high numbers, and with growing vociferousness. He was skeptical when Bryce issued his clarion challenge to them to join in or get used to saying the Lord's Prayer. But people have responded, and he gives much of the credit to India. She has ensured that Ingersoll is not only energized, but focused and organized to be effective.

This may be true to a fault. Anyone who expected the nonbelievers to respond to the churchers' provocations only with measured words and intellectual arguments was in for a shock. Nonbelievers and freethinkers across the country—and particularly in this area—have shown themselves willing to threaten and retaliate. A popular poster around Ingersoll: *The Second Amendment Applies to Nonbelievers Too.*

The tense situation took another turn for the worse last week when someone pockmarked the outside of the auditorium with gunfire. The building was not in use at the time, and no one was hurt. Within twenty-four hours every one of the stained glass windows at Rev. Liston's church was shot out. Someone said looking at the multicolored shards on the floor was like peering into a kaleidoscope.

Roark and his people have become increasingly important as the struggle has escalated. This is true from a defensive security standpoint—and perhaps more. India has become surprisingly close to Roark, and either because Ansel has been distracted or, just as likely, because it is better not to know certain things, he has not inquired too closely.

As for Bryce, it has become obvious that his desire to remain in the background was naive in the extreme. The churchers don't buy into his background role. He's too juicy a target to allow that to happen. They have carried on an incessant campaign against him, trying to discredit him in every way possible. The most he has been able to do is remove himself from day-to-day affairs—though even this has been difficult when it comes to using his personal influence, which does not transfer automatically to Ansel or India no matter how many times he confers a public blessing upon them.

The campaign has gone from name-calling to promises by elected officials sympathetic to the churchers to put Bryce's financial dealings under a microscope. Nothing has stuck to him yet—the accusations have been fatuous and easily rebutted—but they have nevertheless demanded much of his time.

The latest assault involves vague allegations leveled by a former SEC chairman that Bryce has a "Bernie Madoff problem." It doesn't matter that Bryce's trading record—let alone his Ponzi scheme record—is clean. The charges cling. They are red meat to the media and eagerly embraced by the churchers (*just look at the lack of moral fiber in this man who has the effrontery to champion a war on God*).

Bryce is too self-possessed to be undone by such charges. At any other time he would merely shrug them off. In the current environment they cannot be left without a response, and this is time-consuming. Among other things, Bryce has sued the former SEC chairman for slander. Given the lack of evidence against him Bryce has no doubt that he will win, if not money damages (not of much concern to him anyway), at least a public retraction.

Bryce has also mounted a massive publicity campaign to debunk the allegations. To be sure, the churchers will not be persuaded on this score any more than many of them can be persuaded that dinosaurs are more than six thousand years old. The campaign is to protect Bryce's reputation among non-zealots and as much as possible keep the mud from slopping over on Ingersoll or the anti-ratification campaign. Yet the fact remains that whatever happens ultimately concerning reputations, there will be no formal resolution of the allegations or the lawsuit in time for the conclusion of the ratification votes, and this amounts to at least a tactical victory for the churchers.

Ansel was more than aware of these things when he told Bryce that he must see him, and soon.

When he enters the office, Ansel is struck by the expression on Bryce's face, which he reads as one of rapidly transitioning pleasure (the usual response on seeing Ansel) and concern over the problem he is sure is going to drop into his lap at any moment.

They move automatically to the sitting area, each taking their accustomed places in the plush ocher leather chairs. Bryce is at the head of a small, rectangular rough marble coffee table. Ansel sits at a right angle to him; their knees are almost touching.

"All right, what's the mystery that couldn't wait?" Bryce asks, sitting back and mouthing an arm of his reading glasses. His voice is a study in casual control, but there is no doubt that something important needs to be transacted. Neither man would inconvenience the other at this time otherwise.

Ansel leans in, elbows on knees, hands clasped in front of him. "Bryce, I'm afraid something has come up."

* * *

Bryce lets Ansel finish without interruption. Only a few times has he betrayed surprise at what he is being told (he didn't get where he is without a good poker face). As usual, he doesn't need to have the multiple implications of a situation explained to him. He grasps such matters almost instantly, intuitively. Now he says, "I'm very sorry to hear these things, Ansel, not least because of how much their revelation will hurt Erika."

At this, Ansel only casts his eyes down toward the coffee table in silence. No response is needed, or would be useful.

"It's clear to me now why you were reluctant to take on this job. I assume this is the reason."

Ansel nods.

"It did seem strange at the time. I would have bet my last dollar that it would be the kind of job you'd jump at."

"You wouldn't have lost the bet, Bryce. It was—is—the most desirable challenge I've ever had. But I knew the damage that could be done. I also know that you've always appreciated my loyalty to you. The irony is that I thought at the time there was no better demonstration of that loyalty than to turn down the offer."

"But you didn't."

"No, obviously I didn't. You were persuasive and I persuaded myself, foolishly, that I could keep everything under control. In any case," Ansel goes on after a loud sigh and shake of the head, "there aren't many options open to us now. My resignation is the least of it. Maybe we can make up a plausible story to control the damage."

For a long moment Bryce is silent, looking off to an unfixed point across the room. The only outward sign of distress is that he is chewing more purposefully on the arm of his glasses.

"Not so fast," he says finally.

"Excuse me?"

"There may be no choice but for you to resign, but not yet. I'd like to think things over a little more carefully."

"I have thought . . ."

"Hold on, Ansel. I know you've thought it through yourself. You never would have come to me otherwise."

"The hearings are coming up, Bryce, and the voting will not be far behind. The last thing we need is for this news to break then. The least we can do is try to control the news cycle. If I resign now and give some plausible explanation . . ."

"I'm not sure it would help," Bryce says, holding up a hand. "As I'm sure you've concluded, there's nothing to keep the churchers from using this against us anyway. Hell, look what they're trying to do to me! And, obviously, you can't try to deny it; they have all the proof they need."

"Which still leaves me thinking that the best of all the bad choices is to resign now and hope they want to keep the story in reserve. At the very least I'd become a less valuable target to them."

"I still would like to hold off a bit," Bryce says after a pause. "In fact, the more I think about it, the more I think you should carry on at least through the hearings."

"Really, Bryce, I don't . . ."

Ansel is surprised when Bryce puts a hand on his shoulder. "Listen, Ansel, you know it's not my way to bluster. You probably also know me well enough to understand that this doesn't mean I'm not mad as hell.

You've been reckless—not to say immoral, I'll leave that judgment to you."

"Really Bryce, don't you think I know . . ."

"What I know is that I'd like to think through some of the damage control options. You're not aware of *everything* I have at my disposal." He says this with a trace of a smile. "As the man says in one of my favorite films, I still have some friends in this town and a few teeth left in my head. And though, clearly, your personal welfare must come second, that's on my mind too."

"Thank you. It means a lot, no matter how things turn out."

"A couple of other points before you go: First, for what it's worth, I don't think they'll use what they have before or during the hearings. I could be wrong, of course, but if I were in their shoes I'd wait until after they're over—see how they go—and closer to the vote. If there's any benefit to them from the shock value of the revelation, they can only redeem it once.

"Second, no matter how painful this is for you, I have to bring Roark in on it."

Ansel looks up in surprise. "Bryce . . ."

"And you have to explain it to India. She may be a wild woman sometimes, but she's discrete. She's earned our trust and has a need to know."

Still staring at Bryce, Ansel exhales audibly. "It makes me squirm, but I agree. She shouldn't be blindsided. I'll talk to her. But Bryce, I need you to make it clear that she is not to act on this information in any way without consulting us. If her proclivity toward action gets the better of her, there's no telling what will happen."

"Agreed. Now, it's only my two cents, but I feel a need to put them in: If I were you, I would make a preemptive revelation to Erika, if you haven't already done so. I think you owe it to her. Of course, that's for you to decide. It's your business."

Here, too, Ansel knows Bryce well enough to understand that he doesn't really mean this last point.

Chapter 30

Hearings: Thursday

THE HEARING ROOM IS jammed, as it has been all week. Other rooms have been outfitted with television monitors to handle the overflow. But for wanting to be a part of the moment, these people might as well have stayed home and watched in comfort. The proceedings have gone far beyond local interest, garnering a national and even international audience.

The vote has taken on a sense of importance that exceeds the facts—it is not the end of the road for either proponents or opponents of the amendments; a few other states remain to be heard from. Nevertheless, it feels that way. It has been hyped that way, and both sides are aware that because of this the outcome will affect the other states.

The senators and delegates who are members of the Special Commission occupy a horseshoe-shaped raised platform at the front of the room. Various backbenchers, including some legislators who are not on the commission, take up all the seats behind the members, while several staffers occupy a table at floor level, placed between the members and the table for the individuals and groups that will be heard—what people have taken to calling the witness table, even though the hearings are informal, no oaths are sworn, and there is no compulsion to appear (to the contrary, more want to appear than can be accommodated). There is a podium next to the table for those who prefer to address the commission standing.

Three seats in the audience have been reserved for Ingersoll, part of a larger bloc held for interest groups that have a direct involvement in the proceedings. Today's fourth day of hearings has been anticipated with particular eagerness. The Rev. Morgan Fitzgerald is featured, joined by the Rev. Roland Peterson.

As people file into the room, Fitzgerald and Peterson are busy shaking hands. Most audience seating is first come, first served, and both sides have been jockeying to squeeze in as many of their supporters as possible. This has been true every day so far—with a wrinkle: Each side has made a special effort to get in when opposing points of view are being presented. It is as important to show vocal opposition to American Atheists or Right to Life as it is to stay on side.

For all that is at stake, the mood at the moment is festive. Fitzgerald's magnetism, so manifest on TV, is not lost in person. Whatever one thinks of his views, it is hard not to warm to the man.

Ansel, India, and Rachel are also mixing before taking their seats. Their turn will come tomorrow. But the star turn is clearly Fitzgerald's. His size alone would be enough to command the room, but he also conveys charm, warmth and sincerity. His voice may occasionally rise to a boom, which if it belonged to someone else might remind one of a huckster with a flower in his lapel, but on Fitzgerald suggests nothing more than infectious exuberance.

As he observes the scene Ansel is struck by the power of the man. It is easy to see why he has become the face of the evangelical movement. Other Christian groups have made presentations earlier in the week, but this is the show everyone has been waiting for.

Ansel also thinks that the opposition has made a very smart decision not only in featuring Fitzgerald, which is an obvious choice, but in adding Peterson. Even in a minor role, Peterson's presence will help with the black community. They are particularly smart to keep Carter in the background. Carter has his strengths, but likeability is not among them. He is present today, but only as an observer.

It is Carter who was the focus of Ansel's attention when he entered the room. Would Carter be surprised to see him there? Surprised that he is still listed among the presenters for Ingersoll? He was unable to tell when they briefly caught sight of one another. Ansel thought he saw the smallest expression of Carter's being taken aback. The man has a good poker face, though, and he's not likely to give much away.

India, on the other hand, not known for repressing her feelings, is clearly unhappy with the way things are going. As he promised Bryce he would, Ansel has taken India into his confidence. Astonishment at what she was hearing aside, the practical, no-nonsense part of her immediately kicked into gear and turned the conversation to how to respond to any public scandal.

At this point it is unclear to Ansel how much of the coolness he detects in her is the result of his revelations or to the general weight of events. Whether or not there are negative consequences to Ansel's problem, he is deeply embarrassed to have had to explain his actions to her. He is, after all, still India's boss, at least nominally, and their conversation evoked in him the sense of a communist party self-criticism.

On the other hand, he notes that Rachel, who has not been informed, also has a stern demeanor today, so perhaps he is reading too much into what he sees in India.

One of the commission co-chairs, Edward Collins, a Democrat, calls the session to order. His welcome includes the admonishment that displays of emotion like those that occurred the previous day will not be tolerated. Security will remove anyone who fails to act with civility or follow the ground rules for the hearings.

Fitzgerald and Peterson are introduced as representing the National Coalition for Constitutional Reform. Collins emphasizes the umbrella status of the organization, presumably as a reminder justification for excluding some groups that requested to be heard.

Fitzgerald thanks Collins for the introduction and says he can't promise as interestingly dramatic a session as yesterday's, but he and Rev. Peterson will do their best to convince all concerned that ratification of all three amendments is manifestly in the country's interest now and in the future.

There is laughter at Fitzgerald's mention of the previous day's drama. A panel representing an ad hoc coalition of atheists and agnostics had caused an uproar with their no-holds-barred statement and acerbic sparring with the legislators.

Miriam Sterling of American Atheists had read the opening statement for the group and immediately went on the attack, noting that for all the freedoms supposedly guaranteed Americans, atheists had consistently received a raw deal. This was true even before the country was "chartered," as she put it, as the first settlers demanded religious conformity even as they themselves had fled their homelands precisely to escape such demands. She reminded listeners that no less a stalwart of the American Revolution than Thomas Paine had been turned into a nonperson for his atheistic views, just as surely as if he had been subjected to a kangaroo court.

This prompted an angry interruption of her statement by the Republican co-chair, one of the most conservative House delegates, Howard Warrington. "And yet, here you sit," he interjected over a rigid index finger, "telling the court, as you would have it, about your views, no matter how much those views may reflect the minority. I'd say these are hardly the ways of a dictatorship."

"But definitely the ways of Joe McCarthy," Roger Dawes shot back from the atheists' panel, sparking shouts from both camps.

"Oh, please, spare me," Warrington responded, leaning into his microphone and making it boom and screech. "Not only are you free, you are free to run for public office and pass laws as surely as anyone in this room."

This brought a skeptical hoot from many in the audience, while Collins, the commission co-chair, attempted to reassert control.

Dawes was having none of it, as he cut in on Sterling, who was trying to resume her statement. Jumping up, his face florid beneath thin strands of straw-colored hair, he all but shouted, "I'm waiting to hear the usual crap line—I toned the word crap down for you, Delegate Warrington— the usual crap line about every American having a chance to grow up to be president."

"And I would remind you," Warrington overrode Collins, who was cocking his gavel, "that no one thought we'd have an African-American president in our lifetime, but we sure had one."

"Sure had one? Meaning what?" Dawes retorted. "Why don't you say what you really want to say, sir? We sure had one, and look what a screw-up that was. Isn't that what you mean? Don't think we haven't looked up your voting record, you antediluvian racist."

This time Collins had to shout above his microphone, which, when he attempted to shout into it, so distorted his voice that he could have been making a train station announcement. He banged his gavel and threatened to clear the room, but there was no stopping the panelists, as Miriam Sterling gave up on her formal statement and went through the lane opened by Dawes, not letting a millimeter of light in between Dawes's remark and her assertion bolstering it. "How about being honest for a change, Delegate?" she demanded. "The way this country is going, Obama is a never-to-be-repeated fluke, and as for atheists, the American people in their usual dumb cattle-like ways are more likely to elect a pedophile president than a nonbeliever."

At this point Collins had to act on his threat to clear the room.

Tempers were still simmering when the panel reconvened an hour later. Collins opened by warning everyone to maintain decorum.

At first it seemed the atheists would try to cool the rhetoric. Sterling began with an apology, saying it was never her intention to cause a commotion, a remark that drew derisive laughs from the audience, a disgusted look from Sterling in response, and a rap of the gavel by Collins.

"When we speak of hostility toward nonbelievers and the dangers posed to freedom," Sterling continued, "we only need to recall the hateful remarks of prominent religious bigots themselves to prove the point. Pat Robertson lumps atheists and secular humanists together with drunkards, Satan worshippers, greedy money changers, and assassins.

"Randall Terry, the founder of so-called Operation Rescue and the inspiration for the current virulent antiabortion movement—many of whose leaders are present today—advocated hatred against his opponents and said flat out that Christians are called upon by God to conquer the country.

"And no less a personage than George Bush the Elder was widely reported to tell a Republican fundraiser—listen to this, now, this is the President of the United States, and I quote—'I don't know that atheists should be considered citizens, nor should they be considered patriots. This is one nation under God.'

"Astonishing! Is this the Christian nation you have in mind with this execrable amendment?"

"Yes! Yes it is!" a voice pierced from the audience, causing Collins to use his gavel.

"Well, there you have it," Sterling continued. "Q.E.D. Just listen to that guy. Listen to that deluded flatulent pig and remember that a free America will not exist if these amendments are ratified."

The ensuing commotion barely missed another clearing of the room before it subsided.

But the rhetorical temperature continued to shimmer like burning phosphorus with the panelists' responses to every question from the legislators. Some delegates and senators tried to cool things off, as when a distinguished delegate tried in a honeyed old south patois to get the atheists to agree (*Now ahm sure we can awl agree*) that the nation's pastors and rabbis brought philosophical and moral decency to the minions—a hopeful vapidness that was immediately countered by the oblivious aggressiveness of the atheists, who went on to provide a harsh litany of pastoral deficits, the mildest of which was recitation of the adage that where a priest has trod, no grass will grow.

"As a Virginian," Dawes interjected, "I'd like to feel that my state has done *something* right over the last two hundred years. Since we produced the most prominent founding fathers, we've been on the wrong side of every important issue—slavery and Jim Crow, of course, but don't forget that it also took decades after the fact for Virginia to grudgingly concur in women being given the vote."

* * *

Now the Ingersoll Trinity (as the press has taken to calling Ansel, India and Rachel) are fuming as they await what they assume will be the statesmanlike remarks of Fitzgerald and Peterson. Ansel's ire is not directed against their religious opponents, but rather the atheists. As far as he is concerned, they have managed to pull off the not inconsiderable trick of dwarfing every negative stereotype to which they are routinely subjected. He is convinced that, rather than persuading the panel and public opinion of the bigoted unreasonableness of the Christian right, they have succeeded in proving that very point about nonbelievers and secularists, all of whom certainly will be lumped in with militant atheists.

It doesn't help Ansel's mood that India seems to have missed this point. Every time the atheists came up with some self-satisfied witticism, their smirks were joined by India's apparent smiling appreciation—less obvious perhaps, but evident all the same.

"You think this is funny?" a frustrated Ansel whispered to her at one point.

"Funny? I don't know. Humorous, yes. Justified, yes. Funny? I guess that would depend upon your definition."

Which Ansel took to mean, "After the jeopardy you put us in, who are you to criticize?" But whether this was an accurate assessment or a guilty projection, he refused to be put off. "It's goddamned juvenile! They're like teenagers who can't keep from blurting out whatever inanity pops into their heads. Except unlike teenagers, they won't be given a pass as just kids doing what kids do. I'm sure it feels good to vent their spleens, though."

India sat cross-armed, stonefaced. "You're making too much of this, Ansel," she whispered curtly, eyes forward.

"No, I'm not, India," he said, modulating his voice in midsentence in response to looks from people nearby. Leaning in to keep his voice down, he said, "Our whole campaign has been predicated on the idea that it's the Christian right that is irresponsible and putting our freedoms at risk. What we're hearing from these guys," he tossed his head at the atheists and continued, "is every bit as smug and arrogant as what we hear from the worst of the believers. They have the truth, and it is the only truth. Fitzgerald will be seen as the responsible elder statesman, and we'll have to revise our statement for tomorrow."

Rachel, sitting on India's far side from Ansel, seemed to tune in to their conversation at that point. "What's wrong with our statement? If we have to revise it one more time, I'll blow my brains out."

"Well you'd better cock your piece then," Ansel said, leaning past India.

"You're overreacting, Ansel," India responded irritably. "Every time we get the slightest bit aggressive, you want to rein us in."

"That's not true, and I would hardly characterize what happened yesterday as slightly aggressive."

"It is true." India's emphatic response caused heads to turn toward them. "It is," she repeated in a lower voice. "You want to talk about elder statesmen? That's how Ingersoll usually comes across, as some kind of milquetoast elder statesman."

"We might want to have this conversation somewhere else," Rachel interjected. Ansel and India simultaneously sat back in their seats, faces pinched.

Now Ansel is about to make a sotto voce point to India when they are interrupted by the panel co-chair's repeated call to order. In a voice determined to quiet the chatter, he asks Fitzgerald and Peterson to continue.

A cheer goes up at mention of Fitzgerald's name. "Seems like their side did a better job of audience-packing than we did," India says under her breath.

"Look, there's my boy," Rachel says with a nod toward David Bernsen, sitting off to the side.

"If he's your boy, he'd better give us equal time," India responds in a mildly mordant tone.

Fitzgerald is true to form. His opening statement is dignified and rhetorically compelling. He tells the legislators and the audience that there are those who would have us believe that the true essence of a nation and a people cannot be distilled in its constitution.

"Who, exactly, would have us believe that?" India whispers.

"Reverend Peterson and I are here today to tell you that not only can it be so, it must be so if the United States of America, this blessed land, is to live up to its oldest ideals and be that shining example of the good that nations can do if they honestly reflect the most basic values of their citizens.

"I say this with no intention of belittling any other nation, people or religion, but we in our country, which is the product of a Judeo-Christian heritage, are without doubt the world's greatest hope."

The early parts of Fitzgerald's remarks are interrupted frequently by applause, shouts of amen, and a few shouts of derision. However, as he continues in his lofty baritone, the audience adopts a more reverential silence that worries Ansel more than do the outbursts. The silence tells him that Fitzgerald is getting through—that his sermon (for that's what it is) is having the desired effect.

"There are three constitutional amendments before you to consider carefully, and each one of them reflects the noblest ideas of our faith and our culture: Thou shalt not kill the spark of God; we honor the sanctity of marriage as the bedrock of civilization; and above all, we honor the religious heritage upon which are based the greatest accomplishments of our national past and the greatest hope for our nation's future.

"To this end we declare to the world that every day on earth as we await the return of our Lord and Savior will be a day devoted to showing that as a people and a nation we are worthy of His glorious redemption.

"The amendments before you—which have fallen into your power to make a success—do nothing more or less than codify the best of our history and the way toward an even greater future."

When it is Roland Peterson's turn to speak, he introduces himself as the pastor of Christ the King, which has of late been surrounded by the Community of Ingersoll, whose growing opposition to God has become infamous. In a humble but clear voice he tells his listeners that he cannot improve upon the words spoken by Reverend Fitzgerald. "However," he says, "before we take questions, I would like to tell you a few things about my congregation, and in particular about what Christian devotion has meant to African-Americans."

As Roland continues, Ansel thinks that, in a few well-chosen words, he accomplishes what the believers must have hoped he would and one of the few things that Fitzgerald could not—he has explained the essential contribution of religion in saving his people in times of their worst tribulation.

Roland goes on to personalize his story, telling of his family's troubled history from slavery onward. "In bondage and in freedom, our faith delivered us and still delivers us. The amendments before you will ensure that our nation will move forward under the umbrella of God's grace."

"Black people's Stockholm Syndrome" is India's verdict, but most of the people in the room are undoubtedly moved.

As the ensuing question period draws to a close, Ansel's confidence is shaken. He feels like a patient who has just received unexpectedly bad news.

Collins offers "deep, sincere thanks" to Fitzgerald and Peterson, and announces that tomorrow, Friday, the hearings will conclude with the appearance of the Ingersoll representatives.

He is finishing his announcements, when he looks up to a commotion, which this time comes not from the general audience, but from scattered staffers, one of whom steps forward and whispers to him animatedly.

Collins appears to be rattled by what he hears. Yet, he quickly regains his composure and gavels the day's proceedings to a close, thus leaving it to the news media to inform people in attendance that, within the past hour, a car carrying C. Bryce Jones near his Community of Ingersoll has been raked with automatic weapons fire.

Chapter 31

First Aftermath

ANSEL AND INDIA ARE sharing the back seat of an armored limousine, en route to Ingersoll. Just before leaving Richmond they received word that Bryce was not badly hurt. Ansel spoke to him briefly; he relates to India that Bryce has a few cuts on his face from flying glass. His driver had not been so fortunate; he was hit by several shots and died at the scene.

Rachel has remained behind in Richmond. Security details have been juggled to protect her. Friday's commission session has been postponed until Monday.

Ansel and India are making calls from the car, having divvied up the list of people they must speak to and put them in priority order. Each of them is tucked into the opposite corner to minimize confusion in their phone conversations.

Erika is first on Ansel's call list. He sees she has made several attempts to reach him and left voicemails full of concern over Bryce and worry for Ansel's safety. The initial news reports have been conflicting and confusing. India is angry and upset that even after ample opportunity for clarification, the media are focused on stirring the pot rather than providing accurate information. CHRISTIAN ATTACKS ON ATHEISTS! is a common theme in lead-ins and crawls.

"This is horrible," Erika says. She asks if Ansel knows the driver who was shot. He tells her he only knows his name from Bryce, Tim Praeger.

Looking across the back seat, Ansel notices what he takes to be a quizzical look from India when it is clear who he is talking to. She would never say anything, but what must she think? Is every word she overhears interpreted differently or reinterpreted now that she knows about his second family and also knows Erika does not?

"What about you and the others?" Erika asks, worry plain in her voice.

"We're okay. I spoke to Roark. He's up to his ears, as you'd expect, but he laid on extra security before we left. India and I are sharing a car. I guess Roark combined our details. It's probably overkill, but it feels like a Secret Service lockdown, which I suppose is Roark's template."

"Better too much, as far as I'm concerned. You'll be home tonight, then?"

"I'll try. If I don't have to stay at Ingersoll."

"Please do try, Ansel. Maybe it's stupid, but I want to feel you in the flesh and make sure you're all right."

He promises to do his best. He tells her he loves her. And means it, though more than ever the potion is laced with guilt. Somehow he has gone from keeping completely separate lives, with all the denial and rationalization this entails, to gut-punched awareness that, like it or not, his lives are merged, blurred, and vulnerable.

Of course this has always been an accurate description of his existence. Only now, however, does it feel real and present.

He is only mildly surprised not to have heard from Melinda. This probably has little to do with their estrangement. She is tough-minded and practical. After hearing no mention of him in the news, she would have concluded that there was no need to hear his voice. After all, this was the game of self-imposed, disciplined compartmentalization they had played for more than a decade. The call following Sam's accident is the only time he can remember her breaking the no-contact rule. Moreover, unlike Erika, Melinda has no relationship with Bryce.

Ansel will want to carve out time from this unplanned weekend at home to see Sam and Cara. He has no intention of withdrawing from them. Sam has recently been moved from inpatient to outpatient physical therapy, having made much more progress than anyone dared hope for. And if Sam and Cara are home, he will probably see Melinda. The thought reignites the guilt he feels over Erika, as well as the question of whether, or when—he has been thinking of it more as when, though he is hardly rock-sure about this—to confess to her.

The guilt is not new; it has always plagued him, off and on. The necessity of a confession—it is the minimum he owes her given the likelihood of exposure by Carter—*is* new, at least in the sense that while the double life seemed to be working he could convince himself that the worst thing would be to breach the watertight compartment when there was no evidence that someone else would do so first. He had accepted that he was doing something—many things—wrong, but confessing, particularly if he had no intention of breaking things off with Melinda, would be worse. He would then be the stereotypically banal husband who confesses the affair to make himself feel better, while dealing a double blow to her: the affair and then the greater portion of misery over the affair.

And then for a moment (he has had many such moments) he recognizes and berates himself over the enormous knot of rationalization he has tied. He understands he is guilty on every count. He has no benefit of a deity to wash him clean. And since he knows that this moment will pass, he wonders idly about the relative merits of being willfully oblivious to one's sins, or being aware of them and not caring, or being aware of them and caring but not trying to correct them. If he is true to his past, he will parse the ethical arguments into infinitesimal pieces, choose one that seems plausibly defensible, discard it and choose another and then another, and so on, until, too confused and exhausted to take any action at all, he leaves the status quo in place, it only being left to ponder whether credit should be awarded (by whom?) in the category of breast-beating and self-imposed futility.

Of immediate concern is when Carter (Ansel assumes it is Carter calling the shots) will cry havoc. Does he plan to engineer a splashy exposé when Ansel is scheduled to appear before the commission? That's what makes the most sense: distract and discredit. He ponders Bryce's advice not to withdraw until he has had a chance to play whatever cards he might come up with. But he has not heard anything further about this, and he wonders how today's events might affect Bryce or distract him. He resolves not to let the weekend pass without forcing some update. Resigning and formulating some excuse for not appearing before the commission—possibly even just the latter—are still options. The fact that his secret has been revealed to India means at least she will be prepared to proceed without him.

During lulls in their communications with the outside world Ansel and India worry about what they will find when they reach Ingersoll. Immediately after the shooting, Bryce issued a call for calm. But already enraged Ingersoll supporters are taking to the streets. Some have begun pelting churchers with rocks or any object at hand that can wound.

For the first time since the announcement of Ingersoll, the churchers have had to withdraw from the gates out of fear for their safety. Without evidence beyond basic trust that has developed despite their differences, Ansel credits Roland Peterson with orchestrating an orderly retreat. Whoever is responsible, it was wise to pull the churchers out of harm's way.

Some militant atheists had obviously anticipated such a moment, as it took no time before they seized on the shooting to rally supporters. It did not matter that these militants had no connection to Ingersoll, and it did not help that from the beginning some had acted as if Ingersoll should be treated like a de facto capital of some breakaway nation, which in turn got detractors to deride Ingersoll as the White Man's Bantustan.

The militants didn't hesitate to steal the graphic used by the Israeli extremist group Kach: the rifle in the fist held high bearing the single word *Thus*.

Riot police were just about to move in when the churchers left and the confrontation cooled. Still, no one fails to recognize that a situation that was tense but contained now may be nearing what rocketmen call escape velocity.

Riot police or no, there are plenty of cops and other security people in evidence as Ansel and India's car pulls up early in the evening. They've gone through a hastily constructed zebra course of concrete barricades, a stop for an undercarriage mirror check, and inspection of the trunk and engine compartments.

"Overkill," India mutters, looking around impatiently. Ansel agrees, but he remains silent.

They go directly to Bryce's office. He is standing behind his desk, talking on the phone. He holds up an index finger to indicate he'll be off in a moment.

"Hell of a thing," he says. His face has been cut by small shards, the kind Ansel assumes should have been prevented by the limousine's ballistic glass. He has a few Band-Aid dots, and several small points of clotted red that appear from the distance like acne spots.

"I'm just glad you're not seriously hurt," India says.

"Tim," Bryce says through pursed lips, with a shake of the head.

"How did it happen? Ansel asks. "Why wasn't he protected by the car?"

"Hell, Roark will be the first to tell you that there's no bulletproof anything. Anyway, the media got it wrong. We weren't actually in the car when the attack occurred. We'd been on our way to the office, and made a stop at the commercial complex on the south side. It was supposed to be a brief photo-op with a few merchants. I didn't really want to do it, but I know one of the store owners, a big fast food entrepreneur who is trying to launch a new brand here. He persuaded me it would only take a few minutes."

"So this was a planned stop," Ansel says.

"But within Ingersoll, within the compound," India adds.

"Yes. We'd hardly stepped out of the car. Tim had come around to open the door for me. I swear, all hell opened up—gunfire from everywhere. We assume it was some kind of drive-by, but we don't really know yet. It was all I could do to flinch and they were gone.

"Tim was dead before he hit the ground. Between the open car door and Tim blocking some of the shots, I came out alive. There was shattered glass everywhere, but not from the limo. It came from store windows and even shot-up streetlights. I actually fell backward into the car, but not before my face got hit, and my hand too." Bryce holds up his bandaged hand. "I didn't even know I was hurt until the ambulance arrived."

"You couldn't have been in the hospital long," India says.

"I never went. Once I realized I was okay, I insisted that the EMTs patch me up at the scene. The last thing I needed was to be sitting around waiting for a doctor to tell me what I already knew."

The office door opens and Jeanette sticks her head in just long enough to signal to Bryce, who nods. "I have to go. I'm meeting Tim's family. Christ," he adds, shaking his head.

"Who . . ." India starts.

"He's divorced. The ex-wife is coming with his kids—two boys in the eight to ten range, I understand. I hate things like this. There's nothing I can say that won't seem canned and less than useless. I have to go," he says again. "We can get together later."

"Where is Roark?" Ansel asks.

"Dealing with all . . . *this*," Bryce says with a disgusted wave as he heads to the door.

Ansel reaches and puts a hand on Bryce's arm. "Two things, quickly. If anything's clear, it's that someone knew where you'd be."

"Of course."

"I'm thinking of Roark's warning that someone inside may be working against us."

"I know, Ansel," Bryce says impatiently. "That was the first thing I thought of. We'll have to get with Roark later."

"In the meantime," India begins to say, "we need . . ."

"Of course," Bryce says, holding up a hand to interrupt her. "We'll all be extra careful, I'm sure."

"Just one more thing, Bryce," Ansel says. "We need to revisit the question of my appearance before the commission. At risk of seeming callous, we may have an opportunity to turn this mess to our advantage publicly, and we shouldn't undermine that by giving the other side an easy distraction with me."

"We'll talk about it later," Bryce responds as he pulls the door open.

India has taken a step back, as if she is uncertain about where to enter this discussion. The fact that she has been informed confers no invitation. Nevertheless, she is India Ruiz, and she is uncomfortable allowing anything in which she is involved to be derailed by inaction.

"Don't do anything until we talk," Bryce admonishes. He is out the door, where Jeanette is waiting with a packet for him. As they begin to walk away, he startles Ansel by turning and asking whether he has talked to Erika.

Ansel understands what he is being asked, but he chooses to make an unresponsive response. "I spoke to her from the car on the way up. She sends love, of course."

"Of course," Bryce responds with an obvious rolling of his eyes before he turns around and again makes for the elevator. "Of course," he repeats, still walking away.

Chapter 32

Erika

IT WAS NEARLY MIDNIGHT before Ansel got home. I didn't care. He's unhurt, thank goodness. Considering everything that's going on, I'm grateful to have this time with him. I certainly wasn't counting on it. I feel like a prisoner who just got a surprise conjugal visit!

Ansel may not be hurt, but he doesn't look well. His face is more drawn than I can ever remember, with dark shadows under his eyes. He seems heavier around the middle—a little bit of that apple shape men are told to avoid. I limited myself to telling him he looked tired. He takes pride in the self-discipline it takes to keep the age monster at bay. I assume he hasn't been able to find time to exercise. No sense rubbing it in, though. He'd do something about it if he could.

One way or another Ansel and I will get through this hellish time. Whether the country will get through it as a decent place to live in or be proud of is another question. Maybe Ingersoll will have to secede! Declare itself a secular Vatican City!

We made love. It was difficult. I wanted him so much—the nearness of him as much as anything—but my rattletrap body wasn't cooperating. Sometimes I have shooting pains, like electrical shocks, mostly in my thighs. They're unpredictable. Also, I've been dry and tight, and no amount of K-Y seems to help.

Yet, when I had him in bed, I was determined not to let anything get in the way. Ansel seemed almost desperate to be inside me . . . like he wanted to lose himself . . . lose us both, maybe. He's usually so gentle when we make love. I know it's because he's afraid I'll break.

When we found ourselves overwhelmed by the explosive steam reminiscent of first times, I was not going to let my body's inadequacies get in the way. He was deep inside me when the electrical surges hit my legs. The pain was excruciating, but I refused to give in to it. I willed us to continue, and I managed to hide the pain. Not just for his sake. *I* needed us to go on. *I* needed to allow myself to be spent, even as I know the damned disease will find a way to make me pay. If it's true to form, I won't know the price until it's rung up. That's the way it is with a substandard nervous system.

I don't know how we could have been more exhausted when we were done. More than falling asleep, it was like being battered into unconsciousness. We ended up twisted in each other's arms, leg over leg, held in place by his cum that was first hot, then cold, then like a tender adhesive. For this—to have this—the pain was worth it. The lightning in my legs subsided. Then it returned. Oddly enough, when it returned it felt good. I can't begin to describe the sensation, the rapid alternations from pain to nothing to a combined pleasure-pain.

I woke up an hour later and peeled myself from him. Usually I can't move in bed without his knowing, which must be difficult for him, this hair-trigger sleep, always being at the ready. It doesn't matter how often I tell him the vigil is illogical. As often as he's away from home, I couldn't possibly count on having him next to me when something—this damned disease won't even let me know what the something is or could be—hits. He insists that the least he can do is protect me when he is here. Last night, though, he didn't budge. His rumbling snoring (also not typical) was the only thing that kept me from holding a mirror under his nose.

I fell asleep again, but it was fitful. I twisted the sheets into a rope, and finally gave up and went over to my writing desk.

Ansel slept until almost nine—ridiculously late for him. I watched as he peered at the clock and startled himself awake, cursing. He calmed down when he noticed me watching him. "You're vertical," he said.

"Almost. Not quite like a Greek column."

"How do you feel? You look tired."

"Calling the kettle black, are you?"

He pinched the bridge of his nose and mumbled that he needed to get going. As if he needed to prove it, he looked at his phone. "Emails, texts, tweets, voicemails—at least three from Roark—it's fucking endless," he exclaimed, and added, "I don't know how I missed the calls. I guess vibrate didn't cut it."

"For me, either," I laughed. "The real thing was so much better."

He returned the laugh. "Thank goodness for that."

"I'd suggest ignoring all the messages if I thought it was remotely possible . . . and yes, I know you have to deal with the fallout from yesterday."

"Let me get dressed. We'll have breakfast together."

"Impressive effort, husband."

"I know," he answered with a wan smile.

We did have our breakfast—or started to, anyway, before the calls started to pile up. There was only so much I could expect.

It occurred to me that my desire to keep him at home was like a child's desire to have her homework magically do itself. I do believe fervently in the importance of the work he's doing. I am very proud of him—possibly even more than he is of himself.

The most I was able to wangle was a promise to spend tonight here, before he heads back to Richmond. It probably won't happen. But I appreciate the gesture.

Chapter 33

Melinda

SUNDAY. WE HAD AN unexpected visit from Ansel this morning. He was supposed to be in Richmond for hearings on the amendments but came back following the attack on Bryce. He didn't have a lot of time (isn't that always the case?) as he had to return to Richmond today.

It was awkward. We embraced like old friends, not lovers. I was determined to keep my distance. I was the one who decided to change things between us, after all. I'm good at following through after I've decided.

I have to admit, I thought I might have to resist Ansel's wanting to resume things as they were. I was imagining that I'd have to show resolve from the get-go. I was mentally prepared for it. We'd greet one another with kisses, but I was determined to find that strange space where there is warmth without regret or encouragement—showing affection, respecting what we had, but not suggesting a desire to go back. It's the *situation* I came to want to change, not Ansel; Ansel has done nothing to anger me. We made many mistakes (an understatement), but they were our mistakes, not just his.

What I didn't expect—and what against all logic hurt me a little—was that Ansel's greeting was at the same level of ambivalence as mine, as if he had come to the same place in terms of our relationship. I think it's a variation on the old oh-yeah-you-can't-fire-me-I-quit thing. Juvenile, I know. I don't want you until you don't want me.

The hard part is that I do want Ansel. I never stopped wanting him. I only came to the belated realization that things couldn't go on as they were.

In some ways it's hardest on the children. They've been conditioned not to see much of Ansel, and he explained to them some time ago that they would see even less of him than usual until the present political situation was resolved. The question now is whether, when and how to explain things to them before they come to an ugly, public end.

I'm torn to shreds over whether to tell Sam myself. It's the right thing to do if it's going to come out anyway. I'm struggling to find a way to sugarcoat it. I can't in good conscience put the whole thing on Ansel, as if I'm the woman wronged. That just wouldn't be right. Besides, I've always tried to instill in Sam the idea that love is not exclusive.

Every time I get ready to brave the subject, I get cold feet. I tell myself nothing has happened yet, and every day that goes by is another day for Sam to mature, and it would be a shame to tell him now if I didn't have to. Except for the maturity part, it's not that different from Ansel's reluctance to confront Erika—his wishful thinking.

Sam's accident altered the strained equilibrium, for all of us. Ansel did what he could to spend more time with Sam, but especially at the beginning, when Sam was in pain, Sam was hurt not to have more of him. It's that simple. It was a time of need, and a time when Sam, whether it was a conscious thought or an intuitive one, wanted—no, I think he felt he *deserved*—Ansel's attention.

Ansel wants to stay in the kids' lives, and I want him to—I just haven't figured out yet how to make it work, particularly as they get older. (I don't even want to think about how to handle everything if I meet someone else.)

In any event, today at least, both kids were happy to see Ansel. Sam managed to hide his recent-found resentment. Cara seemed a little shy.

It's hard to know if she understands anything beyond the fact, which she may simply accept as normal, that she doesn't see Ansel very often.

I occasionally forget that Ansel has a very commanding presence. He doesn't charm a room, as such, but he fills it—effortlessly, automatically. There's rarely a question about who is in charge. Within no time after his arrival, Cara's shyness was gone. When she fell and skinned a knee, I was amazed (and a little hurt, I have to admit) that she wanted him instead of me to comfort her.

The weather was pleasant for this time of year, and Sam was eager to show off his reacquired mobility—it's happened much faster than anyone expected—and to throw a football with Ansel. It made me nervous. I knew Sam would want to overdo it. But that's a mother's caution taking precedence over a father and son's . . . well, I'm not sure what to call it. I hate the word bonding.

Then Sam did something that made me wonder whether he knows more of our situation than he lets on. I insisted that they not stand too far apart when they threw the ball, so Sam wouldn't strain himself. What started out as easy, arcing passes of about fifteen yards, soon became something else, as Sam threw harder and harder. I told him to take it easy, but there was a tight, almost mean look on his face, like he wanted to hurt Ansel. I'm sure Ansel saw it too.

And then the storm passed, as quickly as it came. Sam lightened up, and we were left to wonder what had been driving him.

As I watched the two of them, I was struck by how much Sam is starting to look like Ansel. You can just glimpse it in flashes. He'll look at me, and for a split second I see the bones in his face shifting outward toward manhood, and it's Ansel. It's a visual equivalent of those moments when a sound or a smell will bring up an old memory—and not just the memory as such; it's more than an intellectual thing, where you'd say yes, I remember when so and so happened. It's a flash of being in the moment. But it's also the opposite of a memory; it's a projection; it's the feel of a memory looking forward. It's a whisper, a transporting instant that may convey a feeling more than something you can actually describe and touch. In that instant Sam was on the verge of manhood, and he was Ansel. And not only in looks. He had the same shrewd self-possession that defines Ansel.

When Ansel announced to Sam that he'd throw one more pass and then he had to go, Sam didn't immediately cop an attitude of childish petulance, as I might have expected. I saw disappointment in his face, not sullenness. Plenty of time for sullen teenage angst, Ansel would be quick to remind me, and I suppose it's a harbinger of things to come that the only resentment I saw in Sam's face was directed at me—*me*, goddammit!—when I asked him to take Cara into the house so I could have a few words alone with Ansel before he left.

At the car, Ansel held me for a long moment, and it was all right. There was none of the heated change of heart I feared he would express and then feel piqued if he didn't. His embrace was affectionate . . . comprehending . . . wistful.

I wished him luck in Richmond. "Save us from the crusading Biblical barbarians." He laughed and said he'd do his damnedest.

Then I said something I probably shouldn't have—the last thing he needs is something else to ponder and worry about. But I said it anyway, either in a what-the-hell moment or to put down a marker for future discussion.

"Ansel, what would you say if I told you that I've become friendly with the Episcopal minister in town?"

He looked at me with an expression somewhere between bemusement, disbelief, and incomprehension—in a way that suggested he would delay his departure long enough to hear the punchline.

"I'm serious, Ansel." I wished I sounded more serious.

"Darling, I'm prepared to lose you to anyone but a holy man. Considering my position, you going to mass would be as near as I can imagine to being cuckolded."

"Only theologically," I laughed. "He's twice my age, married, and a grandfather. He and his wife came into the gallery, and we got to talking. One thing led to another . . ."

"That's usually how it works . . ."

"And before I knew it, I was telling him I did in fact think it would be good for the children to try out a nice, warm, stable, traditional community church."

"Please tell me your pastor doesn't know about me and us."

"I don't think so. Of course, that will be a moot point pretty quickly if that fuck Carter goes through with his threat."

Some of the lightness left Ansel's expression. "We've always been on the same wavelength about religion. We'll need to talk about this as far as the kids are concerned. And you understand that this is not the time to be seen in Church . . ."

"Don't worry, I won't go over to the dark side now."

"For what it's worth, I think we'll know more about Carter's intentions by tomorrow. I've offered to resign, of course, but Bryce asked me to hold off. We'll see. So," he continued with some ease returning to his face, "just tell me you won't sign the kids up for seminary or buy Cara a burqa before we have a chance to talk. On the other hand, if we lose the ratification vote, you might as well go ahead. It will be mandatory anyway."

Smiling, I told him I thought we could hold off until then. I hesitated for a moment, and Ansel gave me a sideways look.

"Well, this is not the time," I said, "but I do want to talk to you about some . . . questions."

"Questions?"

"Life questions, I suppose you'd call them. I'm serious, Ansel. For me, and the kids for that matter."

"Okay, give me a clue."

"Well, for instance, right after Sam's accident, when I was afraid we could actually lose him, I got to thinking about death more seriously than I had in a long time. And I started thinking that the state of nothingness you and I have always presumed is inadequate."

"Inadequate," he echoed.

"Yes, as in somehow there has to be something more . . . more meaningful. Listen, get going," I said with a clearing shake of the head before he could respond. "As I said, this is not a conversation for now."

He nodded, opened the car door and put his right leg in, then pivoted and held on to the window frame. "You know," he said before getting the rest of himself in the car, "one of the victims of our fight with the churchers is tolerance of doubt or inquiry. Both sides are so dug in, afraid any departure from their talking points will be exploited against them. Let me just remind you that I've never been sure in any way about what happens when we die. I suspect it will be the great void, but I don't claim to know.

"What I do know—and what I hope you won't forget—is that the churchers don't know either. Nor do the Muslims, the Mormons, or anyone else. That's all I'm really sure of: I don't know the answer, and I say so. They say they know. And they don't—no matter how much comfort their certainty gives them . . . or might give you."

Chapter 34

Return Engagement

SUNDAY NIGHT, ANSEL, INDIA and Rachel meet over dinner to compare notes on the weekend and finalize plans for the next day's commission hearing. All fairly straightforward and routine, considering the tumult of the previous few days. With one exception.

Soon after they are seated Rachel passes an envelope across the table, saying it had arrived while Ansel and India were gone. Hand-written and apparently hand-delivered, it is marked ANSEL FRYE EYES ONLY. India looks at Ansel intently as he turns the envelope over in his hand. It is still sealed, and there are no identifying marks. Rachel looks at Ansel for a clue, then at India, and finally at Ansel.

"Excuse me," he says, opening the envelope and holding it obliquely so that only he can read the contents. Whatever it contains, he is careful that his face not betray him.

Like the others, the message is terse. It is both sufficiently pointed that the addressee would have no doubt about its meaning, and sufficiently vague to permit whatever denials might be necessary:

It will be most interesting to see what the lead story will be on the Monday evening news. Americans do so love a good soap opera.

Ansel nods, keeping his expression neutral. Folding the note, he returns it to the envelope and inserts it into the inner pocket of his sport coat in a way he hopes will be viewed as nonchalant and yet decisive enough to make clear that there will be no further discussion. Looking directly at Rachel, he asks her to continue with her update.

They are nearing dessert when Rachel excuses herself to go to the restroom, and Ansel takes the opportunity to pass the envelope to India.

"What now?" she asks, refolding the note and returning it to him.

"I don't know. It's seemed obvious to me from the beginning that I should withdraw, either to get Carter and company to hold their fire or minimize the impact if they don't. Bryce keeps telling me to wait. I don't know what he has in mind."

"I don't like keeping it from her," India says as she spies Rachel returning from across the room. "It's not fair."

"Well, something has to give soon. All I can tell you is I know Bryce well enough to trust him."

"You may want to call him anyway, and read him the note."

* * *

Ansel is running on adrenalin and caffeine when they gather in the commission hearing room the next morning. Tom Whist will backbench and handle the loose ends, having accompanied Ansel and India on the return to Richmond.

After spending the night trying to decide whether it was worth struggling for sleep or just giving up, Ansel finally threw the covers off at about five. He was unable to reach Bryce until an hour later. "I'm confident," is all Bryce could say. "I'm waiting for a piece to fall into place. Sit tight and assume you're going on if you don't hear from me, but I'll try to confirm one way or another by nine."

"Jesus, Bryce, we're supposed to start at nine-fifteen."

"I know. I can't do any better than this. If for some reason you need to withdraw, India will be able to manage, as we've discussed. But it's still better if you can run the show."

The room is alive in anticipation of the session. Ansel, India and Rachel are standing next to their seats, waving and greeting people who have approached from all over the room to wish them well or see if there is any news from Ingersoll. (*A relief that Bryce is not seriously hurt . . .*

but his poor driver . . . his name again? Right, Tim. Horrible. Just horrible. Could have been worse, though. Well, the driver . . . not for him. At least not Bryce . . . must be thankful for . . .)

Ansel catches Carter's eye. It's a cold look, but the possible explanations for it are many, and anything Ansel takes from it would be useless projection and speculation. This doesn't stop him from imagining the worst.

The commission members and other legislators have been filtering into the room, responding to familiar faces and shaking hands.

As the nine-fifteen start time approaches, people drift toward the seats they had arrived early to reserve with coats, briefcases, notebooks, precariously situated coffee cups, or any object that signaled their squatter claims.

Ansel, India and Rachel—depending upon the speaker, the Troika, Triumvirate, or Unholy Trinity—take their seats at the witness table.

"Bernsen's here," Rachel says to the others with something of a proprietary nod in his direction. Bernsen takes the nod for a greeting, smiles and gives a slight wave.

"Good. If there's anyone we want here, it's Bernsen," Ansel says.

"Thank you nonexistent god," India says under her breath.

As the commission members begin to take their seats on the rostrum, the co-chairs, Collins, the Democrat, and Warrington, the Republican, approach the witness table. Ansel begins to rise to greet them, but Collins motions him and the others not to bother. Collins and Warrington simultaneously chime good morning. Hands are extended. Ansel notices that Warrington is missing the tips of the ring finger and little finger of his right hand. Not that it matters, but Ansel prides himself on being observant of such things, wonders why he hasn't noticed before, and attributes it to the stress he's been under.

"We're about ready to go," Collins says.

Warrington says, "Before we do, speaking for ourselves and the other members of the Senate and House of Delegates, we wanted to tell you how sorry we were to hear about the tragedy and to give our condolences in particular to the dead man's family."

"We've both spoken to Bryce Jones," Collins adds.

"He mentioned that," Ansel responds. "I appreciate your concern, as I'm sure Bryce does."

"Well," Warrington says, "let's hope for a less dramatic day all around."

Ansel is about to respond, when India says "we hope so too," and adds, "Apparently, none of us has the influence we'd like over our respective radical elements."

"Very true," Collins responds gravely.

Maintaining the stiff posture he has held since he came over, Warrington reminds that they need to get started.

As the two return to the rostrum, India looks to Ansel and shrugs. "Looks like you're staying," she says with a tight smile.

"I hope Bryce knows what he's doing and that something didn't just fall between the stools."

As Warrington calls the session to order, India says under her breath, "Just watch us get a two-hour-old message saying No, Wait!"

Ansel shifts in his seat, hoping to take a look back at Carter without being noticed. But he doesn't see Carter. Fitzgerald is there. So is Peterson. Fitzgerald's face appears set, grim, missing its usual optimistic liveliness as he looks straight ahead.

Collins has begun to introduce the morning's panel, starting with a short bio of Ansel as Ansel pulls his notes together, squaring them off like a deck of cards.

Collins moves on to India, and is just beginning to introduce Rachel when Ansel's phone vibrates in his pocket. There is a text on the screen.

Go forward.

Think we've bought some time.

Ansel nudges India and turns the screen so she can read it. The momentary distraction causes him to miss a beat when Collins asks him to proceed with his opening statement. Rachel looks over, a questioning look on her face, as Ansel regains focus.

"I want to begin by thanking the commission for holding these hearings . . ."

Over the weekend they had decided to further tighten the statement and distill the points they want to make on essential issues. Narrow focus and repetition are the keys now. Ansel hammers at the words they want the audience to absorb. *American tradition freedom of belief freedom to love anyone stay true to tradition chilling effect on freedom reproductive freedom essential to believe not believe according to conscience recapture Virginia's spirit of liberty and individual rights ensure those who infringe today are not infringed tomorrow Jeffersonian vision ensure Commonwealth not trapped in its past vanguard of the future . . .*

The first response to Ansel's remarks, cloaked as a question, comes from a conservative Democrat on the commission, an Old South member of the House of Delegates who makes Ansel glad it is not necessary to defeat the amendments in the House as well as the Senate. Ansel understands from the man's smug self-satisfaction that he believes he is posing the perfect query-statement, one containing the seeds of a desired incontrovertible answer.

"Why," he asks, "should America's great majority not insist on protecting *its* rights? Hasn't the freedom you speak of, Mr. Frye, resulted not in restricting the rights of nonbelievers, but ironically, the rights of the majority? Some might wonder how this can be possible, but every day marks some new assault on the faithful. Has not the atheist left created an environment poisonous to the faithful majority in which government is asked, not to be neutral about religious belief, but to be hostile to it? Atheists never miss a chance to bludgeon the opposition with their unreasonable demands. They sue when they sniff prayer in schools, and also when the September 11 Museum and Memorial displays among its thousands of artifacts the happenstance of girders that survive in the shape of a cross. Is there no limit to their petty effrontery? When does the so-called healthy questioning touted by nonbelievers cross the line to verbal assault and insult? When we heard from the atheists the other day, many of us could only wonder who exactly is threatened in this country. Who really needs protection?"

However smug the delegate might be, Ansel regards his remarks as nothing more than a tiresome variation on the theme that has been prominent since the religion amendment was first proposed, namely, how to protect the hallowed tradition of the majority from the so-called depredations of a bigoted minority.

Still, for all its transparency, Ansel thinks the theme is clever, not because it can't be easily rebutted, but because it is the kind of thing that in its warping simplicity can be seized upon readily by a gullible majority: *We* are the victims, not you. *We*, not you, are defending the country's best traditions. The Big Lie thrives. The questioner is feeding believers from a giant cauldron of confirmation bias, reinforcing what they have believed all along—they, not nonbelievers, are the endangered species.

"Thank you for posing this question, Delegate," Ansel says calmly. "It is important and deserves a considered answer. Fortunately, I believe we have that answer, and it is this, rooted in the experience of all history: The great majority almost never needs protection from the minority. The whole point of our country—what has really made it great—is the recognition from the beginning that the minority needs protection from the majority, not the other way around. Those who are weak must be protected from those who are strong.

"I realize that a vocal minority can seem threatening out of proportion to its numbers. And if you were to say that some of the people who count themselves among our minority are occasionally vulgar, disrespectful and hostile, I would agree. Nevertheless, even the most vociferous among them are no more a threat to believers than the ideas they espouse, for it is the competition of ideas that is at the heart of any great democracy.

"We maintain that calling the United States a Judeo-Christian nation is not the harmless change of brand it is portrayed as. Rather, it is the opening salvo that gives official sanction to one set of ideas or beliefs over another, and this is the road to ruin for a democracy."

"I'd like to add," Rachel says, leaning forward, "that at a moment's notice we can provide you with a catalogue of examples where people who hold minority views and beliefs or are members of minority groups have been oppressed or brutalized by a religious majority, whereas, with the exception of certain brutal political dictatorships, I defy anyone here to provide a comparably extensive catalogue demonstrating the opposite."

Clearing his throat to indicate his intention to interrupt, Delegate Warrington says, "Unless you include the worst of the last century—Nazis and communists, nonbelievers all. And before we get completely derailed by abstractions, I want to point out that we are also talking about the moral reality—the everyday reality—that flows from these ideas."

This brings a cheer from the spectators. When Ansel glances around, he sees that Carter is still absent.

India leans closer to her microphone. "Since you seemed to be looking at me when you spoke, Delegate, let me answer."

A good-natured laugh in the room drowns out the beginnings of a weak demur from Warrington.

"Frankly, Delegate, I thought—or had hoped, at any rate—that we were past having to disprove the fatuous assertions of religious people that one must be religious to be moral or ethical. Is it really necessary for me to list the legions of exemplary people in our society who claim no religion, or of despicable people who do? Is it really necessary for me to explain that nonreligious people are as motivated as anyone to treat their fellow humans fairly and decently, even if the motives may differ, or that nonbelievers have the same self-interest as believers in treating others well so that they themselves will be treated well and will be able to live in a decent society?"

"Well, Ms. Ruiz, you raise interesting points and a natural departure for some of our other topics. I suggest that in the spirit of a moral nation, we include in our discussion the moral realities of homosexual marriage and abortion."

Above competing cheers and catcalls, Warrington adds, "After we take a break, I'd like to show you the difference between religious people and nonbelievers in, say, protecting the rights of the unborn."

As the boisterous response from both sides continues and Collins tries to gavel the room back to order, Warrington clearly thinks his will be the final word before the break. But he's visibly taken aback when India responds, a fortuitous microphone feedback squeal quieting the spectators and returning attention to her.

It is as if for too long the politic India has bottled up the natural impulses of the radical activist, when she says, almost in a shout, "Yes, we'd very much like to discuss these issues, Delegate, just as we hope you'll be prepared to explain why so many religious people only seem to care about the sanctity and wellbeing of the fetus until it's born."

At this point there is nothing left to do but clear the room, Collins's gavel falling with pile-driver regularity in a vain attempt to assert authority over the crowd. For his part, Ansel is visibly displeased that India has taken the bait.

Chapter 35

Bernsens

THE SATURDAY MORNING AFTER the hearings is cold and clear as India and Rachel step out of the car. Gravel crunches loudly under foot; a fresh layer of the stuff, like sand on a beach, makes walking a minor effort. With the votes approaching possibly by the end of the coming week, they have come to Senator Bernsen's estate for another shot at double-teaming him.

Bernsen has agreed to see them today if they meet here, instead of at his office, and if they don't mind occasionally having less than his full attention as he deals with the oft-delayed phone calls and odds and ends of a weekend at home.

As at their first visit, they are both struck by the serenity of the place. It's not that far from the urban scene where they have been spending their time, yet the rural freshness and calm are palpable. The breeze, biting in Richmond, seems bracing here.

Rachel stops for a moment to look up at the large red brick Georgian house. "Beautiful place, isn't it?" she says to India, who has paused next to her. "It's the real thing, not the pretentious prefab copies we're used to. It really is another world out here," she adds.

"In every way," India responds, her tone carrying just enough edge for Rachel (or anyone who knows India well) to understand she means yes, it is beautiful, but don't ever forget that it was built on the backs of a lot of people for whom this truly is an alien world. "And even more so over there," she adds, turning and pointing to the still more impressive adjacent estate of Bernsen's parents.

"Let's get inside," India says, turning toward the crimson-lacquered double door.

"It's not Southern California out here," Rachel laughs, giving an ostentatious shiver.

India, who has never liked the cold, adds, "The one thing the Great Deity got right in his small-minded way was to place a preponderance of the really poor people in warmer climes."

"Also lucky for the people who want to help them on site," Rachel notes.

India presses the doorbell, which is a button inside the mouth of a brass lion's head, then presses it again, saying she can't hear whether it is chiming inside. She begins to lift the heavy brass knocker, also in the form of a lion's head, when Bernsen opens the door. "Sorry," he says, ushering them inside. "I had to come from the other side of the house."

India and Rachel are dressed casually, as Bernsen suggested, but not as casually as he is in faded navy brushed cotton twill pants, blue and white plaid flannel shirt, and low-cut hiking boots.

The house is pleasantly warm, but seems warmer to the women in contrast to the temperature outdoors. They pass through the living room and its large stone fireplace, where a nearly exhausted fire could use tending.

"We'll go back to my office," Bernsen says. "My mother and I were just chatting and going over a few to-dos. We don't see one another as often as you'd think for living next door. We'll be finished in a minute."

"That's fine," Rachel says. "Take your time."

They follow Bernsen around a corner and into the large room that serves as his office. There is another, smaller fireplace, this one going with a good blaze.

A woman is seated on a down-stuffed sofa that is angled into a corner to take in both Bernsen's desk and a view of the fireplace. She stands, smiling, and waits for an introduction.

"Mom, I'd like you to meet Rachel Kennedy and India Ruiz."

"Robin," the woman says, extending a hand. India catches a faint scent of hand cream as she takes it, noting its softness. Robin would be better described as lovely than as classically beautiful. She is wearing a simple gold and lapis ring on her right hand and a platinum wedding band, no engagement ring, on the left. She strikes India as someone who works at keeping fit; India assumes there is a personal trainer on retainer.

Next to Robin's country casual dress, India experiences an unwelcome, but automatic, impulse to feel dowdy—an impulse that typically morphs into annoyed resentment and self-reproach for having such a thought. Robin's outfit is fine and obviously expensive, but not ostentatious, a plain solid shirt brightened by a Gucci scarf, tailored dark blue slacks, Italian flats. Her hair is pulled back, simply, and India notes, not entirely uncritically, that her lean facial elegance is at least in part the product of having had "work."

At the same time, Robin's easy smile and languid grace give India the sense that this is a woman who is comfortable with herself and that the finery is taken for granted and without pretense. (And what would she have to pretend to, anyway, though for whatever reason, India is rarely conscious of great wealth when she is in Bryce's presence, perhaps because he is so wealthy she can't conceive of it.)

"Sorry to interrupt," Rachel offers.

"Not at all," Robin replies. "We were just catching up."

"I warned them they would have to be flexible if they wanted to see me today," Bernsen says lightly.

"And we are," India responds, smiling.

"I have to say, it is really a treat to meet you," Robin says, turning to India. "I've been fascinated by your work on women's rights and your confrontations over helping migrant workers. I grew up in Southern California, you know, so the issue is close to my heart."

India didn't know this, and is not readily convinced, but she recalls Rachel telling her that David Bernsen described his mother as something of a reformed bra-burner and is curious about how much of the activist survives. "Really? Where?" she asks.

"In Orange County."

"Lovely," India says, wondering briefly if she saw a flicker of self-consciousness in the decidedly generic answer. Trying to judge her age, India concludes based primarily on her son's known quantity that Robin would be about ten years her senior.

"When I was in college," Robin says, "I worked to support giving migrant workers rights and benefits. So I've followed your activities with interest."

"But you didn't stay active yourself." India says this matter of factly, hoping not to convey the criticism that arises naturally within her.

"Not really. I haven't had much time," Robin adds with a note of apology and striking another of India's reflexive biases (such a woman has nothing *but* time). "I can still talk a pretty good game though," Robin offers, apparently as recompense, and adding with a laugh, "My views are not particularly popular at dinner parties."

"Or with my father," Bernsen adds lightly.

"Ah, I suppose we have to take personal conviction where we can find it," Rachel says with a smile.

"It hardly compares with the bravery—and I choose that word deliberately—you two display in your work," Robin offers. "You're actually at risk of physical harm. I don't know where you find the courage."

India and Rachel look at each other with a small, mirrored shrug. "Funny," India says, "I never really think of what I do as being particularly brave. There are sacrifices, of course, but speaking for myself, I consider them small and never doubted they were worth it. So I suppose it comes down to believing you can do some good in the world." After a pause, she ventures, "If I may ask, Robin—I'm curious given your interesting background—where do you stand on the constitutional amendments?"

"I'm the family's black sheep," Robin answers with a small laugh. "I'm leaning against all three of them."

"Really?" Rachel interjects in surprise.

"Yes, *really?*" her son follows. He is fidgeting, obviously uncomfortable, though it's not clear whether he's simply awkward in Robin's presence or (India's most optimistic interpretation) he is embarrassed to appear less forward-thinking than his mother.

"Yes, really David," she replies. "You should know that," she adds gently in awareness that the mood in the room has gone quickly from polite pleasantries to something more tenuous.

As if to confirm this, Bernsen says lightly, "Okay mother, time for me to do my job."

Which brings forth a hearty laugh from India, along with a humorously exaggerated plea. "Oh, no, Robin, please don't leave. You're doing *our* job so well."

"Seriously, mother," Bernsen can't seem to resist asking, "even the abortion amendment? I thought you supported it."

"No, I said I wasn't sure."

"And now you are," Rachel interjects, trying to keep the ball rolling.

"Pretty much. I've thought about it a lot. I oppose abortion, and I have no problem with laws that restrict it. But it's just not a constitutional issue to me, and frankly, I'm tired of a lot of old guys telling women what they can and can't do.

"I'm not really sure how I feel about the marriage amendment," Robin continues. "I suppose I could go either way, as it were."

"And the religion amendment?" Rachel asks, hopefully.

India looks at Robin, revising some of her initial judgments, as if she can't believe the good fortune of having such a potential ally and agent of influence but is clearly uncomfortable in this official-personal-maternal wilderness they've stumbled into, and sensitive to the possibility of provoking an adverse reaction from the only person in the room who actually gets to vote.

As if reading India's mind, Robin says, "I think this is where I leave you to carry on with the senator."

"Well, it's been a real pleasure meeting you," Rachel says with enthusiasm, extending her hand.

"For me, too. Maybe we can have lunch sometime when this whole amendment mess is over." Turning to India, she adds, "I'd love to hear about your experiences."

Which leaves India to wonder whether she might be able to treat the suggestion of getting together as more than just something polite to say, and actually invite Robin to lunch.

* * *

"Very nice woman," Rachel says after Robin has gone.

"Thank you. I think so too, if you make allowances for the typical mother-son stuff. So," Bernsen says after a pause, "what can I do for you guys?" He looks from one to the other as he drops into the leather executive chair behind his desk and interlaces his fingers behind his head.

India takes a seat where Robin was on the sofa, while Rachel pulls up an armchair.

"Well," India begins, "the votes are coming up soon. First of all, we'd like your take on the hearings. What were your impressions?"

"Entertaining, for sure," Bernsen tosses out with a smile. "Especially the hardline atheist loonies," he adds.

The flicker of a frown crosses India's face. Not that she necessarily disagrees completely with disparaging remarks about the atheists' showing at the hearings, but phrases like hardline loonies are somewhat disorienting to her when they aren't being applied to the people she normally assigns to the category, principally Muslim fundamentalists, Mormons, Scientologists or Evangelical Christians. Beyond this, she is concerned that, however flippant Bernsen is being, he may have gotten it right—the lasting impression many take away may be the atheist confrontation with the legislators. It was one of the few times she tended to agree with Ansel (or, rather, revised her view, though was still reluctant to say so) about the damage that could be done by overzealousness.

"Of course, the terrible things that happened at your place in Maryland also come to mind," Bernsen adds.

"What about the impact of the various testimonies before the commission?" Rachel asks. "Do you have a sense of that?"

Bernsen is quiet for a moment, considering. Before he can respond, India interjects a clarifying question: "To be blunt, where do you think we stand?"

"I understood the question. Overall, I'd have to say, vote-wise, things are pretty much as they were before the hearings."

A loud pop comes from the fireplace; a bright red ember is thrown against the screen, making Rachel jump and drawing a smile before Bernsen continues. "I don't mean to be flip by saying the hearings were entertaining, but they clearly were, as evidenced by the huge audiences that tuned in one way or another.

"But at the end of the day, my impression is that people had their opinions confirmed more than changed. The Ingersoll panel's remarks were quite articulate, in my opinion, and persuasive, assuming the listener could be persuaded. I don't think many people were persuadable, though. If they opposed the amendments going in, they probably came away feeling reinforced and with fresh arguments to use. And the same for those in favor. So, people opposed to you probably got a charge out of atheist day—*you see, what can you expect from the heathens*—and the people on your side probably said pretty much the same in response to the prolife testimony and the Ingersoll violence."

"Which, in a nutshell, would leave us where?" Rachel asks, her face set in a way that suggests she is preparing for an answer she won't like.

"In the House, it'll be a sweep. All of the amendments pass."

"And in your chamber?" India asks.

"It's iffier, but again, I can't see much change. I'd say abortion and marriage are a pretty sure thing, religion less so."

"What about public opinion?" Rachel wants to know. "What kind of feedback are you getting?"

"That's harder to gauge. Your own polling is probably as accurate as ours. Even before the hearings, the mail, electronic and otherwise, was off the charts. During and after, it's been even heavier, but I can't really speak to effectiveness. Given my general assessment that the vote count is probably unchanged, the logical conclusion is that there hasn't been much movement based on the mail."

"Well, just out of curiosity, is the mail trending pro or anti?" India asks.

"I don't really have a sense of it overall, and I'm not sure you can tell from the gross numbers anyway. A lot of volume is in the form of scripted emails and letters based on a template provided by the respective groups—'Dear Senator So and So, I'm writing today because I believe it's vital to' . . . fill in the blank. I don't know anyone who pays much attention to those. Actual, thoughtful individual letters often will get more than a canned response. In any case, what you really want to know is whether the numbers have shifted within a given district in response to the hearings. In terms of influence, if two thirds of the mail at the start is in one direction—it doesn't matter which direction, and pick a district—it only really matters if more or less than two thirds is in the same place at the end. And the bottom line is that not many districts are really in play."

"What about your own district?" asks India.

"I'd say it's about the same as before."

India looks at him without blinking. "Okay, Senator, you're going to force me to ask this out loud, aren't you?"

Bernsen gives a fleeting smile. India assumes he's being more mischievous than obtuse when he says, "Apparently."

"All right, then." India leans in, clasping her hands in front of her. "Where are *you* now on the issues? Can we count on you to do the right thing?"

"Maybe you should have ended the question with can we count on you. I still haven't completely made up my mind, and the right thing is precisely what I want to do. It just might not be what you believe is the right thing."

Apparently taking a shot at lightening the mood, Rachel smiles and asks, "Well, how's that girlfriend of yours, David? Is she still trying to push you in our direction?"

The remark has the opposite effect, as Bernsen's face pinches in annoyance. "Oh, she's trying, all right. The amendments seem to be all she wants to talk about."

India is deflated as she runs her fingers through her short salt-and-pepper hair. When she speaks, though, there is more last-ditch exasperation in her voice than defeat. "Look, Senator, let me put my cards on the table. Yes, of course we want your vote on all three amendments. We believe in the strongest terms that the country will be hurt if any of them is ratified. But we have to be ready for the possibility that the antiabortion and antigay forces are too strong right now and might carry the day.

"But the Christian nation amendment is different. You—*you*," she repeats for emphasis—"Senator David Bernsen, may be the vote that decides the future of this nation. As much as we're opposed to the other amendments, the country will survive going back to the dark ages on abortion or taking a step backward on equality in marriage. Without a doubt, this is not true with regard to religion. As a lawyer and a student of American history and culture, you must know that the changes to the First Amendment in the Christian nation proposal will irretrievably change the course of the United States.

"I'm asking you to vote with us on all three amendments. I'm *begging* you to vote with us on freedom of religion."

Chapter 36

On Edge

❝WHAT DO YOU THINK?" The question comes from Rachel as she and India settle into the back seat of the Town Car. She appears worried as she asks it. They had been quiet for a long moment after they got in and closed the doors, an unnatural state for both of them.

In a deliberately astringent, sarcastic tone, India responds, "On the whole, I think I'd rather have his mother in the Senate."

This brings a soft laugh from Rachel, who begins to speak but is held up by India's raised hand. India presses a button to close the window separating the passenger cabin from the driver. Usually, she would feel obliged to politely alert the driver in a voice containing a note of apology that she was about to do this, the decent egalitarian core of her discomforted by the lack of trust the closure implied. This impulse was greater if she knew the driver. Today the driver is new, a cheerful twenty-something with close-cropped blond hair, and she is impatient, so she issues only a pro forma excuse me.

A few days earlier they had received a note from Roark cautioning that although Security tried to vet all of the people in Ingersoll's employ, events were moving quickly. In light of the recent incidents, extra vigilance and discretion were called for. No specific reason was given beyond the reminder of the precarious times and the reference to "recent incidents."

Rachel needs no explanation, and waits until the window is closed with a reassuring dull whoosh and while India double checks to see that the intercom is switched off before speaking. "You think he's a lost cause?"

"Not really," India says after a pause. "But I am definitely concerned that at this late hour he's still keeping his intentions vague." India doesn't say so, but she also worries that her heartfelt appeal—her laying the cards on the table, as she put it to him—might have been premature; bullets fired too soon, ammunition low.

"I get the impression that girlfriend of his may be wearing thin," Rachel says. "Do you think he's holding out for something?" she adds. "We've assumed all along that we'll probably have to buy off Harper, but that Bernsen can be persuaded on principle. Could we have gotten this wrong? Maybe Bernsen is more reciprocity-driven than we thought, though presumably for him the inducement wouldn't be money."

"I suppose it's possible," India acknowledges. "Maybe I'm being taken in by his boyish eagerness, but I still think he wants to do the right thing. Unfortunately, as he said himself, we may not agree on what that is."

Nodding, Rachel says, "For what it's worth, I really think that's the heart of the problem. In all the time I've spent with him, wandering around the Capitol and such, I've never for a moment felt he was signaling that he wants a quid pro quo for his vote."

"Maybe that's his lack of experience—like a shy freshman in a singles bar, he hasn't learned to make his desires known without making his desires known, if you know what I mean." There is no conviction in this declaration from India. It is more just something to say in frustration and out of simple exhaustion at the pace they've been keeping.

Rachel seems to sense this as she responds only with a socially amenable chuckle before continuing without directly addressing the comment. "Look, maybe I'm wrong, but I think it's worth keeping up the drumbeat of argument with Bernsen. The basic problem is that he's struggling with a lifetime, short though it may be, of conservative sensibilities, and not necessarily very explicit ones. You know what I'm talking about. He spends his life in a cocoon of privilege, not really knowing anything else, except perhaps in an intellectual sense."

"Well, his mother might have provided some counterbalance," India interjects, "and we don't actually know that much about his father. He seems to be a stereotypical fat cat, but sometimes people fool you."

"True, but I wouldn't bet on an optimistic interpretation. My point is that David's conservatism doesn't have to be of the virulent rightwing variety for him to oppose us. Yet he does show signs of sympathizing with us."

India nods, and both look out their windows in silence as the view turns gradually from farmland to suburban monotony.

"I think you're right," India says, turning back to face Rachel. "He does seem to have human tendencies," she adds, either ignoring or unaware of condescension in the remark. "But then there's that cocoon of privilege—that ritual joining of Young Republicans in the same way you're automatically baptized into the church."

"Also, whether he admits it or not," Rachel notes, "he's dealing with parental approval issues—I'm sure of it. He may be bright and a senator and all that, but he still has thirty-one-year-old parent-child things to work out. And as we saw today, this may not be an easy balance. We assume the mom and dad are not on the same page, so he's bound to disappoint one of them."

"Unless he splits the difference in his votes."

"At which point he'll disappoint them both!"

"Maybe that's his true subconscious desire," India throws in with a laugh. More seriously, she says, "Look, we can only go so far with pop psychoanalysis. I do know where you're coming from," she adds, "and I'm troubled that if you're right, if he really is wrestling with all these demons, he may vote according to whoever he hears from last."

"In that case, I guess we'd better make sure it's us."

"Or his mother."

* * *

The two of them are lost in thought for a few minutes when traffic comes to a bumper-to-bumper crawl. India utters to no one in particular, "Now what?"

"Maybe an accident," Rachel offers, then says, "Getting back to Harper, do we know where we stand? I haven't heard anything in at least a week."

"I spoke to Ansel about him a couple of days ago. The reason we haven't heard much about him is that you and I are apparently not good enough for His Corruptitude."

Rachel affects a hurt expression. "Do tell."

"Without ever making a concrete demand, he declared to Ansel that he had to deal directly with Bryce. Ansel held his ground, though, and told Harper that he had all the necessary authority and that Harper would deal with him or no one. That seems to have got Harper's attention. He said he'd think about it and then called back the next day to say he wanted to meet with Ansel quote-privately-unquote."

"Maybe he doesn't know how desperate we are."

"Maybe, but not likely. It could also mean he's going back and forth between the sides to see who'll offer him the best deal. He probably thinks he's in a great position between two wealthy factions, each of which will do what's needed to buy him off. For what it's worth, Ansel says we've positioned ourselves to pay the price, but then also to take something out of his hide, as he put it. He didn't explain what or how, and frankly, I'd just as soon not know."

"Rough business we're in," Rachel offers. "Can corpses in dumpsters be far behind?"

"Well, I have to give credit to Bryce and maybe to Ansel, too. From the start I've been afraid that the self-venerating great moral majority we're up against would find a way, moral or not, to win this fight. We should understand from church history that any means can be justified if they lead to pious ends. All along I've been afraid our side might be apathetic or too fastidious in responding—you know, retreat into our ivory towers and give dainty intellectual sniffs at the theft of our rights. *Pass me my copy of Sartre, if you please*," India imitates through her nose for the flourish of it.

Rachel laughs, says she agrees. She too feared what she calls an egghead crumble, the downside of having an inquisitive, reflective nature. "But I've been pleasantly surprised at the rallying around Ingersoll. Quite remarkable, really, when you consider the natural resistance of non-joiners to joining—herding apostate cats, as you're fond of saying."

"And also that so far they've stayed the course," India interjects as the car begins to move again. It quickly picks up speed. "Must have cleared an accident," she adds.

"Right. I've also been surprised, less pleasantly, I suppose, that our side has been willing to respond to violence tit-for-tat. I wouldn't have bet on it."

"Me either," India responds, and adds, "Getting back to Bryce and Ansel, I'm surprised and actually encouraged that responding in dirty kind to the churchers is not beyond the pale for them. And I get the distinct impression that Roark is proving his worth beyond playing defense. I am still concerned about our side's resilience, though. If we lose this battle, do our forces fold tents and retreat to . . . to . . . well, wherever will be left to retreat to?"

Rachel's expression is grave, determined. "We won't know until it happens, so let's make sure it doesn't."

Chapter 37

Friday Panic

THE PROMISE OF A cold, blustery day is not enough to keep thousands of demonstrators off the streets of Richmond. The nastiest confrontations have been over abortion. The supporters of the antiabortion amendment are confident, often puffed up to the point of strutting, that after years in the Roe v. Wade wilderness they are about to break into the Promised Land. Their opponents on the choice side are in the opposite state of mind, grim and fatalistic, though no less determined as their leaders flog them on to a resolute last stand.

At night the streets and parks have been filled with candlelight vigils, supplying glittering visual unity that belies the multiplicity of causes the candles represent. There is some synergy, though, as pro-lifers find common cause with antigay activists and Christian Dominionists, while pro-choicers do so with those on the other side of these issues.

There has been some violence, mostly by the lunatic fringes. So far, the police, augmented by large numbers from around the commonwealth, have been able to remain in control.

The gloom is palpable as the Ingersoll three take their seats in the Senate gallery. The votes in the House went almost according to script. Ingersoll and its allies are left to find what solace they can in the numbers. The first two amendments passed by comfortable, but not overwhelming, majorities. However, the religion amendment was closer than either its supporters or detractors predicted, owing to a larger than expected number of abstentions.

"At least it's something," India said as they left the chamber. "Not much, but something."

This modicum of cold comfort unraveled quickly as they faced two new problems. The first involved Harper, who remained unavailable. When Ansel called, the receptionist said Harper was feeling unwell, had not come into the office, and gave strict orders that he wanted no phone calls.

Ansel immediately disregarded these instructions, but there was no response at Harper's home, and no voicemail to leave a message. Emails and texts also went unanswered. Possibly they were read. In any case, this was hardly the sort of mystery anyone wanted at this moment. Ansel (and India and Rachel, when he told them) immediately began envisioning the worst. Based on a meeting Ansel had with Harper on Tuesday, they all believed things had been settled.

As for Bernsen, that morning, Rachel—whom everyone agrees has established the best rapport with him—placed a final call. She wasn't even sure he would be taking calls this close to the Senate session, but it was worth a shot, as the prevailing analysis still concluded that he might be persuaded by the last cogent argument he heard.

Rachel did get through, but Bernsen made it clear he was in no mood to hear her case made again. He was about to hang up when Rachel ventured into the personal relationship they had established.

"Is anything wrong?" she asked, undisguised concern in her voice. "I know you're under a lot of pressure, but is something else going on?"

The answer both surprised and chilled her.

"Yes, as a matter of fact there is." His voice was harsh, uncompromising. It invited no further inquiry.

Rachel tried anyway. And got nowhere. All that was left for her to do was to remind him that much was riding on his shoulders.

"I know," he said. And that was that.

When Rachel relayed the conversation to Ansel and India, there was no doubting the contagion of her alarm.

For both Rachel and India a rotgut fatalism has set in. They are tired of speculating. It is out of their hands (though India still can't keep from wanting somehow to position herself within direct sight of Bernsen, hoping for . . . what?), and neither of them can shake the feeling that they have given their all and come up short. At the moment there is no satisfaction in having given their all.

And the situation is even more dire than they realize.

Shortly before they assembled for the Senate session Ansel called Bryce to give him an update. From the outset Bryce was not himself—or at least not as Ansel had ever heard him. He was tentative, his tone almost apologetic, though Ansel couldn't imagine what he had to apologize for. Just as odd, he didn't appear to react to Ansel's report about Bernsen. He was neither obviously surprised, nor agitated. Rather, what Ansel read in his voice was regret and resignation—two things he never associated with Bryce. He asked, not really expecting a significant answer, "Is something going on?"

The pause seemed endless. "Ansel, I'm terribly sorry."

"Excuse me?"

"Look, there's no sense not getting to the point. It comes down to this: I've made a huge mistake, and there's nothing you can do to rectify it."

"What . . ."

"Just listen for a moment. I can't even tell you what it is over the phone, and it wouldn't matter anyway at this point. We'll just have to keep our fingers crossed for this afternoon."

Ansel was reeling, at a loss. To hear these words at any time would have been a disaster. To hear them now was incalculable. But there was no way he could simply end the discussion, and so he said, barely containing his emotions, "Look, Bryce, I'd never not trust your judgment, but you can't hang us out to dry like this."

"I'm sorry. I'm truly sorry. You'll just have to trust that this matter is out of your hands. The best I can do is have Roark come down this afternoon and fill you in."

"Roark!" Ansel practically shouted into the phone. "What the hell does Roark have to do with this?"

"It'll become clear soon enough."

* * *

Ansel is still puzzling through his conversation with Bryce. Nothing about it makes sense. Only the gravity of the situation feels real. For all the crises they've been through together, Ansel has never registered such a dour countenance in him. Bryce's sorrowful apology makes it all the worse, all the more strange.

He has not yet told India or Rachel about the conversation. He rationalizes this with the thought that there hasn't been a good opportunity to do so. More to the point, what could they do about it? They would be as helpless as he is. He might as well hear from Roark first; he might as well have something more to pass along, even if it is only the substance of a postmortem.

The senators are filing in, somber and purposeful. The debates and pressure sessions are behind them. There is a sense of the moment. No matter how they plan to vote, there can be little doubt that the outcome will have an enormous effect far beyond the commonwealth's borders.

For all of the sadness in her face, Rachel appears still and composed. There is no fidgeting. Her back is straight. Her hands are folded in her lap.

India couldn't be more different. She can't settle in, and continually changes her posture. Her fingers fly everywhere around her. She cranes her neck to take in as much of the scene as possible.

Ansel nods toward Harper's empty seat. Rachel tries to catch Bernsen's eye, but he is rigid, staring straight ahead, jaw set as if he is grinding his teeth.

But something else is out of kilter. The start time for the session has passed by five minutes, then ten, then fifteen. Lieutenant Governor Mitchell Caulkin, the president of the Senate and a vocal champion of all three amendments, is having an animated conversation with two of the more senior committee chairmen. Rachel points out that one of them is chairman of the Rules Committee. As they confer in whispers, conversation throughout the chamber becomes louder and more cacophonous.

Caulkin moves closer to the microphone, begs the senators' indulgence at the late start. He announces that Senator Harper has phoned to say he has been delayed due to sudden illness, but he will be here. Caulkin begs for the courtesy of the chamber. No one is inclined to deny him.

Another fifteen minutes pass, and the senators are becoming visibly impatient. There is more chatter, questioning shrugs, annoyed looks. Harper has yet to arrive. Still, there is no call from the leadership to proceed.

"They don't have to wait for him, do they?" Rachel asks.

India appears puzzled. "No. I'm surprised they've waited this long. It's very strange."

Rachel shrugs, puffs out her lower lip with a perplexed look on her face. "Do you believe he's really sick?"

Ansel responds, with obvious disgust. "No, but who knows what to believe with that oily son of a bitch."

He has hardly gotten the words out of his mouth when Caulkin announces that Harper will not arrive after all. He has tried to make it, but is simply too ill.

India exhales loudly. "What the fuck?"

Caulkin has expanded his coven of whisperers. Both parties are represented. The Rules chairman is thumbing through the Rules of the Senate.

Then without warning three senators, two opponents of the amendments and one supporter, abruptly leave the chamber. On the Senate floor and throughout the gallery people are murmuring and turning to one another with perplexed expressions.

Several minutes pass. Caulkin takes the floor. Senators are now conferring in knots. The gavel falls to call the room to order. "Once again, I would like to beg the Senate's indulgence," Caulkin says. "It seems that three more of our colleagues have suddenly taken ill. They were together at lunch, and may have had food poisoning of some kind. They are quite indisposed. They, as well as Senator Harper separately, have apologized to the chamber for any inconvenience they may have caused, and ask if we will consider postponing the votes until tomorrow. They have every confidence they will be well enough by then to attend."

The buzz of confusion rises. Holding up a hand, Caulkin says loudly over the din, "The senators will be aware that the request is out of the ordinary, to say the least. However, we have consulted the rules of the chamber to be certain, and conclude that, as we are not yet formally in session, there is nothing preventing us from deferring to our colleagues, who I would point out represent both sides of the aisle. Considering the crucial nature of the business before us, I propose that we do so."

"How the hell to read this?" Ansel mutters.

Caulkin raises his hand again, and continues. "Furthermore . . . furthermore . . . I would suggest that, given the circumstances and rather than place further pressure on our indisposed colleagues, we postpone our business until Monday morning."

"I don't know what's going on," India says in a loud whisper. "Whatever it is, I'm pretty sure he's full of shit. He's engineered this little move. I just don't understand why."

"Listen," Ansel says, "whatever the reason, if he wants to postpone, that's okay. We can use the time to regroup. The really weird thing is that everyone seems so eager to go along with him."

"What does that tell you?" Rachel asks, leaning over in front of India.

"I'll tell you what it tells *me*," India exclaims. "It tells me that neither side is sure of its numbers. They're both willing to regroup and count noses."

"That's my take on it too," Ansel adds. "Plus one more thing knocking around inside me: Somehow Harper is at the root of this. And I don't believe for a minute that he, or any of the others for that matter, is actually sick. Caulkin has fabricated an excuse."

India nods emphatically. "In any case, as you say, we really can use the time. Maybe we can unravel some of the day's strange goings on."

Ansel nods, biting his tongue over the thought that India doesn't know the half of it. For that matter, he probably doesn't either. "We definitely can use the time," he echoes after a pause. "But here's the other thing— the really unsettling thing we need to figure out: If Harper really is somehow the reason for the postponement, my guess is that both sides need his vote—and both sides had thought they'd bought it."

Chapter 38

Another Twist of the Knife

LATE THAT AFTERNOON ANSEL calls Bryce from the office to update him, but beyond discussing the fact of the postponement, which Bryce will already know, Ansel is unclear about how to assess the situation. If they have lost both Harper and Bernsen, their cause is dead. But they have two days to either confirm that these doomsday fears are unwarranted, or somehow to try and turn the situation around if they are.

When Bryce answers, he startles Ansel by immediately telling him to call back on one of the reserve phones—sterile throwaways—from a secure location, and hangs up. It is the first time Ansel has been asked to follow this procedure, which only adds to his already heightened sense of doom. He retrieves a phone from his safe and dials the prearranged number.

Bryce answers immediately. He asks Ansel to hold on. Ansel can hear Bryce requesting whoever is with him to leave for a few minutes.

"You're in a secure place?" Bryce asks after a moment.

"Yes. What's going on?" Ansel realizes that his tone of voice is impatient. He's had enough bad news for one day. Now he's bracing for more.

"I told you Roark would be down today to explain, but he's stuck here until at least tomorrow evening, and you need to know the outlines of the problem before then."

Ansel's exhale is pronounced before he says, "All right. Let me have it."

"It involves Bernsen."

In these few words Ansel already detects the rare apologetic tone of the earlier conversation. At the moment he's not interested in hearing an apology. He wants anything that can enlighten him about Bernsen or Harper.

Bryce doesn't wait for a response. "Some time ago, not long after the Ingersoll rollout, in fact, I authorized Roark to . . ." Bryce pauses. "Let me back up. It was more than authorizing. I asked Roark as one of his duties to find out, quietly and behind the scenes, anything that might be useful about the key players in the opposition and among our legislative targets. I deliberately didn't tell you or anyone else about it, and frankly, I didn't give the matter nearly as much thought as I should have. I thought about it even less as time went by and Roark didn't bring anything back. I simply assumed he hadn't been successful.

"Yesterday, Roark asked to see me urgently. At first I thought it must have something to do with another attack by the churchers, or possibly something about your problem with Carter, but this wasn't the case. Anyway . . . David Bernsen has . . . or had . . . a girlfriend. I think you know that."

"Had?" Ansel is beginning to see a vague outline of where this might be going. "Not anymore, then."

"As it happens, she never was."

"Oh, don't tell me . . . Roark?"

"Roark. She was a plant. Roark set Bernsen up with this young woman . . . I don't know her name."

"Rachel will know. She met her."

"Well, it doesn't much matter now. The damage is done."

"So, let me make sure I have this straight, Bryce. Roark wanted this girlfriend to spy on Bernsen and report back to . . . to whom?"

"That never got to be an issue. Anyway, it wasn't just information we were after. Roark thought she could be used to influence him."

"And he would do this without telling you? I can't believe it." When it becomes apparent that Bryce will not respond, Ansel takes an audible breath and continues. "Since everything you're saying is in the past tense, I suppose it's safe to assume that she's been discovered."

"Roark became aware of it yesterday. That's why it was so urgent."

"How was she exposed?"

"Roark still doesn't have the whole story. What we're certain of is that Bernsen knows, and they've split."

"When you say he knows, do you mean everything—that she was a plant from the beginning?"

"Apparently."

"Christ," Ansel says, softly.

"As I said earlier, Ansel, this whole mess is my responsibility—my responsibility entirely. You'll just have to see if anything can be done with Bernsen."

"At least we know why he's been behaving the way he has been. Rachel will have to take the lead. That's assuming he'll talk to any of us. If he trusts anyone, it will be Rachel. She'll have to convince him that she was in the dark . . . that she was taken in too. In the best case, maybe he can be convinced that the issues at stake are more important than anything else—convinced that he shouldn't make the wrong decision just to get back at us."

"There's something else, Ansel."

The laugh is coughed out on reflex. "Pile it on, Bryce. I can take it."

"Yes, well . . . the reason Roark can't make it to Richmond to see you today is that he discovered—he'll tell you how when you get together— Carter is planning to out you, maybe as early as tomorrow."

Ansel is struck weak, thrusts himself back into the chair. "I thought we'd worked that out." His voice is sober, mournful, but doesn't completely disguise the panic, the eternal child in everyone that wants to cry *But You Promised!*—the patient who, thinking he is on the mend, has just been told he's taken a fatal turn.

"We had. Something about today's postponement, though—maybe that's the reason—has caused Carter to pull out all the stops."

"For what it's worth, Bryce, I haven't received any more threats from him."

"I suppose that supports the notion that something recent, like the postponement, is behind it. I'm sorry to say it, but in some ways the fact that you haven't been threatened is even more worrisome. My sense is he's concluded he needs to use the weapon. You're probably not even the target at this point. He'll use anything he can get his hands on."

There is a sort of fatalistic bitterness in Ansel's voice when he says, "Ansel Frye, collateral damage."

"Does Erika know yet?"

"Not yet." As he says this he feels more than guilty; he feels foolish. Amid the press of events and the belief Carter had been beaten back, he convinced himself that the confession could be postponed.

"That's too bad."

"It's worse than too bad. There's no way I can leave here this weekend, and the last thing I want to do is tell her over the phone."

"No, the last thing you want is for her to hear about it on Fox News. Well, I suppose you've gambled this far. You might want to gamble for another day or so that Carter won't put the story out there."

"Why? Why would he hold back?"

Another sigh from Bryce's end. "Another secret, I'm afraid. The two of us seem to be full of them suddenly."

"I don't understand . . ."

"There's some information . . . I was hoping not to have to reveal it. I'm still hoping. It would put someone at serious risk."

"What . . ."

"Look, Ansel, the bottom line is we have some bad stuff to use against Carter. We hope it will dissuade him. It's a mutually assured destruction kind of thing. One way or another, I'll have Roark explain everything when he sees you tomorrow night."

"All right, but listen, Bryce, as far as the Bernsen matter is concerned, we can't wait until then to see if repairs can be made."

"I understand."

"India and Rachel will have to be brought in on all of this. Also, we need to try and figure out what the hell is going on with Harper. I'm afraid to ask what you know about that."

"Only a small part of me is happy to say that I don't have anything for you on that score. I just don't know what's going on with him. So you're on your own there."

"I'll do what I can. At least we have the weekend to work with. I'm afraid to ask this too, but did the zealous Mr. Roark plant any other mines that I don't know about? Any other senators who are going to blow up on us?"

"He assures me not." After a pause: "I really am sorry, Ansel."

"Me too."

Chapter 39

Friday Night Confessional

RATHER THAN HAVE INDIA and Rachel meet him at the restaurant as planned, Ansel calls and asks them to come to the office first. He's not surprised to hear wariness in India's voice after she mentions being in the middle of something with Tom Whist and asks if it can wait and then whether Ansel needs Tom to join them. (No and no.) Given the revelations he's had to make to her recently, it would be reasonable for her to suspect she won't like what they're about to discuss.

He has decided not to tell Rachel about his personal crisis and the renewed threat from Carter. He may update India separately—tell her the Carter mess has not been warded off as effectively as they'd thought.

He wonders if even this much is really necessary with India. It would be more of a courtesy to her, since in any case there would not be much time to do anything beyond implementing the emergency media response they have already put in place. *In the event of total screw-up, break glass, pull handle.* Probably useless all the way around. On the other hand, India wouldn't be completely blindsided . . . again.

After the phone call with Bryce, Ansel had resolved to bring Rachel in on the whole mess. He should have done it when the storm first broke.

She's become essential, and has shown herself to be more than trustworthy and competent.

Then he changed his mind, about his personal crisis, anyway. In for a penny, in for a pound. There is still a possibility that Carter will not act on the threat, in which case the fewer people who know, the better. And if the explosion does come? Rachel will be angry, feel betrayed by not being forewarned. Just a bit more collateral damage.

Like any successful corporate chief, Ansel prides himself on seeing things clearly and acting decisively. But now he is exhausted, foggy, willing to throw up his hands and hope for the best. He is aware of how often he's been permitting himself such irresponsible fatalism lately, as well as how unlike him it is to take the Inshallah Route, as he has called it when criticizing subordinates for the same offense.

He berates himself for not being able to deliver a thought from inception to logical conclusion without being sidetracked by the siren of a related problem whose solution seems, at first, more within reach but whose complications soon cause it to join the initial thought in the Bin-of-the-Easily-Diverted. This is particularly true if the looming logical conclusion is exceedingly painful to contemplate.

Then, too, in such a state of mind one always wins an imagined debate. Any point made by the conjured opponent can be easily, articulately rebutted. Or, if not—if unanticipated problems with the argument occur—can be reframed in such a way as to be more easily handled. That's the seductive beauty of an imagined debate. As a last resort, the whole thought sequence can always be abandoned in favor of a more congenial argument or opponent.

In this instance he rationalizes the decision not to bring Rachel in on the Carter Debacle (which he finds is easier mental shorthand than thinking of it by its more accurate title, the Ansel Frye Debacle), by telling himself Rachel will have enough on her mind when he informs her about the Bernsen Debacle, on which she will have to take the lead.

* * *

When India and Rachel have arrived and seated themselves, Ansel recounts the conversation with Bryce. He gets the reactions he expected.

From India, a woman who uses expletives the way most people use punctuation, the outburst: "What did that fucking asshole Roark think he was doing! Who gave him the right to put every fucking thing we've sweated for in danger!"

"Bryce knows he was careless," Ansel says, feeling a need to rally his sense of loyalty. "He's angry at Roark, but he blames himself. For what it's worth."

"Not fucking much."

But the other thing predictable about India is the sudden shift from explosion to cleanup. Once she exhausts her considerable store of profanity, she focuses clearly and intently on what might be done. She is not one to wallow.

Rachel's normal course has fewer switchbacks. Her passion is never far from the surface, but is of a more calibrated sort, triggering emotion that passes through some kind of internal membrane before it surfaces in the form of actionable resolve. She and India usually end up in the same place in terms of deciding what needs to be done. India, banking on her natural qualities of leadership, will arrive via a path of motivational histrionics, sweeping her followers along. Rachel, more efficient, will skip the catharsis.

But there is another element here. Rachel is deeply embarrassed by the thought that Bernsen feels betrayed by her, and worse, that the betrayal was premeditated. Whatever else happens, she wants him to know—wants him to truly believe—that she had no part in the deception. It is a matter of basic integrity, and a matter of self-image: she thinks of herself, and wants others to think of her, as someone who, no matter how heated things get, can be relied upon for honesty and decency.

She tells Ansel about being introduced to the girlfriend, Laura, in Bernsen's office, and about how vaguely familiar Laura seemed. She still doesn't know why she looked familiar; she's not convinced that she'd ever really seen her before. "But Jesus, Ansel, how will he believe me, especially after the things I said to him?"

"What kind of things?" India interjects, not hiding her alarm.

"It was completely innocent. Before I met her, Bernsen mentioned that his girlfriend disagrees with him about the amendments. We kidded about Laura having more influence over him than I do because she has more things to withhold—I think he was the one who said that. So I said, very lightly mind you, 'well, you should listen to her then.' But how will he look back at that exchange and not revise it to think I was in on the scheme from the start?"

Ansel draws a carafe of water from the center of the table, pours three glasses and passes them around. "My guess is he'll believe you. That's just how people relate to you."

"Look," India says over a pointed index finger, "if you think it will help, you can pin it on me or Ansel. Tell him we deceived you, too."

Rachel ponders this for a moment. "Possibly, but I'm not inclined to do that. The last thing we need is to clutter things up with more lies."

"Besides," Ansel adds, turning to India, "we don't know what the future holds. You and I may need to deal with him again. There's no sense burning that bridge if we don't have to."

India nods, says to Rachel, "Probably right. But we need him now, so use your judgment. We can't afford to hold anything back."

"What about Harper?" Rachel asks. "Roark hasn't screwed that up too, has he?"

Ansel takes a sip of water, feels the cold pleasure in his throat. "Not as far as I know—or as far as Bryce knows, I should say. Anyway, leave him to me. As we discussed earlier, he may have made himself scarce because he's got deals with both sides and is trying to work a final angle."

India barks a laugh that seems to catch her by surprise, says too loudly, "Well, I know how Roark can make it up to us. When all this is over he can kneecap the cocksucker."

Ansel gives a low laugh. "It wouldn't shock me if Bryce had something like that in mind—perhaps not a literal kneecapping, but . . ."

Rachel is clearly not interested in sharing in the banter. "In any case, I think we have to assume we don't have his vote."

"All the more pressure on you to get Bernsen on board, my dear," Ansel responds.

India sweeps her hand in exaggerated disgust. "As long as we're pulling out all the stops, I think I'll see about inviting Bernsen's mother to lunch."

At another time the suggestion might have been preposterous. Now, neither of the others bothers to counter with anything stronger than that it probably won't make any difference one way or the other.

Chapter 40

Saturday: Making Amends

BERNSEN FINALLY TELLS RACHEL she can have ten minutes, and this only after a considerable amount of cajoling. Not that the number of minutes would matter in the end. He'd either give her the time she needed or the time he needed to tell her off.

She had reached him at home Saturday morning after spending a restless night wrestling with what her initial words to him might be. She didn't believe he would hang up outright. He's too decent a person for that. Isn't that what they'd been counting on all along—that he would do the right thing when the time came to vote, because he's a decent person—even if this assumption did occasionally veer too close to condescension (*sweet young guy*)?

Beyond this Rachel wasn't sure what to expect. Outright anger? Cool professionalism? She thought it would be the latter. She imagined it would be a question of self-image, of maintaining the dignified detachment of a mature senator—one wizened enough to take the dirty game of politics in stride. No petulance, no lost composure, nothing he would cringe at in some future time of reflection. He would want to make his point while appearing to be in control of the situation.

She turned out to be right about this. What she read in his voice over the phone as a flash of resentment transformed almost immediately (or was she projecting?) into a crisp, lawyerly demeanor.

He didn't explain his reluctance to see her except to assure her that her point of view was fully known to him and would be given careful consideration, as he had always promised (was there something, the slightest note of sarcasm in that word)?

Rachel anticipated this line of argument and had decided in advance what to say to get him to agree to a meeting. Of course, his actual response when they met was anyone's guess. How would he react to her saying that she had heard about the situation with Laura and had a personal need to make things right? Would it bring out that suppressed petulance?

In the end she decided to say to him simply that with regard to the *situation* (she wasn't totally clear about the exact words she would use to convey this situation), she had some things to tell him in person that he would probably like to know. This itself was misleading, as it implied she could provide details about which he might be curious, when in fact she couldn't do so. But the small deception used in the service of clearing up the larger one would be worth it if it provided an opportunity to offer a heartfelt apology and, perhaps, if not win him over completely, shift him away from anger and resentment and toward, at the least, honest neutrality.

* * *

At first Rachel is afraid Bernsen has decided not to show up at all. There is activity in several of the senators' offices, unusual for a Saturday (but, then, these are unusual times), no doubt to accommodate the requests from supplicants like herself. When she knocks on Bernsen's office door, however, it takes a long minute until he answers.

"Oh, you're alone," she says, mildly surprised when he opens the door.

"No entourage, and even the receptionist is pleading family emergency," he responds. He invites her in with a theatrical sweep of his arm. (Deliberate, jaunty sarcasm? she wonders.) "I can't offer anything to drink, I'm afraid." He holds up a large Starbucks cup by way of explanation. "Self-service today."

When they are seated he takes a sip and says, simply, "What's up?"

So, it will be up to her to make the agenda explicit. "Look, Senator," she begins. (Better to retreat from previous first name intimacies. By his expression he seems to recognize this as deliberate, but he doesn't correct her to the familiar form. Part of her penance, perhaps.)

"Senator, this visit is only partly related to the vote. The larger reason is personal." She is already second-guessing herself. Is he saying to himself that there is no such thing as personal when it is so inextricably linked to a desired political outcome? But she presses on. "Whatever happens in the vote, a question of my personal integrity has arisen, and I have to set the record straight."

"Laura," he says without hesitation or emotion, leaving the name to float back to Rachel.

"Laura," she confirms with a nod. "You have to know that the first time I heard what happened was last night. That is the solemn truth."

"I don't suppose you're really surprised that this war has descended to such nastiness, are you?"

"No. I've been around the block once or twice. I know how these things can get. And judging by your comment I'd guess you recognize that dirty tricks are not the province of only one side. As far as Laura is concerned, I can only convey my sincere apology, as well as the apologies of India and Ansel Frye. I swear to you that none of us knew anything until yesterday."

"None of you?" He seems more skeptical when the list of possibilities is widened. "The rogue operator theory, then," he says evenly, leaning back in his chair.

Rachel is not sure how to read him. Is it a statement of incredulity, or merely something he can bat back at her and demonstrate his sage sophistication, a way of showing that he understands the ways of the world? "You can call it that. As I understand it, the scheme was the result of a casual conversation that occurred some time ago, which didn't include any of us and was subsequently forgotten."

"Not by everyone, obviously."

"Obviously. Senator . . . David, if I may, it's very important to me personally that you believe this, and that you believe that I am very, very sorry about the pain this must have caused you."

Bernsen nods, leaving it for Rachel to go on. She was wondering if he would fill in some of the blanks about how he learned about the deception, but she stifles her curiosity and leans forward earnestly in her chair. "I've been fighting for unpopular causes for most of my life. And I won't tell you everything we've done has been strictly above board. But I will tell you clearly and without equivocation that I have never been even remotely involved in anything as tawdry and unethical as what you've been subjected to."

After a pause, Bernsen says, "I am curious about one thing, Rachel. When you met Laura that day after our stroll around the Capitol, I thought I saw a flicker of recognition on your face, as if you'd met her before."

"You're not wrong," Rachel responds, with a rueful shake of the head. "Frankly, when I heard about what had been done, my mind went to that moment. It was one of the reasons I had to see you. I was afraid you would remember it and conclude I was guilty.

"All I can tell you—and I swear this to you—is that she did look familiar, but I don't know why. I don't know if I saw her in some other context, or if she has a look that simply reminds me of someone, or, yes, even whether I saw her around Ingersoll. But I did not, and I do not, know Laura, or for that matter, whether that's even her true name."

* * *

Now, as she leaves Bernsen's office, Rachel knows nothing more about the details of the deception from his perspective. Whether Bernsen doesn't himself know is also unclear. If he does, he didn't offer to enlighten her.

He made no promises, and though he listened politely and at times seemed to accept what she was saying, she can't be sure he believed her.

She only knows that she has done everything in her power to convince him.

Chapter 41

Saturday Night: Destruction, Mutually Assured

ANSEL PICKS HIS WAY through the hotel lobby. Following Friday's postponement of the ratification votes, all over town people have been scrambling to extend reservations, change plane tickets, impose on hosts for a few more nights. Ansel likens it to a political convention that has deadlocked over choosing a presidential candidate. Instead of folding the tents and rushing home, anyone who can manage it will stick around for the delayed celebration or mourning.

Ansel has made a perfunctory effort to contact Harper. He had no more success than he had the day before, but he's fatalistic about it now. He considered asking Roark if there was anyone in Richmond who could locate him, but decided against it. If Harper didn't want to be reached, he had a good reason for it. Ansel's guess is that he intends to raise his head at the last minute to extort a higher price.

It is not that they need Harper's vote any less. To the contrary, especially in light of Friday's events in the Senate, which for that matter Harper probably had a hand in engineering, and the mess with Bernsen (could Harper know about this?), they needed it more than ever. Harper is reputedly a good head counter. Even if he didn't have a hand in the last-minute maneuvers, there is little doubt he knows the value of his vote has increased.

Which brings Ansel back to Harper's keeping himself scarce. If Harper is angling for both sides' hot pursuit, it is probably just as well that Ansel not play his game. He has already signaled to Harper that he is an eager suitor—not a very desirable negotiating strategy, but Harper knows he has both sides over a barrel and he presumably thinks he can make a final pitch to Ansel and have his terms met. If Harper has solid commitments from both sides, he might even decide to vote one way or another at the last second.

If these conclusions are accurate, it would do little good to reach Harper now; it would only amount to one more round of bidding. If there is no further attempt to contact him, it might cause him to worry about his deal falling apart. With Harper it will be all about leverage.

As a practical matter, Ansel's obsessing less about Harper means more opportunity to obsess about Carter.

He scans the lobby, looking for Roark. He has dressed down, as Roark suggested, which for Ansel means he's removed his tie. He sees Fitzgerald holding forth to a cluster of men and women who are quite obviously in his sway, unabashedly enjoying the moment of preferment and no doubt hoping someone will capture the image, publish it, upload it, and watch it go viral before it ends up years later framed on a desk or hung on an ego wall.

Nearby there is a smaller knot of less genial, more furtive, more intense men. Almost predictably, they are engaged with Carter. Ansel notes approvingly that Carter appears drawn, tensile, angry. They briefly catch sight of one another, and both men are momentarily caught out. There is no mistaking the reflexive disgust that takes over their expressions. The entire exchange, including the discharge of mutual animosity well formed over the last months, passes in a few seconds as Ansel moves on.

He spots Roark near the main entrance. They shake hands automatically, with a mutual nod that acknowledges there is much to discuss. Neither one alludes to the Laura fiasco, a conversation for later. Ansel gives Roark a taut smile and pro forma thanks for making the trip to Richmond, and asks deadpan whether either of them could have thought when Roark came on board that he would become the center of gravity at Ingersoll.

"Not quite, Mr. Frye," Roark answers with a self-deprecating laugh and a smile that quickly turns somber. "Not enough to help Tim Praeger, anyway—and almost not enough to protect Mr. Jones."

Ansel nods, forces a more upbeat tone. "I'm famished. Let's get going. And please, I can't relax if you keep calling me Mr. Frye. I'd call you something other than Roark, but I don't think I've ever heard you called anything else."

"Probably not. I decided a long time ago that I didn't like Warren. Roark suits me."

"It does, actually."

"Besides, Warren is useful. When some glad-hander calls me Warren, I know we don't know each other."

Ansel notes Roark's definition of dressed down. Jeans, cotton sweater under a brown scuffed leather bomber jacket, boat shoes that look like they've actually spent a lot of time on a boat.

"I hope you like Italian," Roark says.

A black SUV with tinted windows pulls up under the hotel's large porte-cochere, and they climb into the back seat. Ansel briefly wonders whether the lone car is secure given recent events, then dismisses the thought. The recent events notwithstanding, Roark is one of the best in the business. Meanwhile, there is no shortage of things to worry about.

When he spoke to Erika late last night, it was all he could do to follow through with his decision to hold off on a confession. Having finally become resigned to having the conversation, he nevertheless wanted to do everything possible to avoid having it over the phone.

Still, he had almost caved in when he spoke to her, almost went at least as far as trying to alert her that a painful discussion was on the horizon. And he might have done so if he had been able to find the words.

This failure of vocabulary or courage (or to look at it another way, the victory of the hope that the conversation would keep until he got home) was made more difficult by Erika's total sympathy for the pressure he was under. Unlike men who sought confrontation as an opening to confession (*You've earned my transgression!*), Ansel was moved more by Erika's fundamental love and compassion for him, which magnified his offenses, engorged his guilt, and made him eager to have it out and rebuild, assuming she would agree to rebuild.

He might have given in, too, but for Erika's sudden announcement that she had to get off the phone, followed by her quick, parting, "Hang in there, I love you, speak to you tomorrow."

Now the moment had passed—not the feelings of remorse or determination to make it right between them, but the return of the in for a penny, in for a pound sentiment that had driven his decision to wait in the first place.

Like a gambler who has thrown in his last chip, he can only hope the wheel brings redemption.

They have only just pulled away when Roark turns to Ansel and says, "The Laura thing."

"Right. The Laura thing."

"Listen, Mr. Frye . . . Ansel, I won't mince words. It was a cluster fuck, and it's my fault. Period."

"Interesting that you put it that way. Bryce blames himself."

Roark gives a dismissive wave. "He's a stand-up guy, you know that. I'd expect nothing less. But it was my operation. I won't burden you with excuses for what went wrong. It's irrelevant. If Mr. Jones is taking the blame on himself it's only in the same way a government big shot offers to resign because some scandal happened on his watch. The only possible reason he might blame himself is that he gave this kind of vague instruction at the beginning and then didn't follow it up, which I mistook for his wanting to keep a distance—a wink and nod kind of thing, plausible denial, so I didn't try to keep him in the loop. You should know that I offered to resign."

"Well, I wouldn't have expected Bryce to accept. I have to admit, I was so angry when I heard, in his place I probably would have. And India and Rachel . . ."

Roark holds up a hand. "You don't have to say it. I know how much this may hurt us."

They drive through a cold sleet. A few minutes later they pull up to a corner that looks better suited to a drug drop than dinner.

"Here?" Ansel asks.

"Best Italian in town. Just ask any of them," he adds, pointing to a line of people outside, huddling against the raw. "They don't take reservations, of course. I checked with Rachel. She said you wouldn't mind waiting in the rain for good Italian," Roark smiles. "I brought umbrellas."

"She knows me well, apparently." Looking at the brick and forest green plywood exterior, Ansel is reminded of the kind of low-rent neighborhood storefronts that turn out to be Mafia headquarters—things with names like the Columbus or Garibaldi Club, if they have names at all. This particular place bears the sign *Mamma `Zu*. Beneath the sign, carved out of a brick wall next to which the patient customers are waiting, is a small, square window trisected horizontally by two iron bars; it strongly suggests a car on a prison train.

Roark nods to the driver and steps outside with two large umbrellas, one of which he begins to open as Ansel follows, taking the awkward high step down from the SUV. "I guess I'm not dressed down enough," Ansel says. "I don't suppose this place looks any better in dry daylight."

"Worse, actually. You can see what you're looking at," Roark says, grinning as he puts up the second umbrella into a wind gust. "You're dressed fine as long as you don't lean up against anything sticky in the men's room."

The wait turns out to be only about twenty minutes, and seems shorter amid the high spirits of the people in line. The odor of sizzling garlic reminds Ansel he hasn't eaten all day. To Roark's question, he responds that there's nothing he doesn't like and he'll leave it up to him to order. No pressure, he tells him with mock severity. It's only his job on the line. In reality, no matter how the meal turns out, he's thrilled to be anywhere else for a little while.

"Bring me up to speed," Ansel says as soon as Roark has ordered.

"For the most part, I'm just a messenger for Mr. Jones. He doesn't trust the phone, encrypted, sterile or otherwise—not a bad thought just now. Anyway, I only mention this to explain that I'm not privy to everything that's happened in the past few days. Some things Mr. Jones took care of himself, and he won't say how. Maybe he'll tell you, but I don't get the impression he wants to share it with anyone."

Ansel nods as a large bowl of salad and a plate of hot antipasti are placed in the center of the white laminate table. "So, I'm hoping this means that Bryce . . . or you and Bryce . . . found a way to get Carter to back off." In response to Roark's please-you-first signal, Ansel takes salad onto his plate.

"Actually, I'm not sure how much credit is due either of us. We got lucky. Basically, Carter overreached and screwed himself."

"Ah, more good news, then. Maybe the son of a bitch will contract self-inflicted syphilis. Anyway, so tell me."

Roark pours wine into a tumbler for Ansel, then pours a little too much for himself, coming near the rim. "I like the noise level in here," he says, smiling and nodding toward the general din. "Makes me feel more secure." He lightly slurps the excess off his glass, wipes his mouth, and sets the glass back on the table.

"A few weeks ago, I got a call from the security officer at the lobby desk. He said there was a woman who would only give her first name. She called herself Ellen, which turned out to be her real name. We found out later that her last name is Preston. The officer said she was insisting on speaking to Mr. Jones, that she had something to tell him. Something vitally important were the words she used.

"The officer called Mr. Jones's secretary, it was Beth that day, who responded with the standard line for these kinds of walk-ins—we've been getting quite a few of them lately, as you might expect—that Mr. Jones was busy and could she talk to someone else etcetera, etcetera.

"But the woman was insistent. She said she was an Evangelical Christian—not exactly the usual way people identify themselves to a security guard—and she had something she needed to profess. I think that's the word she used. It was something very important to Mr. Jones, she said, and she had to speak to him, no one else.

"Beth apologized, saying she couldn't interrupt him. Normally she'd just send the woman on her way, but she told the officer she would call me first. She told me later that there was something about her that seemed . . . how did she put it . . . real. Maybe she used the word authentic.

"Anyway, I told Beth to sit tight and told the officer to ask the woman if she could wait a few minutes. By this time he'd gotten her to tell him her last name, so I was able to do a quick-and-dirty background check."

Roark pauses while the waitress clears away empty plates. He uses the interruption to pour more wine.

"What turned up?" Ansel asks when the waitress has gone.

"Nothing, really. Which was fine. At least she wasn't on record as some kind of religious loony, not that it would necessarily show up anyway.

"So I came down and introduced myself as Mr. Jones's assistant. The Ellen woman said she was happy to meet me, but she repeated for the umpteenth time that she had something important she felt compelled—I remember that was the word she used—to tell Mr. Jones, and no one else. Needless to say, considering how nasty things had gotten by then, no way I was going to say, well of course, ma'am, Mr. Jones would just love for you to walk in off the street and see him.

"Still and all, I have to tell you, Mr. Fr . . . Ansel, I could see why Beth didn't just send her away. There was something . . . sincere, I guess, about her. She was youngish, late thirties, I'd say. Kind of pretty in that scrubbed-shiny way evangelicals have about them. Short, brown hair. A bit wide-eyed. She wore a dress. Very earnest. She was polite, but she never smiled, and she was clearly nervous. Anyway, I told her I'd see what I could do, but that since Mr. Jones was busy at the moment, would she mind waiting in my office for a little while and so forth."

"Okay," Ansel says, wiping his mouth. "I get the picture. I think you can cut to the chase."

"Stay with me. This is important. We talked for a while, and gradually she let out some interesting things. For example, first she says she teaches religion at Liberty U. Okay, fine. And then she mentions that she spends a lot of time working on pro-life stuff—it's the most important question facing the country and so on. And then she says she's taking a sabbatical from teaching so that she can work to get the abortion amendment passed.

"I asked what kind of things she was doing, not really expecting to get more than some blather about picketing abortion clinics or something.

But what she says is, 'I'm working for Mr. Carter, in his office at the NCF.'"

Watching Ansel's interest spike, Roark says, "Exactly! And then something else that got me going. Jeanette walked into the room, and Ellen didn't say anything, but I was sure I saw some kind of recognition in her face. It wasn't obvious, like she knew Jeanette and was trying to keep her composure so that I wouldn't realize it. It was more a look of disorientation, like haven't I seen that girl before?"

Ansel nods, recalling the early warning meeting with India and Bryce, when Roark sent Jeanette out of the room. "So . . . Jeanette . . ."

"Hang on, it gets more interesting."

The two stop long enough to have the waitress put down a huge platter of sweetbreads (best on the planet, Roark pronounces) and a bowl of linguini.

"All right," Roark resumes. In his excitement, a drip of sauce from the sweetbreads escapes down his chin. He catches it with his napkin, which Ansel notes is already doing yeoman work.

"So of course I went to tell Mr. Jones what I'd learned. He said I should bring her in.

"Now, the rest of this is mostly second hand, from Mr. Jones. Ellen was very polite, apologetic, but she was firm that she would say what she had to say only to Mr. Jones, not with me in the room. So I left the two of them. I should mention that I had taken the precaution of telling her she couldn't bring anything into the room . . . her purse or what not. She had to understand . . . with what was going on and all. She was okay with that.

"About half an hour later, the door opens. Ellen comes out, Mr. Jones at her side. He asks Beth to help her—show her out, get a taxi, whatever she needs. He was so goddamned pleasant to her . . . that's not the right word, but you get the picture."

"I understand," Ansel offers.

"After she'd gone, Mr. Jones called me into his office. He seemed . . . I don't know, not rattled exactly—I don't think Mr. Jones gets rattled. Maybe just surprised. He had kind of a don't-that-beat-all look on his face.

"He said Ellen spent the first five minutes or so explaining how conflicted she was, how normally she would never dream of blah blah blah, and how her being there shouldn't in any way be taken as a sign that she was weakening in her faith or approved in any way of Ingersoll. She was there because her Christian conscience demanded it. She had prayed on it and prayed on it, etcetera, etcetera. In fact, she said, it was exactly the opposite. She had no qualms about fighting hard for the amendments and against Ingersoll, but there were certain lines her conscience wouldn't let her cross. Well, I guess especially that last bit got Mr. Jones's attention."

"And the crossed lines were?" Ansel asks, with a narrow look at Roark.

"Do you remember Nixon's dirty tricks department that came to light during Watergate?"

"Of course."

"It seems Carter has been running something like that out of his office—you know, sabotage and smear campaigns against people, and the like."

"Present company included, I presume. But just between us, I think I also know a certain someone in our present company who might have engaged in a bit of skullduggery for our side. Not a department of dirty tricks, maybe, but we can play rough too, and I assume Carter is sufficiently aware of that to counter any of our allegations against him."

"Yes and no. You have to follow the saga, because even this part gets overshadowed. According to Ellen, Carter explicitly sanctioned the violence in Ingersoll, beginning with the arsons, and he worked with a pastor at one of the atoll churches. She didn't say which one, but it doesn't take a genius to figure it to be Liston."

"Hold on," Ansel commands. "How does she know these things? Even if she works for Carter, he's not stupid enough to take too many people into his confidence. Though on second thought, arrogance can trump smarts."

"Mr. Jones asked her about that. She said it was true not many people knew, but that Carter trusted her, and this kind of trust is in the water over there. She said it's difficult to make an outsider understand, but all of the people she knows at the NCF believe absolutely in their cause, and there is a presumption of trust. Pretty naive from my point of view, but that's what she said.

"Ellen told Mr. Jones that the rough stuff bothered her a lot, but as long as no one had gotten hurt, she persuaded herself to keep quiet—for the greater good of God's cause and all. But she kept praying on it, asking herself if this was how God would really want her to behave—what if someone did get hurt, wouldn't she have some responsibility?

"Mr. Jones asked why she came to him, instead of going to the police. She said—get this—she respected Mr. Jones. He was doing wrong things with Ingersoll, but she could respect his honest intentions and understand why he has a good reputation. Also—and I think this is really the heart of it—as well connected as Mr. Jones is, she hoped he could do something without opening up a criminal can of worms. She didn't want anything to go public, and in any event, she couldn't prove what she was claiming. It would be embarrassing to Carter, but it would end up as her word against his. More important, she may not like Carter, but she didn't want to play into the hands of the anti-amendment people. So she seemed to be giving Mr. Jones just enough behind the scenes to get Carter to back off. And, of course, this would protect her from retribution, though I don't know how much she was really concerned about herself. She may have enough of the martyr in her to step onto the kindling and wait for someone to toss the match. Probably has images of Ingrid Bergman doing the Joan of Arc thing."

Ansel gives a short, sardonic laugh. "That's a Christian zealot for you—either glorying in the fire or anxious to start it."

"Well, anyway, when you think about it, things went pretty much as Ellen hoped. When Mr. Jones gave you the go-ahead before you testified, it was because he had contacted Carter and made it plain that two could play at the defamation game."

Ansel is nodding as the pieces are coming together. He's feeling a bit miffed that Bryce kept him in the dark about Ellen, then reminds himself that what he should be feeling is absolute, unadulterated gratitude.

As if Roark has read Ansel's mind, he says, "Just FYI, Mr. Jones told me what Ellen said wasn't to be shared with anyone else. Which, no offense, probably was a good idea."

"Maybe so." Ansel nods, takes a sip of wine and laughs. To Roark's quizzical look he says, "I just had a memory of that day at the hearings. India said the real mystery in all this is that Bryce could send a text. She loved the image of his executive thumbs working the tiny keyboard."

"That is a great image," Roark says with a laugh. "So anyway, what we had was a good old fashioned standoff. Carter had a story that would embarrass us, and Mr. Jones had a story that would embarrass Carter—or worse, if he could prove criminal activity. Ellen went away, and we all resumed our day to day activities.

"But then came the Thursday shootings and Tim's death, and Ellen was having a big-time attack of conscience. This time she called me from Richmond, and said she needed to talk to Mr. Jones in private again. Per Mr. Jones's standing orders, I told her I'd arrange it *tout suite*, which of course I did."

"How did you work it?"

"Long, not very interesting story. If you don't mind, let me tell you the rest first. It gets more and more fascinating."

"Go for it."

"Ellen swore to Mr. Jones that she didn't know about the attack beforehand. Maybe that's true, maybe it's not. And she doesn't think Carter had a direct hand in it. Maybe *that's* true, and maybe it's not. But piecing together various things she'd heard leading up to the attack, it was clear that at the very least Carter was aware of it and did nothing to stop it. Personally, I think he had to be close enough to have stopped it if he'd wanted to.

"Ellen said she was sick at heart when Tim died. She was afraid more attacks might be in the works, and she couldn't stand by and let them happen. Her conscience wouldn't allow it. Mr. Jones said she raised her hand in that professing thing the evangelicals do."

"So," Ansel says, "we got some leverage."

"You can't imagine how much. And it couldn't have happened at a better time, either. Before Bryce could act on the information, you got Carter's new threats."

"So, at that point obviously the gloves were off. I guess we had it figured right that they were so scared about how close the vote looked that it would be worth calling Bryce's bluff."

"Right, but this time we had something really nasty on them."

"Even nastier?"

Roark gives an eager, satisfied smile. "The way Mr. Jones tells it, by this time he and Ellen and established a level of trust between them—not agreement, of course, but personal trust. Mr. Jones ventured to voice a suspicion with her. He said, 'Look, I appreciate your courage in going against Mr. Carter, but I can't shake the feeling that you have a dislike of him that goes beyond the violence issue, and you're leaving out something important.'"

"And what did she say to that?"

"She said she had lost all respect for Carter, that he's a hypocrite and not a true Christian."

"Well," Ansel says snidely, "I could have told her that."

"Wait until you hear why. A little after Ellen came on board in Carter's office, she began hearing about a woman on the staff who had found out something really bad about Carter, and who had resigned in a huff. One day, this woman—Ellen didn't give her name—came in demanding to see Carter. She barged into Carter's office and slammed the door. Of course, this got the staff tittering, and even more so when there was a lot of shouting followed by the woman storming out. Everyone was standing around, stunned, and as the woman kept moving toward the door, she did an about-face and said . . . yelled, I guess . . . 'Don't look at me like that! If you want to know the truth about the holier than thou guy you're working for, I have two words for you: Michelle Jarvis.' And she turned and marched out."

"Michelle Jarvis," Ansel echoes. "This is what? An affair?"

"Worse—for him." Roark leans in, barely able to contain himself. "Long story short? College sweetheart. Junior year. Pregnant. Abortion. He paid."

Ansel throws himself back in his chair, wide-eyed. "Well, I've got to say, you don't disappoint. Maybe you shouldn't resign, after all. But can you prove it?"

"Ansel, please, some credit! Of course I can. For one thing, Ms. Jarvis said she's had enough and would just love to go public."

With a big smile, Roark continues. "Mr. Jones contacted Carter directly to make it clear that if he outed you, we would nail him. It was a delicate dance. He needed to be credible, but we want to protect Ellen, if we can, by not revealing more than we have to. Carter blustered, of course, said he didn't know what Bryce was talking about and so on. But I guess he heard enough to convince him we're not bluffing."

"And you got him to back off of me," Ansel interjects, matter of factly. His first thought is relief. But this is short-lived, as he remembers that this is hardly the end of the story. He will still have to confront Erika. And another rock to add to the pack of guilt: At least for now, there will be no reckoning over Tim's death—no one held to account— and Ansel blames himself for this.

"Actually, Mr. Jones said it was a pretty easy sell. He didn't even have to get into the details on the violence or dirty tricks. He only had to say the two magic words: Michelle Jarvis. Carter must have been floored, because this time the pause was too long before the denial. Mr. Jones knew damned well the denial was bogus.

"Oh, before I forget, Mr. Jones did say one thing he wanted me to pass along to you. I didn't understand it, though. He said to remind you about his having a few teeth left in his head."

Ansel laughs.

"You understand, then?"

"I do," he says, still smiling. "Oh, what about Jeanette?"

"Yeah, this is interesting too. It turns out Ellen did know her. It seems sweet Jeanette was planted here some time ago, even before anyone knew for sure about the Ingersoll rollout."

"So, your instincts were right."

"They were. But there's more. Tom?"

"Him too?"

"Him too."

"I'll be damned. Well, obviously we'll have to hold a little come to Jesus meeting, so to speak, when I get back to the hotel."

"I don't think you'll find Tom when you get back."

"Please tell me that's not as ominous as it sounds."

Roark gives a bark of a laugh. "I wish. Ah, for the good old days. The son of a bitch certainly deserves it."

"Whatever *it* is."

"One more thing."

"Hard to believe anything can top all this."

"Well, not top maybe. But pretty damned interesting anyway. Jeanette and Tom?"

"Yes?"

"Holier than thou Christians, let me tell you. They're married to each other."

Chapter 42

Sunday: Thin Reed

RARELY IS GETTING TO the point a problem for India. Patience is another matter. She knows herself. She understands that she has to make a conscious effort to allow person-to-person rituals to unfold at a natural pace. This lesson has been hard-won. Especially when she was younger, how many struggles were provoked simply because she didn't have the self-discipline to let the line play out? She has come to understand that taking the time for pleasantries (how's-the-wife-how're-the-kids?) doesn't equate to softness or lack of will, and that patience and indirection in the hands of a skilled practitioner can be more effective than confrontation.

None of which accrued wisdom necessarily made it any easier for her to hold back. Her eagerness to get down to it (here's how I see things . . .) cannot always be suppressed, as evinced when she adopts a tense, forward-leaning, strike-ready posture or an inability to allow an interlocutor to finish his sentences. The physical resemblance to Joan Baez that people often remark on (and, for that matter, their shared strength of will and similar philosophical and social views), is misleading. India lacks much of Joan's sweetness. Given a choice, winning a chess match is less gratifying than winning a brawl.

There is nothing pugnacious about Robin Bernsen, but India is pleased to find her direct. At Robin's suggestion, they are meeting for Sunday brunch at "my club." This is the CCV, the Country Club of Virginia, est. 1908, and when India drives up to its perfect antebellum white Doric columned entrance, every one of the egalitarian cells in her body enters into rebellion.

Even in winter drear, it is hard not to be struck by the imposing I-am-white-person magnificence of the place, with its perfectly manicured spaces outside and in, burnished parquet floors, fine oriental carpets, Queen Anne furniture, and so on and so on in stereotypical traditional splendor.

In what would seem a deliberate effort to meet all of India's preconceptions, the door is held for her by a carefully groomed black man of a certain age. India expects this to be the last bit of pigmentation she'll see for some time, and so far, as she walks into what she thinks of as a Confederate Holy of Holies, her indignation has not been given cause to be deflated, at least as far as the membership is concerned. The CCV's ultra-thinly veiled claim to "traditional private membership" sticks in her craw as Jim Crow exclusivity writ large.

India is wearing a simple print dress, adorned with a gold and silver sculptural necklace. Robin had issued what India took as the club-prescribed caution against "dressing down," as if she might not have figured it out for herself. It's true that in other times and circumstances she might have worn banned denim just to make the point, but she's not stupid enough to do such a thing today. She's happy Robin invited her, though clearly she would have preferred to have been invited someplace else.

Because she arrives first, she is asked kindly to make herself comfortable, and would-you-like-something-to-drink-while-you're-waiting. Fortunately, she doesn't have to stew for too long before Robin walks in. As on their first meeting, Robin is dressed finely, unpretentiously, and exudes a natural friendliness that immediately captures India.

They are seated at a table with a wintry vista overlooking one of the club's fifty-four holes of golf. It's on the early side for brunch, and they are among only a few people in the dining room. (Here, too, India assumes with automatic disdain that it will be more crowded as soon as the misguided faithful get out of church.)

"I take it you want to talk about David," Robin says matter-of-factly, mimosa newly installed in hand. "You do know he's a grown man more likely to resent his mother's influence than to be grateful for it?" she adds with a pleasant smile.

"I do," India replies. She wonders if Robin is aware of the business of her son's girlfriend, which causes her to flash momentarily to a desire to kick Roark in the ass. "It's no secret that we've been working hard to get him to vote with us tomorrow. Whether you would, or could try to convince your son . . . well, I have to be honest, it would be nice, but I have no illusions."

"Just so we're clear."

"Of course."

"Well," Robin says with a big smile and a theatrical sigh, "I suppose that takes care of our formal agenda."

India, who has just sipped from her water glass, gets the liquid caught in a spontaneous cough-laugh.

"Or perhaps not," Robin adds, still smiling.

India exhales a final cough into her napkin, then returns the smile. There is something about Robin that makes India feel camaraderie despite how little the women would seem to have in common. Perhaps she is trading on Robin's proclaimed nostalgia for India's activism during their last encounter.

"Okay, okay," India says in mock surrender. "I confess, I want your help even without knowing what form it could take. I put two things together and leaped. First, I'm always intrigued by people who engage in noble causes in their youth only to think back on them wistfully, as if they'd put away the things of childhood and moved on."

"Well, you know, India, Paul said when I was a child, I thought like a child . . ."

"Yes, and when he became a man he gave up childish things. You see? Even atheists can know their bible—First Corinthians, by the way, and also by the way, the good folks at Pew have shown that atheists know more about religion than believers do. In any case, Paul notwithstanding, I'd say there's nothing childish about fighting for justice or freedom of belief."

"What was the second thing . . . you said there are two you put together."

"I love it when people pay attention," India says with a good-natured laugh. "The second thing is simply my observation, based on the brief interaction I witnessed between you and your son, that there is an easy relationship between you, and he just might not dismiss your opinions out of hand."

Robin nods and raises an eyebrow in a way that suggests she is impressed by India's perspicacity. "But as you said, India, I may not agree with you on the issues, in which case why would I try to convince David even if I could. You've set yourself a pretty high hurdle to jump over brunch."

"You're right. It is."

"Fortunately for you, we're not as far apart on the issues as you might assume."

"Actually, when I called you it was at least partly because that day when Rachel and I met you, you went out of your way to stress your possible disagreements with David. I suppose it could have been for effect, but I have to admit, we were pleasantly surprised."

The waitress brings coffee. India stirs in half a packet of sweetener, shakes the remainder to the bottom, and folds the top with a neat crease. "Look, Robin," she says, leaning in as the waitress moves to the next table, "this is hardly a typical approach to gaining votes in a legislature. But I have to assume you appreciate how great the stakes are. They're great for poor women who are on the verge of returning to the days of underground abortions. They're great for anyone who believes in the right to choose who they love and not have the choice relegated to a second-class relationship. And they're positively enormous when it comes to preserving the most basic First Amendment rights Americans have given their lives for. I also don't have to tell you how close this vote will be, or that as implausible as it may seem to you, your son's vote may be decisive on all of these things. So, yes, this appeal may be unconventional, and yes, it may not end up doing any good." India sits back and shrugs. "I have to try."

This time, when Robin nods, she is not smiling. She is earnest, as she leans in and fixes her gaze on India. "Just between you and me, you may be wasting your time in one sense: I'm certain you'll honor confidentiality when I tell you that since the day I met you and Rachel, I have in fact been walking that fine line between trying to persuade David to vote down the amendments and being so maternally overbearing that he is driven in the opposite direction. I'd like to think he's past that kind of thing, and in truth I do, but you never know, especially since our family dynamic is something of a wildcard. You do realize that my husband supports the amendments?"

"I'm not looking to split up your family, Robin—well, I suppose I am, on these issues anyway. I understand that your husband is, how shall I say this, of old Virginia stock. There is nothing I'd like more than for Virginia to reclaim its progressive heritage. Never mind its record on race—that's bad enough but at least slightly understandable in a historical context. But as a woman, I'll remind you that Virginia opposed suffrage and didn't come around on it for decades after that amendment squeaked by. For what it's worth, it was a mother's letter to her son that was responsible for the fact that we can vote."

"Really?"

"Really. It's a great story, and even better because it's true. The fate of the suffrage amendment had come down to Tennessee—not exactly a hopeful scenario for its supporters. Needless to say, there was an all-out struggle for the legislators' votes. It was a hot as hell August, and the so-called 'suffs' and 'antis' were pulling out all the stops. It became known as the War of the Roses, because pro-suffrage legislators identified themselves with a yellow rose in their lapels, while opponents wore red ones.

"After lots of legislative maneuvering, the anti-suffrage Speaker finally allowed a vote to proceed—mostly because he thought he had the votes to table the measure and effectively kill it. What he didn't count on, or miscounted I suppose you might say, was the youngest legislator there. His name—here comes another freaky sign for you—was Harry Burn, and he wore a red rose.

"Well, at the last minute, Harry Burn switched his vote, and the amendment passed. Some accounts say he had to run from the outraged antis."

"Do we know why he did it?" Robin asks.

"Oh, Robin, I love when you play the straight man," India says with a laugh. "He had just received a letter from his mother, who was quite progressive. It said, 'Don't forget to be a good boy . . .'"

"Oh, come on . . ."

"I swear. I can even show you a copy of the original letter. It said 'don't forget to be a good boy and help Mrs. Catt'—that's Carrie Chapman Catt—'with her Ratts.' And that's why you and I can vote."

"It's a nice story, India, but I'm not sure sons are quite so obedient nowadays."

"Maybe," India nods. "What can I say? I'm hoping against hope that there are good Virginia gentlemen in the Senate who will look to the future. And I believe your son can and will be counted among them."

Chapter 43

Monday: Showdown

❝WELL, WELL, JUST LOOK at that smarmy, glad-handing son of a bitch."

Neither Rachel nor Ansel needs any help figuring out who India is talking about. Harper is standing at the center of a clutch of senators, smiling, confident, apparently at ease. A burst of stentorian laughter emanates from the group, including one laugh in particular that cuts through the general din. It strikes Ansel as a nervous laugh, and worries him since it comes from one of the Antis he's counting on.

"And look how healthy he is!" Rachel exclaims. "Why, I tell you, it's a miracle!"

"A MEERACLE!" India echoes, giving her take on a tent revival preacher, an image straight out of *Elmer Gantry*.

Mitchell Caulkin motions to some of the senators that they are about to begin.

The Ingersoll representatives take their reserved seats in the gallery. From their position slightly back and off center they have a good view of the Senate floor and also the rest of the gallery audience, or at any rate the members of the opposition they are most interested in.

Fitzgerald has jammed his extra-large corpus into the generic medium seat. He cranes his neck to talk to someone behind him. Despite the obvious difficulty of this maneuver, he is smiling, his usual genial self.

Disconcerting to Ansel, a few seats away Carter also is smiling his rat-tooth smile. Is it bluff confidence, or does he have something to smile about? Both, maybe.

Outside, the crowds have swelled; many people never left, but remained camped through the weekend to keep a favored spot, or improve on one. They were bundled against the cold when Ansel arrived, but at least it had dried out from the weekend rains, and there is a warm-up into the fifties promised for the afternoon. Chants and staccato cheers are audible in the Senate chamber.

From what has become her accustomed position to India's right, Rachel leans in and asks, "Are we making odds today on whether there will be actual votes on the amendments, or more maneuvers?"

"I'm betting votes," India responds. "It looks like everyone is present. The sick guys have recovered," she adds in a tone of unmistakable sarcasm.

"We'll know soon enough," Ansel adds, looking straight ahead at the president's dais. "If Caulkin proceeds, it's probably because he's confident of the result."

"Great position to be in," India says. "Either we're stuck in limbo or we lose. How 'bout them apples?" she adds with a shake of the head.

"Call the body to order," Caulkin intones in a voice full of the moment. "The clerk will record attendance."

"I guess here we go," Rachel says.

India nods. "We have a quorum for sure, so unless there's more parliamentary legerdemain on the horizon . . ."

Ansel is scanning the room. "I think another indication as to where we stand will be whether or not the amendments are reopened for debate. If not, it's because one side or the other—unfortunately, it's probably the other side—believes they have the votes and they want to get on with it."

Caulkin gavels the room to order, striking hard twice, then raising it again without completing the motion as the chamber comes to attention. "We'll begin with our customary period of devotions."

"Just great!" The outburst comes from a United Atheists representative in the gallery.

Caulkin looks as if he is about to use the gavel, but he holds up as the chaplain begins an invocation to the Creator for wisdom.

India smiles, annoying Ansel once again for what he regards as her inability to suppress her sympathies—a recklessly puerile reflex, a lack of self-discipline. "Glad you find it amusing," he mutters. "We're walking a tightrope over Niagara Falls and those assholes are determined to poke us with a sharp stick."

"I like irony," India shrugs.

Jaw set, Ansel replies, still looking forward: "They've been leading off with a prayer for centuries, as has the U.S. Congress for that matter. Let U.A. choose some other time to confront them over it."

Caulkin thanks the chaplain and turns his attention to the gallery. "Let me remind visitors that presence in this chamber is a privilege. As in all of the General Assembly's previous proceedings, we will not tolerate disruption.

"I want to begin this morning by thanking the senators for the flexibility and spirit of cooperation they displayed on Friday. We are now prepared to proceed with the voting. However, there is a motion before us to reopen debate on each of the U.S. Constitutional amendments under consideration. All in favor, say aye. All opposed," Caulkin continues without hesitation after the paucity of aye votes makes the result a foregone conclusion. "The nays have it. The motion is defeated. The clerk will read the first of the three amendments."

"Answers that question right smartly," Rachel says.

The clerk, a jowly, pleasant-looking, middle-aged woman, stands at her post on the rostrum just below Caulkin's. "Thank you, Mr. President. Before we continue, I have one announcement. As you may have surmised from the random flashing of the electronic voting board, once again the system has decided on its own—apparently invoking the law of digital supremacy, as it does from time to time—not to cooperate. Therefore, we will revert to the tried and true roll call vote, which will proceed in the order established by the Rules Committee.

"Our first order of business is consideration of proposed U.S. Constitutional Amendment number twenty-eight, which reads as follows:

Section 1. Marriage is defined as a legal union between one man and one woman.

Section 2. Congress and the several States shall have power to enforce this article by appropriate legislation.

"Mr. President, I will call the roll."

Rachel is hurriedly thumbing through a file folder in her lap. Before India can ask, she says, "I'm looking for my Senate lists, alphabetical and by district. So we can follow along," she adds for clarification. "The electronic vote board registers everyone instantly, so usually there's nothing to follow in real time. Since we're doing an old-fashioned roll call . . ."

The clerk begins calling names, and two aye votes are recorded quickly. "Senator Norton," she continues.

"No."

"That one surprises me," Rachel whispers. "I had him pegged for a yes on all of the amendments. Maybe it's a good sign."

"Ever the optimist," India responds. "I wouldn't count on it."

Leaning in, Ansel says, "For all the effort we've put into it, let's hope at least our targets come through."

He doesn't have to wait long before Barbara Reich votes aye, followed soon after by Carl Armstrong, who does likewise.

India shakes her head. "Well, we predicted we might not carry them with us on this vote."

"This is going to be a bloodbath," Ansel says quietly.

The tally moves to 18 for and 11 opposed. With each yes vote the anticipation rises in the gallery. Fitzgerald is all smiles.

Then, a mild surprise: no votes by two senators they had predicted would be solidly pro-amendment.

"I'll be damned," Rachel exclaims in wonder.

But the delay on the march to the magic twenty-one majority is brief. Shortly thereafter, the vote goes over the top, and remaining senators, including Harper and Bernsen, add their votes to the aye column.

"Take that, gay people!" Carter exclaims with a low fist pump. Cheers follow from the gallery and can be heard on the street, swamping the boos from the losers.

The Ingersoll contingent sits glumly as Caulkin crosses the T's. "If all the senators have voted and none wish to change their vote, the clerk will close the roll."

"I have recorded twenty-seven in favor and thirteen opposed," she declares. "The amendment is ratified."

The formal certification of the inevitable brings another wave of cheering. Caulkin does not try to suppress a smile as he announces that the chamber will recess for fifteen minutes and then reconvene to consider the second proposed amendment."

India looks up. "We thought we might lose this one, but it wasn't close. Not to mention Bernsen's aye vote. And that fuck Harper went against us, which I have to assume means we've been outbid by the dark side."

"Possibly," Ansel agrees. "It's also possible that since the vote wasn't close, they both decided there was no point bucking the trend."

"Well, listen to Mister Denial," India responds with a sardonic laugh. "I'm sure we'll all feel a lot better after the abortion vote."

* * *

When the senators return there is a new wrinkle. They are wearing their abortion position on their lapels. Carter's NCF has handed out buttons to supporters declaring, *"Choose Life. Choose the 29th Amendment."* They would have had the field to themselves but for the free enterprise zeal of the company that printed up the buttons. A company rep had mentioned them enthusiastically to an amendment opponent, asking whether his side would be wearing similar buttons. This resulted in an order for models saying *"Choose Choice—Vote NO on XXIX."*

"Makes it easier to count heads," I suppose, India says gloomily, watching the manifestation of another prospective loss.

"David's pro button is really depressing," Rachel responds, nodding in Bernsen's direction. "I actually thought we might turn the tide with him."

Ansel is looking into his lap, dejected. "Oh, hell, it probably doesn't matter," he declares, turning to the women. "Look at that puffed up S.O.B. Carter. He knows the score. Goodbye sanity, hello coat hangers and back alleys."

"But Bernsen," India says, shaking her head. "I really thought we had a shot with him."

"I'm more bothered by the last vote," Rachel says. "David told us all along that he supported the antiabortion measure as a matter of principle. He's never wavered on that. But I thought we had a chance on marriage. Now it looks like three strikes when the religion amendment comes up."

"I don't know what more we could have done," India responds, lowering her voice as the senators take their seats. "Hell, we even tried to get his mother to help. If that isn't going the extra mile, I don't know what is."

* * *

It's over practically before it's begun. Whatever give there might have been on the marriage amendment, and conceivably might be on the religion amendment, very few senators were unsure of their votes on abortion. Pro-life buttons aside, the signs have been there for years as pro-choice forces essentially have been engaged in a holding action, working on several fronts simultaneously to push back the tide that long ago shifted against Roe v. Wade and ended in today's let's-not-waste-any-more-time effort to gut that decision once and for all.

Even before the vote is formalized, fixed in legislative amber, there is a mushroom cloud of rapture. These are the people who since 1973 have been single-minded in saving souls, mourning the souls that were lost, and sometimes murdering those who would take them. No longer would it be necessary to stand on street corners decrying murder of the innocent babes; to man booths at state fairs and line up rubber fetuses at various stages of gestation like a deconstructed matryoshka doll; to stamp things with tiny baby footprints; to wave jarred fetuses in the faces of abortionists and legislators; to come just near enough to the abortion pit to violate the judge's order of separation—and then to come closer (what is jail for a holy cause, after all); to plead with, pray for, and blockade the so-called pro-choice murderers; to kneel in the rain and light candles in the night; to threaten the medical butchers, and sometimes visit their own crimes upon them; to go state to state, legislature to legislature; to redefine the rules governing women's health; to buttonhole congressmen, senators, judges. All of these things and more. A cause fought for and won, and worthy of unbridled whoops, shouts, applause, tears and prayers.

When the spectators in the gallery are commanded to behave in keeping with the dignity of the place, many turn to the tried and true, oft-practiced practice of kneeling in silent prayer. Even Carter, after the hand grasps are done, the joyful noises silenced, even he has moved into the aisle and knelt.

Inside the chamber and outside, the noise belongs overwhelmingly to the anti-abortion people. It is their moment, and it leaves the pro-choicers bereft—their noise a moan lost in the victors' din. There are tears unlike those of the victors, bitter and without the comfort that might come, maybe, eventually, in accepting the finality of loss. It is over. Whether their best was good enough or not, it is done. For now, here in Virginia at least.

Ansel, India and Rachel do not have the luxury of regret or self-pity; they have to keep their wits. After two huge losses, the biggest vote is yet to come. Call the U.S. a Judeo-Christian nation and all of the other things are beside the point. It goes without saying that there will be no same-sex marriage in a Christian nation, or abortion, or who knows how many other things?

As if a reminder of these things were needed, Carter stands and turns obviously toward Ansel. *Two down*, he mouths.

And there is only this final fight to come. During the break, alarmed at the prospect of the next vote being swept up in the euphoria of this one, the Ingersollers do the only thing they can. They corner their supporters and beg them to push for a postponement. Caulkin will resist, of course, for the same reason the Ingersollers want one. Momentum. Big Mo.

An hour, then, they plead with their supporters. Push for an hour. Stall. Stretch the fifteen minute break. Let the steam cool. Any way they can.

Chapter 44

A Nation in His Image

THE THIIRTIETH AMENDMENT TO the Constitution of the United States. The clerk is reading it for the record, just as she has read the two previous amendments. And like the previous two, the Senate chamber and gallery are filled with people who don't need it read to them. They are mouthing the words along with her.

Congress shall make no law abridging . . . nor by law or regulation . . . constrain beliefs and practices related to the preeminent place of Judeo-Christian principles . . .

Ansel turns to India, watching as she utters the phrases, low and in clipped diction, which becomes more clipped as she says the words *preeminent place of Judeo-Christian* and then, when she and the clerk together say the words barring the *denial of the role of the Creator*, and get to the next section, where India is practically spitting the words *right to pray . . . on public property, including schools.*

A few rows over, Fitzgerald is also saying the words; also, as Ansel can see, articulating them clearly, but unlike India, appearing to take deep satisfaction from them.

The vote tally sheet is damp where Rachel is clutching it in her left hand, while the right is squeezing the life out of a pen poised inches above it. She has color-coded the names: Blue solidly in their camp, red opposed, yellow uncertain. She had updated the list just the night before, irritated as she placed Harper in the yellow field, less irritated but more deeply disappointed as she did the same for Bernsen.

Now, as she sits here, rigid, she whispers to India that she is feeling even less confident about Bernsen. Earlier, during the break that they managed to stretch like putty from fifteen to forty-five minutes, she and Bernsen had passed one another, and Bernsen gave only the briefest acknowledgment before turning away in what Rachel could only hope was the kind of self-conscious embarrassment over the earlier votes that would bring him around on this one, even as she forced herself to admit that, if it was embarrassment at all, it might just as well have been over his decision to go the other way now, too. The pro-life button he was still wearing did nothing to relieve the near panic she was feeling.

The voting commences with the first two senators supporting the amendment. No surprise there, as Rachel's sheet has them solidly in red.

But the two senators have created a different mood. Rather than simply call out yea or nay, each one stood dramatically and locked eyes on the rostrum before declaring, with voices starting deep in the chest, YEA!

The third vote, also a yea, is given with a similar performance. The fourth through seventh give the Ingersollers reason for cheer as all go against and, taking their cue from the ayes, all stand boldly before enunciating their nays.

Before long half the Senate has declared: eleven for and nine against, thus far tracking perfectly with Rachel's tally sheet.

And then, fourteen all.

Since the start of this amendment session, Bernsen has been taking discrete glances at his phone. Ansel notices that once or twice he looked at the screen in annoyance. "Anyone know what he's doing?" Ansel whispers after he points to Bernsen. India and Rachel shake their heads and shrug.

Sixteen-fifteen in favor. With each vote, the tension ratchets up, the gallery buzzes just below Caulkin's gavel threshold, while the people in the streets, under no stricture, send forth volcanic bursts.

Seventeen-fifteen. But a few moments later, a hopeful shift: eighteen-seventeen against.

The tally is tied at eighteen when Harper's name is called.

"Come on, you fucking weasel," India says under her breath.

For the first time, a senator breaks the chain and fails to come to his feet. But the word that comes out of Harper's mouth is nay.

"Fuck yes!" India says, too loudly.

Ansel looks over to see an enraged Carter and a clearly surprised Fitzgerald. "I'll be damned," Ansel says, shaking his head in wonder. "The fucking weasel came through."

But nineteen to eighteen opposed quickly becomes tied again at nineteen, before Bernsen's name is called.

Rachel moves to the edge of her seat, as Bernsen breaks the rhythm of the voting when for a long moment he neither rises nor calls out his vote. He glances at his phone again and, just as the clerk begins to call his name once more, he stands erect and announces.

"I vote nay."

India whoops and embraces Rachel. Now, at twenty to nineteen the room is in near tumult, and Caulkin, his face set and grim, does have to gavel the volume down.

Rachel has India's arm in a death grip as she leans over with the tally sheet, madly jamming her pen against the one remaining name to be called: Seth Cornish, Democrat, in blue. "He's going to give us twenty-one!" Rachel all but shouts as Cornish's name and district is called. "He's going to put us over the top!"

Like the others with the exception of Harper, Cornish brings himself to his full height. He is well over six feet tall, fiftyish, burly but not fat, with a bald spot that is particularly pronounced from Ansel's vantage point above.

Cornish looks around the room briefly, reveling in his moment before he says in a ringing voice, "I vote aye."

And at twenty-twenty the room erupts. Ansel feels like he's been gut-punched. Tears flood Rachel's face. India's face is not visible as she covers it with her hands.

And Caulkin, his expression gone from despair to ecstasy in the span of a three-word phrase, barely bothers to gavel the room into silence as he makes the ritual declaration, "All senators have voted. Do any senators wish to correct their vote? The clerk will announce the total."

The words are hardly out of her mouth—"In the matter of the ratification of the proposed Thirtieth Amendment, there is a tie of twenty in favor and twenty opposed"—before Caulkin declares, "Commensurate with the provisions of the Constitution of the Commonwealth of Virginia, as President of the Senate, I hereby break the tie with a vote of aye. The Thirtieth Amendment to the Constitution of the United States is hereby ratified by the Commonwealth of Virginia."

Amid the bedlam Caulkin has unleashed, it is difficult to hear him say, "Thank God for delivering our great nation."

Chapter 45

Come to Jesus

LOSING ON EVERY COUNT is hard enough. But there is no time to mourn, and barely enough for the postmortem, a word that doesn't feel the least bit metaphorical. They will have to fight what is now by anyone's estimation a lost cause in the remaining states. The momentum is all behind the amendments.

There is no time to waste. The Richmond operation is drawing down, moving on. There will be a crucial meeting at Ingersoll within the next day or two.

Before this happens, Ansel must confront his past and his future. He must attend to this long overdue reckoning.

At home he is greeted with all the compassion Erika can muster. She tells him she's worried about his health. He appears haggard, and there is still so much he must do. She wants to pamper him a little, pour him a glass of something, get him to relax. She is surprised and a bit hurt to find that he doesn't want to be comforted, actually rebuffs her overtures.

Clearly he's not himself. Even taking into account the defeat in Richmond, this is not Ansel. He is edgy, irritable. He can't stand still. In the kitchen he accepts a glass of water. He sits. He stands. He doesn't know what to do with himself. This is not the Ansel Erika expects, the one who will not accept defeat. The one who will regroup and fight again.

In the living room he takes his favorite seat, the one with the ottoman, but he doesn't put his feet up. He pushes it away so that he can sit on the edge of the chair. He leans forward, hands together, looking down.

She has no way of knowing that he is not rebuffing her, but rather that he is caught up within himself, on the verge of his confession and what it will mean. He can't get much lower. He has failed professionally. He has lost Melinda, and a cloud hangs over his future with the children. He is about to cause enormous pain to Erika, and he may lose her too.

Erika takes a seat opposite Ansel. She mirrors his rigid posture. At a loss, she makes a weak overture to just be together like last time, when they made love.

Ansel can't respond. He has to do this first—has to set the earthquake in motion. He looks up at her, says there is something he must tell her, and that nothing will be the same after he does.

She loses some of her normally stoic composure. She sits erect, fearful, hands in lap, preparing to listen and willing herself to hear, but even before he speaks her eyes are welling.

He says: "There are some people in my life you don't know about."

"People?" she interjects, trying for a lighter incredulity. "The way you began, I was bracing to hear about another woman. But people?"

"It's complicated, Erika . . . more than you can imagine."

"Try me. I've got a good imagination." She is still trying to hold on to a brave smile, but it is weak, and her voice betrays her, a mixture of anticipation and fear. Before he can go on, she interrupts. "I know I haven't always been able to be . . . together . . . physically I mean."

"It's not that."

She rushes on. "Ansel, you have to know I've been prepared for a long time for the . . . the possibility you might need to . . . see someone else. I can underst . . . I think . . . "

"Wait, Erika, don't say it! That's not it!" As horrible as he imagined this scene would be, this is worse. To hope for forgiveness is one thing. To be offered it before the fact—for Erika to, in essence, blame herself— is something else, and unbearable. And the real confession is still to come.

He looks at her now, straight on. "I have a lot to tell you, and you'd better let me finish."

She emits a nervous laugh. "You know I always want to know the ending first. I want to know who committed the crime at the beginning. So just tell me: Are you leaving?"

Ansel is startled by the question. He recovers, says, "That's the last thing I want."

"But?"

"But I'm afraid you'll leave me." He adds in a rush, "No matter what, you must understand that I love you."

Erika pauses, about to say something. She seems to change her mind, gain some control. "You'd better tell me from the beginning then."

He takes a breath, exhales a gust, starts haltingly. "A little over ten years ago, more like eleven I suppose . . . I met a woman. Her name is Melinda Staunton."

As he goes on, debriding a layer at a time, he is watching her face contort. The tears are the least of it. He knows this woman as well as he knows anyone on earth. She is doing everything in her power to maintain her composure, maintain her dignity. She is fighting so hard.

"She . . . this Melinda . . . she's still in the picture then."

"We're not together. But, yes. She really can't ever not be in it. Not completely."

Erika appears perplexed by this answer. What does it mean? She settles for asking, "Does she live near here?"

"Near enough."

"But . . . ten years. So, when we lived in New York and Connecticut she . . . what? Lived there too?"

"Some of the time, yes. Let me finish, Erika."

"She's not the only one then?" An expression of incredulity breaks through new tears.

"Erika, listen . . . Yes, she's the only one . . ."

"And for more than ten years, you loved her."

"Yes."

"You still love her."

"We're not together anymore."

"Answer the question, Ansel! Do you still love her?"

He looks at her directly, with new resolve. "I don't know if I'll ever stop completely. I'm sorry . . . more sorry than you can imagine. But I don't want any more lies."

She gives a short, bitter laugh. "Lies are sometimes undervalued."

"Do you want me to go on?"

She nods, looks through him.

He says, "I have never loved you any less, not for one moment."

"You might wonder why I don't find that comforting."

"There's more . . ."

The tears are still there, but now they are competing with indignation. "So you said."

Ansel pauses to gather himself again. "Ten years ago we had a child . . . a boy."

Erika is taking shallow breaths. Her hands are shaking. She manages to get out . . . "You . . . you and she . . . you have a ten-year-old son?"

"Yes."

"Yes," she echoes, as if into an ether.

"Erika . . . we have a daughter too. I'm so sorry."

"Sorry?" The repeated word is caught somewhere between outrage and a shocked laugh. "No, Ansel, you left the realm of sorry when I thought you might have had a fling. What you've had is another marriage!" The thought startles her. "You're not married to her, are you?"

"No."

She shakes her head. "Isn't it amazing . . . how I can feel relief?"

Ansel is silent.

"Well," she says, "if ever there was an inadequate word . . . sorry."

"I know, but I am sorry. And I do love you so. If you believe nothing else, believe that. There has never been a moment when I have not loved you."

She exhales, takes a deep breath, exhales again. "I can't recall any time in my life when I have felt at such a loss for words, or emotions." She pauses, collects herself, goes on. "Why now? Why are you telling me this now?"

Ansel answers with a fatalistic shrug. "Everything just came to a head."

"You said you're not together now. Why not?"

"As I said, things came to a head—the Ingersoll rollout, the amendments fight, and I guess most of all, Sam."

"Sam is your son?"

Ansel nods. "He was badly hurt in a car accident, and because of everything that was going on and the need to keep all of this secret, I couldn't spend time with him. That was hell for me. For Melinda it was the breaking point."

"But not for you . . ."

"I don't know. Maybe."

"Maybe," Erika repeats. "Is he all right? Sam?"

"Yes. He's had a hard time, but he's doing well."

Erika is silent, unsure what to say next, or how to mix sorrow, anger and shock. It seems an impossible challenge. At this moment, anger is winning out. She looks at him sharply. She says, "Ten years. More." She's not shrill. She's never shrill. But the anger is profound: "You deceived me. No, you did more than deceive me. A deception might have been a brief affair—something off the rails and then set right."

As she continues, she picks up steam, picks up momentum. "This wasn't a deception, Ansel. This was an entire existence as a lie . . . as a monstrous betrayal. This was me trying to be understanding all these years as you kept Bryce's world in orbit, as you crusaded for Ingersoll. All of those trips. All of those nights away—hell, weeks away! Were any of them for what you said they were?"

Ansel is silent, determined to take the blows without flinching.

But her question is not rhetorical. "Well, were they?"

"Erika . . ."

"I want an answer, Ansel!"

"Yes, most of them."

"Most of them," she echoes. "And how often did she accompany you?"

"Never."

"Really? Oh, right, she had to stay home with the children."

"Stop it, please . . ."

"Are these unreasonable questions, Ansel? Do you think you don't have them coming?"

"I do. Melinda never came away with me because we didn't want anyone to find out. We kept our lives separate, or we tried to until now."

"So you never had a vacation together—a week, a weekend . . . in ten years?"

"We did. A few times."

"I thought you said . . ."

"I meant we never went anywhere when I was traveling on business. That was the context of your question."

"I see." She says this with a short laugh of incredulity. "Since we're parsing to the nth degree, let me clarify: When you said you were going away on business, sometimes you didn't. You were really away with her . . . or your . . . family." And now the anger morphs again. Tears of hurt and indignation give way to tears of sorrow.

"Erika," he says quietly. "I'll answer any question. I will. But this is . . . this is not helping the situation."

And here the anger flares again. "Sorry, Ansel, you don't get to decide what's helpful. When you come home from your wars and deceits and turn my life upside down—turn our lives upside down—you don't get to decide that."

"No. I don't."

Chapter 46

Ingersoll, Spring

AND HERE ANSEL IS, sitting on the same stage he sat on for the rollout all those months before. In the same chair in the place behind the podium. India, too. She is right beside him. Rachel is an addition to the core group—a plus-up, as the jargon goes.

And here comes Bryce, walking toward the podium. The pinstripe suit is indistinguishable from the one he wore that day. The tie may even be the same one. It's not the kind of thing Bryce frets over.

The audience, however, is different in almost every way from the day of the rollout. Casual curiosity has been supplanted by purpose and energy. The business beat drones have been replaced by correspondents of national and international stature.

Something else is different. As of this moment, Amendments Twenty-eight through Thirty are the law of the land, part of the national charter, each bearing the same weight, mass and specific gravity as the ones before them. Instead of bestowing new rights, the Constitution is now eviscerating old ones.

Abortion clinics are artifacts of history. It didn't take long, rebuking those people who said the uproar was exaggerated and who predicted that in the end not much would really change. (Ostriches, as far as Ansel was concerned, though he would be the first to admit that unlike revenge, served cold or otherwise, vindication makes an unsatisfying meal.)

The forces that since Roe were arrayed against abortion in all of its manifestations shifted effortlessly and with equal zeal to enforcement. Moving the procedure underground is harder than it's ever been. Unlike the pre-Roe period, where abortion was simply presumed to be illegal and dealt with as the occasion arose, now there are legions of antiabortion veterans with nothing better to do than sniff out baby killers.

Planned Parenthood still exists, and may even counsel women, provided of course that only approved remedies for pregnancy are discussed—meaning not quite remedies, then, but adoption alternatives. Enforcement by the various groups' peculiar brand of secret shoppers is another function easily assumed by the Pro-Life Army. (There actually is such a thing, comprising "soldiers" organized into active service from their brief retired-reserve status—Carter's brainstorm.) There is talk that the DEA will have to direct more of its already enhanced resources toward stanching the flow of illicit morning-after pills.

Decertifying gay marriages has been a trickier business, with much stronger and more focused blowback coming from the gay community and a surprisingly diverse array of allies. States are under enormous pressure to grandfather in existing same-sex unions, and amendment supporters are discovering that putting the new law of the land into practice can be daunting. It may be that marriage is only between a man and a woman, but civil union, under a variety of more palatable names, such as social partnership, has yet to be struck down by the courts (though it may well be), and try as they might, the opponents of same-sex marriage have not been able to stop civil unionists from referring to their partners as husband or wife.

In short, as India frequently tells a newly energized crop of activists, "The churchers are discovering the power of civil disobedience, and it's driving these styptic-hearted fools crazy."

There never was any doubt that, win or lose, India would be leading this fight for as long as it took—with Ingersoll's continuing imprimatur if possible, without it if necessary. These months since Richmond have been strange for her. On the one hand she is bitter over what she refuses to consider as anything but her own abject failure. (Though not entirely her own—she does hold some residual bitterness toward Ansel for the distraction of possible scandal and his reluctance to adopt confrontational tactics.) She does occasionally smile at the thought of Bernsen. Sometime after the vote on the religion amendment she found out that what he was reading when he kept looking at his phone was a text from Robin urging him to "do the right thing," which of course he did, even if it did turn out to be futile and possibly will cost him his Senate seat.

At the same time, tempering her thoughts of failure and defeat is her natural love of a fight, and there is no shortage of worthy causes—vital causes—to fight over now. Moreover, the failures of January have been an excellent recruiting tool. India is hardly the only one who believes there is still something to fight for.

When Bryce reaches the podium, the place boils over. Beyond his any expectation or reason, Bryce and his project are no longer amusing oddities. In the brief time since he stood on this stage to announce his strange idea—Ingersoll, his quasi-Utopian vision, which one wag labeled Bryce's Canon and many critics dismissed as the plaything of an eccentric rich man, a shameless for-profit gimmick, a Disney-esque gated community for the wonkily liberal (*New Homes . . . Well-Priced from the Mid-$400s*), the fatuous notion of a dilettante who said those who are disinclined to be joiners had better change their minds in their own defense—Ingersoll, the "Community for Reason and Progress," has become something far different. It has become a center of gravity.

Bryce's purpose today may be all seriousness, but the standing ovation he is receiving has clearly caught him off guard and pulled the expression of grim determination on his face into, first, a bemused smile, and then a moist-eyed moment as he brings his hands to his heart in gratitude.

Behind him, the Ansel-India-Rachel Troika is also caught by the moment. When the applause won't die down, Bryce turns to look at them, giving a self-conscious shrug. Ansel stands and encourages the audience, sweeping his arm in Bryce's direction. "Take a moment," he mouths with a smile, "you've earned this," and the others on the stage stand and applaud, undercutting Bryce's now seriously self-effaced efforts to motion the crowd down.

Among those in the front row section reserved for honored guests, standing with difficulty but determination, is Erika. Ansel nods in her direction, tries for something like a smile. She tips her hand toward him, a gesture Ansel understands is a sincere measure of the respect she has for his part in bringing Ingersoll about.

It is a tightly bounded moment that briefly transcends the pain of his revelations to her—the anguish of the day after the disastrous defeat in the Battle for Richmond, when he walked into the house steeled to finish the job, to add private anguish and humiliation—so richly earned—to public ones.

He still told himself that one love didn't diminish another. In any event, his enforced separation from Melinda had made his feelings easier to take, eroding their strength to the point where (and perhaps this would be helpful) he had moments of questioning whether he had really loved, or if he had, when this love began to wane.

But nothing did as much to rattle the marriage to the core or to hurt Erika more than the revelation that he was the father of two children. This was devastating news, the unassailable, undeniable evidence that this was no dalliance. Just sex? Hardly. How could it be? An accidental child was possible. But two? With the same woman who gave them to him over more than a decade (constant subtext: *which I couldn't*)?

If not for the children, some of these questions might have been addressed over time by artful ambiguity—by the fading memory of Melinda, on the one hand, and Erika's conscious and unconscious desire to find some kind of equilibrium she could live with, on the other. If not for the reality of Sam. If not for the reality of Cara.

Ansel's love for his children *is* real, is unchanged and unchanging, and perversely, the thing that may save his marriage, because it is the one thing, however painful, Erika insists on if the marriage is to continue: He will not repudiate, will not ignore, and will not salve his conscience by merely providing financial support to his children. To Erika, this is a moral imperative. Whether or not the marriage survives, Erika will not allow—will not allow herself to become an excuse for— two fatherless children.

She has told herself that she would feel this way if the children had come from a previous marriage. She will force herself to make the necessary adjustments and rationalizations to feel this way now. She has even said that some time in the future, when everything is less raw, she would like to meet them, and perhaps find a way to have some kind of relationship with them.

He will try to make this happen. In the meantime, at this moment, he is grateful beyond measure that Erika is standing there, joining in the swell of enthusiasm, joining in this strangely exalted moment with people who have suffered such a resounding defeat.

Bryce is at pains to capitalize on this mood, as the audience finally settles down enough for him to speak. The test, he tells his listeners, will be whether these feelings of warmth and unity can be converted into sustained action.

"At this moment, slabs of concrete, granite and poster board containing the Ten Commandments are springing up in public spaces—in town halls, schools and on courthouse lawns. In some places, it's more conspicuous. The courthouse in Montgomery, once the site of victory for freedom as such displays were banned, is now the site of a large-scale reproduction of Calvary.

"Schools across the country—not all, but many—have reintroduced the kinds of rites and religious education that the courts once had the wisdom to forbid. Public school graduation ceremonies make appeals to the Lord and Savior. High school football games begin with prayers for victory—a practice which, in any case, many schools have carried on illegally for a long time, the difference being that now they have the power of the Constitution behind them.

"When we created this Community of Ingersoll, it was with the hope that it would be, as advertised, a center of free thought and unencumbered research and exploration. We—or I, at any rate—underestimated the need for it to be a center of political action as well.

"Yet, thanks to the exigencies of our times, it has had to become that. It has had to become the place, the headquarters, if you will, for a long, arduous battle to reclaim the promise of our nation.

"When we announced the creation of Ingersoll, I warned that people who are not known to be joiners had better change their ways, or get used to beginning the day on their knees.

"Well, we're not there yet—at least not in most places. But we are well on our way. Indeed, because we fell short in our efforts, the Constitution of the United States, which was truly a sacred document"— Bryce pauses and smiles, says, "but not for the reasons our opponents believe," which draws a round of cheers—"is no longer the impediment that it was to official, sanctioned, and in some future worst case, mandatory religiosity.

"To say that our purpose now is to resist this trend, and reverse it if we can, is to beggar the obvious. What I feel I must say, however, is that as difficult as it is for you and our supporters to hear—as much as it plays against type—our success depends upon becoming modern crusaders. Alas, we must be prepared to adopt the rabid tenacity shown by our opponents. Whatever their faults, we must give them this: They never let up for a moment.

"The heart of our community may be reason, but the heart of our effort must have more in common with the methods of the antiabortion movement than with those of the Ethical Society. In the end, a society based on reason is only possible if reason is the society's supreme value.

"Whether we succeed in making it so or end up on the heap of failed experiments is in our hands."

And now the people on stage are on their feet again, joining a rapturous wave of applause that stops Bryce short of finishing his speech.

But Ansel sees that he really has finished it. Bryce's audience must know that the corollary to accepting the absence of a guiding, concerned god, loving or otherwise, is being able to hold fast in trying times to the hard, lonely truth of the universe's indifference to the fate of all things. Viewed through this lens, the success of—the very continued existence of—the planet, let alone the prospects for an entity as arbitrary and frivolous as a single nation, is of concern only to those with the capacity to comprehend existence on its own terms and take responsibility for the future.

These people are here in this place, rallying around this idea, this particular totem and all it stands for, in the perversely arrogant belief that the future will depend on their supremacy.

Automatically, without irony, Ansel thinks, Amen to that.

THE END

Acknowledgments

No writer publishes a book without help. *Ingersoll* is no exception. Many people helped in the research and writing. In particular, I'd like to thank several who read the manuscript at various stages of gestation and who offered perceptive, often no-holds-barred critiques (the only kind worth having, after all).

John Steiner, who has experienced the believer-nonbeliever wars firsthand and whose depiction of them in *Answering Aunt Bertha*, a book that deserves wider distribution than it has received, provided a window into the world of Evangelical Christians. Invaluable comment on the manuscript was provided by Jessie Thorpe, Laura Flaherty, Donna and Jack Salem, and Angie Gray. My wife Jo's eyes have surely glazed over by the endless iterations she has read voluntarily, not to say masochistically. Friends and family offered encouragement. To all, many thanks.

The source material on the issues raised by *Ingersoll* is just about infinite. This is certainly true of believer theology, less so but still enormous on the nonbeliever-agnostic side. To cite just a few valuable and compelling works: Susan Jacoby's *Freethinkers: A History of American Secularism*; many of the writings of Richard Dawkins, Christopher Hitchens, and Sam Harris; *The Gnostic Gospels*, by Princeton's Elaine Pagels; Gina Welch's *In the Land of the Believers*; and Orvin Larson's venerable biography of Robert Ingersoll, *American Infidel*.

Like my other books, *Keeping Gideon* and *An Imperfect Certainty*, *Ingersoll* is a work of fiction that strives to explore in an entertaining way some of the wider dilemmas of the human condition. While taking the usual novelistic liberties with people, events and places, I have endeavored to create a true sense of the contentious issues depicted in the story. I apologize in advance for any errors or misrepresentations; they are inadvertent but in any case my responsibility alone.

Richard Samuel Sheres
Alexandria, Virginia, 2020

About the Author

Richard Samuel Sheres is a writer and former foreign affairs and intelligence senior executive. He is the author of the acclaimed novels *Keeping Gideon* (a San Diego Book Awards finalist) and *An Imperfect Certainty*. Born and raised in New York City, he has visited or resided in over sixty countries. He and his wife live in Alexandria, Virginia.

9 780989 060264